SHADOW OF DOUBT

Shadow of Doubt

A THRILLER

Brad Thor

EMILY BESTLER BOOKS

ATRIA

New York London Toronto Sydney New Delhi

**EMILY
BESTLER
BOOKS**

ATRIA

An Imprint of Simon & Schuster, LLC
1230 Avenue of the Americas
New York, NY 10020

First Emily Bestler Books/Atria Books hardcover edition August 2024

EMILY BESTLER BOOKS/ATRIA BOOKS and colophon are trademarks of Simon & Schuster, LLC

Simon & Schuster: Celebrating 100 Years of Publishing in 2024

For information about special discounts for bulk purchases, please contact Simon & Schuster Special Sales at 1-866-506-1949 or business@simonandschuster.com.

The Simon & Schuster Speakers Bureau can bring authors to your live event. For more information or to book an event, contact the Simon & Schuster Speakers Bureau at 1-866-248-3049 or visit our website at www.simonspeakers.com.

Manufactured in the United States of America

1 3 5 7 9 10 8 6 4 2

Library of Congress Cataloging-in-Publication Data has been applied for.

ISBN 978-1-9821-8223-6
ISBN 978-1-9821-8226-7 (ebook)

For the magnificent Al Madocs, who has been with me more years than I can count, and who, with each book, helps me look much better than I deserve.

The truth is rarely pure and never simple.

—OSCAR WILDE

PROLOGUE

An airman first class peered at the message on her screen and announced, "Estonian Air Defense is tracking five Russian military aircraft launched from Soltsy air base, Novgorod Oblast. Currently heading due south."

The watch commander set his coffee down and sat up straighter in his chair. "That's part of Russia's 22nd Heavy Bomber Division," he announced. "I want a screen up in the next sixty seconds with everything we've got on their inventory. Also, grab whatever geospatial is live and feed it to the big board."

As the first airman got to work on her orders, another chimed in with an update, "Latvian Air Defense is confirming the launch. Looks like an Antonov AN-124 cargo aircraft accompanied by four Sukhoi Su-57 fighters. Took off eight minutes ago."

"57s?" the watch commander repeated.

"Yes, sir," the second airman replied. "That's what the Latvians are saying."

"Destination?"

"Unknown."

"Payload?"

"Also unknown," the second airman stated.

The watch commander looked at the screens. *What kind of cargo could that Antonov be carrying that required an escort of Russia's newest and most sophisticated fighters?*

"Ping the National Reconnaissance Office," he ordered. "I want all the overhead satellite imagery from Soltsy air base for the last seventy-two hours."

"Yes, sir. Right away."

Within twenty-minutes, the NRO had uploaded the imagery to the DoD's secure cloud. The watch commander was just about to dig in when he received another update.

"According to the Latvians, all five Russian aircraft have just entered Belarusian airspace," the first airman stated.

"Lithuanian air defense confirms same," said the second airman.

"All right," said the watch commander, "let's see where they go."

After twenty more minutes, the planes began to make their descent and the Pentagon watch team had their answer.

The Russian aircraft were on approach for Machulishchy air base, twenty kilometers outside of downtown Minsk.

Once the planes had touched down, the team watched as the cargo aircraft taxied to a large hangar and disappeared inside. Shortly thereafter, the Su-57 fighter jets took off and headed back to Russia.

The watch commander entered everything in the logbook, wrote up a report, and submitted it to his chain of command.

Two days later, standing in front of what appeared to be some sort of military storage facility deep in a forest and surrounded by military vehicles, the president of Belarus made the following statement to the Russian state TV channel Rossiya-1 and the Belarusian state news agency's "BelTA" Telegram channel, "The Republic of Belarus has now received from Russia shipments of both missiles and bombs three times more powerful than those dropped on Hiroshima and Nagasaki."

With those words, alarm bells began going off around the world.

If the assertion was true, the nuclear doomsday clock had just clicked one minute closer to midnight.

CHAPTER 1

Jean-Jacques Jadot had spent a rainy weekend at his seaside cottage in Brittany, only venturing outside for a short walk along the wind-swept coast.

The remainder of the time, the snowy-haired, sixty-two-year-old French intelligence officer had pored over his files.

The rot can't be this widespread, he had thought to himself. *The treason this deep.* Yet the evidence was all there.

Not a single agency appeared to have been untouched. Not even his beloved DGSE, France's equivalent to Britain's MI6 or the American CIA.

Worse still, the penetration ran right to the top, compromising a key member of the French president's cabinet. The gravity of the situation was clear.

What wasn't clear, however, was its raison d'être. Russia didn't need French nuclear technology. Neither did it need France's submarine technology. It was a rather poorly kept secret that the Russians had already stolen schematics for France's new Barracuda-class nuclear attack subs.

So then what was it all about? Why go to such extraordinary lengths? The investment in this kind of espionage operation, not to mention the risks, was almost unfathomable. *What intelligence did France have that the Russians wanted so badly?*

That question had spun endlessly in Jadot's mind over the last two and a half days.

Rising only occasionally to place fresh logs on the fire or to prepare another mug of tea fortified with cognac, he had sat in his favorite chair, trying to connect the dots and deconstruct the Russian plot.

But no matter how much of his considerable intellect he had applied, the answers refused to reveal themselves. Before he knew it, the weekend was over and it was time to leave.

While a local taxi idled in the drive, Jadot closed up the cottage and then made himself comfortable for the twenty-minute drive into Saint-Malo. There he picked up dinner from his favorite brasserie along the Place Chateaubriand, walked the rest of the way to the station, and boarded the last TGV to Paris.

As the high-speed train raced through the darkened countryside, Jadot ignored his food and stared at his reflection in the window.

He was no longer a young man. He had been with the Directorate General for External Security for over three decades. His time in the espionage game was coming to a close. This case would be his legacy.

Exposing the breach of the French intelligence community was not only his duty, it was his chance to leave a deep and indelible mark. It was critical, therefore, that he choose his steps with caution; that he get everything right. There was zero room for error.

Turning his eyes from the window, he forced himself to eat. It was important to keep up his strength. He was about to step into a minefield. Tomorrow he would meet with a colleague from the CIA's Paris station—one of the few people he felt he could trust. Then he would put his plan, as ill-conceived as it was, into action.

Two and a half hours later, his train arrived at the Gare Montparnasse in Paris's 15th arrondissement.

The rain, which had lashed the windows of his cottage throughout the weekend, had pushed inland and was now pouring down on the capital. Finding a cab would be impossible, so Jadot opted for the Métro.

He rode for seven stations, transferred at Châtelet, and then reemerged above ground at the Hôtel de Ville. Turning up the collar of his jacket against the elements, he headed for his apartment in the Marais.

Even though it was getting late, there were still several establishments doing a brisk business along the Rue Vieille-du-Temple. Under soft lights, patrons laughed over bottles of wine, chatted over cups of coffee, and enjoyed each other's company over plates of food. *Conviviality. Human contact.*

He thought about popping into Robert et Louise—the little restaurant across the street from his apartment—just for a nightcap. The glow from its wood-fired oven, the rumble of the dumbwaiter as it shunted up and down, the heavy "neighbor's pour" the barman treated regulars to—all of it had a way of putting him at ease. There was, however, an additional, more professional reason the idea appealed to him.

Ever since stepping off the train in Montparnasse, he had felt eyes on him, as if he were being watched.

Per his training, he had conducted multiple surveillance detection routes. He covertly scanned the faces he saw on the Métro, changed carriages several times, and literally took the long way home once he had exited the subway system. Still, he hadn't seen anything.

Either he was being followed by someone exceptionally skilled, or his mind—and maybe even the rain—were playing tricks on him. A stiff calvados and a perch on a barstool with a view of the street would help him sort it all out.

Inside Robert et Louise, he hung his wet coat on the rack. The air was redolent with the scent of roasted pork, chicken, lamb, beef, and veal. He could practically hear the sizzling of fat as it dripped from the spits in the open kitchen.

Grabbing a seat at the end of the scarred *comptoir,* he didn't even need to place his drink order.

Within seconds of his sitting down, the barman was busy uncorking a bottle filled with gold-colored liquid.

"Quel putain de temps," the man said as he set a generously filled snifter of apple brandy in front of Jadot. *Pretty shitty weather, eh?*

"Plus mal demain," the intelligence officer replied. *Worse tomorrow.*

They made small talk for a few moments before a waitress signaled that she needed the barman to make a round of drinks for her.

Sipping his calvados, Jadot kept his eyes on the front door of his building across the street.

Beyond a few cars and a person or two with an umbrella, no one passed. No one stopped. No one came into Robert et Louise. It was simply a rainy Sunday night in Paris. Nothing more.

When he got to the bottom of his snifter, the barman asked him if he wanted a refill. Jadot politely waved him off. If he had a second, he'd probably have a third. That wouldn't be good. He needed to be sharp and fully focused tomorrow.

Laying a bill on the *comptoir*, he thanked the barman and told him to keep the change.

As he put on his coat, a waiter offered him a Styrofoam to-go box of food—roast potatoes and meats they would only be throwing out when they closed in twenty minutes.

Jadot didn't have much of an appetite, but he was a good man, a good neighbor, and so he graciously accepted.

Stepping outside, back into the rain, he paused briefly on the sidewalk to scan up and down the street. Still nothing.

He tucked the to-go container under his arm and fished for his keys as he crossed to his front door.

Inside, he ignored his mailbox. There was nothing in it that couldn't wait another day.

He ignored the elevator as well.

Stairs helped keep him in shape. He had spent most of his life as a rugged outdoorsman, a committed alpinist. Nothing crazy. No Kangchenjunga, no Nanga Parbat. And definitely no K2 and no Everest. Jadot was a sub-25,000 man.

Summits such as Baintha Brakk in Pakistan, Cerro Torre in Argentina, and the Eiger in Switzerland were much more his style. An intelligent, technical athlete's climbs—with far fewer fame-seeking Instagram assholes to contend with. He had yet to see any dead bodies on his summits.

To that end, he had nothing but disdain for those who chased the biggest mountains only for the bragging rights. Climbing, in his book, was like making love. You didn't become an expert overnight. It was something you got better at with practice.

When he reached his apartment, he kicked off his boots and hung his coat on a peg in the vestibule to drip-dry. His was the sole unit at the top of the five-story building.

Inside, the centuries-old dwelling was complete with hand-hewn wooden beams, three antique fireplaces, and original tiles. The *portes-fenêtres* in the living room gave onto the Rue Vieille-du-Temple, while the smaller windows in the back looked out over a hidden courtyard and a slice of the expansive National Archives complex.

The walls were covered with framed photographs from his adventures abroad—both his climbing trips as well as the far-flung locations where he had carried out assignments on behalf of the DGSE. There was no evidence to indicate the presence of a spouse or any sort of romantic partner in Jadot's life. By all appearances, the man was unattached.

Entering the kitchen, he dropped his keys on the counter, placed the to-go container in the fridge, then pulled out his cell phone and plugged it in to charge.

As he did, he heard a noise. It sounded like it had come from the master bedroom. Jadot froze. He wasn't alone. *Someone was in the apartment.*

Being careful not to make a sound, he opened the cupboard beneath the sink and retrieved the old Manurhin double-action revolver he had taped inside.

His first instinct was that maybe he was being robbed. Over the last six months, multiple apartments across the Marais had been hit. But none of them, to his recollection, were late on a Sunday night. The thieves had preferred to strike during the day—while people were at work. That could only mean one thing: someone had come for him, specifically.

Quietly cocking the pistol, he brought the weapon to the ready position and crept toward his bedroom.

He placed his steps carefully, avoiding the handful of floorboards that were guaranteed to groan and give his approach away.

At the door, he took a deep breath, applied pressure to his trigger, and then peeked around the frame. *The room was empty.*

Not only was it empty, but he believed he might have discovered the source of the sound he'd heard.

Lying on the floor next to his book-strewn nightstand was a large tome on European history. *Could it have fallen by itself?*

Anything was possible, but just to make sure, Jadot checked under the bed, and inside his closet and the master bath. They were all clear. Picking up the book, he returned it to the nightstand. Then he heard something that stopped him dead in his tracks. Out in the hall, one of the floorboards *creaked*.

For a fraction of a second, he was tempted to fire right through the wall. But not knowing who was on the other side made such an act incredibly reckless.

If it did turn out to be some poor kid forced to steal or some junkie just trying to support a habit, those weren't the kinds of deaths he was prepared to have on his conscience. And if it wasn't a thief but someone sent to attack him, he needed that person alive. Dead men were somewhat difficult to interrogate.

Taking another deep breath, he steadied his pistol and prepared to peek into the hall.

He counted down from three and then leaned out only far enough to steal the quickest of glimpses before pulling back. He didn't see anything. *There was no one there.* His hands slick with sweat, he gripped the pistol tighter.

Stepping into the hall, he swung his gun toward the kitchen, but it appeared just as he had left it—empty—and he headed toward the living room, carefully clearing each of the rooms he passed.

By the time he reached the front of the apartment, adrenaline was wreaking havoc on his body. His heart was pounding so hard that all he could hear was the sound of blood thrumming in his ears. His breath came in short, shallow snatches and his hands had developed a tremor. But there was a good sign—the front door was ajar.

Whoever had been in the apartment must have made the smart decision to flee. Jadot felt his pulse begin to slow.

He wiped each of his palms on his trousers, before reacclimating his grip on his weapon. There was one last thing he needed to do.

Opening the door the rest of the way with his foot, he cautiously stepped out onto the landing. There was no one there.

He strained his ears but heard no sound of footfalls on the stairs. He then glanced over the railing, gun first, but couldn't see anyone. Perhaps the intruder was hugging the walls on the way down or had heard him coming and paused on a lower floor. All he could be certain of was that whatever the threat had been, it had passed.

Retreating into the apartment, he closed the door behind him and made sure it was locked.

Inhaling, he filled his lungs with air and stood there for a moment, willing his body to reset, before exhaling it all out.

He needed to do a thorough, top-to-bottom search of the place to make sure nothing had been taken. But because his hands were still shaking, the first thing he was going to do was pour himself a drink.

Padding down the hallway in his stocking feet, he tucked the pistol into his waistband as he entered the kitchen.

From a cabinet above the sink, he took down a bottle of bourbon and placed it, along with a glass from the dish rack, on the countertop.

He had just opened the freezer for some ice when he heard it again—a floorboard had creaked. *This time right behind him.*

In one fluid motion, Jadot spun while pulling his pistol, but he was a fraction of a second too late.

The last thing he saw was the tip of a climbing axe as it came crashing down into his skull.

CHAPTER 2

S cot Harvath hadn't thought twice about splurging on a first-class ticket. He'd been through hell.

After fighting his way into an active war zone in Ukraine, rescuing an American hostage from behind enemy lines, and fighting his way back out, all he wanted was a nice, long chunk of uninterrupted recovery time. The more luxurious, the better. He had earned it.

Boarding his flight to Norway, he'd been accompanied to his seat by a flight attendant who asked what she could bring her handsome passenger before takeoff. His answer—three Ziplocs packed full of ice and a glass of bourbon.

He'd had the shit kicked out of him and could feel it from the crown of his head to the soles of his feet. His body was tattooed with bruises, his left shoulder felt like somebody had driven an ice pick through it, and his ears were still ringing. *He probably needed to see a doctor.*

Making himself as comfortable as possible, he placed the bags of ice where he had the most pain and then sipped his drink while the rest of the passengers boarded.

He hadn't told anyone back at the Carlton Group where he was going. It wasn't any of their business. If the world suddenly caught fire over the next week, he was content to let it burn. For the time being, he was out of the spy business.

Closing his eyes, he envisioned what awaited him in Norway.

Sølvi Kolstad had appeared at the lowest moment in his life and had given him a reason to live, something he hadn't imagined would ever again be possible.

They were two shattered vessels—he broken by the murder of his wife, she abandoned by her husband because she couldn't bear children. Yet what had felt like the end was actually the beginning, a form of *kintsugi,* the Japanese art of putting pieces of pottery back together with gold. They had merged their flaws, their loneliness, and their pain to create something beautiful, something stronger. And despite their age difference, with Sølvi several years his junior, they shared a lot in common.

Harvath had been a U.S. Navy SEAL, first with the cold-weather specialists of SEAL Team Two, and then with the storied SEAL Team Six. Sølvi had also served with an elite Special Forces unit—Norway's all-female Jegertroppen. Both of them had eventually wound up in the espionage game.

Like him, she was a highly skilled operative and had made an exceptionally good spy. In fact, Harvath was willing to admit that she was smarter and even better at it than he was. His only advantage over her was that he had been at it for longer.

Unlike him, however, when a plum leadership position had become available inside the Norwegian Intelligence Service, she had jumped at the chance.

Promoted to deputy director status, Sølvi had been placed in charge of a top-secret program critical to Norway's survival. If the Russians ever overran their shared border, her covert unit was responsible for standing up a shadow intelligence service.

She loved her new job. Her career was taking off and her future was filled with nothing but possibility.

Harvath, on the other hand, couldn't bear the thought of ever coming out of the field only to ride a desk. He had been handpicked by the Carlton Group's founder to run the organization after his passing, but had repeatedly turned the position down.

It wasn't just the corporate bullshit and office politics he couldn't stand—it was the fact that hanging up his cleats would mean that he had aged out. And as far as he was concerned, he wasn't there yet. He could still do his job better than any of the younger operatives.

Did it require increasingly tougher workouts and a mix of performance-enhancing drugs in order to keep his edge? Sure, but in his world, there was no Marquess of Queensberry, no rulebook.

In fact, the Carlton Group had been created to level the playing field. It was a private intelligence agency—operating beyond the gaze of Congress—empowered to hunt down enemies of the United States who refused to respect the international order.

The idea was that if bad actors were going to choose to ignore the Geneva and Hague Conventions, then America needed a way to defend itself. Fighting with both your arms and legs tied behind your back wasn't a winning strategy. That's where Harvath came in.

The powers that be could let him off the chain, look in the other direction, and know that the job would get done.

It wasn't a calling for a sadist or a maladjusted personality. You couldn't have someone in the role who took pleasure in inflicting pain on others or who enjoyed breaking the rules simply for the sake of breaking them. The position required a person with a strong moral compass who only broke the rules when necessary. That was Harvath.

He lived by the SEAL maxims that the only easy day was yesterday and that when tasked with an assignment, success was the only option.

His personal motto was that there was no American dream without those willing to protect it.

More and more, however, he had begun to ask himself what *his* American dream looked like. Once he was ready to lay down his sword and remove his armor, what would life be like? What was there for *him* to look forward to?

The obvious answer, as the plane pushed back from the gate and taxied out to the runway, was Sølvi. Over oysters, a fabulous bottle of champagne, and a terrific view of the Oslofjord, he had proposed and she had accepted.

Yes, things had moved fast. But having known excruciating heartbreak, neither of them wanted to risk letting something so good slip away.

Since her job required that she work at NIS headquarters in person, he had spent the summer with her, burning through all of his vacation and sick days. It wasn't until the Carlton Group had threatened to fire him that he had gotten serious about returning to work himself. And no sooner had he made that decision than his operations tempo had been pushed into overdrive.

Assignment after assignment rained down. In less than two months, he had been to Tajikistan, Afghanistan, India, Romania, Poland, and Ukraine. During that time, he had been unable to see Sølvi. And therein lay the biggest problem in their relationship—the intense demands of their careers. Something had to give.

Right now, though, he didn't want to think about it. All he wanted was to see her, to touch her, to quiet their busy lives long enough to reconnect and reassure each other that they were doing the right thing and that what they had was worth making any sacrifice for.

As the plane roared down the runway, Harvath felt the familiar feeling of the stress leaving his body. It was like this every time he finished an assignment. Lifting off instantly helped him relax.

Within minutes, his exhaustion overcame him and he fell into a dark, dreamless sleep. But it didn't last.

About an hour later, somewhere over the Baltic Sea, he was jolted awake by the sound of screaming coming from the rear of the aircraft.

CHAPTER 3

Harvath leaned into the aisle to get a look at what was going on back in the economy section. Flight attendants were trying to get control of an unruly passenger.

The man, who was in the rear galley, was largely obscured from view. But when Harvath caught a flash of one of his beefy, heavily inked arms, that flash was enough to identify him. He had seen him downing drinks in the airport bar before the flight.

Standing about six foot eight and weighing upwards of 275 pounds, the guy was a monster. He was also extremely agitated. Maybe someone had made the mistake of cutting him off. Maybe they had run out of peanuts. Or maybe the man was having some sort of a mental breakdown. None of that, however, was Harvath's problem.

At least it wasn't until the not-so-gentle giant punched one of the female flight attendants in the face and sent her crashing to the floor in a spray of blood.

The passengers screamed again.

If there had been any security officers on board, it was now officially time for them to get involved. Harvath waited, but when no one did, he knew he was going to have to serve as the cavalry.

Unbuckling his seat belt, he scanned the space around him for a weapon—anything that might help even up the odds.

He grabbed an in-flight magazine, which could be rolled up into a baton, and began twisting it as he stepped into the aisle.

As he did, he saw the other flight attendants in the back wrestling with the monster as they called out for help. He didn't relish what lay ahead.

Knowing that this could be the beginning of a hijacking, with sleepers lying in wait to take out any passengers attempting heroics, he kept his guard up and scanned every face and every pair of hands as he moved toward the rear of the plane.

Before he could get to the galley, another flight attendant, this time a male, was struck with a devastating punch to the head and knocked to the floor.

Two passengers decided it was finally time to do something and, leaping from their seats, charged the tattooed combatant . . . with blankets.

Blankets? For what? To tie him up? To throw them over his head so he couldn't see?

The only thing Harvath knew was that as brave as these paunchy, middle-aged guys were, they were going to get their asses kicked. *Bad.*

And he was right.

As soon as they entered the galley, the giant shoved the remaining flight attendants aside and kicked the first of the middle-aged men square in the chest. The blow knocked the wind out of the man, cracked his sternum, and dropped him right there.

The second man received one of the worst headbutts Harvath had ever seen. The blood gushed from his nose like a hydrant. As he blacked out and fell backward, he hit his head on the way down, *hard.*

It was at that moment, scanning for additional threats, that the monster locked eyes with Harvath. He paused, sizing him up.

Harvath stood five foot ten and a muscular 175 pounds. Though the giant outweighed and towered over him, he radiated the unnerving, icy calm of a man conversant with violence.

He put his left hand up and attempted to deescalate the situation. "Hey, it's okay. Let's just take a breath. Nobody else needs to get hurt."

With his nostrils flaring and the whites of his eyes exposed, the giant resembled some sort of enraged bull. His chest heaved as he sucked in air.

It was hard to tell if he spoke English or if he even understood what Harvath was saying. Right now, though, he wasn't attacking anyone. He was standing completely still. That was the right start.

"Do you want to sit down?" Harvath asked. "I'll sit with you. Any place you want. How does that sound?"

There was a grunt from the heavily tattooed man as he balled his massive hands into fists. Things were going in the wrong direction.

Harvath remained calm and continued to try to dial down the situation. This wasn't a hijacking. It was a troubled individual having some sort of a psychotic break. "Is there someone waiting for you in Oslo?" he inquired. "Someone you'd like to talk to? Your wife? Girlfriend?"

The man's eyes narrowed and before he had even started moving, Harvath knew that he had crossed some sort of line. He had screwed up and triggered the guy into action. *It was on.*

Exploding across the galley, the giant charged. And when he did, Harvath was already two steps ahead.

Pivoting out of the way, he used the makeshift baton to deliver a strike to the man's kidney.

The giant roared in pain. His knees buckled and he almost went down. *Almost.* Breaking his fall with his right hand, he pushed off the floor and lunged again.

Harvath waited until he got in close, threw his left hand toward the man's eyes, and then drove the baton into his solar plexus. The giant stumbled.

Sidestepping out of his path, Harvath was certain the tattooed man was going *all* the way down this time, but he was mistaken. The giant regrouped and came at him again.

Even for a wide-body jet, the galley made for one of the world's narrowest cage matches. Harvath wasn't going to be able to keep slipping out of the man's grasp like this. If the giant took him down to the ground, things were going to get ugly.

He had no choice but to increase the pain he was subjecting the man to; to deliver a blow that wasn't fatal, but that was serious enough to take him out of the fight, at least until they could get the plane safely on the ground. With a guy this big, that usually meant one thing—going for his knees.

To do that, however, he was going to have to square up with him; stand face-to-face as he charged, which was exactly what Harvath did.

The giant thundered across the galley. Harvath held his hands up, palms out, as if signaling he didn't want any trouble. Simultaneously, he focused on the man's left knee and got ready to deliver a kick so hard, the man wouldn't be able to walk without assistance for a long time.

But just as the giant got in range, he changed his attack. He lowered his head and bent over at the waist, as if to tackle his opponent, making it impossible to take out his knee. Harvath barely had time to react.

He knew he had to be ready to shoot his hips forward and drive his legs backward, out of the way, in order to prevent being taken down to the ground. It was a defensive technique known as a "sprawl." The only problem was, Harvath had totally misread what his attacker was planning.

The giant wasn't interested in taking out his legs. Instead, he wanted to use his upper body to hit Harvath, as hard as he could, right in his midsection. Which was exactly what he did.

It was like being struck by a freight train. Harvath was lifted off his feet and driven full-force into the emergency exit. But the giant didn't stop there.

Using his meaty palm, he slammed Harvath's head against the door. Harvath saw stars.

In response, he delivered a series of blistering punches to the giant's ribs, one after another. None of them seemed to have any effect.

The giant again slammed his head into the door and this time, his vision began to dim. Harvath was in serious trouble. If he didn't get out from under this guy, it was going to be game over.

Planting his feet, he tried to thrust upward and knock the giant off balance, but the beast didn't budge.

Instead the man pulled Harvath's head back once more and was preparing to pound it against the door when there was a loud, metallic thud.

Dazed, the giant paused. One of the flight attendants had bashed him with a coffeepot. Harvath knew it was now or never.

Using all his strength, he exploded, pushing his attacker off him and sending the man tumbling over backward into the middle of the galley.

Harvath leapt to his feet, but he'd had his bell rung to such a degree that his balance was temporarily off. He needed to place his hand against the wall to steady himself.

Shaking his head, he tried to clear his vision. He could see the flight attendant, but the giant was no longer where he had thrown him. He was on the other side of the galley.

It took Harvath a moment to realize what the man was doing, but when he did, only one word popped into his mind—*Fuck*—as he bolted back into action.

The man had deactivated the safety mechanisms on the opposite emergency exit door and was about to open it, when Harvath launched himself the final few feet, landed on the giant's back, and put him in a rear naked chokehold.

Because the man was so big, Harvath had to modify his grip, but within seconds he reduced the blood flow from the man's heart and had cut off the oxygen to his brain. The giant collapsed unconscious onto the floor.

Loosening, but not completely unlocking the chokehold, Harvath gave instructions to the flight attendants and nearby passengers. A man this big and this unstable was going to need a lot more than a pair of plastic flex-cuffs to keep him restrained until the plane landed.

Once he had been secured, Harvath released his grasp. Moving several feet away, he rested his forearms against his knees and took several deep breaths.

As the flight crew attended to each other, as well as the injured passengers, one of them offered Harvath a bottle of water. "Thank you," she said.

Harvath accepted the water and nodded.

When he felt good enough to stand, he got up and headed back to his seat in first class. A group of economy passengers, eager for a piece of the action now that the actual danger had passed, had deputized themselves to keep an eye on the bound passenger until the plane landed.

After a pit stop in the lavatory to verify he wasn't bleeding, he sat back down and asked for a fresh bourbon, along with a few more icepacks.

The pilots had decided that with the giant subdued, they didn't need to divert and would land in Oslo as planned.

With that piece of good news, Harvath settled back in his seat, focused on his drink, and tried to relax.

•   •   •

When the plane landed, the pilot came back over the PA system to explain that airport police would be meeting the plane at the gate and that all passengers should remain in their seats.

It took six tactical officers to remove the giant from the aircraft. The passengers clapped and cheered as he was marched off.

But no sooner had he been led away than another officer boarded. After speaking with the lead flight attendant, he entered the first-class section and stopped at Harvath's seat.

"Passport," he said in an officious tone, holding out his hand.

Removing the document from his pocket, Harvath handed it to him, noting the three gold stars and two stripes on the man's epaulets. Whoever the man was, he was very high in rank.

The officer checked the name and photo, and then, looking at Harvath, ordered, "Come with me."

CHAPTER 4

Grabbing his bag from the overhead, Harvath followed the officer, stopping briefly at the main cabin door to receive additional thanks from the flight crew.

As he and the cop deplaned, they had to step aside to allow medical personnel to board and see to the injured.

But once they had passed, the officer didn't lead him toward the terminal. Instead, he opened the door to the jet bridge stairs and took him down to the tarmac.

The air was chilly and awash with the smell of jet fuel. Two ambulances were standing by, as was a BMW X5 crisscrossed with thick neon yellow stripes, a lightbar, and the Norwegian word for police, *Politi.*

Harvath was about to ask whether he should sit in the front or the back, when the cop preempted him. Taking his bag, he opened the rear door, gestured for him to sit, and then closed the door once he was inside. After tossing Harvath's bag in the trunk, the cop got behind the wheel, activated the lightbar, and, without saying a word to his passenger, took off across the airport.

Harvath had no idea what was going on. He wasn't in handcuffs and hadn't been patted down, so that was a minor check mark in the plus column.

On the other hand, he had been escorted off an airplane and was riding in the back of a police car being driven with its lights on by a cop who had not returned his passport.

This wouldn't be the first time he'd been taken in for questioning by the Norwegian Police Service. In fact, somewhere in Sølvi's apartment he still had the card of the lawyer who had previously gotten his passport back and had walked him out the door in record time. If this turned out to be anything more than the cops taking his statement about what had happened on the plane, he might need to call her to dig it up for him.

The officer rolled to a stop and killed his lights outside what looked like some sort of private, VIP terminal.

After retrieving his bag from the trunk, the cop opened the door, handed it to him, and motioned for Harvath to follow him into the building.

The lobby, with its polished reception desk, resembled something out of a boutique hotel. The cop nodded at the woman behind the desk and kept moving, leading Harvath down a brightly lit hallway decorated with pieces of modern art.

On a glossy orange door with "Suite 7" written in an oversize font, he swiped a keycard and then stepped inside followed by Harvath.

"Wait here," the officer ordered, stepping back into the hall and closing the door behind him.

The room was decorated with chic Scandinavian furniture and had a private, marble bathroom, complete with a walk-in shower, just off to the side. A large flat-screen TV was tuned to a local Norwegian station. There was a buffet with fresh fruit, an array of snacks, a full bar, and a coffee station. Harvath made a beeline for the coffee.

As he dropped in a pod and waited for his espresso, he opened a drawer and found a range of amenities, including individual packets of pain relievers. Tearing one open, he popped the two pills, chased them with a water from the mini fridge, and put the rest of the packets in his pocket. He also grabbed a fresh toothbrush and some disposable razors. If this was the level at which the Norwegian police were conducting interviews these days, he was all for it.

When his coffee was ready, he walked over to the long leather couch and sat down. The floor-to-ceiling windows provided a terrific view of planes taking off and landing. Removing his boots, he put his feet up, and grabbed the remote. As long as he was being detained, he figured he might as well enjoy himself.

He dialed around until he found an English language news station and then only half paid attention as the host ran through the headlines.

In his mind he was in the city center, forty minutes away, already halfway through a great bottle of wine with Sølvi, catching her up on everything that had happened since they had last seen each other.

Part of him regretted not having picked her up a gift. He had searched for one at the airport shops in Kraków, but there hadn't been anything special. It was all either too crappy or just not her style. He knew she'd understand. Making it back to her in one piece was the only thing that she had said she truly wanted.

The more he thought about her, the more he wanted his passport back and to be on his way.

He was also getting to the point in his pain threshold where ice packs were no longer going to do the trick. He was going to need a full-on ice bath. Where the hell he was going to buy large bags of ice in Oslo, however, was beyond him. That American culinary specialty had yet to pierce the Scandinavian market.

After polishing off his espresso, he was about to hop up and brew another one when there was a knock on his door, followed by the chime of a keycard opening the lock.

He looked up, expecting to see the officer who had brought him over from the plane, but instead he was greeted with the sight of Holidae Hayes, chief of the CIA's Oslo station.

"Bumpy flight?" she asked, stepping into the room.

"I've had better," Harvath replied, taking his feet off the table and sitting upright. "What are you doing here? Is Sølvi okay?"

Hayes held up her index finger, pointed toward the ceiling, and drew imaginary loops with it, indicating that the room might be bugged. "She's fine. I came to give you a ride."

"I can't leave yet. Some cop has my passport."

The tall, redheaded CIA operative removed Harvath's passport from her pocket and tossed it to him.

He opened it and flipped it to the most recent page. "Even got it stamped for me."

"Professional courtesy."

"They don't want a statement?"

Hayes shook her head. "Only if you want to press charges."

It was now Harvath's turn to shake his head. The man on the plane was already going to be facing a host of charges. He was also probably going to get added to Europe's no-fly list. He needed psychiatric help, not Harvath piling on.

They brewed two coffees to go and Harvath followed Hayes out to her black Chevy Suburban with its yellow diplomatic plates.

After throwing his bag in the cargo area, he hopped into the front passenger seat and they drove out of the airport.

"Safe to talk now?" he asked, checking his side mirror as they got onto the pine-studded A10 highway, which led into the city.

"I want to save the shop talk until we're back at the office."

Interesting, he thought as he nodded in response and took a sip of his coffee.

When Hayes had indicated her reluctance to speak because the VIP private jet suite might be bugged, that hadn't been surprising. Corporate espionage, even among allied nations, was big business. The French and Israelis, some of the worst offenders, were even said to bug the business and first-class sections of their national airlines.

But the fact that she didn't even want to speak in a moving U.S. Embassy vehicle was significant. Whatever this was, it was serious. Very serious.

CHAPTER 5

Tilting his seat back, Harvath had tried, without much luck, to get comfortable, and they had passed the rest of the drive making small talk.

Hayes was a fascinating woman. She was exceedingly bright and exceedingly ambitious. In an arena still dominated by the old boys' network, she had carved out quite a career for herself. She had even come to the president's attention and there was talk of her jumping from CIA to the State Department for an ambassadorship after the next election.

He also knew that Sølvi really admired her—especially as Hayes had succeeded despite her good looks, not because of them. No one had given her anything. She'd had to fight for every single thing that she had achieved.

Arriving at the ten-acre embassy campus, Harvath was reminded of the attention to detail that had gone into its design. Horizontal roofs were meant to honor traditional Norwegian longhouses, while boulders placed throughout mimicked the landscape of the Norwegian fjords. The most impressive design element, however, was the copper cornices, which were identical to the copper used for the Statue of Liberty, which was also mined in Norway. The entire project was a testament to the enduring friendship between the two nations.

Hayes badged Harvath in and after leaving his bag in her office, they headed for the sensitive compartmented information facility, also known as the SCIF. It was an ultra-secure room, about the size and shape of a shipping container, designed to foil all manner of high-tech eavesdropping. As such, they were required to leave their cell phones in a cubby outside.

Once in the SCIF, with the door securely closed behind them, the CIA station chief pulled out the chair at the head of the conference table. Harvath took the chair to her right.

"You did an exceptional job in Ukraine. Langley, the White House . . . everyone's very happy."

"Good. That's what I'm paid for," he replied, following up with the first of many questions he had. "What was all of that back at the airport? Why pick me up? In fact, how'd you even know I was going to be on that flight?"

Hayes smiled. "I'm CIA."

"Don't jerk me around, Holidae. I'm not in the mood. Not today. Okay?"

"Fair enough," she responded. "I apologize."

"So what happened? The pilots called in the disturbance, the Norwegians ran the manifest, and what? They contacted the embassy to let you all know there was at least one Amcit on board?"

The station chief shook her head. "I wasn't aware of the disturbance until I got to the airport and Chief Inspector Borger filled me in. He was the officer who escorted you off the plane and got your customs and immigration expedited for me."

Now Harvath was even more confused. "If you didn't show up because of what happened during the flight, what were you doing there?"

"I needed to see you before you saw Sølvi."

In the back of his mind, alarm bells began to go off. "Holidae, if you've got something to tell me, *tell* me."

Hayes took a breath and cut to the chase. "The Norwegians have a Russian defector. Came across a couple of days ago. Sølvi's in charge of him."

"I know."

She looked at him. "You know?"

"Yeah. She told me."

"What else did she tell you?"

"Nothing else. It's none of my business."

Hayes removed a folder and pushed it across the table to him. "His name is Leonid Grechko," she said as Harvath opened the man's jacket and began flipping through it. "High-ranking operative in Russia's Foreign Intelligence Service. He was in charge of their Active Measures Department. His job was to shape world events via political warfare. Espionage, sabotage, assassination, propaganda . . . he had every conceivable tool in his toolbox and he used them all. With a frightening level of precision."

Harvath closed the folder and slid it back to her. "This guy's a walking, talking golden ticket. He could have defected anywhere. You guys at CIA would've showered him with so much money, he'd have drowned. So with all due respect to the Norwegians, why defect here?"

"That's what we want to know."

"So ask your counterpart over at Norwegian Intelligence. You and Vice Admiral Iversen are friendly enough, right?"

"The Norwegians don't know that we know that they've got him."

Harvath reached into his pocket and pulled out another packet of pain pills. Hayes was beginning to give him a headache. "Sounds to me like a *you* problem."

"All we want you to do is to keep your ears open. Maybe ask a few questions—"

"*We.* Meaning the CIA."

The station chief nodded.

"And by 'keep my ears open and ask a few questions,' what you want is for me to spy on Sølvi—the woman I'm about to marry."

"We've picked up intelligence that suggests the Russians are up to something."

"For fuck's sake, Holidae. It's the Russians. They're *always* up to something. Sorry. I'm not your guy. I'm not going to spy on my fiancée."

"You're the only person we've got."

"Technically speaking, you don't *have* me. I work for a private agency that contracts with you guys. I get to say 'no' anytime I want. And for the record, the CIA should've known I'd say 'no,' especially to something like this."

"To be honest," she replied, "they actually anticipated that would be your answer." There was something about her tone that unsettled him, but before he could respond, she produced another folder and slid it across the table.

"I want you to know that this wasn't my idea. In fact, I was against it."

More alarm bells.

He opened the folder and looked inside. There were only a few sheets of paper. The executive summary made clear what he was looking at. Slowly, he flipped through it.

When he was finished, he closed the folder and gently slid it back. "I have no idea what this is."

"Now who's jerking who around?" she asked.

Harvath looked at her, his expression flat, unreadable.

"Since we're getting things about the CIA on the record," Hayes continued, "I want you to know that I pushed for using a carrot. It was Langley that decided to go with the stick."

"Well, wrong stick."

"That's not the way the seventh floor sees it. They think the evidence is pretty compelling."

"What evidence?"

"After your wife was murdered, you launched a far-reaching revenge campaign. Right up to and including the drug-addled, psycho son of President Peshkov of Russia. But what you hadn't banked on was the boy's oligarch godfather putting a one-hundred-million-dollar, winner-take-all bounty on your head.

"Of course you being you, you ignited another kill chain and took out everyone involved with that plot too. Everyone, that is, except for the man who put up the bounty—the boy's aforementioned godfather, Nikolai Nekrasov. For some reason, you let him live. And that's where it starts to get interesting.

"After running Nekrasov to ground, you left your team in a parking garage while you went into the building, alone, ostensibly to finish him off. But for some reason you changed your mind.

"Shortly thereafter, Nekrasov's long-suffering wife, Eva, gets a magic deposit of fifty million dollars, half the value of the bounty, in an account in Bermuda. Then that same day, another account, this one buried in a web of shell companies in Switzerland, its ultimate beneficiary unknown, also receives a fifty-million-dollar deposit."

"That's amazing," Harvath deadpanned.

"What? That the CIA tracked it all down?"

"No. That you don't know who the second account belongs to."

Hayes smiled. "We didn't know bin Laden would be in that house in Abbottabad either, but we had a high enough level of confidence to move on it."

"You took your shot and it paid off."

"As this could for you. Fifty million is a hell of a nest egg. And no one is blaming you."

"Blaming me for what? I told you, I don't know what you're talking about."

The station chief put up her hands in surrender. "Maybe you and Mrs. Nekrasov came to some sort of an understanding. I don't know and I don't care. The Russians are butchers. They killed your wife. And you made them bleed, *big-time*. If that bleeding also meant keeping the bounty Nikolai had placed on your head in exchange for letting him live, even better. All I want you to do at this point is think about it. Okay? It's a big ask. I get it."

"What's the carrot?"

"Excuse me?"

"You said Langley opted for the stick, but you wanted to offer me a carrot. What was it?"

Hayes smiled again. "It doesn't matter. That Swiss account, stuffed with fifty million dollars, isn't yours."

"But," said Harvath, pausing for effect, "if it was."

"If it was, then I'd do you two favors. First, I'd let you know that an elite unit at the U.S. Treasury has it ringed with tripwires."

He rolled his eyes. "Sounds dangerous."

"They don't mess around at Treasury."

"And the second favor?" he asked.

"The second favor is the carrot. I'd help make all those tripwires, in fact the entire file, disappear."

CHAPTER 6

By the time Harvath exited the SCIF, he had already made his decision. It wasn't easy. In fact, it went against almost everything he stood for. That said, it was the only way forward.

Retrieving his phone from the cubby, he powered it back up and was greeted by several messages from Sølvi. The news about what had happened on the flight from Kraków must have made its way to her.

He texted back that he was okay and would be at the apartment soon. Grabbing his bag, he left the embassy and picked up an Uber a block away.

He made two stops en route to her apartment. One was for a bouquet of flowers. The other was for a bottle of Krug and a small tin of Desietra caviar. Harvath had a few, very specific reasons why he bought this particular brand. Yes, the caviar tasted great and was the perfect accompaniment to champagne—although so were pizza and popcorn, he had found—but Desietra was completely sourced in Western Europe, not Russia or Iran, and the brains behind the company belonged to a successful American entrepreneur from, of all places, Wisconsin. Harvath's patriotism didn't stop at the U.S. border; he took it with him wherever he went.

When they arrived at the address he had provided, Harvath thanked the driver, tipped him via the app, and gave him five stars.

Once the car had driven off, he turned and walked the two short blocks back to Sølvi's. It was a minor inconvenience; an investment in making sure that he wasn't being followed and that the apartment wasn't under surveillance.

It also gave him a few more minutes to sort out his words. He had never been placed in this kind of position before. The territory was completely foreign. In his mind, he knew what he had to do. His gut, however, was ripping him apart.

When he arrived at the entrance of the building, he took one last look up and down the street. Confident it wasn't being watched, he stepped inside, locked away any misgivings in the attic of his mind, and headed up to the apartment.

Sølvi was already there waiting for him.

He threw his arms around her and they shared a long hug, followed by an even longer kiss.

Once they had peeled themselves off each other, he handed her the flowers and said, "These are for you."

"They're beautiful," she replied. "Thank you."

He couldn't believe they were finally together again. "*You're* beautiful. God, you have no idea how much I missed you."

"I think I've got a *little* idea."

She flashed her megawatt, million-dollar smile that he loved so much, and for the moment, nothing else mattered.

"Bedroom or living room?" he asked, holding up the bottle of Krug.

"Neither, I'm afraid."

"Balcony?" he pressed, seductively raising an eyebrow.

Sølvi laughed. "For now, *refrigerator.* But later . . ." Her voice trailed off as she leaned in and gave him another kiss.

"So you're not staying."

"I wish I could, but I have to get back to the Woods."

The Norwegian Intelligence Service was located just outside the city center, on a lake, surrounded by heavy forest. The nickname for their headquarters had practically created itself.

"Maybe dinner?" he asked.

"I'd love that," she replied, kissing him again. "And you can tell me all about what happened on your flight. And in Ukraine. And everywhere else you've been since we last saw each other."

"I'd love that too," he said.

But there remained an item they needed to discuss. Something he wasn't content to let wait. Holding up his phone and pressing his index finger against his lips, he motioned for her not to speak.

She didn't know what he was up to, but nodded in response. When he held out his hand for her phone, she pulled it from her pocket and gave it to him.

"I brought you something from my trip," he continued as he opened the fridge and quietly put both phones inside. "It's in my suitcase."

Once he had closed the fridge door, he activated the dishwasher and then led her back to the master bath. Closing that door behind them, he turned on the shower and pulled her close.

"Scot," she began in protest, "I've missed you too, *tons,* but they're expecting me back at the—"

He pressed his lips up against her left ear and whispered, "When was the last time you had the apartment swept for bugs?"

"A couple of weeks ago," she whispered back. "Why?"

"The CIA knows about your Russian defector. They know it's Leonid Grechko."

"How?" Sølvi asked, stunned. "I didn't even tell *you* who it was."

"I don't know. Holidae wouldn't reveal her source."

"So this comes from Oslo station."

Harvath nodded. "She met me at the airport and drove me straight to the embassy to discuss it."

"Does the CIA have my apartment bugged?"

"I asked her and Holidae said no, but . . ." This time, it was his voice that trailed off.

"But what?"

He took a deep breath before responding. "You can't trust her."

Sølvi didn't understand. "She's going to be at our wedding. She's your colleague, Scot. And my friend. What do you mean I can't trust her?"

It was the moment of truth. He was about to cross the Rubicon. And once he did, there'd be no crossing back.

Using the words he had settled on outside, he replied, "The CIA wants me to spy on you. Holidae is their point person. She made it clear what would happen if I didn't."

Her eyes widened. "She threatened you?"

"I don't think she wanted to, but I also don't think they left her with much choice."

Sølvi didn't respond.

Pulling his mouth away from her ear, he looked at her face and could see that she was pissed-off. *Very* pissed-off.

A fraction of a second later, she pulled him back in close, pressed her lips up against his ear, and said, "First, fuck her *and* the CIA. There's no way in hell we would have held back intelligence critical to the United States. She could have come to me. We're NATO allies. The fact that she didn't, tells me something. But the fact that she sent *you* to get information, tells me something even bigger."

"Which is?"

"Washington is scared. They must have a piece of the puzzle that we don't. And from the little bit I've learned, they should be scared. In fact, the United States should be terrified."

CHAPTER 7

K arine Brunelle was angry. As soon as the body of Jean-Jacques Jadot had been identified, the next call should have been to her office at the DGSI—the Directorate General for Internal Security—France's equivalent of the American FBI or the British MI5.

Instead, the Paris police—who, like most of the French public, gorged themselves on action movies depicting DGSE agents as glamorous, globe-trotting James and Jane Bonds—had called Jadot's agency, the Directorate General for External Security.

By the time Brunelle arrived at the crime scene, the place was crawling with Jadot's colleagues. There was no telling how much evidence had been disturbed. They might make good spies, but they weren't homicide detectives and they definitely weren't evidence technicians.

Flashing her creds at the door, she pushed past a burly patrol officer and called out for the lead homicide detective, "Gibert!"

As she passed the living room, she caught sight of three men in tailored suits with stainless-steel dive watches, perfectly polished shoes, and expensive haircuts who were sitting on Jadot's couch, smoking.

"I'm sorry for your loss," she said, stopping to address them. "But you can't be here. This is an active crime scene."

"You don't even know who we are," said one of the men.

"You're DGSE," she replied, working hard to keep her temper in check. "That's why I extended my condolences. Here's my card," she continued, setting it on the vestibule table. "Feel free to reach out at any time and I will share with you whatever I can. But like I said, this is an active crime scene and you're not authorized to be here."

The men looked at each other as Karine, all five feet four inches of her, held her ground and slowly tapped her foot. She was in her thirties, with a thin nose, full lips, and jet-black hair cut in a short, shaggy bob. She looked more like a graduate student you'd find reading Baudelaire or Rimbaud in some café near the Sorbonne than a federal cop.

She was an introvert who understood people. And because she understood them, they often exhausted her—especially the dumb ones.

She preferred to work alone; no partner. It wasn't that she couldn't summon the requisite social skills, she could. In fact, when she needed, she could be quite charming—though it rapidly depleted her social battery. The problem was that she'd yet to find anyone who could keep up with her mentally.

Like most humans, she was complicated. A perfect night could mean a good book, a great bottle of Burgundy, and her phone set to *do not disturb*. Or it could mean a little hash, an old Nouvelle Vague film from Truffaut or Chabrol, along with a warm, naked body in her bed, male or female— as long as they knew when to stop talking and when it was time to leave.

She was the embodiment of Chhinnamasta, the goddess of contradictions. And as such, she was often difficult to read.

Now, however, was not one of those times. She was radiating a total boss bitch vibe.

Finally, it had the desired effect as one of the DGSE operatives stood up, but not before moving to stub out his cigarette in Jadot's overflowing ashtray.

"Stop," Brunelle ordered. "That ashtray may contain evidence. Jesus, toss your butts out the window or throw them in the street downstairs like real Frenchmen."

The trio glowered at her as they rose and filed out of the apartment.

The patrol officer, apparently a fan of seeing people up the ladder from him get their asses chewed, smiled and flashed her the thumbs-up.

Brunelle didn't find it amusing. She found it unprofessional. "What's your name?"

"Leconte, madame."

"Officer Leconte, before I was DGSI, I was a police officer. I had the same training that you do. So, I have no problem asking you—what's your number one responsibility here?"

It had been so drilled into him that the young officer didn't even need to think about his reply. "To protect and preserve the crime scene, madame."

"Does that mean letting DGSE agents traipse through it?"

"No, madame."

"Are you going to see to it that no further unauthorized persons are allowed in?"

"Yes, madame."

"Good. Now, how many more are back in the kitchen with the body?"

"Two, but—"

Brunelle held up her hand. "No buts. I'll deal with them. You see to your post. Is that understood?"

"Yes, madame," Leconte replied.

Nodding at the young officer, she turned and headed back toward the rear of the apartment, where homicide detective Vincent Gibert was exceeding his authority by allowing two DGSE operatives direct access to the corpse.

She was a detail person and took in everything as she walked. She paid special attention to the framed photos on the walls of Jadot in different exotic locales. The ones of him mountain climbing were where he appeared happiest. He wore a broad smile that stretched from ear to ear. It was hard to believe that a man filled with so much vitality had just been discovered by his housekeeper dead on the kitchen floor.

She peeked briefly into each room she passed, developing a better feel for the victim and the scene. Arriving at the kitchen, she paused and registered it all in one chaotic snapshot—the partially open freezer door, the keys on the counter, the empty glass next to the bottle of bourbon, Jadot's corpse, the gun lying on the floor next to him, and the three additional men gathered in the room.

Gibert, a sinewy cop in his mid-forties with a buzz cut and permanent bags under his eyes, was a senior inspector with the Brigade Criminelle, also known as the BC or "la Crim." His department was in charge of homicides, kidnappings, bombings, and investigations of personalities "of mention," which could be anyone from a politician to a celebrity actor. He stood chatting with two rough-looking guys whom she didn't recognize.

They were in casual clothes—jeans, dark T-shirts, and boots. The men were about Gibert's age, fit, and also sported short, military-style haircuts.

One of them was using his personal phone to take pictures of Jadot's corpse, leaning down to get close-ups of the ice axe embedded in the dead man's skull.

Sensing her presence, the man taking pictures turned and looked up.

"Have budgets gotten so tight that forensics specialists now use their own iPhones?" she asked.

"Agent Brunelle," Gibert replied, trying to keep things cordial, "I thought I'd heard your voice. How are things at the DGSI?"

"Nice try, Vincent. I thought we had more respect for each other. Why is this crime scene crawling with DGSE operatives?"

"If one of your colleagues was murdered, wouldn't you want to receive a call from me?"

"I would expect it. I would also expect you to preserve the crime scene until representatives from my agency had arrived. Under the Ministry of the Interior, the murder of a federal officer makes us the oversight authority."

Gibert pursed his lips and shot her a look that clearly indicated he thought she was being unreasonable. "Contacting DGSE was a small professional courtesy."

Brunelle didn't want to argue. She knew she was right and, more important, so did Gibert. Jurisdiction over this case was not in question.

Shifting her attention to the casually dressed men, she asked, "Who are you two?"

Neither spoke.

"They're old colleagues of mine," Gibert answered for them. "We served in the army together. They're with DGSE now."

It was starting to make sense. Pointing at the men, she said, "But you're not just DGSE, are you? You're from Action Division."

Action Division was the DGSE's covert operations unit. They recruited from elite French military units and handled some of the nation's most sensitive black ops—up to and including assassinations.

Again, neither man responded.

"I'll take that as a yes," Brunelle went on, piecing it together. "So, three suits in the living room, a couple more milling around downstairs, and two operators from Action Division. Obviously, DGSE doesn't think this is some random act of violence."

"That's why you're here," she said. "It takes a thief to catch a thief and all that. You guys are not *unfamiliar* with assassinations. You're here looking to rule it in or rule it out, right? How am I doing so far?"

The men remained silent.

"What exactly did Jadot do for the DGSE?"

More silence.

"Judging by the photos in the hallway, he wasn't some lowly paper pusher in the Paris office. He got around. Pretty global. What kind of stuff was he working on?"

No reply.

"Who do you think might want him dead? Any clue? No? Nothing at all? C'mon, guys," she chided, shaking her head. "This isn't how it's supposed to work. Help me out here."

The men were a brick wall.

Gibert could see this was going nowhere.

Shaking their hands, he chatted with them for a brief moment and then sent the operatives on their way. "I'll let you know if anything develops," he said as they exited the kitchen and headed for the front door.

"Great talking with you guys," Brunelle quipped.

Once the men were down the hall, she rounded on Gibert. "What the actual fuck, Vincent? The scene hasn't even been processed yet. Now thanks to your pals, we've got extra hair, fibers, and God-knows-what-else all over the place. Is this how la Crim rolls these days?"

"Don't bust my balls, Karine."

"Don't give me a reason to."

"Fine."

"No, it's not *fine,*" she replied. "What were you thinking?"

"What was I thinking? I was thinking that whatever this is, it runs straight through DGSE. Look around. If this was a robbery, how come nothing's missing? They didn't even take his gun. Do you know what that would fetch on the black market?"

"How do you know that's Jadot's gun and not the killer's?"

"We ran the serial number. He also has about five hundred euros, cash, in his left front pocket. They didn't take his phone either."

"Where is it?"

Gibert pulled a clear plastic evidence bag from his jacket pocket and showed it to her. "I'm going to take it back to Trente-Six," he said, using the slang term for his office, which corresponded to its address at 36 quai des Orfèvres, "and have my people go to work on it right away."

"And anything you come up with, you're going to share it with me and *only* me, correct? No more of this old-boy network with the DGSE. You need to respect the chain of command."

"What could it hurt? Why not give them a taste?"

"Because they're not permitted to work inside France. They work *exterior* of the country—that's literally the *E* in DGSE."

"I know what the *E* stands for," he said, pivoting to her animosity. "Are you still angry with me? Is that what this is all about?"

"Don't flatter yourself, Vincent."

"I'm just saying, if you don't want to work with me, if you can't put our personal stuff aside, you can hand this case off to someone else."

"First," Brunelle replied, "anything personal between us is in the past. And—"

"Are you sure?"

"And second," she pressed, not allowing him to derail her, "I wasn't angry until I walked in here and saw that you'd turned this crime scene into an open house for your buddies from the DGSE. That's unprofessional. I won't have that. Am I clear?"

"Crystal," Gibert responded. "But I'm telling you, Jadot's murder is work-related. That's why I said it runs straight through the DGSE. We're not going to solve this without them. Anything we can do to keep them cooperative, benefits the investigation."

"What if it's not work-related? What if this was a crime of passion or opportunity?"

"That's not what my gut's telling me."

Brunelle looked at him.

"I've been a homicide inspector for over two decades," he continued. "You learn to trust your intuition. And mine tells me this is work-related."

"And what did your intuition tell you about me?"

"Fuck off, Karine."

"No, tell me. I'd like to know."

"Honestly?" he asked.

"Honestly," she replied.

Gibert traveled back in his mind, back to when they had first worked together, before their relationship had crossed the line.

"I thought you were smart," he said. "Maybe a little too smart. And weird. You were standoffish. The other cops thought you were cold, bitchy even, but that wasn't it."

"No?"

"No. You were lonely. You probably still are. You push everybody away. Of course every time you do, you've got a perfect excuse why, but somewhere, deep down, you know you're lying to yourself. You're a misanthrope. And until you truly learn to like yourself, you're going to be incapable of liking, much less loving other people."

After a long pause, Brunelle began to clap, slowly. "Well said. It's like having the great Molière himself right here in the kitchen imparting his wisdom."

"Go ahead, make jokes," Gibert responded. "Deflect. I should've washed my hands of you a lot sooner."

She could have let that go, but she was still angry. "Speaking of hands," she replied, needling him, "I see you've started wearing your wedding ring again. Was that your idea? Or your wife's?"

"Fuck you, Karine. I mean it. Fuck you to hell. I don't know why I bother with you."

At that moment, patrol officer Leconte approached the kitchen to let them know that the evidence technicians had arrived.

Whatever this was between them was, for the moment, over.

"You know the rules," said Gibert as he left to go talk with the techs. "Look all you want. Just don't touch anything."

If only you had obeyed that rule, she thought to herself, *we could have saved each other a lot of heartache.*

Tired of the back-and-forth, she nodded. No additional venom. No more witty rejoinders. Just seeing him again had taken a lot out of her. She needed some air.

She glanced around the kitchen one last time, committing everything to memory, looking for anything unusual or out of place.

Her eyes landed on the set of keys sitting on the counter. There wasn't anything strange about them per se, but attached to the ring was a car's key fob. It gave her an idea.

Searching the neighborhood for Jadot's vehicle would allow her to get out of the apartment and away from Vincent while continuing to move the investigation forward.

Pulling a pair of latex gloves from her pocket, she put them on and walked over to the counter. Picking up the keys, she studied the fob.

It was black, with chrome accents, and had three buttons—door lock, door unlock, and trunk release. Pretty standard stuff. Separating the fob from the key ring, she slid it into her pocket and texted a colleague back at the office to run Jadot's name through their vehicle registry database.

Crouching down, she inspected the revolver. It was a Manurhin MR 73, chambered in .357 Magnum. The wooden grips were worn and the weapon itself was scratched up. It was an old gun that had been around. Parts of it appeared to have some sort of gunk on it. She didn't have to touch it to know what it was. She had a pretty good idea what she was looking at.

Straightening up, she withdrew her flashlight and opened the cabinet doors beneath the sink. It only took a moment to find it. Underneath the counter were the strips of duct tape that had been used to hold the weapon in place.

Jadot had obviously known he was in trouble, but whatever had gone down, he hadn't been able to get the upper hand.

Examining the corpse, she saw the same tacky tape residue from the pistol where Jadot's shirt met the top of his trousers. At some point, he must have tucked the revolver into his waistband.

After taking one last look around, Brunelle exited the kitchen. At the front of the apartment, she saw Vincent chatting with the evidence techs.

For a moment she thought about letting him know what she was up to, but then decided against it. The last thing she wanted was him trying to accompany her.

She took the stairs to the ground floor, crossed the vestibule, and pushed the electronic door release, which allowed her to step out onto the sidewalk. The moment she did, she was reminded why owning a car in Paris was such a pain in the ass. Parking, especially in some of the older neighborhoods like the Marais, was almost nonexistent.

Jadot's street was too narrow for parking, so she'd have to try some of the wider streets nearby, like the Rue des Francs Bourgeois and the Rue des Archives. If she didn't get lucky on any of the immediate streets, she'd have to google the neighborhood parking garages. To make things even more difficult, the break they had been granted in the weather was going to end soon. More rain would be moving in.

She was noting the position of security cameras outside the apartment building, wishing she'd packed an umbrella, when her phone chimed. It was a text from her colleague back at the DGSI. The vehicle registry search had been a bust. According to their records, Jean-Jacques Jadot didn't own a car.

After texting back a *thank you,* Brunelle made a mental list of possibilities. The most likely was that it was a rental or might belong to a friend. The lack of a plastic tag wired to the fob with the details of the rental agency made her lean toward the latter. Either way, she was going to have to walk up and down the streets, and in and out of parking garages, pressing the unlock button until she heard a chirp and saw a pair of headlights blink.

It would help if she at least knew what make of car she was searching for. Renault? Peugeot? Mercedes? Nissan?

Removing the fob from her pocket, she turned it over in her hand. *That's weird,* she thought. There was no logo.

She didn't own a car herself, but she had driven plenty of them. Automakers branded everything. She couldn't recall ever seeing a fob without a car company's logo.

Looking at it some more, she wondered if maybe it was a replacement—something from a third-party vendor. Taking her phone back out, she snapped a photo, opened her browser, and did a reverse image search. A fraction of a second later, the results loaded.

It turned out not to be a remote key fob at all. It was only designed to look like one. In reality it was a USB flash drive. She had a decision to make. It took her less than a second.

Since Vincent had already laid claim to Jadot's phone, she had no qualms about "liberating" the fob. A healthy division of labor, she told herself, was good in any high-profile investigation.

While she understood that it was important that they share information, she also understood what kind of a man Vincent was. She'd be as forthcoming with him as he was with her. And she'd do it on her timetable.

The sooner she figured out who had murdered Jean-Jacques Jadot, the better. She just hoped Vincent was wrong. If the killing was related to the intelligence officer's work, there was no telling what kind of a Pandora's box they might be opening.

CHAPTER 8

The safehouse was hidden in the middle of one of the city's trend-iest neighborhoods, Tjuvholmen.

Roughly translated, the word meant "isle of thieves," which was exactly what it had been for hundreds of years—a small island where pirates, cutthroats, and other ne'er-do-wells set up shop in hopes of es-caping the long arm of the law.

Now connected by a series of bridges, Tjuvholmen and the adjacent Aker Brygge area boasted some of Oslo's hottest restaurants, bars, night-clubs, museums, boutiques, apartments, condos, and townhouses.

Wrapped within shimmering glass and steel structures, every com-mercial and residential space took advantage of unparalleled views across the sprawling Oslofjord.

One such waterfront apartment had been quietly leased by a fictitious British investment banking firm, allegedly as a corporate residence for its visiting executives. The true holder of the lease, however, was the Nor-wegian Intelligence Service.

The stunning unit had five bedrooms, five and a half baths, and three adjacent parking spots in the massive underground garage complex that served Tjuvholmen like a web of catacombs.

With its marble countertops, high-end fixtures, and gallery-level art, the apartment looked like something out of *Architectural Digest.* The icing on the cake would have been the vistas through the floor-to-ceiling win-dows, but all of the drapes had been pulled. What was happening inside needed to stay inside. The debriefing of Leonid Grechko wasn't meant for public consumption.

Sølvi looked at her watch. They had been at it for over five hours. It was long past time for a break.

The session had been taxing. The Russian spymaster had changed tactics and was no longer being forthright. He was playing games.

She wasn't surprised. In fact, she had been expecting it. They were getting closer to the most valuable intelligence he had to offer. And the closer they got, the harder he was going to bargain. She was going to have to get much tougher with him. Before that, however, she needed a mental reset.

It had taken all of her professional strength to set aside everything Scot had told her back at her apartment and to focus solely on Grechko's debriefing. Right now, that's what mattered most.

Nevertheless, she felt betrayed, unable to give Holidae Hayes even the slightest benefit of the doubt. It was a personal and professional gulf that would never be bridged. As far as she was concerned, Hayes was dead to her. *Completely.*

After letting the security team know that they were taking a break, she allowed Grechko to leave the debriefing room and stretch his legs. Her only prohibition was that he wasn't allowed to leave the apartment—that included not stepping out onto the balcony.

Once he had exited, she spent a few moments jotting notes—avenues of conversation she wanted to pick back up on after their break.

After getting everything down on paper, she closed her notebook and went in search of some coffee.

The apartment had a machine that used pods, but she much preferred the pour-over method and had purchased a glass Chemex system to keep there. For a coffee aficionado, it was well worth it.

"Can I interest you in some tea?" the Russian asked as she joined him in the kitchen. He was standing at the sink filling a kettle.

"No, thank you," she replied, opening the cabinet where she kept her coffee beans. Taking them down, she popped the top off the burr grinder she had brought from home and filled the hopper.

The Russian shook his head and laughed. "Norwegians and their coffee."

"Russians and their tea," Sølvi said with a smile. "Not to mention their vodka."

"Touché."

Looking over at the leader of the security team—a tall, muscular man in his mid-fifties seated in the living room—she asked, "Coffee, Martin?"

"Yes, please," the man replied.

"You're sure you don't want tea?" Grechko interjected, attempting a little good-natured competition. "I can even do it Moroccan-style for you."

All business, Martin stated, "I'm only interested in Norwegian-style. Coffee, black."

The Russian turned his attention back to Sølvi. "You people don't produce a single bean, yet you're the world's second-largest consumer per capita. Amazing."

She knew what he was up to. He was being a chameleon.

Away from the debriefing room and its video cameras and microphones, Grechko had shifted back into "charm" mode. He was trying to build rapport with her, to get her to trust him. It was what all good intelligence officers did.

Except in this case, he wasn't the debriefer, *she* was. And she had no intention of being drawn into any of his games.

That said, she could understand how he had risen so high through the ranks of Russian intelligence.

He was a distinguished-looking man in his early sixties with an above-average intellect. He carried himself with poise and a heap of self-confidence. But beneath that confidence, behind the charm that he turned on and off like a light switch, he was tired, world-weary. He was a man who had seen enough—particularly the unspeakable things that men could do to other men.

He had done many of those unspeakable things himself—all in service of his nation. A nation, if he was to be believed, that he had lost faith in and no longer wanted any part of.

With only the clothes on his back, he had driven across the Norwegian border at Storskog—one of the few European crossings still open to Russia after its invasion of Ukraine. It was a trip that citizens of Murmansk Oblast made every day. The prices in Norway, not to mention the quality of the goods, were far superior. It wasn't until the next day that anyone realized he had fled. By then Sølvi had already whisked him the nearly two thousand kilometers south to Oslo.

He was now a man without a country, completely dependent on the Kingdom of Norway for his survival.

For that reason alone, Sølvi was eager to dispense with the "cooperative" defector, "reluctant" defector nonsense and get to the bottom of what he had to offer.

"That's a shame," Grechko said, staring into an empty tea tin. "You're all out of black tea."

Dumping the coarsely ground coffee into the moistened filter of her Chemex, she told him, "There's more. Check the pantry."

He set the tin down and walked around the corner of the gourmet kitchen. The large butler's pantry was lined with well-stocked shelves containing everything from breakfast cereal to barbecue supplies for the currently off-limits outdoor grill. Through a connecting door, there was a laundry room, which could also be accessed from an additional door off the main hall.

The Russian searched for a few moments, before shouting, "I can't find any."

Sølvi rolled her eyes, stopped what she was doing, and went to help him.

As she did, Martin rose from his chair in the living room. "Do you hear that?" he asked.

From where she stood, all she could hear was the pressure building inside the kettle on the nearby stovetop as the water began to boil. She shook her head and continued to the pantry. There she waved Grechko out of the way.

The safehouse was meant to support the entire team for up to two weeks if necessary, without anyone having to enter or leave. She knew the contents of the pantry like the back of her hand—right down to the large nylon duffel bags and hard-sided plastic cases on the bottom shelf of the far wall. They included everything from an advanced tactical medical setup complete with surgical equipment, vials of morphine and epinephrine, a pulse oximeter, tourniquets, and defibrillator, to a high-end vehicle diagnostics and repair kit, capable of handling almost anything one of their vehicles downstairs might throw at them. Every single item was meant to reinforce their self-sufficiency.

Moving a couple packages of Knekkebrød, Sølvi retrieved a fresh tin of black tea and handed it to him.

"Huh," Grechko replied, having practically been staring right at it.

Back in the kitchen, the kettle began to whistle.

Pushing past him, she reached the pantry door and was about to exit when she noticed Martin across the living room. He had pulled the drapes partway open and was staring at something.

Sensing her presence, he spun to warn her.

"Stay away from the windows!" he ordered. "Get down! There's a drone outside with—"

But before the security team leader could finish his sentence, a massive explosion tore through the living room, sending glass, steel, and molten fire everywhere.

CHAPTER 9

The violent shock wave knocked Sølvi straight back into the pantry, where she crashed into Grechko. As the pair tumbled to the floor, five more explosions rocked the apartment.

Her training kicked in and she rolled over, completely covering the Russian defector with her body. They were under attack. There was no time to figure out by whom. Her only job was to keep Grechko alive.

She waited for a seventh explosion and when it didn't happen, she leapt to her feet, pulling a 9mm CZ pistol from her holster. Her head was throbbing from the blasts. The air was obscured by smoke and debris.

After quickly assessing Grechko, she gestured for him to stay put and stay quiet, while she peeked out into the kitchen.

Approaching the pantry door, she readied her weapon, held her breath, and risked a glance.

The kitchen and dining and living rooms were on fire and had been completely ripped apart. The bloody, shrapnel-riddled upper half of Martin's body lay only feet away from the pantry door. Where his bottom half lay was anyone's guess.

Fighting back her shock, she glanced in the direction where she had last seen him—standing by the large living room windows. But as the curtains of smoke parted, she received an even bigger jolt.

A black-clad, four-man assault team, complete with ballistic helmets, full face masks, and H&K G36 automatic rifles, had rappelled down from the roof and were making entry via the shattered windows. None of them were members of Martin's security team.

Sølvi retreated into the pantry and helped Grechko to his feet. "Stay right behind me and don't say a word."

When the Russian nodded, she led him into the adjacent laundry room and stopped at the door to listen for any sign of activity from the other side.

She couldn't hear anything, but she didn't know if that was because there was nothing, or because her hearing hadn't fully returned after the explosions.

Gesturing for Grechko to take a step back, she cracked the door and was about to peer out when the hall erupted in a barrage of automatic weapons fire.

She leapt back, kicked the door shut, and pushed Grechko out of the way just as a line of bullets pierced the wall and went straight through the laundry room.

That exit was out of the question. They would have to take their chances in the living room.

The good news, at least for the moment, was that judging by the back-and-forth tempo of the gunfire, some of Martin's six-man team had survived and were still in the fight.

Steering Grechko back into the safest part of the pantry, she once again instructed him to stay put and stay quiet. This time she was going to do more than just peek into the kitchen. *Much* more.

Squatting down, she did a press check to make sure her pistol was hot, and then, counting to three, she swung into the kitchen and, ignoring Martin's corpse, kept her attention focused forward as she used the long, marble-clad island for cover.

Gunfire could be heard from up and down the main hallway—as if the assaulters were going room to room. In between bursts, it was quiet. No one was firing back now. That was a bad sign.

Moving to the end of the island, she made sure to use the cabinets for support and not the floor, which was pebbled with shards of broken glass. She was absolutely silent.

On the counter was a toaster crafted from high-gloss chrome. Sølvi craned her neck, trying to get just the right angle. She was hoping to use it as a mirror, to see what was happening beyond the kitchen. It was at that very moment that she heard the *crunch* of a footfall on glass.

The sound had been close; just the other side of the island. Whoever it was, they were standing only inches away.

She gripped her pistol tighter and applied pressure to the trigger. Planting her feet, she prepared to spring. The moment she fired her weapon, it was going to be like a starting gun going off. Unless some of Martin's men were still alive, she was going to draw all the heat down on her.

But she had no choice. She and Grechko were trapped. The assaulters would search every room until they found what they were looking for. And she felt pretty certain as to what it was they wanted. They had come for him. She was determined not to let them succeed.

There was another crunch of glass and then another. Looking up at the toaster, she could see one of the black-clad men approaching. He was so close, she could hear him breathing behind his Kevlar mask.

In a tense microsecond, her mind processed all of the data available to her and formulated a plan. She'd be lucky not to catch a bullet in the skull, but there was no time left. Action beat reaction every time. When the assaulter's left boot became visible, she sprang her trap. Her first shot went through the man's foot.

As he screamed in pain, she popped back around the end of the island and shot him twice in the groin. The screaming grew even louder.

The assaulter wildly fired his weapon, chewing up the cabinets and countertops, as he stumbled backward to get away.

Sølvi didn't give him any quarter. Popping out once more, she drilled him twice through each kneecap and was on top of him before he even hit the floor.

Placing the muzzle of her pistol just under his Kevlar helmet behind his left ear, she fired, killing him instantly.

Slamming the butt of her weapon against the man's chest, the solid *thunk* confirmed that he was also wearing a chest rig with a bulletproof ceramic plate. Probably had one in back too. She had been right to aim for his lower extremities. It was the only Achilles heel the assaulters had. At least until you could get in close enough to finish them off.

Working fast, she stripped the man of his rifle and one spare magazine, just as one of his colleagues came around the corner and began firing.

Sølvi raced back behind the island and kept moving. Her new attacker seemed to have known exactly what she was up to because he went full auto, tearing up the island and everything around it. If not for the marble cladding, she never would have made it back to the pantry.

The assaulter from the kitchen was going to be on them any second. Worse still, she had no idea if the other two were still alive and if they were, *where* they were. She needed to come up with a plan, fast.

Covering the doorway, she gave Grechko a set of rapid instructions. As the Russian sprang into action, she pointed the muzzle of the dead assaulter's rifle into the kitchen, depressed the trigger, and raked the room back and forth with bullets, sending their current attacker diving for cover.

Moments later, Grechko held up what she had asked for. "Like this?"

Sølvi nodded. "Take the cap off and light it," she instructed as she inserted her one and only fresh magazine into the rifle.

The Russian did as she asked, dragging the scratch strip across the black flare igniter button.

Holding the rifle in her left hand and snugging the stock against her left shoulder, she used her right hand to accept the improvised explosive device from Grechko. The next step was the most dangerous part of her plan.

Tilting the barrel of the rifle around the door frame, she exhaled, pressed the trigger, and charged into the kitchen as soon as the weapon started firing.

She only needed to clear the island. It was a meter and a half, tops. She could cover the distance in three strides. The only question was whether her ammo would last.

She saw two assaulters, partially behind cover, who were actively returning fire. Adjusting the rifle, she focused her shots on them, keeping the pair pinned down.

As she neared the island, she drew her right arm back, and then—just as she cleared it, she snapped her arm forward and released the IED.

Like a granite stone in the sport of curling, the twenty-pound propane tank slid across the polished marble floor of the kitchen, the red road flare duct-taped to its side burning brightly.

The moment she let it go, she spun and raced back toward the pantry. Her weapon ran out of ammo halfway there.

Without losing a step, she dropped the rifle, pulled her pistol, and continued to rain down rounds on her assailants.

The IED had just drawn parallel with the assaulters as she reached the pantry door. Gaining a rapid sight picture, she fired two rounds and dove for cover.

There was an enormous explosion as fire engulfed the living and dining rooms and kitchen. Shrapnel from the ruptured propane tank sliced through the flame-filled air.

Sølvi didn't wait to see what had happened to the attackers.

Getting to her feet, she swapped out the magazine in her pistol for a fresh one and led Grechko into the laundry room.

After having him stand back, she cracked the door and checked the hall once more. It was clear.

Repeating her previous command, she told him to stay right behind her. There was no telling what kind of reinforcements the assaulters had. They needed to get moving. *Now.*

Slipping into the hallway, they headed toward the apartment's front door. With each room they passed, Sølvi did a quick peek inside and then positioned herself on the opposite side of the doorway to protect Grechko as he moved safely past. The bodies of Martin's security team members lay everywhere, their corpses littered with shrapnel, bullets, or both.

Sølvi and Grechko were approaching the final bedroom when her eyes picked up something—the briefest glimpse of motion.

Pressing Grechko against the wall, she motioned for him to be silent and crept forward. The fourth assaulter sprung before Sølvi was even fully at the door.

Releasing her left hand from her weapon, she leapt forward, grabbed the barrel of his rifle, and pinned it against the frame, making sure to position her body outside his line of fire. As she did, she pumped round after round into his Kevlar face mask, hoping to penetrate one of the eyeholes and take him out.

The man was much bigger than Sølvi and used his size against her. Ducking his head, he pivoted off the door frame and brought the butt of his rifle crashing into her exposed rib cage.

A white-hot pulse of pure pain shot through her body and caused her to let go of the rifle.

No sooner had she done so than the man began to raise the muzzle to finish her off. Sølvi, however, refused to cooperate.

Her training had drilled into her never to surrender her advantage. And, if it was ever taken from her, to recapture it. *Immediately.*

She renewed her attack, launching herself into him, firing anywhere she might be able to avoid his armor until the slide of her pistol locked back, empty. There was no time to insert a fresh magazine. It was hand-to-hand now.

Unable to bring his weapon to bear, the assaulter wrapped himself around her like a giant crocodile and rolled her to the floor. There he began hammering her in the head with his Kevlar helmet.

With her arms pinned to her sides, there was no escaping the blows. Her only hope lay in a small Kydex sheath along her belt. In it was a backup knife, known as *Sgian Dubh.*

Using her thumb to hook the curved, steel handle, she pulled it from the sheath, drove the scalpel-sharp blade deep into the inside of the man's wrist, and ripped the knife down his forearm toward his elbow. The assaulter howled in pain.

As the man released her from his grasp, Sølvi didn't waste a single second.

Pulling out the knife, she used her opposite hand to drive the man's head straight back, exposing his throat.

She plunged the knife into the left side of his neck and, in one fluid motion, ripped it straight across to the other side.

With both his carotids severed, the assaulter began spurting blood all over the place. Sølvi scrambled quickly away from him.

Picking up her pistol, she inserted a fresh magazine and, ready to engage any additional threats, slipped back into the hallway.

The expression on Grechko's face said it all. Sølvi could only imagine what a mess she looked like.

She hadn't even bothered to assess her own injuries. There wasn't enough time. Her number one priority remained. She needed to keep Grechko alive at all costs. It was imperative she get him out of the building and move him someplace safe.

"Let's go," she ordered.

With the Russian following tightly behind her, she led him to the front of the apartment, only to find that the heavy oak door had been blown completely off its hinges. The vestibule beyond was also destroyed and smoke was pouring out of the charred elevator shaft.

Judging by the looks of it, their attackers had not only used explosive-laden drones to attack the apartment from the outside but had also sent up a pretty good-size explosive via the elevator. *Who the hell were these people? And how the hell had they found this location?* The whereabouts of the safehouse, and the fact that it was occupied, were two of the most closely guarded secrets of the Norwegian Intelligence Service.

Figuring that out was going to have to be put on hold. Right now she had to concentrate on their escape. The only way down was going to be the stairs.

As they descended, the building's internal fire alarms continued their earsplitting blare. They were joined in the stairwell by streams of frightened evacuees. Not wanting to add to the panic or draw additional attention to herself, she concealed her weapon.

Floor by floor, she moved Grechko deliberately, carefully, paying attention to every face and every set of hands they encountered. There was no telling who was friend and who was foe.

When they got to the ground level and everyone else pushed out into the lobby, she kept descending. There was no way to know who or what was waiting for them out on the street. She didn't want to find out. She would take their chances in the garage. In the garage there was cover. And if there was cover, they wouldn't be sitting ducks. They'd at least have a fighting chance of getting away.

At the garage level, she opened the door and scanned the vicinity. It looked safe. Nothing but parked cars and fluorescent lighting, but even down here, the fire alarms were still blaring.

Keeping Grechko close, she wove a path through the vehicles, ready to drop down at a moment's notice if they heard or saw anything at all suspicious. They just needed to put a bit of distance between themselves and the apartment building. Once they had done that, she could take a moment to catch her breath. They were almost there.

Suddenly, tires squealed. The noise was accompanied by the roar of an engine. Sølvi looked over her shoulder to see a van racing toward them.

"Get down," she ordered Grechko, pulling out her pistol.

As she did, the van's driver flipped on his high beams and picked up speed. Another figure leaned out the passenger-side window. When Sølvi saw the gun in his hand, she began firing.

The shooter returned fire with a bigger, fully automatic weapon, which shattered the windows, windshields, and mirrors of the cars all around her. Sølvi, however, was relentless.

Alternating her rounds between the passenger and the driver, she didn't let up. She used her cover as best she could and held her ground.

When she ran her pistol dry, she slammed home her final magazine and got right back in the fight. With the van almost on top of them, she changed her point of aim, taking out the right front tire.

The vehicle careened wildly as the driver lost control and slammed into a row of parked cars.

The impact was so severe, the passenger was jettisoned from the cab. He slammed against a concrete support and landed only fifteen feet away. Motioning for Grechko to stay put, Sølvi crept forward.

She used parked vehicles for cover for as long as she could. When she stepped out into the open, it was only long enough to check the defenestrated passenger for a pulse. He didn't have one. He also didn't have a phone, any identification, nor any pocket litter that might give her a clue to who was behind the attack.

Leaving the man where he lay, she raised her pistol and cautiously approached the van.

The driver was still alive, but only barely. Blood ran from his nose and both ears. He wheezed as he drew in short, painful gasps of air. The van was older and didn't have airbags. The steering wheel had crushed his rib cage and likely punctured both of his lungs. No doubt there were all sorts of other internal injuries as well.

Seeing her approach, the man lifted a Beretta 9mm and arced it in her direction. Sølvi shot him in the head, killing him instantly.

Quickly she patted him down, but once again she came up empty. No phone, no ID, no nothing. The glove box and the van's rear cargo area were also a bust.

Leaving everything where she had found it, she hurried back to Grechko.

"We're not safe yet," she said. "Follow me."

The Russian did as he was instructed. They wove their way through the honeycomb of parking areas, careful never to step out into the open unless they absolutely had to, and even then, only for as long as was necessary.

Finally, they arrived at a large set of steel doors, which Sølvi pushed her way through before walking over to an elevator call button.

When the elevator doors opened, they stepped inside. Sølvi pressed a black keycard against a reader and selected the fourth floor.

"What is this place?" Grechko asked.

"Plan B," said Sølvi, motioning for him to be quiet. She wasn't in the mood to answer questions. Her mind was spinning, trying to put together everything that had just happened to them.

At the fourth floor, the elevator doors gently chimed and opened onto a sumptuous, carpeted hallway. The walls were covered with blond wood and each numbered door was painted a glossy black. Theirs was a corner room at the end of the hall. Sølvi used her keycard once more.

When the lock released, she stepped inside to make sure everything was okay and then waved Grechko in, telling him to take a seat on the couch.

Opening the sliding glass door to the balcony, she dissembled her phone and threw the pieces into the water below. Already she could hear the Klaxons of police and first-responder vehicles approaching. Closing the door, she locked it and drew the drapes.

Grechko was studying the directory of services that he had picked up off the coffee table.

"The Thief," he stated matter-of-factly. "Interesting name for a hotel."

"Stand up," Sølvi responded.

"Why?"

"Just do it," she ordered.

When he complied, she patted him down from top to bottom.

She went over every square inch of him, searching for anything her people might have missed—any sort of subcutaneous tracker that might have led the assaulters to the safehouse. She couldn't find anything. They had already swapped out his clothes and provided him with new shoes. A male operative had even checked his anal cavity, or his "prison wallet" as it was colloquially referred to. By whatever means the attackers had found the safehouse, Grechko, it would appear, hadn't led them there.

That brought Sølvi back to the unimaginable possibility that someone inside Norwegian Intelligence had betrayed them—all of them, including Martin and his security team.

She had a lot to untangle, but now wasn't the time. Prebooking a room at the Thief under a false name and credit card had only been a just-in-case contingency and was only meant to provide a short-term sanctuary. They couldn't stay here. Not for very long.

Walking into the bedroom, she slid the bench away from the foot of the bed, removed her blood-caked knife from its sheath, and sliced along the seam where she had expertly reglued it.

In the shallow cavity inside were several items she had prestaged, including a burner phone. Powering it up, she waited for a signal and then sent a text message to the only person right now she could trust.

Moments later, Scot Harvath texted back.

They had a shorthand that, even if someone was intercepting their communications, no one would be able to decipher.

He told her to sit tight. He was on his way.

Sølvi urged him to hurry. She was concerned that they hadn't seen the worst of things yet. Not by a long shot.

CHAPTER 10

A ndrew Conroy had been with the Central Intelligence Agency for almost forty years. During that time, he had gone through four wives, three peptic ulcers, two brushes with cancer, and one assassination attempt.

Over his career, he had helped the Agency navigate coups, wars, foreign interventions, and untold other global and regional crises.

For his dedication and hard-won experience, he had been promoted to Deputy Director of Operations.

As such, he was responsible for overseeing the collection of foreign intelligence, most specifically *human* foreign intelligence, as well as covert action by CIA operatives around the world. It was a job he had not only excelled at but also had enjoyed. At least until recently.

His failed marriages notwithstanding, he liked to think that he performed better under pressure, but the relentless force being applied by the White House at the moment, as well as the intelligence committees in Congress, was withering. They all wanted answers. And rightfully so. He did too.

For three weeks, the powers that be had been pushing the CIA to turn over every rock, leaf, and blade of grass that they could find. It was critical that the Agency get to the bottom of what the Russians had transferred to Belarus. But so far, the entire Directorate of Operations had come up empty.

They had hit so many dry holes, in fact, that some were wondering if it might be a wild goose chase—some sort of psychological operation cooked up by the Kremlin to spook Western powers into reevaluating their support of Ukraine.

But on the other hand, if the story was accurate, all bets would be off. It would mark an incredibly dangerous escalation—the first time since the Cold War that Moscow had moved nuclear weapons into a country outside Russia.

And not just any country. Belarus was a bellicose, regional backwater with a rightly deserved inferiority complex and enough bubbling paranoia coursing through its leadership's corrupt bloodstream to make even the most fervent of conspiracy theorists blanch.

The Belarusians weren't just unstable nutcases; they were now unstable nutcases who may have been handed nuclear weapons.

As to what type of nukes they could be in possession of, the consensus, based on best guesses, as well as recent public statements from Russian president Fedor Peshkov, was that they were tactical nuclear weapons—smaller, shorter-range devices that could be put to devastating effect on the battlefield.

While experts debated the degree of likelihood that the transfer had taken place, Conroy and his people had already moved on to the next question—if Belarus did have Russian nukes, where were they being kept?

The most obvious answer was at one of its old Soviet-era nuclear storage facilities. The USSR had built dozens of them across the country. But after the collapse of the Soviet Union, all of the facilities had, presumably, fallen into disrepair. That meant that one, or more, must have been refurbished.

Though the CIA couldn't have eyes everywhere at every moment of the day, if the Agency had missed such a refurbishment—at the very same time they were unable to confirm or deny the presence of Russian nuclear weapons on Belarusian soil—it spoke to a massive intelligence failure. It was the Iraq WMD debacle all over again. Langley would have failed to develop the proper well-placed, knowledgeable sources necessary for the U.S. government to make vital national security decisions.

It would be a black mark on the CIA's record. More specifically, it was a stain on the Directorate of Operations—especially with how deeply invested America was in the war next door in Ukraine.

There were other divisions, departments, and American intelligence community partners that had played a role in the current failure, but ultimately Conroy saw it as his responsibility and therefore his problem to fix.

As such, the Agency was playing a dangerous game of catch-up—shoveling mountains of currency, man-hours, and resources into Belarus, all in the hopes of quickly developing as many high-value human networks as possible.

Until they received evidence to the contrary, the CIA had no choice but to operate as if there were indeed Russian tactical nuclear weapons in Belarus. That raised the stakes for everyone, including the Russians, to a dangerously high level.

It was a level that the White House deemed absolutely unacceptable. American president Paul Porter had no intention of accidentally stumbling into war with Russia, nor did he intend to allow the Russians to purposely drag him into one.

In a face-to-face with the Director of Central Intelligence, President Porter had made his position crystal clear—he wanted the gloves to come off. The Agency was to do everything in its power not just to clip Russia's wings, but to remove them.

Since its most recent invasion of Ukraine, one of the greatest fears had been that if Peshkov and the Russians were allowed to succeed, they wouldn't stop there and that history would repeat itself. The history they were all afraid of was what had happened in the run-up to World War II.

After Adolf Hitler had been allowed to annex Austria and then the Sudetenland, the Nazis went after the rest of Czechoslovakia. In the absence of meaningful international pushback, Hitler became even more emboldened and, after staging several false-flag attacks as a pretext, next took Poland, and World War II began.

In 2014, despite having signed an international treaty known as the Budapest Memorandum, which stated that Russia would respect the territorial integrity of Ukraine, the Russians invaded and took both the Donbas and Crimea. Eight years later, without provocation, the Russians invaded again, hell-bent on capturing the rest of the country.

From there, before even the thought of nuclear weapons being transferred to Belarus, analysts had seen Peshkov possibly going one of two ways. He had massed troops in Transnistria, a breakaway region of Moldova—a tiny, former Soviet Republic—where he was running a similar playbook as he had in the Donbas. He was already claiming to just be looking out for the interests of "ethnic Russians" who happened to live in the sovereign nation of Moldova. It was the same line he had used before invading the Donbas and Crimea. It was also eerily similar to Hitler's claim that he was simply protecting "ethnic Germans" in the Sudetenland.

The other option was that the Russians could invade one of the smaller, Baltic nations like Latvia, Lithuania, or Estonia, all three of which had also been members of the former Soviet Union.

Of course today, Latvia, Lithuania, and Estonia were members of the North Atlantic Treaty Organization, the greatest military alliance in history and Article 5 of the NATO charter stated that an attack on one member was an attack on all.

Peshkov, however, had been doing all he could to weaken that alliance, to sow doubt as to whether it was worth fighting for, or whether it would fall apart in the face of actual war against Russia.

Analysts across NATO members' intelligence services put the odds of a Russian attack on a member nation in the next ten years at fifty-fifty. In response, NATO headquarters in Belgium had been completely reorganizing itself into a full-on war command center. It was a level of activity not seen since the very height of the Cold War.

And the sudden threat of nuclear weapons being based in Belarus had only made things worse.

President Porter came out and publicly denounced Russia's alleged deployment of tactical nuclear weapons to Belarus, declaring any such transfers as "absolutely irresponsible." It was a statement he made repeatedly and forcefully.

In keeping up the public pressure, the White House hoped to discourage the Russians from doing anything stupid and kicking off World War III.

But hope wasn't a plan. A plan required a concrete course of action. That's where Conroy came in.

Once the CIA confirmed that the nukes were in Belarus, they would be able to present options to President Porter and the National Security Council. To get to that point, however, he was going to need a lot of luck and a lot of brainpower.

Looking up, he saw the personification of both standing in his outer office. Maggie Thomas, as always, was precisely three minutes early for their daily meeting.

CHAPTER 11

Margaret Jean Thomas, or "Maggie" to the people who knew her, was a "skip leg"—a legacy employee whose family service had skipped a generation.

Maggie's grandmother Jean, from whom she took her middle name, had worked for the Agency's precursor, the Office of Strategic Services, during World War II. The woman's exploits had been legendary. When the OSS was dissolved after the war, Jean became one of the CIA's first female intelligence officers and served with continued valor and distinction until her retirement.

The resemblance between grandmother and granddaughter was uncanny. They were both tough, broad-shouldered women who stood over six feet tall. Maggie, like her grandmother, had no problem holding her own in the male-dominated world of espionage. She could outdrink, outsmoke, and outpoker the best of them.

She had been a Russian, Eastern European, and Eurasian studies major at Smith College in Massachusetts and had gotten her master's of science in global studies and international relations at Northeastern. Thanks to a pair of flower child parents, she had spent most of her youth overseas and could speak four languages. The CIA couldn't have scripted a better résumé.

It's been said that great intelligence analysts were like great painters or musicians. You didn't teach them their craft, you helped them perfect it. It was a God-given ability that you either had, or you didn't. Which was why the great ones, like Maggie, were so rare.

She was fearless, curious, and absolutely tenacious. Once she had zeroed in on something, she didn't give up until her objective was complete. Nothing and no one could stand in her way.

Adept at spotting patterns, she was patient and methodical in her approach, especially when it came to piecing together the bigger picture. She was also humble, willing to admit when she had gotten something wrong, to learn from her mistakes, and to adjust accordingly.

Maggie and her husband, Paul, a State Department employee, lived in a storybook Cape Cod that had belonged to her grandmother Jean. It was only three and a half miles from CIA headquarters. Maggie could make the drive in under ten minutes, but preferred, when the weather was agreeable, to ride her bike.

Considering her high-profile position at the CIA, it was a dangerous means of travel, which she and Conroy had butted heads over countless times. But no matter how often they'd argued, Maggie always came out the winner.

From Bangkok to Berlin, she had grown up on a bicycle. Since she was a child, it had given her a sense of freedom. She loved the outdoors, being in the fresh air—especially with how much time she spent cooped up at Langley. It was a mental health issue for her, something she wasn't willing to compromise on.

Though Conroy never stopped disliking it, particularly from a security standpoint, he chalked it up to her being quirky. It was simply who she was. It was also part of what made her so good at her job.

In her mid-forties, with almost two decades at the Agency, she was smarter than most of the people in the building, which was why he'd put her in charge of Russia House. It was a specialized, highly secretive unit focused on Russia and the former Soviet states.

Despite falling under the CIA's Mission Center for Europe and Eurasia, because of the extremely sensitive intelligence it dealt with, Russia House was fully self-contained. It had its own offices, its own computer network, and even its own SCIF.

As an example of how the culture had come full circle at Langley, post-9/11, the Middle East and counterterrorism assignments had been all the rage. Today, however, Russia House had once again become the coolest table in the lunchroom. And with all of the pressure raining down from the White House over Belarus and the nuke situation, Conroy was exceedingly grateful to have Maggie sitting at the head of that table. Getting her attention, he waved her into his office.

"Good morning, Maggie," Conroy said as she entered and they both took their usual seats at his conference table.

"Good morning, boss," she replied, removing a tablet and two folders from her briefcase, which she placed in front of her.

"What have you got for me?"

Maggie was a skilled briefer. She knew what her boss was interested in, as well as what he didn't want his time wasted on.

"Norway's Russian defector," she said, opening the first folder. "Leonid Grechko. I heard back from our Oslo station chief."

"Holidae Hayes," Conroy stated. He prided himself on knowing the names of all his NATO country chiefs, as well as those based in the nations most hostile to the United States.

Maggie nodded. "Harvath bit, but he didn't like it. Hayes said it got quite heated, yet in the end, he agreed to cooperate."

"I told you he would. Nobody walks away from a pile of money like that. Not for a woman. No offense."

"None taken."

"How soon until he starts producing?"

"Hayes put him on a short leash. She told him that she expects results ASAP."

Conroy smiled. "Good. What else?"

She moved to her second folder. "This morning, a senior French DGSE officer named Jadot no-showed for breakfast with our Paris station chief."

"Ray Powell."

Maggie nodded again. "Turns out, he couldn't make breakfast because he had been murdered at some point last night. His housekeeper found his body."

"Why did it hit your desk?"

"Powell says Jadot had requested the breakfast. He believes the dead operative discovered something, possibly Russia-related, and wanted to discuss it. Other than that, Powell has no clue. Paris police are investigating. He'll stay on it and update us as soon as he has anything."

"I only see two folders today. Is that it?"

"Pretty much."

Conroy cocked an eyebrow. *"Pretty much?"*

Maggie didn't want to lead him down a dark alley until she knew what was in it. "We've found a new thread. It's interesting, but we need to pull on it a bit more."

"How *interesting?*"

"It has to do with Cape Idokopas."

Mention of the tiny promontory on the Black Sea instantly captured Conroy's attention. "I'm listening."

Cape Idokopas was the location of the Russian president's $1.5 billion palace. It was the physical manifestation of his arrogance, his thievery, and his pillaging of the Russian people.

When some brave anticorruption bloggers had drawn attention to the massive, chateau-style complex, Peshkov had moved quickly to camouflage its ownership. He substituted bogus paperwork and got a conglomerate of Kremlin-friendly oligarchs to stand up and claim that they were the true owners.

"Peshkov's Palace," as it was known, was the most closely guarded facility in Russia. At over 190,000 square feet it included multiple helipads, an Olympic-size ice rink, an amphitheater, casino, hookah lounge, movie theater, swimming pools, and an arboretum—just for starters.

The adjacent grounds contained vineyards, greenhouses, a stable, livestock barns, and even an Orthodox church that had been moved stone by stone from Greece.

But it was what lay fifty meters below the palace that the CIA and the U.S. government found most interesting—a gigantic, heavily fortified doomsday bunker with its own electrical, water, sewer, air filtration, and fire suppression systems.

If there were to be some sort of Armageddon—nuclear or otherwise, this was where the CIA believed Peshkov and his inner circle would ride it out.

"I wanted to widen the aperture," Maggie continued.

Opening her iPad, she pulled up a series of photos and slid the device over to Conroy, who swiped through a handful of equestrian images.

"What am I looking at?" he asked.

"The Ukraine invasion rendered the Russians persona non grata at pretty much every international competition. So wealthy Russian elites began creating their own, like this equestrian event in Volgograd."

"And?"

"And the rider you're looking at is Peshkov's mistress, Valentina Usova. She's a former gold medalist who still loves to compete. The Volgograd event gave her a chance to do just that. The photographs you're looking at are from the day before yesterday."

"Who took these?" Conroy asked.

"We pulled them from local press coverage, as well as Rossgram—Russia's version of Instagram."

"Am I missing something? Was Peshkov in the crowd?"

"No," Maggie said, taking the tablet back. "This was a real rich people's event and Peshkov's no fool. If he had been there, publicly supporting Valentina, there would've been photos of him splashed all over the place. He won't hand his opposition, much less Russia's angry citizenry, who are shouldering the weight of international sanctions, a let-them-eat-cake moment like that. He's too cunning. But would he come in under the radar? Maybe adopt a disguise of some sort? That's what we were wondering."

"Did he?"

Maggie shook her head. "As we know, he's paranoid about assassination attempts and travels with a large security element. The sheer number of men and vehicles would have been impossible to hide."

"Then what am I missing?"

"This," she replied, swiping right to a new set of images and handing the iPad back. "Satellite footage taken from after the event."

"It looks like a horse being loaded into a trailer."

"Correct. That's Valentina's trailer. But that isn't her horse."

Conroy looked closer. "How can you tell?"

"The first giveaway is the color. Valentina's horse, Balthazar, has an autosomal dominant gene. It creates a dilute phenotype in black-pigmented horses."

"In English, please."

"It's referred to as silver dilution. A horse with a black coat will actually be chocolate in color with a flaxen or silver-gray mane and tail. Balthazar's are flaxen."

"And the horse I'm looking at here, its mane and tail aren't?"

Maggie reached over and zoomed in on the photo. "No. We believe this horse is a bleached blonde."

"I'm starting to understand why you didn't bring this to me sooner."

"Bear with me," she replied, committed to making her case. "The second giveaway is even more revealing."

"Which is what?"

"The horse's height. Balthazar is an Arabian. Arabian horses stand fourteen to fifteen hands high."

"And how tall is the horse in this photo?" Conroy asked.

"Based on our calculations, it's at least sixteen hands, and while it looks similar, it isn't an Arabian. Our best guess is that it's probably a breed known as an Oldenburg."

He studied the photo for a few more moments. "For the sake of this conversation, let's say they are two different horses. Why do we care?"

Leaning over, Maggie swiped to the next series of photos and replied, "Because about twenty minutes after Valentina's trailer with Balthazar's look-alike left for Moscow, another trailer departed, heading south toward Idokopas."

Conroy scrutinized the new series of photos. "Remind me where Volgograd is again?"

"It's along the Volga River. Halfway between Moscow and Idokopas."

"Were you able to see what was inside the second trailer?"

"Only partially," she said, advancing to the next images. "They backed it up so tight, it was practically touching the stable door. Where we do catch a glimpse of the second horse being loaded, the animal's been covered in a full Lycra body wrap, right down to what I've learned is called a tail bag."

"How do you know that's Lycra?"

"Because of how tightly the material hugs the musculature of the horse, and because by isolating the pattern, we were able to source the product manufacturer."

"Why would you wrap a horse in Lycra?"

"It's normally used pre-event to keep braids in place or dust and bedding out of the horse's coat."

"Is it possible that it's also used to keep flies and other biting insects away?" Conroy asked.

"Lycra doesn't work for that. You'd use a mosquito mesh or a ripstop nylon."

She had done her research. He had to hand it to her. "So what's the point of all this? Why the decoy?"

"That's the thread we keep tugging on. Valentina has been spotted back in Moscow, so we know she didn't head south with the horse."

"Do we have confirmation that the ultimate destination was Peshkov's palace in Idokopas?"

"No," Maggie admitted. "The satellite window closed before we could get confirmation."

"And nothing from subsequent passes over Idokopas?"

She shook her head. "The Russians know when our satellites are coming. Pretty simple to only let the horse out of the stables when it's safe to do so."

Conroy swiped through the photos once more. As he did, he asked, "Worst case, what *might* we be looking at?"

"You don't want my worst case. Like I said, just let me pull on this thread a little longer and see what we come up with."

"You can keep pulling, but I want to know what you're thinking."

Maggie paused for a moment before responding. "Okay. Here's what I'm thinking. I think Peshkov knows his mistress loves that horse more than anything. I think that if he and Valentina needed to get out of Moscow in a hurry and get to someplace safe, say Idokopas, they could hop on a helicopter or a jet at a moment's notice. Moving humans in a time of crisis is one thing. But a horse? That takes advance work. And *that's* what I think we could be seeing here."

Conroy handed back her iPad. "Nuclear weapons have only been used twice in war. Both times, it was by the United States—Hiroshima and then Nagasaki. That was almost eighty years ago. If Russia is preparing to do the unthinkable, we need to know, so we can stop it. And to do that, the intel has to be something we can actually take to POTUS and the National Security Council. A horse wrapped in Lycra isn't going to cut it. Is that clear?"

"Yes, sir."

"Good. Get back to work and find me something."

"Yes, boss," she responded as she gathered her things and headed for the door.

"And Maggie," Conroy called after her. "Do it fast."

CHAPTER 12

The exploding drones had drawn first responders from across the city. Emergency service vehicles, their light bars flashing, were parked and double-parked everywhere. With only two small bridges, both of which Norwegian police had already closed, no one was getting on or off of the island of thieves. At least not via land.

Once Harvath was in place, he sent Sølvi a final text. It contained just one word. *Now.*

Positioned at the water's edge, it was not unusual to see guests from the Thief Hotel's spa, wrapped in thick terry-cloth robes, venture out for a plunge in the Oslofjord. When Sølvi and Grechko exited, that's exactly what they looked like.

Sølvi's long blond hair was wrapped in a towel and Grechko had slung one over his head like a hoodie, so as to help disguise themselves. They wore rubber spa slippers and had rolled their pant legs up under their robes. Other than that they were fully dressed. Sølvi carried their socks, shoes, and the gear she had predeployed in the hotel room, in a backpack slung over her shoulder.

Slipping her arm through Grechko's, she encouraged him to walk slowly and to focus straight ahead. She kept her free hand wrapped around the grip of her pistol, which was tucked inside her robe. It was less than two hundred meters to the water.

As she walked, she kept her head down, occasionally leaning it against Grechko's shoulder in what looked like an affectionate gesture, but which in actuality allowed her to steal glances off to the sides.

So far, so good. No one appeared to be following them. Everyone she saw was headed in the opposite direction, back toward the scene of the explosions.

After a few more moments, she spotted Harvath, his boat bobbing on the water. He had spotted her as well. She could hear the gurgling of the engines as he put the vessel in gear and came in toward the shore.

She guided Grechko down to the swim platform, where Harvath ignored the NO BOATS signs and pulled alongside the landing.

As he did, he saw a flash of recognition ripple across the Russian's visage. But just as quickly as it had materialized, it vanished. Had Harvath not been trained to notice such things, he might have missed it.

He had never seen Grechko before in his life, yet the man appeared to know who he was. It was slightly unsettling.

Setting it aside for the moment, he helped the Russian climb aboard and then extended his hand to Sølvi, asking, "All good?"

She looked back in the direction they had come, scanned the shoreline one last time, and then, not seeing anything that would suggest that they had been followed, accepted his hand and stepped into the boat.

"All good," she replied. "Where do you want us?"

"Down there," he stated, gesturing at the small cabin under the bow. "Just until we get away from the city."

"Thank you," she said, giving him a quick kiss before disappearing with Grechko below.

Pushing away from the swim platform, he put the engines back in gear and headed out into the fjord.

Most of the police marine units were on the other side of the island, but one did come flying past and he was glad that Sølvi and Grechko were out of sight. There was no telling if anyone was actively looking for them yet. If they weren't, they would be soon. It was going to be up to Sølvi how she wanted to handle that.

He had a bunch of questions, all of which would have to wait until they got to their destination. His only focus right now was getting them there safely.

•   •   •

Once they had passed the lighthouse at the tip of the Nesodden peninsula, the coast, as well as the water around them, was clear. Reaching down, he opened the cabin door and let his passengers know that it was safe to come up topside.

Sølvi made introductions, first names only. "Scot, Leonid. Leonid, Scot."

The two men shook hands.

As they did, Harvath decided that he wasn't in the mood for all the cloak-and-dagger bullshit. "Have you and I met before, Mr. Grechko?"

"No, we have not."

"Interesting. Because back at the dock, it was clear that you recognized me."

"I wouldn't have been very good at my job if I didn't. Your reputation, particularly in Russian intelligence circles, preceeds you, Mr. Harvath."

Harvath took a smug pleasure in hearing that. It was a matter of personal pride that he kept so many Russians awake at night.

"Glad to know my work is appreciated," he replied.

Grechko frowned. "Some of it, perhaps. But definitely not all of it."

Sølvi patted the gunwale and changed the subject. "Good to see the old girl again," she stated.

Harvath knew her well enough to know what she was doing. Grechko was her assignment; her responsibility. He didn't need to like the Russian, but he did need to maintain his professionalism. If nothing else than for her.

"We were lucky," he replied, accepting the subject change. "With the warmer-than-usual weather, they hadn't pulled her from the water yet."

It also didn't hurt that the boat's owner liked Harvath. Not many Americans who came to Oslo rented a boat for the whole summer, paid in advance, and brought it back in pristine condition.

The owners of the cottage they were headed to felt the same way. Harvath had been the perfect tenant, paying in advance for the summer and fixing anything he saw in need of repair. Just like the boat owner, when Harvath had called at the last minute in need of a favor, the cottage owners had been more than happy to oblige. The key was in the same spot and he was welcome to stay as long as he wanted. There were no other renters on the books.

It was only late afternoon when they arrived, but the sun was already going down. After tying up the boat and opening the cottage, Harvath walked into the village for supplies.

He hadn't realized until halfway through the summer that the village had played an important role in the Norwegian resistance movement during World War II.

A small, clandestine radio station had been hidden in one of the cottages. It was manned by three brave undercover agents who belonged to the main Norwegian resistance organization, Milorg.

In April 1944, the Nazis finally zeroed in on it and launched an ambush, killing the resistance operatives and leaving their bloody bodies behind as a warning to the rest of the village.

A brass plaque, which Sølvi translated for him, had been placed to commemorate the station and the valiant men who lost their lives.

The whole story had only endeared the village even more to Harvath's heart. It was full of good, neighborly people who were happy to engage in conversation, while at the same time respecting boundaries and not being too nosy. They were solid.

The stockboy at the grocery store remembered him from over the summer and, after checking with his assistant manager, agreed to give him a lift back to the cottage. This allowed Harvath to buy not only the groceries he wanted, but also a couple of bundles of firewood, and to hit the government-owned liquor store known as the Vinmonopolet, or Polet for short. Eschewing his credit card, he paid for everything in cash.

Back at the cottage, he tipped the stockboy two hundred kroner, about twenty bucks, thanked him for the ride, and told him he didn't need any help getting the groceries inside.

Once the young man drove out of sight, Sølvi stepped outside to give Harvath a hand. But before she could touch a single bag, he pulled her in tight and just held her.

They stood there in their embrace without saying a word. Neither needed to speak. He had made it back from his string of operations without being killed only to almost lose her today. And in downtown Oslo of all places. They both knew how lucky they were to be holding each other.

He could feel some of the stress leaving her body as her muscles relaxed. After a few more moments, however, he sensed a shift. The tension had returned. She had clicked back into work mode. He gave her an extra squeeze and let her go.

Tucking a lock of her long blond hair behind her ear, she looked down at all the groceries.

"You even went to the Polet," she remarked.

"After the day you've had, I thought you might need a drink."

"You have no idea."

Together, they carried the bags inside, where Harvath slid the bottle of vodka into the freezer and then helped unpack everything else.

Once they were done, he got a fire started in the fireplace and suggested they sit down and debrief about what had happened at the safehouse while it was still fresh.

CHAPTER 13

The details of the assault were brutal. The knowledge that Martin, a man Harvath had known, had been ripped in half by one of the explosions was gut-wrenching. Every part of the attack was terrible. It had been an absolute bloodbath.

Once they had each shared their version of events, Harvath had walked them back through, probing for even the smallest of details. Nothing in a situation like this was ever inconsequential. The smallest clue could have the biggest of impacts, but only if it was surfaced and brought to light.

Unfortunately, what Sølvi and Grechko remembered were the explosions, the fire, the smoke, and the gunshots. These were the strongest, most overwhelming elements of the nightmare they had just been through.

To her credit, Sølvi could also remember some of the details about the assaulters and their equipment. It was all top-of-the-line gear. The men themselves were disciplined and well trained. Rappelling in through broken windows suggested an advanced military or special police unit background. Not carrying phones or ID further suggested the attackers were professionals. In the end, these were not a handful of thugs rounded up at a local biker bar.

The exceedingly indiscriminate use of force, coupled with the audacity of an attack in broad daylight, also told him something. Subtlety was not their calling card. The entire operation had "Russia" written all over it. It had probably been planned and carried out by a team of Russian Special Forces Spetsnaz soldiers.

Regardless of who the assaulters were, there was no question in Harvath's mind as to what their objective had been—*Grechko*. But was their assignment to kill or to capture him? As far as Harvath was concerned, the answer was probably either.

Detonating high-grade explosives outside the curtained windows of the safehouse meant they could not know who would be killed or injured inside. The van waiting down in the parking garage, while providing exfiltration for the attackers, could have also been used to spirit Grechko away. If the assaulters could have taken him alive and interrogated him, it would have allowed Moscow to learn how much top-secret information he had already revealed to Norwegian Intelligence.

Which brought Harvath to the next piece of this entire debacle—how the *hell* had they found the safehouse?

It was a discussion he didn't want to have in front of Grechko. Grabbing a blanket, they left the Russian inside and walked out onto the deck, where Harvath poured them each a glass of wine.

"I have no idea how they found us," said Sølvi, after taking a long sip and closing her eyes for a moment. "The only answer is that we must have a leak somewhere."

"How many people knew about the safehouse?"

"To be honest, I don't know the exact number."

"Approximately," Harvath replied. "Five people? Fifteen? Twenty?"

"We rotated two security teams on and off, so that's twelve people right there. The safehouse is paid for out of a secret budget, which less than five people at Norwegian Intelligence have access to. Weapons and vehicles needed to be approved, but that doesn't involve the location of the safehouse."

"Anyone else?"

"I'm not the first person at NIS to have used that safehouse. Others knew about it, but its existence was classified."

"As was Grechko's defection," Harvath stated.

Sølvi nodded. "I used a special tactical team to handle it. From the moment he drove up to our border, we had eyes on him. We even had one of our people in the booth, assessing him. He was followed and surveilled all the way to the rendezvous. Not until we were completely sure that it wasn't some sort of Russian trick did we make contact."

"And then what?"

"Straight to the airfield and, after guaranteeing he was clean of any hidden electronic devices, we brought him back to Oslo via private jet."

"That's it?"

"That's it," she replied, taking another sip of wine, before asking, "How did you know we had him?"

"Holidae didn't say."

"Did you ask her?"

Harvath nodded. "All she said was that the intelligence was solid."

"It would appear that both the Russians and the Americans each have at least one spy inside the Norwegian Intelligence Service. That's not good."

"No, it's not. What do you want to do?"

"I want to do my job and complete Grechko's debrief."

"Here?" Harvath asked.

"Why not?"

"Because by now, the NIS already knows you and Grechko are missing. They are going to stop at nothing to find you. That means interviewing your friends and colleagues, several of whom spent time with us here over the summer. I give it twenty-four hours tops before someone is sent to check out the cottage."

"Damn it," Sølvi muttered in frustration.

Harvath tried to reassure her. "You've got a protocol, right? A PACE plan. Primary, alternate, contingency, emergency order of communications?"

She looked at him. "There is no protocol, no PACE plan when your agency has been compromised. I have no idea who I can trust."

"I hear you. But none of this is your fault, okay?"

"This was my assignment. I'm responsible. For *everything*."

"Shit happens. Sometimes it can be really bad. Missions go sideways. You were a soldier. You know that. Even if you did fuck up somewhere, none of that matters now. You got Grechko out of there, you're both alive, and you've bought yourself a little breathing room. Those are wins. *Big* wins. Take them. Keep trusting your instincts. That's all that matters."

Sølvi didn't know how to respond. After another sip of wine, she glanced over her shoulder, back inside the cottage. Against the light from the fire, she could make out Grechko's silhouette.

"He's one of the highest-ranking defectors we've ever had. With what he knows, we'll be able to set parts of Russian intelligence back decades, if not longer. But that won't happen if I can't keep him alive. And right now, I don't know if I can do that in Norway. Not alone. Not by myself."

"Then it's a good thing you're not alone," said Harvath, swirling the wine in his glass and taking a drink.

Grechko was a massive get for the Norwegians and, by extension, for NATO and all its allied partners. He wasn't going to let Sølvi fail.

In fact, he had already begun formulating possible next steps in his mind. That was who he was. When he saw a problem, he charged right after it and fixed it. Or he smashed it into so many little pieces that it wasn't a problem anymore. But Sølvi's approach was different.

She was more measured, more of a tactician. If she had to, she could apply brute force to a problem. Before that, however, she methodically ran through each and every scenario—sifting, weighing, and then rejecting whatever didn't give her the highest possible chance for success. It was one of the biggest reasons he thought she would turn out to be a better spy than he was. She had figured out how to weaponize both her intelligence *and* her patience.

As they sat quietly together in the crisp evening air, the scent of wood smoke curled from the chimney and hovered over the deck. Harvath, ever the mariner, tilted his head back and tried to identify the first stars in the night sky. From somewhere off in the trees, a pair of tawny owls called back and forth to each other as they readied to hunt.

"I know what I want to do," Sølvi suddenly said, breaking the silence between them. "I want to make a deal."

"With whom?" he asked.

"Holidae Hayes."

The response took him by surprise. Of all the potential scenarios he had been running through his mind, that was *definitely* not one of them.

He looked at her. "Are you sure?"

"I'm positive," she replied, pulling the blanket off and standing up. "But first, I need a favor. I want you to speak with Grechko."

"*Grechko?* Why?"

"Because we'll need his buy-in. And for that to happen, he's going to have to trust you."

CHAPTER 14

"Kebab, falafel, *and* couscous," said Brunelle as she set the plastic bag filled with to-go containers on her colleague's desk.

It was amazing to her that a man so slim could eat so much food and never put on an ounce of weight.

Mohammed Motii, or MoMo for short, was a digital forensic specialist for the DGSI's Computer Analysis Response Team. CART's job was to crack, extract, and preserve any and all digital evidence during DGSI computer investigations.

MoMo had agreed to keep on working on the key fob Brunelle had given him, in exchange for her going out in the rain and picking up dinner from the Moroccan restaurant around the corner.

"You didn't let them forget my fries, did you?" he asked.

"They're in the box with the falafel. And here's your Fanta," she replied, pulling the bottle from her bag, which contained her own dinner of chicken tagine. "Any luck with that flash drive yet?"

MoMo shook his head. "Whoever did the encryption on this thing, it's first-class."

"I'll be in my office. Let me know when you break it."

Eyes glued to his screens, MoMo gave her a thumbs-up and she continued down the hall.

In her office, Brunelle closed the door behind her, kicked off her shoes, and hung up her coat before sitting down at her desk. A muted TV on the wall, tuned to a 24/7 cable news channel, was showing scenes from Oslo.

Unwrapping the plastic utensils, she tore off a piece of *khubz* bread and tucked into her tagine as she checked her emails.

There was plenty of the bureaucratic nonsense that clogged her inbox on a daily basis, along with a reminder that she had a pistol and sub-machinegun requalification coming up, and an RSVP for a counterter-rorism seminar in London. Buried at the very bottom was an update from Inspector Vincent Gibert. She opened it.

The email included his case notes thus far, a handful of witness state-ments, and links to the CCTV footage his officers had pulled from cam-eras around Jadot's apartment building, which had been uploaded to the cloud.

According to a brief note Gibert had written, they were still working on getting access to the phone. If it was encrypted nearly as thoroughly as the flash drive, they were going to have their hands full. La Crim's spe-cialists were good, but none of them were at MoMo's level.

As she ate, she scrolled through the witness statements. All of Jadot's neighbors had been contacted, but none of them had seen or heard any-thing. The staff at Robert et Louise, the restaurant across the street, said that Jadot was a regular, and had come in last night for a nightcap, shortly before closing. There was nothing in his speech or his behavior to have given any of them cause for concern.

When he left, the barman remembered watching him cross the street in the rain and enter his building. He didn't recall seeing anyone else fol-low him inside. Brunelle decided to check for herself.

Clicking on the link for the cameras with the best views of Jadot's building, as well as the entrance to Robert et Louise, she toggled back and forth, fast-forwarding and rewinding until she had what she wanted.

She was able to pinpoint the exact moment Jadot arrived at the restau-rant and the exact moment he left. The barman's witness statement was correct. Judging by the CCTV footage, no one had followed Jadot into his building.

No one had come out either. At least not until the next morning, when residents, or what she assumed were residents, began leaving. One man exited with his dog. A young woman with two children departed not long after that. Then a smartly dressed couple stepped outside, only to realize that the man had forgotten his umbrella. He reappeared several moments later with it and they departed.

She kept watching until the woman identified as the housekeeper arrived, followed shortly after by uniformed police officers.

According to the housekeeper, she had found the door fully locked, and she had used her own set of keys to gain entry. She was unaware of anyone else who might have keys of their own.

Wanting to be completely thorough, Brunelle rolled the security footage back a full twenty-four hours and took note of everyone who had come and gone via the front door of Jadot's building. According to Gibert's email, his team had done the same. Everyone had been contacted, identified, and accounted for.

As she reviewed the footage, she kept thinking about Jadot's pistol and what must have happened to cause him to pull it from its hiding place.

By all appearances, he was winding down; relaxing. He had returned home, had taken off his shoes at the front door, hung his coat, and was pouring himself a drink back in the kitchen. At some point, he had pulled his gun from under the sink.

The only logical answer was that something had spooked him. He had grabbed the gun because he sensed a threat. And then what? What would she have done in his position?

That answer was simple—she would have gone looking for the threat. She would have searched her entire apartment until she was satisfied the threat no longer existed. Was that what Jadot had done?

It would explain why he might have tucked the gun into his waistband. After searching the apartment, maybe he was confident enough that the threat had passed, but not so confident that he was ready to return the gun to its original hiding spot. Or perhaps he wanted to have his drink first. Either way, he let his guard down.

Judging by the partially opened freezer door, he had probably gone for some ice and that was when the killer had struck.

She was content with the credibility of that scenario. It made sense. It also allowed her to eliminate Jadot's murder as a crime of passion. When someone was angry enough to go for a gun, the odds normally remained in their favor.

Which left assassination or a crime of opportunity—and this was where it got tricky.

By definition, a crime of opportunity was not premeditated. A burglar, for example, gets caught in the middle of a home invasion, picks up an ice axe, and kills the homeowner. That could very well have been what happened to Jadot. The fact that the murderer hadn't stolen anything didn't make the scenario any less plausible. The killer might have fled in a panic.

In whatever state the killer had fled, it wasn't via the front door. That much was clear. The murderer had entered and exited Jadot's fifth-floor apartment via some other means. This took the degree of difficulty and therefore the sophistication of the crime up a notch.

There was no back door to the apartment, no rear stairwell. Pulling up recent satellite imagery of Paris, Brunelle drilled down on Jadot's building.

The killer would have had to have accessed the enclosed courtyard behind the building and then climbed up, or made their way across the adjacent, steeply pitched rooftops and dropped down. This person would have also had to have done so during inclement weather. It seemed to her that a burglar that determined wouldn't have left empty-handed. Which begged a totally new question. How did she know they hadn't?

Just because the killer hadn't taken his gun, or his cash, or his phone, it didn't mean that they weren't there to steal something else. Jadot was a spy after all and that was exactly what Gibert had been driving at; what his "intuition" and his "gut" had been telling him. The killing had been "work-related."

Despite keeping her mind open—and hating to admit it—Brunelle was beginning to move in his direction. Paris was full of much easier apartments to rob. This wasn't random. Jadot's had been targeted for a reason—because someone either wanted to get to him, or get to something he had in his possession. Once MoMo cracked the encryption on the flash drive, she'd hopefully have that answer.

In the meantime, Gibert and his team needed to widen their net—beginning with interviewing the residents of the surrounding rooftop apartments to determine if they had seen or heard anything unusual, and following up with an investigation of the walled courtyard.

Finally, they needed to expand their search cordon and scoop up a lot more neighborhood CCTV footage. The killer might have been clever and might have been determined, but they were human, and humans made mistakes; they all left clues. Brunelle only needed one.

She was about to reply to Gibert's email when her phone rang. Looking down, she saw his name on her caller ID.

"Brunelle," she said, answering the phone.

"I think I may have something," the inspector replied.

"I'm listening."

"No. Not over the phone. In person."

She glanced out the window. It was still pouring outside. There'd be no taxis available. "It's pissing down rain, Vincent. If you want to do this in person, you'll have to come here."

"I'll meet you halfway," he offered.

Then, before she could utter the one place in Paris she would not agree to meet him at, he said it, and disconnected the call.

"Botaniste. Forty-five minutes."

CHAPTER 15

The Shangri-La was a five-star luxury hotel with jaw-dropping views across the Seine to the Eiffel Tower. Tucked away deep inside and out of sight was its sumptuously decorated, yet intimate, Le Bar Botaniste.

Green velvet sofas, strewn with tiger-print pillows, sat beneath enormous oil paintings of brightly festooned Bedouin horses. Heavy draperies, tied back with knotted silk cords, sat at each end of the bar. Hand-fashioned copper cups filled with fresh herbs had been placed on every table. Terrariums and exotic plants kept under glass were scattered throughout.

In the quietest and darkest corner, Gibert sat at a table—*their* table. This was where their affair had started, meeting halfway between their offices at Le Bar Botaniste.

It was a perk of Gibert's job. Tasked with high-profile, celebrity cases as part of his portfolio for the Paris police, he was known at all of the top hotels in town. Each of their general managers had his direct cell phone number and could call him at any time. In exchange for Gibert's discretion and his ability to handle situations in such a way that the hotels' reputations were protected, he was afforded certain perks. Among them were free drinks, free food, and the occasional complimentary suite.

There was one thing Brunelle could say for her time with him—it hadn't been boring. In fact, it had been quite exciting. He was an excellent lover and highly intelligent. What he wasn't, however, was honest.

The picture he had painted of his marital situation wasn't even close to the truth. His wife had not moved out of their home, he was not six months into a trial separation, and he had no intention of seeking a divorce.

Once the real truth became known, Brunelle had cut off all ties with him. But instead of taking it like a man, owning up to what he had done, and moving on, Gibert had doubled down, telling her that he was profoundly in love with her and that he was, in fact, going to leave his wife. It was quite a spectacle.

The more he pressed his case, the less respect she had for him. She ignored his phone calls, his texts, and his emails, yet they kept coming.

Then one night, absolutely hammered, he had shown up at her apartment. He had done it, he claimed. He had left his wife and he begged Brunelle to take him back. She stood her ground. Things got heated. When he refused to leave her apartment, Brunelle called the police.

As she wasn't interested in pressing charges, just getting him to leave, they took Gibert back to his office and let him sleep it off. The next morning, he crawled back to his wife.

Brunelle had not seen or spoken with him until this morning at Jadot's apartment. She didn't know what to make of his choice of the Botaniste for their meeting. If there was some kind of subtext to it, he had wasted his time. She had absolutely zero interest in rekindling anything with him. This meeting was business and *only* business.

Entering the hotel, she had made her way back to the bar and had found Gibert exactly where she knew he would be. Had he had the temerity to have ordered for her, she would have been hard-pressed not to throw the drink right at him. It was bad enough that he had picked this spot. At the very least, she expected him to remain professional.

When she arrived at the table, she saw that he hadn't ordered anything for her, just a cocktail for himself. It was his usual, and one of the most expensive things on the Botaniste menu—a Sazerac made with Hennessy X.O cognac.

"Thank you for coming," he said, sliding his chair back in order to stand and greet her properly.

Brunelle waved him off. "Don't get up," she said, pulling out her own chair and sitting down.

"Have you heard about Oslo?"

"Only what's been on the news. We haven't had an agency-wide update yet. You?"

"Email and text blasts went out to officers calling for enhanced vigilance. Other than that, all quiet."

A tense moment of awkward silence passed between them. It was difficult being back in this setting under such different circumstances.

"Something to drink?" he asked, trying to reduce the tension.

She loved the Botaniste's Golden Martini. It used to be her all-time favorite, but this wasn't a social event. Not wanting to send the wrong signal to Gibert, she opted for something nonalcoholic. "Tisane," she replied. Considering the weather, the infusion of herbs and spices, simmered in hot water, was probably exactly what she needed.

After getting the waiter's attention and placing the order, Gibert was all business. He removed a manila envelope from his briefcase and handed it to her.

"What's this?" she asked.

"A summary of Jadot's service file, most of which is redacted."

Brunelle opened the envelope and pulled it out. "How'd you get your hands on it?"

"Like I said, a little professional courtesy goes a long way."

"The boys in Action Division."

"They want this solved just as much as we do. Probably more."

"Speaking of which," she replied, flipping through the pages of the summary, "I sent you an email before I left the office. Did you receive it?"

Gibert took a sip of his drink before saying, "I did and I'm already ahead of you. Forensics found some chipped paint near one of the apartment's rear windows."

"Outside or inside?"

"Inside, on the floor. But the paint appears to be from the exterior side of the window. We think that's how the killer made entry."

"Have you spoken with the neighbors in the adjacent buildings?"

"We're in the process, along with expanding our search for additional CCTV footage."

"Good," said Brunelle, pausing as the waiter brought her tisane and set it on the table. Once the man had departed, she said, "Based on the summary, it looks like Jadot was a career intelligence officer, charged with re-cruiting and running spies. He had postings at a variety of French embassies around the world, eventually rising to senior positions toward the end."

Gibert nodded. "Correct."

"His last posting was just over a year and a half ago at the embassy in Beirut," she stated, looking up from the file at Gibert. "Isn't that about the time the French ambassador there died by suicide?"

"That's how it was reported," Gibert replied, taking another sip of his drink.

"Meaning what? It wasn't a suicide?"

He shrugged. "No one knows for sure."

Brunelle pulled up a news article about the incident and checked the dates. "It looks like Jadot got pulled from the embassy and returned to Paris right before it happened. He didn't finish out his rotation. Why not?"

"According to what I was told, off the record, Jadot believed the am-bassador had been compromised."

"Compromised by whom? The Lebanese?"

Gibert shook his head. "The Russians."

Jesus, she thought. It was always shocking when someone in government service was suspected of being an asset for a foreign country, much less an actively hostile foreign country. "So, what happened?" she asked. "Did Jadot blow the whistle? Is that what caused the ambassador to take his own life?"

"Allegedly, he was told by his superiors to back off."

"*Back off?* Why?"

"They wanted to mount some sort of counterintelligence operation."

"And?"

"And," said Gibert, "he didn't think they were moving fast enough. He kept pushing. That's what got him recalled."

"So Jadot returned to Paris and shortly thereafter the ambassador died by suicide."

"Yes, but according to my guys, Jadot claimed never to have con-fronted the ambassador."

"Then who did?" she asked.

"They think Jadot, angry over being recalled, may have told someone else before he left."

"Such as?"

"No one knows," he replied with another shrug.

"That's it? That's all you've got?"

Gibert shook his head, reached back into his briefcase, and withdrew something else. "There's also this."

"Is that what I think it is? You actually cracked it?"

"Yep," he replied, punching in the passcode and sliding Jadot's phone across the table to her. "We've got a new guy in digital ops. Crazy good."

She couldn't believe they had opened Jadot's phone before MoMo could open the flash drive. Picking it up, she began scrolling through it. "Did you learn anything?"

"A little bit," said Gibert, taking a sip of his Sazerac. "We know he spent the weekend at his cottage in Brittany. We know what train he took to Paris from Saint-Malo. And we can map his movements via the Métro as he made his way to Robert et Louise from the Gare Montparnasse."

"And you're pulling all the corresponding CCTV footage?"

"Again, one step ahead of you."

Brunelle continued to look through Jadot's phone. "Anything else?"

"Have you looked at his calendar yet? He had a breakfast meeting this morning, which he obviously didn't make."

Clicking over to today's date, she read the name of the man Jadot was to have met with and her eyebrows went up.

"So," said Gibert, marking her expression, "you recognize who his rendezvous was with."

"Ray Powell," she replied, nodding in a bit of disbelief. "The CIA's Paris station chief. Why would the two of them be having breakfast together?"

"I asked my guys at the DGSE the same question. They couldn't figure it out either. But they did tell me something interesting."

"What was that?"

Leaning back in his chair, Gibert raised his glass to finish off what was left of his drink and responded, "Powell was in Beirut at the same time as Jadot."

CHAPTER 16

In the age-old tradition of how Russians built trust, Grechko picked up the bottle from the dining room table and poured them each another shot of vodka.

"Za zda-ró-vye," the man said.

Harvath clinked his small glass against his and replied, "Za zda-ró-vye."

They had a decision to make. Remaining at the cottage was not an option. Eventually, the Norwegians were going to find them. Once that happened, there was no way of knowing how far behind the next team of assassins were. The attack on the safehouse in Oslo had been so massive, Harvath didn't doubt there'd be more to come. Grechko didn't doubt it either. But he also knew he had leverage at this moment. He didn't intend to waste it.

"Explain to me," the Russian said, "if we go with your plan, how you see all of this playing out?"

"I contact the CIA station chief in Oslo, she sends a team down here to pick us up, and we all go back to the U.S. Embassy compound."

"And what does your fiancée tell her people at the Norwegian Intelligence Service?"

"As little as possible," Harvath replied. "Until she gets to the bottom of who the leaker is, it's the only way to keep you safe."

"Which you believe you can do at your embassy."

Harvath nodded.

"Let me ask you something, Mr. Harvath. If the Norwegian Intelligence Service has a mole, what makes you believe that your embassy
doesn't?"

It was a fair enough question, but it was a hypothetical that could be
applied to any organization. "Right now, I think it's the safest place we can
put you. We'll limit who knows you're on-site. The fewer people in the
loop, the better."

"And then what?" Grechko asked. "An embassy isn't a hotel. If yours
has a medical unit, maybe you've got one or two hospital beds. Or perhaps there are a few army cots that have been tucked away someplace in
case of a crisis. Not exactly a sustainable solution."

"Our first objective is to keep you alive. We can worry about everything else later."

"If by *later* you're envisioning whisking me off to the United States,
I'm not interested."

Harvath smiled. "You'd be the first Russian I ever met who wasn't."

"Do you know why I chose Norway to defect to?"

"Besides the ease of crossing its shared border with Russia?"

"That was a definite advantage," Grechko admitted. "But it wasn't my
main reason."

"Then what was?"

"Norway is one of the most robust democracies in the world. It respects the rights of its citizens, its journalists, and the rule of law. Elections here are free and fair. The Norwegian government stands up for
what it believes in and keeps its word. In every meaningful way, this
country is the exact opposite of Russia."

"All things the United States offers too. Plus, we can give you more
agreeable winters and much better beaches."

Now it was Grechko's turn to smile. "I'm well aware. I did a fair bit of
traveling when I was based at the Russian Embassy in Washington. America
has many things going for it, but in the end, Norway is where I want to be."

"I understand. In the short term, I still think the U.S. Embassy
compound is the safest place for you. After that, maybe—and it's a big
maybe—if you're willing to cooperate and share information with the
CIA, we might be able to help establish a safehouse somewhere for you.

At least until the Norwegian Intelligence Service is able to fully reassert control over your security."

The Russian thought about it for a moment, a plan beginning to take shape in his mind. "What if we split the difference?"

Harvath wasn't sure he understood what the man meant. "That would depend. What are you thinking?"

"I'll agree to a temporary CIA safehouse, but I get to pick the location."

Harvath laughed. "That's not how it works."

"And my deal with the Norwegians has to change."

"Change how?" asked Sølvi. She had been sitting in the living room monitoring the TV for updates. Coverage of the attack in Oslo was on every channel.

"My bonus," Grechko responded as she walked into the dining room. "I want it up front."

"The bonus is yours if you fully cooperate. It's an incentive. That's why it comes at the end. We're going to need surveillance, new passports, transportation . . . It's going to take an entire team to make it happen. For the moment, I'm all you've got."

"Technically," the Russian corrected her, pointing at Harvath, "you've also got him, in addition to whatever resources the CIA is willing to contribute."

Harvath looked at Sølvi. "What's he talking about? What bonus?"

"It's not a what," she replied. "It's a *who*. Her name is Inessa Surkova and it's going to be a nightmare getting to her."

"Russia?"

Sølvi shook her head. "South of France. But he's insistent it look like an accident. He wants to be absolutely certain no one ever comes looking for her."

"If you do this," Grechko said, addressing him, "I promise I will make it worth your while."

"Hold on," Harvath stated. "I haven't agreed to do anything. The only thing we're talking about is getting you someplace secure."

"Then let's make it a safehouse in the South of France. It gets us out of Norway and my debriefing can run simultaneous with planning the Inessa operation, for which you need me on the ground, in person."

This was getting out of control, fast. "All of this is above my pay grade," said Harvath. "Your arrangement is with Norway. They expect you to honor your end. Any change will have to be approved by her." As he pointed at Sølvi, he continued. "And any contribution I, or my country makes, is going to have to be approved by the CIA. That's who compensates me. I don't want or expect anything from you."

"Then we'll consider it a bonus," Grechko responded. "An incentive, provided at the end of the operation, to ensure your performance."

"Again," Harvath stated, "that's not necessary. The CIA will make sure I'm covered."

"The CIA can't give you what I'm offering."

"What's that?"

"An opportunity to repair an oversight."

"What oversight?"

"When you took revenge for the murder of your wife, you went straight to the top," the Russian stated. "You inflicted maximum pain on President Peshkov via his son, Misha. You also killed the head of the GRU's special missions group, the man who masterminded your kidnapping and the death of your wife and colleagues, General Konstantin Minayev."

"I don't know what you're talking about. Peshkov's son died of a drug overdose and General Minayev by autoerotic asphyxiation. If memory serves, he was found to be in possession of some very disturbing pornography."

"Quite," Grechko agreed. "These were good and, dare I say, righteous acts that you committed. But while they went a long way to evening the score, I imagine nothing would ever make you feel as if the debt had been completely paid."

Harvath was beginning to dislike this conversation, *intensely*. He could feel the heat and the anger he kept locked away inside himself starting to seep out. "If you've got a point to make, make it," he stated.

"You didn't finish the job. You missed one."

"And who was that?"

"Someone who worked for Minayev. This person helped assemble, coordinate, and dispatch the team that killed your wife and your colleagues and took you hostage."

"If I didn't know any better," Harvath replied, "I might think you were referring to a certain GRU colonel named Josef Kozak. But shortly after being admitted to Moscow City Hospital Number 67 for complicated spinal surgery, that colonel died in his bed of a heart attack."

Grechko smiled wryly. "Yes, all of those unfortunate incidents. Back-to-back-to-back. All of them befalling prominent Russians directly or indirectly connected to what happened to you. But as I said, you missed one—someone between Minayev the planner and Kozak the team leader who carried out the operation. So, here's my proposition. Get me to Inessa Surkova and I will not only give you the missing man's name, but I'll also tell you how to find him."

CHAPTER 17

C onroy had multiple international news stations playing quietly
on the TV monitors in his office. Almost all of them were relay-
ing footage of the aftermath of the attack in Oslo.

"Tell me you've got good news for me," he said as Maggie Thomas arrived for an impromptu meeting.

"Unfortunately, no," she said, joining him at the conference table
and taking her seat.

"Have we heard anything from Holidae Hayes regarding what took
place in Oslo?"

Maggie glanced at her notes. "So far, it's pretty thin. What she has
been able to uncover is that the Norwegians are treating it as a terrorist attack. They're saying multiple drone-borne explosive devices."

"How about the target? That part of Oslo is mixed-use—commercial
and residential. Any insights there?"

"If the Norwegians have identified the target, they're not saying.
Ditto for who may have been behind the attack. Hayes was able to learn
that there are multiple fatalities, both in the apartment building, which
she believes was the primary target, and in the underground parking garage where some sort of protracted shoot-out happened."

"I have to ask," said Conroy. "Any chance this is related to their Russian defector, Grechko?"

"Good question. I asked the same thing. Hayes isn't sure. She has reached out to Harvath, but he hasn't responded yet. She's hoping to speak with him shortly."

The DDO poured himself a glass of water from the carafe on the table. "The minute she does, I want an update."

"Understood."

"What did you need to see me about?"

Maggie turned to her next page of notes. "According to sources in Ankara, forty-five minutes ago the Russian defense minister reached out to his Turkish counterpart to express concerns over an alleged plot by Ukraine to detonate a dirty bomb."

Conroy couldn't believe his ears. "Are you kidding me?"

"No, and apparently the Turks didn't believe it either."

"Where are the Russians getting their alleged information?"

"They claim to have sources inside Ukrainian military intelligence," said Maggie. "Which sounds like bullshit to me. I don't think the sources or the intel exists. I think they're making it all up."

"Why?"

"Because they did something similar at the beginning of the war. Remember when they spread disinformation that we were helping the Ukrainians develop bioweapons at U.S. government–funded labs over there?"

Conroy nodded. "Beyond insane. Not only have we signed a treaty with Ukraine assuring both of our nations will never develop or use biological weapons, but the labs over there the U.S. was helping were involved in farming. They dealt with anthrax, plague, hemorrhagic fever . . . all of which can infect birds and pigs. The idea was to make sure none of that stuff spreads to humans."

"And it's not just the United States who backed Ukraine's efforts. It was Canada, the European Union, and the World Health Organization. Practically every nation in the world studies these diseases, but the Russians wanted to make it seem like something nefarious.

"We're talking about public health and veterinary labs, all working alongside the Ukrainian health and agriculture ministries. Not only were none of them involved in biological warfare, but their only contact with the Ukrainian military was to provide mobile rapid-testing labs in case of emergency. All of it was out on the internet, open-source. Nevertheless, Russia began spinning tales of secret, U.S.-backed bioweapons labs in hopes of painting itself as a 'truth teller' with valid reasons for its invasion, Ukraine as a sinister country engaged in biological weapons development, and America as an evil force whose support of Ukraine was totally suspect.

"It was prime Russian propaganda, which unfortunately found a home in certain corners of the American citizenry. It didn't matter that the claims were easily disproven with a modicum of research. For some people who were angry with the world, their government, or whatever— it fit a predetermined narrative that was simply too good to challenge. And that's what continues to get me—the angrier people are, the more they are susceptible to malign foreign influence."

Conroy had been around long enough to know how effective Russian propaganda could be. And right on their heels were the Chinese. The billions of dollars those two nations were spending to impact the cultural conversation and harm the United States was mind-boggling.

He longed for a return to the days when Americans realized that there was more that united than divided them. He prayed the country wouldn't have to live through another 9/11 just to get to the national unity that arose on 9/12.

"Okay, let's say they're making the whole dirty bomb thing up," said Conroy, steering them back to the matter at hand. "What's the point?"

Maggie didn't need any notes for this part. This was the part where her analytic skills shone best. "I can think of three reasons," she said. "First of all, it raises the psychological stakes. It refocuses the world on Ukraine and makes the Ukrainians appear desperate. Russia must be winning and the Ukrainians must be losing if the Ukrainians are going to resort to something so damnable.

"Second, it makes the Russians appear more reasonable. By calling out such bad behavior, the Russians are attempting to place themselves above it. Look at us, we're so much better than those guys. The world should be on our side in this. Especially the United States. This is terrorism. How could anyone have as neighbors monsters who would use dirty bombs?"

When, after a lengthy pause, Conroy didn't hear Maggie articulate her third reason, he cocked an eyebrow and asked, "What's number three?"

Taking a deep breath, she replied, "That's my worst-case scenario. It's the Russians prepping the public relations battlefield. By pointing to anticipated bad behavior by Ukraine, they're trying to create a permission structure, which would allow them to engage in even worse behavior. In other words, we're justified in doing X because Ukraine is going to employ dirty bombs.

"If I'm right and it is number three, the Russian defense minister will be making several other phone calls to his NATO contemporaries. I think he's trying to purchase top cover. The Kremlin wants to be able to say it informed NATO members of the threat and that NATO did nothing to rein Ukraine in. Because of NATO's inaction, Russia was left no choice but to strike first."

"Meaning a nuclear strike."

Maggie nodded. "If those devices are in Belarus, I don't think it's for show. If the Russians put them there, it's because they intend to use them."

Conroy didn't waste a moment responding. Reaching for his phone, he buzzed his assistant. "I need five minutes with the Director. Maggie will be coming with me. We need to see him ASAP."

CHAPTER 18

Ray Powell lived in a small but elegant apartment in the heart of the Latin Quarter on the Rue des Écoles. Had he been willing to travel further out, his salary as the Paris station chief would have secured him more space, but he preferred to be in the center of the action. The Sorbonne, Notre Dame, the Luxembourg Gardens, and the famous Shakespeare and Company bookstore were all within a five-minute walk.

It had taken Brunelle a series of after-hours phone calls to arrange the meeting. Her section chief had called the deputy director of the DGSI, who in turn had reached out to the director general herself, who was in the middle of dinner atop the nearby Peninsula Hotel at L'Oiseau Blanc.

A no-bullshit woman, Audrey de Vasselot had asked for Brunelle's cell number so she could speak with her directly. De Vasselot wanted to know what Brunelle had learned, why a face-to-face meeting was necessary, and why it couldn't wait until tomorrow. Brunelle made her case as professionally and succinctly as she could.

Ten minutes later, the director general texted her with Powell's address and his invitation to discuss her case at his apartment.

Gibert was able to secure one of the Shangri-La's chauffeur-driven Mercedes and after tipping the waiter and barman, they headed out.

It was still raining as they crossed the Pont des Invalides and headed down the Quai d'Orsay. At Boulevard Saint-Michel, they headed away from the Seine and deeper into the Latin Quarter.

Two blocks after Boulevard Saint-Germain, they turned left onto Rue des Écoles and soon arrived at Powell's building. It was nineteenth-century Haussmann-influenced architecture—creamy Lutetian lime-stone with wrought-iron balconies and a four-sided, steeply slanted mansard roof. Inside was a large, atrium-style staircase where you could look all the way up to a skylight in the roof.

As the station chief lived on the sixth floor and, as neither Brunelle nor Gibert were keen on that many flights of stairs, they climbed into the uncomfortably small elevator and rode up together.

A cordial man in his late fifties, Powell greeted them at the door in jeans and a gray V-neck sweater over a white oxford shirt. Along with his calfskin loafers and tortoise-shell glasses, he looked more like an architect or a stockbroker than a spook.

"Let me take your coats," he offered as he gestured his guests inside.

Brunelle and Gibert thanked him, and after he had hung their jackets in the vestibule, they followed him into the living room.

The apartment was tastefully decorated. There were leather sofas, plenty of books, and a sturdy brass bar cart loaded with liquor. Various black-and-white photographs, as well as a series of paintings and sketches, were hung salon-style in a myriad of gold and silver frames. Two worn Persian carpets, a marble bust of what may have been Julius Caesar, and a pair of highly polished Art Deco accent tables rounded out the look.

There was not one but two balconies and even on a rainy night, the views through the rain-dappled *portes-fenêtres* were worth whatever Powell was paying for the place. It was one of the chicest bachelor pads Brunelle had ever seen.

"Can I offer either of you something to drink?" the station chief asked, nodding at the bar cart. "I've got just about everything."

Not one to ever turn down a freebie, Gibert sauntered over to examine the selection. "Is that what I think it is?" he asked pointing to one of the bottles.

Powell nodded. "You've got a good eye. Pappy Van Winkle. One of the best American bourbons you'll ever taste." Uncorking the bottle, the station chief poured some into a Glencairn glass and handed it to him.

Gibert swirled the bourbon to help aerate it. Then, after taking a moment to appreciate its rich color, he brought the glass to his nose and inhaled. The aromas were amazing. It was now time to taste.

Taking his first sip, he allowed the warm liquid to cover his palate. The taste was incredible; better than he had imagined it would be.

"What do you think?" Powell asked.

"Marvelous," Gibert replied.

"That's the ten-year," the station chief replied. "And you're right, it is absolutely marvelous. Best thing I've ever tasted. The ambassador is a huge Pappy fan as well. He keeps a bottle of the 23 at his residence, which he breaks out for V-VIPs. Crossing my fingers that someday I'll make the cut." Smiling, he turned to Brunelle and asked, "What can I get for you?"

"Thank you, but I'm okay," she replied, still in business mode.

"Are you sure?"

She nodded. "Positive."

"Shall we sit then?" Powell asked.

After pouring a small portion of the bourbon for himself, he took a seat on the sofa facing his guests. "Director General de Vasselot asked me to help in any way I can. So what can I do for you?"

Brunelle had made it clear to Gibert in the car that she would be doing the talking and that he should follow her lead.

"Are you familiar with a French national named Jean-Jacques Jadot?" she began.

Powell nodded. "Yes, I am."

"Are you aware that he was found murdered this morning?"

"Yes. It's absolutely terrible."

Brunelle studied him. "How did you learn about it?"

"Most U.S. embassies employ a retired high-ranking police officer as a liaison. Ours put the word out as soon as he heard. Jean-Jacques and I were actually supposed to meet for breakfast this morning. He never showed."

"Did you report this to the Paris Police, DGSI, anyone?" Gibert asked.

"No."

"Why not?"

"I felt it was premature."

Gibert looked at him. "Premature? How so?"

The station chief chose his words carefully. "Jean-Jacques was a friend. He was also a colleague. I had a lot of respect for him. With that said, I don't know anything about who killed him or why. Injecting myself into the story, especially before I had more information, could have brought un-wanted attention to the embassy. It's our policy to avoid that kind of thing."

"Did you and Monsieur Jadot often meet for breakfast?" Brunelle asked, taking back control of the conversation.

"No. If we saw each other, it was normally over drinks," he replied.

"Whose idea was it to meet for breakfast?"

"It was Jean-Jacques's. He was at his cottage in Brittany over the weekend and reached out. He said he needed to talk about something and asked if I could be available first thing this morning. I told him he didn't have to wait, that we could talk over the phone if he wanted, but he turned me down. He said that it had to be in person."

"And you didn't find that a little unusual?"

"Maybe," said Powell. "But that was Jean-Jacques. He was old-school."

"How so?"

"He was a spy's spy. Moscow Rules and all that. Don't call when you can write and don't write when you can meet in person. That was one of his favorite maxims."

"Then you believe he wanted to meet with you in order to discuss something intelligence-related?"

"I don't know what he wanted," Powell replied.

"Whatever it was," Gibert interjected, "it was obviously important be-cause he wanted to see you first thing. Was he having romantic problems? Money problems?"

"We didn't discuss those things."

"I thought you said you were friends."

"We were friends," the station chief responded. "But those weren't the kinds of things we talked about. Jean-Jacques was a confirmed bachelor. I never heard him discuss women, or men. He didn't talk about money either. With an apartment in the Marais and a cottage in Brittany, I figured he was doing fine."

"So what did you talk about?" Brunelle inquired. "As friends."

Powell thought for a moment. "He talked a lot about climbing. He enjoyed sports. History was also another favorite subject. And movies. He loved American movies."

"Did you ever discuss business?"

"Define *business.*"

"Your work as intelligence operatives."

"On occasion. As appropriate."

"Did you first meet each other here in Paris?" she asked, testing his truthfulness.

The station chief shook his head. "No. In Beirut. We were both stationed there at the same time."

"From what I understand, Jadot was recalled. He didn't finish out his time in Beirut."

"Correct."

"Do you know why?"

Powell swirled the bourbon in his glass. "Jean-Jacques discovered that the French ambassador had been turned by the Russians."

Brunelle looked at him. "He was absolutely certain of that?"

"One hundred percent. But when he transmitted the information back to Paris, there was quite a bit of foot-dragging. The ambassador was extremely well-connected. If he was outed, it was going to cause a lot of headaches and a lot of embarrassment for the Élysée Palace."

"So what happened?"

"Well, while he waited for an answer, Jean-Jacques kept sending updates to headquarters, along with ideas on how they might take advantage of the ambassador having been compromised. His ultimate desire was to double the ambassador back against the Russians. But failing that, he wanted to limit the classified material the man was receiving and possibly even start feeding him bogus intel in the hopes that it would be passed along to Moscow."

"And was he successful?"

Once more, the station chief shook his head. "The DGSE was getting ready to send a special counterintelligence team to Beirut to handle the situation. Jean-Jacques believed that they were going to quietly remove the ambassador and do any necessary damage control. When he yet again confronted headquarters about it, they accused him of insubordination and brought him home. Shortly after Jean-Jacques arrived back in Paris, the ambassador died by suicide."

"You seem to know a great deal about the situation," said Brunelle. "How is that?"

"Beirut is a big city, but it's a small town when it comes to expats, especially those in our line of work. The DGSE and the CIA cooperated on several intelligence-gathering assignments. That's how Jean-Jacques and I became friendly. At the end, when he was being recalled, he was pretty angry. He was also concerned."

"About what?"

"He was worried that the French ambassador might not be the only one who had been compromised. The deeper he dug, the more convinced he was that he was correct. If the ambassador wasn't removed, if he was left in his position, Jean-Jacques was concerned what kind of damage could be done going forward."

"So he read you in?"

"Yes," said Powell, taking a sip of his drink. "He didn't trust anyone at the DGSE or at the embassy any longer, but he trusted me and asked me to keep an eye on things."

"Did you or Monsieur Jadot ever confront the ambassador?"

"No, neither of us did."

"Then what pushed him to suicide? The timing seems incredibly coincidental."

"I agree," the station chief replied. "According to Jean-Jacques, the ambassador had no known history of depression or suicidal ideation. His thinking was that if the Russians had indeed compromised other people working for the French government, maybe one of them had leaked Jean-Jacques's reports back to Moscow. If the Russians learned that the DGSE was on to the ambassador, maybe they murdered him and made it look like a suicide."

"Why not just murder Jadot instead?" Brunelle asked.

"I think by that point, considering all the reports he had sent back to headquarters, the cat was already out of the bag. It was probably just easier to murder the ambassador, make it look like a suicide, and cut their losses. But you're not incorrect. I think part of the reason Jean-Jacques told me everything was in case he ended up dying, especially if it was under suspicious circumstances, at least someone would still be alive to pursue the truth."

"Perhaps that's why he wanted breakfast with you this morning," she said, thinking out loud. "Maybe he needed to share something with you in case anything happened to him. Any idea what that might have been?"

"*Might* have been?" Powell replied. "Sure, I have an idea. But without additional information, without evidence, it would only be speculation."

"*Speculation,*" Brunelle offered, "is just another word for hypothesis. It's ninety percent of what we do at this stage."

Once again, the station chief chose his words carefully. "After returning from Beirut, Jean-Jacques was preoccupied with the possibility that the Russians had turned other people in the French government, including inside the intelligence services."

"Do you know if he ever found any proof?"

"Every time I saw him, he was pulling on a new thread, yet he never seemed to have uncovered anything. At least nothing he ever shared with me."

"Did he have any enemies that you know of?"

"Anybody who'd been in the game as long as Jean-Jacques probably made a lot of enemies. He absolutely hated the Russians. I'm guessing it was probably mutual." There was a pause before Powell added, "Speaking of which, can you confirm for me how he was murdered."

"We purposefully haven't made the information public yet."

"We heard it was an ice axe."

Brunelle shot Gibert a look. She had no doubt the CIA station chief had gotten that information from his own contacts within the DGSE, possibly from the very men Gibert had allowed access to the crime scene.

"That's correct," she conceded, "but I would ask that you please keep it confidential."

"It's almost too on the nose," Powell mused.

"Excuse me?"

"If it was the Russians who killed him, it's rather unimaginative, regardless of Jean-Jacques's love of history. Or maybe I'm totally wrong. Maybe it was designed to send a message."

"I'm sorry," Brunelle replied. "I'm not following you. What are you talking about?"

"August 1940. When Stalin decided Trotsky had become too much of a threat, he sent an assassin to kill him. The weapon the assassin used was an ice axe."

CHAPTER 19

Nice Côte d'Azur was the third-busiest airport in France, handling almost three million passengers a year. Even its glitzy VIP terminal experienced a constant churn of arriving and departing flights. It was the perfect place to go overlooked, which was exactly what Harvath wanted.

Grechko had put him in an untenable position. Dangling one of the people responsible for his wife's murder, but refusing to give up that person until Harvath did something for him, left him with few options.

He also had Sølvi to consider. For her to be successful, she needed Grechko to be cooperative. And for him to be cooperative, he wanted Inessa to be "rescued." The larger question, however, was whether that was what Inessa wanted. Harvath had his doubts.

Inessa Surkova was, to use the most charitable word available, a courtesan. She traded sex for money—and had done so on several occasions with Grechko. For his part, Grechko had not only willingly given her money, he had also fallen in love with her. He said she felt the same about him, which in Harvath's experience was what most men who fell for hookers or strippers said. The fact that Grechko's feelings might be unrequited wasn't his problem.

His problem was putting the two of them together long enough for Grechko to make his case and then, if Inessa agreed, helping her disappear. A task that was going to be much easier said than done.

On top of all of this was Holidae Hayes, the CIA, and their threat to both freeze him out of his off-the-books bank account and to come after him for taxes and penalties.

If he walked away from the account and never touched it again, there was zero chance they could ever tie him to it. But he had no intention of walking away from it. That money was his. He had more than earned it.

The irony that the money had come from a Russian oligarch in Antibes, only twenty kilometers down the coast from where they had just landed, was not lost on him. Nor was the fact that Inessa was being "kept" by a different Russian oligarch a mere twenty kilometers up the coast from where they now were, in Saint-Jean-Cap-Ferrat.

In a different time and under different circumstances, it might have made interesting grist for a comedic opera, but neither Nikolai Nekrasov, who had previously put the largest bounty in history on Harvath's head for killing his godson, nor mining oligarch Arkady Tsybulsky, who had installed Inessa as his mistress, were men to be trifled with.

Both were close friends of President Peshkov, exceedingly dangerous, and absolutely ruthless. They owed their fortunes and their positions in life to cold-blooded, cutthroat acumen and were driven by a thirst for power, lust, and greed.

Capable of incredible cruelty, they took pleasure in the suffering and misfortune of others. Harvath had no problem helping karma catch up with either of them. And, if he was able to help magnify their pain in the process, he was more than happy to do it.

After a brief discussion at the cottage in Norway, both he and Sølvi had agreed on what needed to be done. Once they had worked out the details, Harvath had contacted Holidae Hayes, who arrived an hour and a half later in a blacked-out Mercedes sprinter van with a small, heavily armed security team she had handpicked herself.

By 10 p.m., they were all tucked safely away inside the U.S. Embassy compound back in Oslo, the framework of their deal having been hammered out on their drive up.

Sølvi would remain in control of Grechko's debriefing. Harvath and the Carlton Group would be in charge of security. The CIA would provide logistical support, including helping smuggle Grechko out of Norway, a safehouse in the South of France, clean passports, and any other items that might prove necessary. In exchange, the CIA would be allowed to remotely observe Grechko's debriefing and ask questions via Sølvi.

While not perfect, it was the arrangement that offered the best possible outcomes for all involved.

As part of his mission planning, Harvath had asked Hayes to provide him with everything the Agency had on Arkady Tsybulsky, as well as satellite imagery of his estate on the tiny peninsula of Saint-Jean-Cap-Ferrat. He also asked for anything they could dig up on Inessa Surkova.

Overnight, Hayes set them up in a part of the compound where they wouldn't be seen by any staff. One of the security team went out for Chinese food.

When it was time to turn in, Harvath and Sølvi were given an office together and Grechko got one across the hall. The rollaway beds Hayes had scared up weren't the most comfortable in the world, but they were definitely better than army cots. Not that anyone much cared. They were all exhausted and fell asleep almost instantly.

The next morning, Hayes and her team accompanied the trio to the Oslo airport, where Chief Inspector Borger, the police officer who had previously escorted Harvath off his flight from Poland, was waiting for them in his car outside the private jet terminal.

Hayes exited the van and walked over to him. When he rolled down his window, she handed him three freshly minted U.S. passports. Rolling his window back up, he drove off to get everything processed. He hadn't asked the passport holders to present themselves.

Once Borger had gone, Hayes texted the pilots of the jet that the CIA had coordinated. When the pilots texted back that they were ready for boarding, Hayes and her team escorted Harvath, Sølvi, and Grechko out to the plane.

Hayes waited on the tarmac for Borger to return with the passports. As soon as she had them in hand, she thanked the cop, headed up the airstairs, and delivered them to their new owners.

There wasn't any prolonged goodbye. With their friendship having iced over, there wasn't much to say. It was a business transaction and this current phase was complete. Hayes wished them good luck and, along with the security team, deplaned. They were on their own.

The flight from Oslo to Nice took just under three hours. The trio cleared customs and passport control in a private lounge at the Nice Côte d'Azur VIP terminal, much the same way as Harvath had when he first arrived in Norway. And as he had done then, he helped himself to a strong cup of coffee, some snacks, and all the packs of pain medication that were in the sundries drawer.

When he received a text that their ride was waiting out front, he gathered everybody up and they headed outside.

There, standing next to a black Audi S8, was one of his Carlton Group teammates, Mike Haney.

Like everybody else on the team, Haney was usually a wiseass—gallows humor being a prerequisite for their line of work. As ex–Special Forces operatives, the compulsion to make fun of each other, as well as the dangerous situations they found themselves in, had been developed early in their military careers and honed to perfection going forward.

But when the situation called for seriousness and professionalism, as it did now, every member of the team could be counted on to deliver.

This wasn't a game. They were on the clock. Grechko was a Russian defector with information that was expected to be of great value to Norway, NATO, and the United States. The Carlton Group was here to keep him safe, to support Sølvi in debriefing him, and to carry out whatever assignments Harvath deemed necessary.

Haney wore a black suit, a wired earpiece, and a pair of Oakley Contrail sunglasses. The six-foot-tall former Force Recon Marine looked every inch the executive protection specialist.

Idling behind the Audi was a Black Mercedes G-Wagon filled with four more of Harvath's teammates—ex–10th Forces Group soldier Kenneth Johnson; ex–5th Special Forces Group soldier Jack Gage; ex–Navy SEAL Tim Barton; and another former Force Recon Marine, Matt Morrison. Harvath nodded subtly in their direction and the men in the vehicle nodded back.

"Good to see you, Mike," said Harvath as he approached.

"You too, Scot," Haney replied, head on a swivel, scanning for threats.

As Grechko was their protectee, they loaded him in first. Sølvi then walked around to the other side and got in back next to him. The moment Haney climbed behind the wheel and put the car in drive, Harvath hopped into the forward passenger seat and gave him the thumbs-up.

After confirming with the men in the G-Wagon that they were ready to roll, Haney radioed the command to move out.

"I brought you a little something," Haney said as the green security gate retracted and he exited the VIP parking lot.

Harvath raised the armrest to find a very sexy, highly concealable personal defense weapon. Built on a SIG Sauer P320, the Flux Raider X replaced the weapon's frame and turned it into a pistol-style carbine complete with a spare magazine well, picatinny rails, and a lightning-fast, spring-loaded, retractable brace. Haney had added a TacDev Ripstik charging handle, a SureFire weapon light, and a compact Trijicon red-dot sight. Sitting underneath it were four fully loaded thirty-round magazines and an Applied Defense Concepts tactical holster.

"Very nice," Harvath responded, lowering the armrest. "How's the house?"

"It's seen better days, but it's quiet. Just the way we like it."

"Everything in place?"

Merging onto Avenue Didier Daurat, Haney headed for the A8 autoroute to avoid the coastal traffic. "Palmer and Ashby are in Saint-Jean-Cap-Ferrat doing surveillance and reconnaissance," he said. "Staelin's setting up perimeter security at the house and Preisler's helping Nicholas with all the remaining electronics issues."

The location the CIA had secured as their safehouse was in the hills above the French village of Eze, halfway between Saint-Jean-Cap-Ferrat and the Principality of Monaco.

After stopping to unlock a set of tall iron gates, they proceeded down a long, dusty driveway lined with ancient sycamore trees. On one side, beyond the trees, rows of vines could be seen. On the other, groves of olive trees. Harvath rolled down his window. Though it was well past summer, the car filled with the unmistakable scents the region was famous for—wild thyme, rosemary, and lavender.

At the end of the drive, they came upon their destination—a run-down, two-story, stone villa.

Left to wither in the intense southern sun, the villa's once-vibrant yellow façade had been bleached to a pale straw. Its previously azure-blue shutters were now dull and faded. The terra-cotta tiles adorning its crooked roof had given up their dark red hues and had been replaced by an aging palette of apricot, coral, and pale orange.

They parked in the circular motor court and, gathering up his personal defense weapon along with the spare magazines from under the armrest, Harvath exited the Audi.

After helping Sølvi out of the vehicle, they left Grechko with Haney and walked back to the G-Wagon to say hello to the other members of the team.

The last time Harvath had seen most of these guys was when they had been tasked with recovering a high-value intelligence asset and his family from Afghanistan. The team had been involved in a brutal firefight with the Taliban and almost didn't make it out. Had Harvath, against the wishes of his teammates, not offered himself up as bait, they all might have been killed.

As usual, the men acted more excited to see Sølvi than to see him. They rehashed the same lame jokes and reminded her that it would only be a matter of time before Harvath screwed up, in which case any one of them would be available to help console her.

From the jibes about replacing Harvath as the man in her life, they quickly pivoted to asking how many of her "hot" friends were going to be coming to their wedding in the United States. They were beyond shameless, and Sølvi, smart aleck that she was, gave as good as she got. She had an excellent sense of humor.

It went back and forth like this for a few more moments until Harvath saw a diminutive figure appear at the front door, bracketed by two huge white dogs. Smiling, he told his team to get back to work and led Sølvi away.

He was a handful of feet from the Audi when he noticed the shocked expression on Grechko's face.

"You," the Russian exclaimed.

"Hello, Leonid," Nicholas replied from the doorway.

CHAPTER 20

Harvath's eyes flicked to Nicholas's Caucasian Ovcharkas. The dogs were incredibly intuitive. When it came to reading people, especially people intent on doing their owner harm, Argos and Draco were unparalleled. If there was going to be any kind of trouble, they would pick up on it first.

But while keenly alert and practically glued to the little man's sides, the dogs didn't seem unduly concerned. Harvath took that as a good sign.

"I didn't know you two knew each other," Harvath said.

"I could say the same to you," Grechko responded.

"Leonid used to be one of my best customers," Nicholas stated. "Absolute VIP status."

The Russian grinned. "Though not always willingly. In fact, I can't count the amount of our highly classified intelligence that you stole, which we were forced to buy back."

The little man smiled in return. "Like I said, you were one of my best customers."

"Then, one day, you vanished. We all assumed," Grechko continued, before stopping himself. "No, we all *hoped* that you were dead."

"As you can see, I'm alive and well."

"And working for the Americans."

"Working *with*," Nicholas clarified, giving his dogs a command. In unison, Argos and Draco both laid down at his feet.

"It would appear we're both on the same side now."

"Let's see how long it lasts."

"You don't trust me?" Grechko asked.

"Trust has to be earned."

"Do your American colleagues trust you? Are they aware of your past?"

"Yes, on both counts," Harvath stated. "He has been an incredible asset."

"Interesting," Grechko remarked.

Eager to get to work, Harvath gestured toward the interior of the villa. "Shall we head in?"

While Haney showed Grechko to his room, Harvath and Sølvi stopped to say hello to Nicholas and the dogs.

After Nicholas and Sølvi had hugged, the dogs had been petted, and Harvath had shaken hands with his friend, Harvath asked, "How are Nina and the baby?"

"Nina is great and the baby is perfect," the little man responded. "We just got the rest of the genetic testing back. Healthy as a horse."

"That's wonderful news," said Sølvi.

"Congratulations," said Harvath. "I told you everything was going to be okay."

"Yes, you did," the little man replied. "Multiple times."

As someone with primordial dwarfism, one of Nicholas's greatest fears had been that he would pass down the malady and that his baby would be forced to endure the same fate. Harvath, while not an expert in genetics, had read enough to know that unless Nina was predisposed, the baby was going to be fine. He had done the best he could to keep his friend focused on the odds being in the baby's favor. It was a relief to now know that everything was okay.

"We'll have to celebrate tonight," Harvath stated. "Do we have any champagne in the house?"

"We're not getting the champagne out yet," a voice from deeper inside the villa said.

Harvath looked past Nicholas to see ex–Delta Force operative, and the team's de facto medic, Tyler Staelin entering from the veranda.

"Why not?" Harvath asked, as he greeted his teammate.

"Nicholas didn't tell you?"

"Tell us what? We just got here."

"The operation has to be carried out tonight."

"What part of it?"

"*All* of it," said Staelin.

"You've got to be kidding me," Harvath replied as he turned to look at Nicholas. "He's joking, right?"

The little man shook his head. "We've intercepted some of Tsybulsky's communications. He's packing up and heading back to Russia."

"Good. Without him around, our job with Inessa will be that much easier."

"She's going with him."

"What the hell are they headed back for?"

Nicholas shrugged. "It's something to do with Peshkov and his place on the Black Sea."

"Who trades the South of France for the Black Sea?"

"When the president of Russia summons you? Arkady Tsybulsky does."

"How much time do we have?" Harvath asked.

"Tsybulsky's jet is scheduled to leave tomorrow morning."

"*Tomorrow morning?*"

"Yup."

"Fuck."

"Not the first word that came to my mind," the little man replied, "but it aptly sums things up."

Harvath shook his head. He needed days, not hours, to properly put together and pull something like this off. If there was one thing he was certain of, it was that tight timelines jacked the danger factor through the roof.

If this were a hostage situation, which it wasn't, a race against the clock would be baked in. Instead it was this bizarre three-legged race. Grechko had to get close enough to Inessa to make his pitch, then—if she agreed—she had to be extracted, after which Harvath had to make Tsybulsky believe that she was dead so that he didn't expend his vast fortune and close relationship with the Kremlin searching for her.

Impossible wasn't a word Harvath allowed himself to entertain. At this moment, however, it sure seemed to be the only word that applied.

"Listen," Nicholas continued, sensing Harvath's trepidation. "Palmer and Ashby will be back in about a half hour. We should know more then. Why don't you get cleaned up. There's fresh clothes in your room. Tyler can show you and Sølvi the way. We'll do a team meeting in forty-five minutes and go through our options. Sound good?"

None of it sounded good to Harvath. Nevertheless, he nodded. Then he and Sølvi followed Tyler upstairs. Already his brain was spinning, trying to come up with solutions.

CHAPTER 21

The team meeting was held in an old library off the living room, which Nicholas had set up as his operations center.

From the carpets and drapes, to the furniture and light fixtures, the villa looked like it hadn't seen a decorator since the late 1970s. Harvath grabbed a seat on one of the orange Togo sofas as Ashby and Palmer, the team's youngest members, walked in.

While Palmer was ex–Delta Force, Ashby was the only person in the group, besides Nicholas, without a Special Operations background. She'd racked up more confirmed kills in Afghanistan than most male soldiers and had wound up on an Al Qaeda hit list. Fearing for her life, as well as the propaganda victory it would give the enemy, the U.S. Army had denied her request to be sent to Iraq and had pulled her from combat. As soon as she could quit, she did, and was scooped up by the Carlton Group's founder. He knew an exceptional operative when he saw one.

Harvath said hello to them and then Nicholas called the meeting to order.

"You want the good news first?" Nicholas asked. "Or the bad news? You're the team leader, so it's your call."

Harvath definitely didn't like the sound of that. "There's *more* bad news?" he asked.

Palmer nodded. "We took a small drone with us and were able to get a look at Tsybulsky's property. As you can imagine, for a guy with more money than God, it's wired tight. Very heavy security. Lots of cameras. The whole thing's fenced and the driveway's gated. We're guessing that there's probably a bunch of other things we couldn't see, but should assume are present, such as ground sensors and other motion detection systems."

"There were also fur missiles," Ashby added, referring to Tsybulsky's dogs. "We counted at least three. They looked like Belgian Malinois."

"Could be worse," Haney deadpanned. "There could be a moat."

"Filled with alligators," said Staelin.

Harvath ignored them. "What's the good news?" he asked.

"Tsybulsky has a yacht in the port of Saint-Jean-Cap-Ferrat," Palmer continued. "A sixty-three-foot-long Lamborghini Tecnomar he named *Hermes*. They're getting ready to go out tonight."

"Where?" replied Harvath.

"Monaco," said Ashby. "The crew is all muscled-up Russians, but one of them was very flirty and happy to chat. He said their boss has a standing card game on Tuesday nights at the Casino de Monte-Carlo. They travel there by boat and the casino sends a car to pick him up at the dock."

"Did the crew member say how long they're normally gone?"

"Not in so many words. But he did invite me back for drinks tonight. Said they're heading out from Saint-Jean-Cap-Ferrat around six o'clock and will probably be back around eleven."

"Do we know who's going with him?"

"No, we didn't get that far. He had to get back to work," she said. "Besides, I didn't want to make him suspicious by asking too many questions about Tsybulsky."

"Smart," Harvath replied. "Good call. Okay, so we know where Tsybulsky is going to be tonight and we know his mode of transportation. What about Inessa? Do we have anything else on her?"

Despite his request, Holidae Hayes had been able to come up with very little on the woman. She had no arrest record. She had never served in the Russian military. All Holidae could find was that Inessa was listed as the chairman of several shell corporations based out of Cyprus.

"No, nothing," said Nicholas. "She may be going to the casino with Tsybulsky. She may be going out somewhere else. She may be staying home and packing for Russia. We don't know."

"Does Grechko have a way to contact her?" a voice asked from the corner of the room. It was Peter Preisler, a former MARSOC Marine who had been a heavy hitter in the CIA's paramilitary detachment known as Ground Branch.

"He's got a cell number for her. Conceivably, he could call or text," Harvath replied.

"Do we know if Tsybulsky monitors her communications?"

"That's unclear."

"Have we looked at her social media?" Ashby asked. "Is there anyone she follows who we might be able to use as a cutout to pass on a message?"

It was an excellent idea and Harvath could kick himself for not having thought of it sooner. He wasn't a social media guy and didn't think in those terms.

Pulling out his phone, he texted a name across the room to Nicholas. "See if you can find any connections between them," he said when the little man's phone chimed.

Looking at Ashby, he remarked, "You're a regular good idea fairy today. Tell me what else you're thinking."

"If we can get Inessa out in public, even if she has bodyguards, which she probably will, all we need her to do is to make a trip to the ladies' room. It's not the most romantic location to reconnect, but it's the only place she'll get a few moments of privacy. Then, it's up to Grechko. He's going to have to make his case quickly."

"Let's put ourselves in that moment," Harvath responded, playing it out. "What comes next?"

"That depends on how she replies," Ashby conceded. "Just because she agrees to a clandestine rendezvous, doesn't mean it's a fait accompli. She could simply be there to say goodbye, once and for all. If that's what she does, if she says no, then obviously we let her leave the ladies' room and it's over."

"And if she says yes? If she's willing to ditch Tsybulsky?"

"Then we're off to the races and it's a whole new ballgame. But for everything to work, we have to go to the end and work our way backward. Have you given any thought as to how you want to make her disappear?"

"I've had a bunch of ideas," Harvath replied, somewhat flippantly. "My current favorite is creating a month out of thin air to cruise the back alleys and drug dens of Marseilles in hopes of finding a body, about her size, that I can match the dental work, and then burn to a crisp in a house fire or car crash."

"In other words, you've got nothing."

"Yet."

Another voice in the meeting spoke up. This time it was Kenneth Johnson. "Why not just kill Tsybulsky? Hard for him to come looking for Inessa if he's dead."

The man wasn't wrong. Harvath had to give him that. And even though Johnson could be a bit overzealous at times in how he responded to threats, there was a simplicity to his logic.

At the same time, it was possible that if Tsybulsky were killed and Inessa vanished, it might appear as if she had been involved. Peshkov could decide that he wanted one of his intelligence agencies to dig into it and they might attempt to hunt her down. That would completely negate Sølvi's deal with Grechko. The Russian defector had been clear. He wanted things handled in such a way that no one would ever come looking for Inessa.

That meant that Harvath was back to square one. Without a woman's burned body, he was out of luck. They needed to keep thinking.

After twenty minutes of going around in circles, the subject of alligators came back up, and Harvath adjourned the meeting. Designing an operation by committee wasn't getting them anywhere. That said, something had begun tapping at the back of his mind.

Once everyone had filed out of the library, Nicholas waved Harvath over to his desk.

"What have you got?"

Turning his ruggedized laptop around, the little man showed him. "You were right. Nikolai Nekrasov's wife, Eva, is friends with Inessa on Facebook and Instagram."

"So now we've got a cutout we can use. We just need to decide on the right message."

"Are you sure Eva will cooperate?" Nicholas asked.

"I spared her husband's life."

"Which she asked you to do for the sake of their children. She also let you keep half of the hundred-million-dollar bounty he'd placed on your head. I imagine both Mr. and Mrs. Nekrasov would like you to remain in their review mirror."

Harvath smiled. "Believe it or not, Eva has a soft spot for me. I was very clear to her shitbag husband that if he ever mistreated her again, or mistreated one of the kids, I'd be back. I'm kind of their guardian angel. We'll consider my unannounced visit a welfare check."

"You're going to go see her in person?"

"I need to get the full download on what she knows about Inessa, as well as Tsybulsky. At this point, she may be the best source of information we have."

Nicholas let out a long, slow exhalation of air. "Since I'm not going to be able to change your mind, who do you want to take with you?"

"Nobody," Harvath replied. "I'm going alone."

"If Nekrasov gets the chance, he'll kill you."

"Then I better make sure he doesn't get the chance."

The little man shook his head. "What do you need from me?"

"I need one of the cars and an encrypted cell phone."

"Anything else?"

Harvath put his hand on his friend's shoulder. "Keep an eye on Sølvi while I'm gone. And make sure everyone is ready to roll by the time I get back."

"Roll where? We don't even have a plan yet."

"Are the Brits still training some of the Ukrainian commando units at Poole?"

"Yes, the Special Boat Service is. Why?"

"I've got an idea," he replied, tapping his temple with his index finger. "If I'm right, there may be a way out of this. And, believe it or not, we may have Johnson to thank for it."

After providing Harvath an encrypted phone and a set of keys to the black Range Rover Palmer and Ashby had been using, he wished his friend good luck. He had no idea what Harvath was about to do, but he had a bad feeling it was going to be very dangerous.

CHAPTER 22

Harvath knew two things about Eva Nekrasova. One, she would be traveling with a security detail, and two, she would know how to get rid of them.

After receiving his cryptic text and agreeing to meet, she had given him an address. The moment Harvath arrived, he knew why she had selected it. It was the one place her husband wouldn't want her bodyguards to accompany her.

Secreted away in the Old Town neighborhood of Nice, the address was for a lingerie boutique called Trésor Caché. While Eva shopped inside, her two-man security detail sat on the terrace of the café across the street, keeping an eye on the shop's front door.

With no one watching the back, Harvath had arrived ten minutes early via a small courtyard whose gate had been left unlocked. The owner of the boutique, a friend of Eva's, had shown him to her upstairs office, where she opened a bottle of champagne and set it on the table, along with two glasses and a pack of cigarettes. After searching, she found a lighter and handed it to him.

Politely, Harvath put up his hand and said, "Thank you, but I don't smoke."

"It's not for you," the owner replied, as she turned to go back downstairs. "I'll send Eva up when she gets here."

The room was dimly lit, with a hand-carved wooden desk, low-slung, pillow-strewn couches, and multiple brass lanterns. With its Moroccan mirrors and other Arabesque details, it looked like something straight out of Bousbir, the historic red-light district of Casablanca.

He made himself as comfortable as he could. Despite the dose of ibuprofen Staelin had given him back at the villa, his body was still quite sore. It was going to take time until he was one hundred percent. He closed his eyes and tried to focus on pushing through it.

Moments later, he heard someone on the stairs. Opening his eyes, he stood just as Eva walked in.

The last time he had seen her had been at the Centre Antoine Lacassagne, Nice's premier cancer institute. Since then, her face had been hollowed out and there were dark circles under her eyes. Even though she tried to hide it in a billowy kaftan, she had lost way too much weight.

Nevertheless, there was still an elegance to the way she carried herself. He met her at the door and she kissed him on both cheeks—a greeting as much French as it was Russian.

"I didn't think we'd ever be seeing each other again," she said, holding him out at arm's length and inspecting him. "You look like you've been through it just as bad as I have."

"My work has definitely been on the upswing," he responded with a smile.

He led her to one of the couches and immediately offered assistance when he saw how much pain it caused her to sit.

"I'm all right," she said softly. Then, eyeballing the bottle of champagne, she asked, "How about a drink?"

Harvath didn't have the heart to say no. Filling both glasses, he handed her one and then sat down next to her.

"What should we toast to?" he asked.

"It's very Russian," Eva said, raising her glass and leaning into her Russian accent, "but let's toast to health."

"Perfect," Harvath replied. "To health."

The pair clinked glasses and took a long sip of champagne.

"So," she began, "what's your interest in Inessa Surkova? Please God, tell me it's not romantic."

Harvath laughed. "No. It's definitely not romantic."

"Then it must have to do with that shit, Arkady Tsybulsky."

"I take it you're not a fan?"

"My husband loves him. The rest of us think he's an asshole. His wife, Polina, is even worse."

"I read his file."

"Then you should know you want nothing to do with him. Trust me."

Harvath appreciated the warning. "Where is Polina?" he asked, digging for more details. "Why isn't she here with him?"

"Polina is a Russian nationalist. She believes all Peshkov's lies about Ukraine. She thinks it's unpatriotic to spend money in France while the French are backing the Ukrainians."

"And what do you think?"

Eva pondered her answer for a moment. "I think if she wants to stay behind in Moscow, that's her choice. But choices have consequences."

"Inessa being one of those consequences."

The woman nodded.

"To be honest," Harvath admitted, "I was surprised to learn that you are friends with her. I didn't think you would approve."

"It's not my job to approve. They're adults. They can do what they want. All my husband's friends have mistresses. I don't like it, but it is what it is. At least in the case of Inessa, she makes it a bit easier to be around Arkady. And if you spend the time to get to know her, she's a good person. A bit sad, but good."

"What's sad about her?"

"She's had a rough life. No little girl grows up dreaming of being the plaything of a monster like Arkady Tsybulsky. I'm sure she lays in bed every night wishing he were dead, but knowing that if he died, she'd be out in the cold. Men like him have no honor. I guarantee you he's made no provisions for her. She's disposable. He doesn't care what happens to her after he's gone. I've told her to stockpile as much jewelry as she can get. It's all she can do."

"Does she listen to you?" Harvath asked.

Eva motioned for him to hand her the cigarettes, which he did. There was an ashtray on the end table and he set that near her as well.

She opened the pack, lit one of the cigarettes, and took a deep drag. Exhaling, she remarked, "God that tastes good. Nikolai won't let me smoke. Not since my cancer came back. He's turned the entire staff against me. I have to sneak around like a criminal."

"What do your doctors say?"

"They agree with him, of course."

Harvath smiled. She knew what he meant. Finally, Eva said, "It's more aggressive this time. They say my odds are fifty-fifty. I've already begun treatment again."

"I'm sorry it came back."

"Thank you."

"At least you're in good hands here. The Centre Antoine Lacassagne is an excellent facility."

"Tell that to Nikolai," she replied. "He wants me to go back to Russia with him."

"For treatment?"

"No. Peshkov wants him back. He won't say why. He told Nikolai to bring the whole family. That it was important that we all return. He offered to set me up with my own private medical team."

"All at his compound on the Black Sea?" Harvath asked.

"Yes," said Eva, stunned. "How did you know that?"

"Tsybulsky was asked to go too. He and Inessa are leaving tomorrow."

"Why?"

Harvath shook his head. "I don't know."

"Well, I'm not going. And neither are my children. I don't care what Nikolai does. I've told him that. I'm not leaving my doctors and I'm not pulling the children out of school."

This was the second oligarch that Harvath had learned Peshkov had reached out to. It was alarming. There was something ominous about the man summoning his closest friends and confidants back to Russia. On top of that, he was encouraging them to bring their families. The Russian president had even offered to dedicate a medical team to Eva. *Why?*

It was a question that would have to wait. Better yet, it was something the CIA could worry about when he sent his next update to Holidae Hayes. Right now, he needed to get to Inessa. And for that, he needed Eva's help. He decided to tell her the truth. Or at least as much of it as he could.

Looking at her, Harvath said, "You asked me why I reached out to you about Inessa Surkova. It's because I need a favor. I need you to put me in touch with her."

"Is that all?" Eva asked, taking another drag on her cigarette. "We didn't need to go through all of this. I could have texted you her phone number."

"It was important that we do this face-to-face."

"Because?"

"Because there's a man from Inessa's past. He says he loves her and he thinks she loves him too."

Eva, a hardened cynic, rolled her eyes.

"I know," Harvath replied. "I had the same reaction, but trust me, it's important that he see her."

"So I'll text *him* her phone number."

"He already has it. That's not the problem. The problem is that if she decides she wants to go with him, he thinks Tsybulsky won't let her leave."

"Well, he'd be right. Arkady sees Inessa as his property. Whoever this man is, you should tell him to find another girlfriend. This one is only going to get him killed."

"I wish it were that easy," Harvath continued. "The first part of my job is to get the two of them together without Tsybulsky, or any of his men, knowing."

Eva laughed. "Good luck. He's even more obsessed with security than my husband. Everyone on his staff is ex–Russian Special Forces and he pays ridiculously inflated prices for them. The saying in the Spetsnaz community is that you haven't truly made it until your invitation to Spetsgruppa 'D' arrives."

Harvath was familiar with the different Spetsnaz units, but he hadn't heard of a Spetsgruppa "D." He figured it was some kind of wordplay. "What does the *D* stand for?"

"Денежный meshok," she replied. "In English, it means 'money bag.' In Russian as well, but for us it's considered quite derogatory. It refers to a boorish person with a crass amount of wealth." Smiling, she added, "I think it fits Arkady perfectly."

Harvath smiled back.

Taking another sip of champagne, she asked, "What's the second part of your job? Once you get these two supposed lovebirds together."

"If Inessa decides she wants to go off with this man, I'm supposed to help her disappear."

Eva shook her head. "If you do, Arkady won't rest until he's killed all three of you."

"I don't think I'll lose any sleep over him," Harvath responded.

"He's not like my husband. He can't be reasoned with. And you should know that he doesn't select his ex-Spetsnaz soldiers solely for their skills and experience. He picks them for their moral flexibility. They are not honorable men. They're bad people."

"Understood. I intend to stay as far away from them as possible."

"Why don't I believe you?" she asked.

Once more, Harvath smiled. "Everything's going to be fine. I just need you to do one thing for me."

"Which is?"

"Contact Inessa. Tell her you want to see her before she leaves. Get her to meet you for dinner tonight."

Eva looked at him. "That's it?"

"That's it," he replied, topping off her champagne. "I'll take care of everything else."

CHAPTER 23

Though Maggie was an excellent cook, her husband, Paul, was also quite skilled in the kitchen. This morning he had whipped up a classic French *omelette aux fines herbes* incorporating chives, parsley, and tarragon from their own garden. He served it with fresh-squeezed orange juice, French-press coffee, and a perfectly crusty baguette from their favorite little bakery in McLean.

Maggie relished unhurried mornings like this—the sun streaming through the windows, she and Paul sharing different sections of the newspaper, simply easing into the day. It both grounded and reminded her of what she was grateful for.

They were halfway through breakfast when the call came in. One of her analysts overseeing the Belarus desk had uncovered something. How soon could Maggie get to the office?

The answer, of course, was right away. Though she drew a bright line between work and home, she understood that there were certain times, especially involving matters of national security, where that line needed to be crossed. Like a surgeon who was on call, it was simply part of the job.

Because of the time element, Maggie was forced to forgo her beloved bicycle and drive one of their cars to work.

In addition to her beautiful Cape Cod, Maggie's grandmother had also left her an indomitable red Volvo, which, despite having almost one hundred thousand miles, was still in fine shape. Conroy hated it almost as much as he did her bike.

With its manual transmission, crank windows, and factory-installed

AM/FM radio, it was a reminder for Maggie of simpler times and all of the wonderful trips she and her grandmother had taken—Colonial Williamsburg, Assateague Island, Gettysburg, Harpers Ferry . . . adventure was only a drive away.

Those had been the days. Life had been so new, so exciting. There was a carefreeness to that era. No cell phones. No computers. No email. You really could disconnect and disappear. People didn't expect to be able to reach you instantly, day or night.

Yes, back then the U.S. was still embroiled in the Cold War, but people took vacations. They left the office behind, in every sense of the word—physically, mentally, emotionally. You didn't feel constantly tethered, nor did you feel as if you could receive a yank on that tether at any moment, pulling you back to headquarters.

It really was a simpler time. It was probably why she enjoyed sitting down to breakfast with Paul, riding her bike, and, when forced to drive, rolling into the CIA in a car that probably ought to be in the Smithsonian Institution. It was her silent protest against the speed and hyperconnectivity of current times. Things only slowed down if you applied your own brakes and took control of the precious short time allotted to you in life.

Rolling through the front gates and security checkpoints at CIA headquarters, Maggie parked her old red Volvo and, grabbing the insulated mug of fresh coffee Paul had pressed for her while she was getting dressed, headed inside.

Having spoken with Holidae Hayes, she knew today was going to be an important one. It had made waves not only in Russia House, but across the entire leadership at the Agency, when it became quietly known that Harvath had succeeded in securing Langley a role in debriefing Leonid Grechko. While she hadn't approved of Conroy's methods, she had to give him credit: leaning on Harvath had paid off, big-time.

That said, moving Grechko to a makeshift safehouse in the South of France wasn't anyone's idea of the proper way to keep him safe. If Langley had its way, the Russian defector would be sitting in a much more secure facility. But it wasn't up to Langley. It was up to Grechko and, for the moment, Sølvi Kolstad, which created an added headache for the CIA.

The Norwegians were exceptional allies. The relationship between

the CIA and the NIS ran deep. Norway's ambassador was beloved in
D.C. Keeping a secret, like the whereabouts of Grechko and Sølvi, from
Oslo was like juggling a hand grenade with the pin removed. The damage
it could cause to U.S.–Norway relations was incalculable.

The CIA Director wanted the pin put back in the grenade. He didn't
care how Sølvi communicated with her superiors, or what she said. She
did, however, need to let them know what was going on, ASAP. Langley
did not want their Norwegian partners blindsided.

The message was transmitted to Conroy, who made it Maggie's responsibility, as she'd become the conduit for all things Grechko. Maggie then passed it to Hayes, who promised she would communicate with
Sølvi. It was CIA bureaucracy at its finest, but it kept people in their lanes
and actually allowed for things to flow.

The revelations that the attack in Oslo had been on an NIS safehouse,
and that Harvath was bringing Grechko and Sølvi in, had happened after
Maggie and Conroy had met with the CIA Director to discuss Russia's
warnings of an alleged dirty bomb plot by Ukraine. All of that information was in the special update briefed to President Porter and his national
security team.

Now Maggie had been called in early because even more intelligence had been developed. It needed to be reviewed and a decision
made as to whether or not to include it in the president's daily intelligence briefing.

This was exactly the kind of thing Maggie didn't like to rush. She preferred to let the intel speak to her, to make its own case as to what it was.
The less guesswork, the better. In short, she was at her best when she was
being patient and methodical. If you moved too fast, you risked missing
the big picture. To find an actual pattern, you had to sit, sometimes for a
while, surrounded by the noise.

She hoped that wouldn't be the situation this morning. Supposedly,
the Belarus team had seen some interesting things on the newest satellite
imagery.

Badging in, Maggie dropped her briefcase in her office and then, insulated mug in hand, walked down to the collection of cubicles referred to
as the "Belarus desk."

A junior analyst greeted her. "Good morning, ma'am," he said. "They're all waiting for you in the conference room."

All? Maggie thought to herself. *They must have found something pretty interesting.*

Following the analyst, she crossed the hall and entered the conference room. Satellite footage was playing on the large, flat-screen monitors. Members of the Belarus team sat around the conference table, briefing books and notepads scattered in front of them.

Standing at the head of the table was the team's lead analyst, a man in his late forties, named Christopher Dunlop.

"Okay, Chris," Maggie said, sitting down in the closest chair. "I left a hot, homemade breakfast with my husband to be here. What've you got for me?"

Dunlop didn't waste time. As he spoke, he drew attention to everything with a laser pointer. "We've been scouring every inch of Belarus that we have imagery for. Essentially, we're looking for any haystack where needles might be hidden. Early this morning, we think we found one.

"This is a military depot just east of the Belarusian town of Asipovichy. It originally had a double-layer security perimeter, which isn't enough fortification to securely house nuclear munitions. That, however, has changed. It now has quadruple-layer security fencing, all the trees within thirty meters of the outer fences have been cut down, and right up front, there's a new roof-covered checkpoint and a guardhouse. Several additional structures have also been erected that appear to be garrison garages, possibly for storing warheads, as well as Russian Iskander missile launchers."

Another piece of the puzzle had just fallen into place. "What about personnel? It takes a lot of manpower to guard and service the type of weapons we're talking about."

"Welcome to Tsel," Dunlop replied, pulling back on the imagery. "It's a village twenty klicks northwest of Asipovichy. Previously, it was a Soviet missile base. The name Tsel literally translates to—"

"Target," Maggie replied, finishing his sentence for him.

"Correct. After the Soviets left, it became headquarters for the sole active ballistic missile brigade of the Armed Forces of Belarus—the 465th.

Five years ago, the 465th shut it down and moved to a new location. Ever since, we assumed that it had been abandoned. Apparently, that's now changed. In addition to trenching for cables, the barracks have gone through upgrades, and there's been a decided increase in activity in and around the base."

"Is there an actual around-the-clock presence?" Maggie asked. "Are there personnel living in the barracks?"

Dunlop nodded. "Affirmative."

"Has the 465th returned? Or is it another unit?"

"They're not Belarusian Armed Forces," he replied, advancing to fresh imagery. "They're actually Russians. We've traced several of their vehicles. They belong to the Wagner Mercenary Group."

"Why would Peshkov be using Wagner mercs to protect his nukes?" Maggie mused aloud. "That's the purview of the 12th Main Directorate back at Russia's Ministry of Defense."

"Two birds, one stone?" one of the analysts sitting nearby suggested.

"Go on."

"Even though Belarus is a satrapy of Russia, Peshkov can't fully trust the security of his nuclear weapons to them. He also can't afford to redeploy any competent troops away from the war in Ukraine. But by using Wagner Group operatives, he gets battle-tested Russians guarding Russian nukes without upending current Russian Army deployments."

Maggie nodded. "And sprinkled in with those battle-hardened mercenaries, he can include the specialists and engineers with the know-how needed to maintain those weapons."

Around the table, the analysts nodded their heads in agreement.

"Any other updates?" Maggie asked.

"Right now," Dunlop replied, "that's our most current intel."

Maggie stood from her chair. "Excellent job, everyone. I'm recommending this for today's PDB, so please get a write-up to my office straightaway."

As she exited the conference room, she checked her watch. Conroy would be in soon and she wanted to be the first person he saw.

CHAPTER 24

"This is the last meal I'm buying until you crack the encryption on that flash drive," Brunelle said as she set down two Styrofoam containers on MoMo's desk, loaded with halal food.

"I'm working as hard as I can," the young man replied.

"La Crim cracked the same guy's iPhone yesterday."

MoMo wasn't impressed. "It's a six-digit password. Everybody thinks iPhones are impossible to crack. They're not. *Obviously.*"

Brunelle was in a disagreeable mood. Shortly after she returned home from Powell's apartment last night, heavy thunderstorms had moved in, keeping her awake. To top it off, in the elevator on the way down, Gibert had suggested they go for a drink before calling it a night.

He was concerned about the "tension between them" and wanted to "clear the air." She said no to the drinks and told him to get over it, as she had done awhile ago. Either that, or he should see a therapist. His guilt wasn't her problem.

When the storms finally abated, it was nearing 5 a.m. She fired off an email to her superior saying that she would be following a lead this morning and wouldn't be in until later. Then she rolled over and, after more tossing and turning, was able to grab a few hours of sleep.

Rolling into the office, having consumed two coffees at her apartment, one at the Métro station and another just outside DGSI headquarters, she stopped by MoMo's desk and tried her best to be nice. She knew what she could be like when she hadn't slept well. Sometimes all the coffee in the world was incapable of improving her attitude.

Without looking up, MoMo offered to work through lunch, but only if she agreed to go get it for him. The urge to choke him, right there at his workstation, was strong, yet she maintained her professionalism, took a breath, and waited for it to pass.

On the way back with the food, she made a decision. DGSI often hired outside hackers. If MoMo couldn't get the job done by the end of the day, that was going to be her next move.

Normally, she would have to get approval, as well as funds, from higher up, but since she'd removed the flash drive from the crime scene, that could pose multiple problems for her. Better to keep it under the radar. Heading back to her office, she reread a text Gibert had sent on her way to work.

His officers had canvassed residents of the rooftop apartments adjacent to Jadot's and, as Brunelle had suspected, at least one of them had heard something the night of his murder.

It was described as a thud of some sort. Too heavy to have been a pigeon, but the resident wasn't sure if it had been a person. It was raining pretty hard, she only heard it once, and she had been listening to an audiobook with AirPods in her ears at the time.

Officers had done a full search of her roof, as well as the others nearby, but hadn't found anything. The same, unfortunately, was true for the new dump of CCTV footage they'd received. In the race to solve Jadot's murder, Gibert and his vaunted la Crim were starting to fall out of medal contention.

She was halfway back to her desk when something clicked in her brain. *That was it!* Turning around, she trotted back to MoMo.

"Still nothing," he replied. The irritation was evident in his voice as he ate his lunch and continued to work on the flash drive.

Brunelle let his attitude slide. "Do you remember the Depeche Mode concert a couple of months ago? It was at the Accor Arena."

"I don't like old-people music."

"A, it's not *old-people* music," she responded, "and B, would you stop what you're doing and look at me, please?"

MoMo did as she asked, leaning back in his chair and gnawing on a skewer of kofte.

"That was the concert where they first introduced AVS."

"Algorithmic video surveillance?" he asked.

Brunelle nodded.

In the run-up to the Olympics, France had introduced a ton of new, high-tech security measures. The idea behind AVS was to use artificial intelligence to help thwart terror attacks such as the 1996 Olympics bombing in Atlanta and the 2016 truck attack in Nice. France was the first country in the European Union to employ AI-assisted surveillance and it was only accessible to a handful of law enforcement and intelligence agencies.

"I forgot they tested it at that concert," MoMo stated. "What about it?"

"We're one of the agencies that has access to it, right?"

"Correct."

"And everyone in your division has been trained on it."

It was now MoMo's turn to nod. "Where are you going with this?"

"From what I've read, the AI is capable not only of facial recognition, but also of gait recognition. So even if we can't see someone's face on a CCTV camera, we can recognize and track them by their walk."

"Technically speaking, yes. That's true. Legally speaking, no. We're not allowed to do that."

Brunelle looked at him. "What are you talking about?"

"The National Assembly crafted very specific parameters as to how and where the software can be used. Only at sports, recreational, and cultural venues to help prevent public order offenses."

"That's all I'm asking for."

"I'm not following you," said MoMo.

"Jean-Jacques Jadot's killer hasn't been spotted entering or leaving the murder scene. There's evidence that the killer came and went via a window at the rear of the apartment. We now know that a neighbor in a close-by building heard a noise on the roof shortly after the time we believe Jadot was murdered."

"And?"

"And my hypothesis is that the killer used the rooftops for ingress and egress. Specifically, I believe the killer did this to avoid being seen by other people and by CCTV cameras."

MoMo took another bite of his kofte and, despite having his mouth full of food, asked, "What's this got to do with the AI software?"

"The fact that we haven't found the killer yet in any CCTV footage doesn't mean he's not there, it just means we're not looking in the right place."

"Still not following you."

Brunelle broke it down for him. "Jadot's apartment is on the Rue Vieille-du-Temple. Do you know what else is on that street?"

"It's a long street."

"The National Archives of France.

"Suppose, just for a moment, that we're dealing with a very sophisticated criminal, possibly even an intelligence operative for a hostile foreign country. Paris isn't London or New York, but we've got a lot of CCTV cameras. This operative knows we're going to be going backward and forward in the footage, trying to find them and identify them. So how would they prevent that?"

"A disguise of some sort?"

"Exactly," Brunelle agreed. "But I'd take it one step further. Jadot was killed shortly before eleven p.m. on a rainy Sunday evening. Not many people are out at that time and in that kind of weather. If I was the killer, I'd wait to make my escape. And if I could, you know where I'd wait?"

"The National Archives?" MoMo asked, midway into another bite.

"Yes," she responded. "The archives are open to the public. I would have come in during the day on Sunday and, having previously surveilled the building, hidden myself shortly before closing. Then, once I was ready, I could climb out onto the roof and cross over to Jadot's building. There I would drop down and enter the window at the rear of his apartment and wait for him to return home. Once he did, I would kill him, retrace my steps, and return to the archives. Then, Monday morning, once it got busy enough, I would walk right out the front door with a group of tourists and disappear."

The forensic digital specialist took his time chewing his kofte. After swallowing what was in his mouth, he replied, "That's a pretty wild hypothesis."

"It also makes sense."

"Maybe, but it doesn't meet the parameters for use of the AI software."

"Of course it does," Brunelle argued. "The National Archives of

France is a cultural venue and murder is most definitely a crime against public order."

Raising his left hand, the young man tilted it from side to side as if to say, *Maybe yes, maybe no.*

"Come on, MoMo. Help me out here," she implored as she pinched her thumb and index finger together. "We could be this close to catching whoever did this. Jadot was a fellow intelligence officer. We owe it to him to do everything we can to solve his murder."

The young man thought about it as he pulled the last piece of kofte off the skewer with his teeth. "There might be one way we can do this," he said. "At least so it's all aboveboard."

"How?"

"We treat it as a practice exercise. We're searching for a fictional bomb suspect who has planted a device at the National Archives. The goal of the exercise is to help DGSI officers better understand how the software can be used. Once we're done, we delete everything. As long as none of the results are used to violate anyone's rights, we haven't run afoul of any of the rules."

"I promise," Brunelle replied, tracing the sign of the cross on her chest. "I will not violate anyone's rights."

MoMo knew her too well. "Just don't get caught. And if you do, don't tell anybody where you got your information."

After accessing the cloud that the National Archives used for its CCTV footage, MoMo entered the time and date range Brunelle had given him, and then set the AI loose.

As the software wasn't perfect, the process had a few hiccups. On multiple occasions it stopped and needed to be redirected. It was young and still learning.

Nevertheless, the amount of faces it could tag, sort, and account for in a matter of minutes was amazing. For each person it identified, the AI cataloged their clothing, any objects they were openly carrying, and their gait.

Brunelle remembered when gait recognition was in its infancy. She had been astonished to learn that each human being's walk was as unique as their fingerprint. Being able to match subjects to their gait was a huge advantage for law enforcement. Bad guys could obscure their faces and change their clothing, but still give themselves away simply by walking past a camera.

The biggest help of all would have been if the French government had erected "readers" across the city to covertly tag and gather cell phone information. It was the logical next step. Once someone had been identified on CCTV, you could then match them to their cell phone and search for their signal. But France wasn't there yet and Brunelle figured she ought to be thankful. If the tech kept going the way it was going, she'd probably be out of a job soon.

Finally, the AI reached the end of its search and MoMo scrutinized his screen. He was toggling between two images.

"What do you have?" Brunelle asked, leaning in closer.

"Studying all entrances and exits at the National Archives, everyone who entered on Sunday, the day of Jadot's murder, is confirmed to have left by the time the archives closed."

"Including security staff?"

"Security staff included," MoMo replied. "The overnight shift can be seen arriving Sunday evening and then departing the next morning."

"So what are the two images you're looking at?"

"According to the AI, these are two different people. The one on the right entered the archives on Sunday, but never exited. And the one on the left exited on Monday, but never entered."

"You can't see the faces very well in either shot."

"Agreed. That's why the AI is defaulting to gait recognition. These two individuals don't have the same walk," said MoMo.

"Play the clips for me."

Brunelle watched as Figure One entered the archives on Sunday, a ball cap pulled low, avoiding the security cameras. Then she watched as Figure Two, wearing a different hat and clothing, while also avoiding the cameras, left the archives on Monday morning. Unlike Figure One, Figure Two was walking with a slight limp.

"He's faking it," she said.

"What?"

"The guy who's leaving the archives. Right there. He's faking that limp."

"How do you know?"

"I just know."

MoMo leaned in and rewatched the footage. "You can't fake your gait. At least not long enough to throw off the AI. Your brain can't keep up the charade. You end up defaulting to your normal stride."

"Unless you put something in your shoe."

"Are you serious?"

Brunelle nodded. "All you have to do is put a rock in there. Guaranteed limp. And your brain won't give you away. It's enough of a change to throw off gait recognition."

"The software guys neglected to mention that in our training."

"Of course they did. They want the French government to think the AI's bulletproof. It's good, but it isn't perfect."

"So whose walk are we looking for?"

"Both," she said. "Have the AI flag each of them. In the meantime, can you use the software to tap into the street cameras and see where the figure with the limp goes after the archives?"

"You mean the would-be bomber in our training scenario?" MoMo clarified, reaching for a fresh skewer. "Sure."

A few moments later, he tapped into a series of neighborhood cameras and was tracking the man with the limp.

The man walked for several blocks before stopping in front of a narrow building with a tiny blue door. Producing a key from his pocket, he unlocked the door, stepped inside, and disappeared from view.

"What address is that?" Brunelle asked.

"One Rue de Chapon."

"Run it for me."

"Already ahead of you," said MoMo. "And you're not going to like it."

She watched as a message popped up on his screen.

Removing her cell phone, Brunelle pulled up Gibert's contact and hit dial. When he answered, she said, "I'm texting you a location. Meet me there. And bring a flashlight."

CHAPTER 25

"You know there's a much better bar right around the corner," Gibert said as he joined Brunelle at her outdoor table.

She knew the one he was talking about. The Hotel Sinner was a kinky, very risqué, five-star hotel housed in a building that looked like it had once been a medieval monastery. All the cocktails had Latin names, the staff ran around in black cassocks, and the stained-glass mosaics were loaded with depictions of naked bodies. It was exactly her kind of place, which was why she had told Gibert to meet her at Café Berry instead.

The tiny café was open daily, only served brunch, and brewed some of the best coffee in Paris. In addition to a couple of tables on the sidewalk in front, there were a handful more in the partially covered Passage des Gravilliers next door. That's where Brunelle was seated, working on her second coffee, when Gibert arrived.

He removed a small handheld flashlight and clicked it on and off to make sure it was working. "As requested. Now will you tell me what we're doing here?"

"We're delving into the underworld."

"In that case, I think it really would have been much more appropriate to meet at the Sinner."

"I'm sure you do," Brunelle replied, paying for her coffees and standing up. "Let's get going."

As they walked to the end of the block, she explained what she had been able to uncover thus far and why she believed Figure One and Figure Two were the same man.

Gibert agreed, but had a different spin on what the AI had uncovered. What if the man wasn't faking the limp? What if, as he made his way across the rooftops from Jadot's back to the National Archives, he slipped? Maybe that's what the woman who was listening to an audiobook at the time had heard?

It was a decent enough hypothesis and Brunelle told him so. She may have been giving the killer too much credit by assuming he would actively try to avoid gait analysis. There was, however, no question that he had taken great pains not to have his face captured by CCTV.

"And what about the ice axe?" she asked. "Ever since Powell mentioned that's how Trotsky was murdered, I keep thinking about it."

Gibert shrugged. "I'm confident that the killer was already in the apartment, waiting for Jadot. Perhaps he was there long enough to look around. Maybe he found the axe and thought, *This would be a pretty cool way to kill somebody.* More than likely, the assassin is a Russian and being aware of the whole thing about Stalin and Trotsky thought, *This'll make for a great story back at the Kremlin.* That's what these guys do. They did it in Spain too."

"Spain?"

"Remember the story about Ukrainian intelligence convincing a Russian helicopter pilot to defect?"

"Kind of."

"It's an amazing story. Not only did the man defect, but he did so with his military helicopter *and* a bunch of top-secret intelligence. In exchange, the Ukrainians gave him a new passport under a false name and five hundred thousand dollars. While the pilot was incredibly brave, unfortunately, he was also a total idiot. He used the money to buy a flashy Mercedes S-Class and moved to a coastal town in Spain popular with Russians and Ukrainians. Even dumber, he reached out to an old girlfriend back in Russia and invited her to come visit him.

"So, surprise, surprise, two hooded assassins showed up in his parking garage one day. They waited around for him for a few hours and when he finally showed up and got out of his car, they shot him. *Multiple* times. But they didn't do it with just any old ammunition. They used nine-millimeter Makarov rounds, a pistol cartridge from the old Soviet Union. They didn't even bother to pick up the shell casings. Then they drove over the guy with their car. It was all caught on video and is all part of a larger trend.

"Whether it's using a nerve agent like Novichok to attempt to kill a former double agent in the UK, or bicycling by a former Chechen commander in a Berlin park and blowing his brains out with a suppressed pistol, the Russians are going back to their old, Stalinist ways. The Soviet-era practice of killings abroad is now back in full swing. The Kremlin isn't even trying to hide it. Their assassins are actually drawing attention to the murders. And, as Peshkov is a devoted Stalinist, I'm sure he loves it. The less subtle, the better."

They were all solid points and Brunelle nodded as he spoke. "The only thing I can't fully scratch off my list," she stated, "is the *why*. For Jadot to have brought down the wrath of a Russian hit team, he had to have crossed some sort of line with Moscow. What was it?"

"That's the million-dollar question," Gibert replied. "If we can find the killer, hopefully we'll also find an answer. By the way, the Germans caught the Berlin assassin. Do you know where he had traveled from?"

"Don't say Paris."

Gibert smiled. Pantomiming a gun, he fired it at her and said, "Yep, *Paris.*"

Terrific, she thought to herself.

Arriving at 1 Rue de Chapon, Brunelle was glad to be able to change the subject. "Here we are," she said.

Gibert looked at the front door and then at her. "You've got to be kidding me."

"I wish I were. This is the last place our man with the limp was seen."

"How the hell did he get in there?"

"With a key."

"But where would he get *that* key?" Gibert asked. Then, seeing Brunelle produce one herself, demanded, "And where'd you get one?"

"A fireman," she replied. "He must have forgotten it at my apartment."

The Parisian cop felt his cheeks flush. As fucked-up as she was, the thought of her being with another man sent a surge of jealousy through him.

At the same time, he knew she took a certain pleasure in causing him pain. It was her way of getting even.

Not wanting to encourage more of it, he got himself under control. "How the hell would a Russian know about this building?"

"It's not a state secret," Brunelle admitted. "These fake façades are all over the center of Paris. Umberto Eco even had one in his book *Foucault's Pendulum* back in the 1980s. One Forty-Five Rue Lafayette was supposed to be an entrance to the underworld for high-level occultists."

"I'm familiar with that book, which is fiction, as well as these buildings. They're nothing more than airshafts for the Métro system. They've all been disguised to blend into their neighborhoods, like something from a movie set."

"They're also the perfect way to disappear. Once you go through one of these doors, *poof*, no more cameras."

"I suppose," Gibert agreed. "And probably not impossible for the Russians to get a hold of a key."

"Shall we?" Brunelle asked, sliding hers into the lock.

When Gibert nodded, she unlocked the door and pushed it open. They were greeted with a whoosh of cold air racing up the shaft. Looking up, she could see that the fake building had no roof, just a grate.

Gibert had been correct, these faux buildings were all over central Paris. Many of them were painted with trompe l'oeil details, like partially open windows, and some even showed people inside.

Brunelle stared down into the semi-illuminated shaft. A ladder, surrounded by a safety cage, went all the way to the bottom. The descent was broken every ten to twelve feet by a landing of metal grating.

"Ready?" she asked.

"After you," Gibert replied.

The shaft was filthy. No matter where she placed her grip, her hands came away covered in a fine, dark soot. Already, she was envisioning a long, hot bath in her near future.

When they finally got to the bottom, she wiped her palms on her jeans, leaving black streaks. Looking up, she guessed that they were about five to six stories underground. They were now in some sort of concrete and steel rotunda. Piping and flexible, brightly colored conduit lined the walls. Two fans, with blades the size of a small aircraft propeller, sat behind grime-caked, metal louvers. They clicked on and off, as necessary, to help circulate the air.

"Which way?" Gibert asked.

There was really only one direction and Brunelle pointed to it. *Straight ahead.*

As they walked, they could hear and smell the underground subway system. While there were the occasional pungent whiffs of urine, the overwhelming odor was of burnt rubber, as many of the train carriages didn't operate on steel wheels, but rather on rubber tires.

"I suppose it makes sense that a Russian assassin would choose to disappear down here. Paris has the busiest subway system in Europe. Want to guess whose is even busier?"

"Don't say Moscow," Brunelle warned.

Raising his finger gun again, the cop aimed it at her and fired.

She shook her head and kept walking.

"Just out of curiosity, what exactly are we looking for down here?" he asked.

Brunelle removed a map she had printed back at her office and replied, "A way out that would allow our killer to remain invisible."

"Meaning someplace with no cameras."

"Correct."

"But that's pretty much impossible," Gibert said. "Any Métro station he walks down these tunnels to, the moment he steps onto a platform, he'll be photographed. He could climb up another shaft, but he'll have the same problem. As soon as he steps out onto any given street, there's bound to be cameras. Either he's counting on us being unable to check all the feeds, or something else is going on."

"You're getting warmer," replied Brunelle, as they arrived at an intersection and she paused to read plates affixed to the walls with the names of the streets running above them.

Gibert followed as she took the tunnel branching off to the right.

"You're not going to give me anything?" he asked. "Nothing at all to work with?"

"At this point, all I have is a guess," she admitted.

"Which is?"

"Using the rooftops and camping out in the National Archives shows a detailed level of planning."

"As does securing a master key to access the air vent," Gibert added.

"Exactly," Brunelle replied. "So why would it stop there? Our killer has dropped off the CCTV system. Even if his limp was faked, we have his natural gait on record from when he entered the archives. I actually agree with you and think he may have been injured at some point Sunday night. Regardless, he's not going to appear on camera again. That made me wonder how he could continue to fully stay off of it. Then it hit me."

Gibert waited for her to explain. Instead, she pulled out her flashlight and began shining it along the wall of the tunnel. Up ahead was a narrow recess that contained some sort of door.

As they neared, they could see that the door had a large sign warning of high-voltage electricity housed within. Producing her key, Brunelle unlocked the door and pushed it open. "Moment of truth," she said, stepping inside.

Gibert followed and as they entered, the lights automatically turned on. The space was filled with industrial-level wiring, breaker boxes, and various other electrical and mechanical equipment.

"What is this place?" he asked.

"From what I was able to figure out, it connects to an electrical substation and helps distribute power down here to the tunnels."

"And we're interested in it, because?"

"Of that," she replied, pointing at a door on the other side of the room. On it was another large sign, reading DO NOT ENTER.

Walking over to it, she examined the lock and noticed something along the frame.

"Do you have a key for this one too?" Gibert asked, seeing that it was different.

"Don't need one," Brunelle replied, pulling the door open.

A metal shim had been inserted into the deadlatch, which she removed and handed to the cop. "Souvenir."

The door let out onto the bottom of a stairwell. Examining the frame from the other side, she saw a pair of contact pads that had been reconfigured so that the door could be opened without setting off the alarm. As she stepped through and held open the door for Gibert, she drew his attention to it.

With no other door at this level, they had to climb up a flight of stairs. Judging from the sounds coming from above, Gibert had a pretty good idea of what kind of structure they were in.

When they opened the next door, everything clicked for him. To her credit, Brunelle had actually figured it all out.

CHAPTER 26

The clock had begun ticking before Harvath had even returned to the safehouse. He had the rough outlines of a plan and was trying to put the pieces into place. But for the plan to work, all of the dominoes had to be perfectly aligned. If one of them was even the slightest bit out of line, everything was going to rapidly unspool. And the moment that happened, bullets were going to start flying. It was his job to make sure that didn't happen.

Part of the plan involved following Tsybulsky from Saint-Jean-Cap-Ferrat to Monte Carlo. In order to do that, they were going to need a very specific type of boat. And while the Agency had all the specs and was working with a yacht broker out of Nice to find and charter the right vessel, Harvath wanted to make sure it didn't get screwed up and assigned Tim Barton to keep an eye on the process. He was the only other Navy operative on the team and, as such, was the only other person with the proper experience necessary to handle a boat like that.

Setting up shop in the villa's library, Harvath sat next to Nicholas and monitored their flight-tracking software. The Ukrainian commandos had been given the green light and were already wheels-up out of Bournemouth Airport, a short helicopter hop from Royal Marines Base Poole. Their flight to Nice Côte d'Azur would take less than two hours. Haney and Staelin would meet them at the airport and drive them back to the villa.

While the longer lead items had been set in motion, Harvath was concerned that he hadn't yet heard back from Eva. She had promised to text him as soon as she'd received confirmation from Inessa. He tried not to think about it and instead focused on the other elements of the operation.

The idea had been to make Inessa an offer she couldn't refuse. Dinner, or at the very least just drinks, at Muse—one of her favorite spots in Saint-Jean-Cap-Ferrat. Even if she was busy packing for Russia, the hope was that she could peel herself away long enough to have a quick visit with Eva and say goodbye.

Muse was perched directly above the harbor and offered breathtaking views of the Mediterranean. It had upstairs and downstairs dining, a busy bar scene, and a terrace that was consistently jammed. Even more to Harvath's liking, there were multiple forms of ingress and egress. Eva had recommended the perfect spot. She also had enough pull (as the wife of the owner of the Hotel du Cap in Antibes) to reserve a table at the last minute.

Naturally, Harvath would want to get there early and see everything for himself, but the little bit he was able to discover online had given him a high degree of confidence that the location would suit their needs. Which left him with the last, and most difficult, stage of his plan.

Everything would come down to Inessa. And the more he thought about her, the more he was plagued by one very important question. *How good an actress was she?*

Courtesans, by profession, were skilled liars, but convincing men that you found them attractive and that they were good in bed was a lot different than lying to your highly trained security team. They were practiced in the art of deception. It was the single most important skill in keeping them alive and employed.

After seeing Grechko, would she be able to keep it together? Or would she inadvertently give herself, and the entire plan, away?

It had eaten at him during the drive in to see Eva. If Inessa buckled, if Tsybulsky or his men sensed something was amiss and pressed her, she could burn a lot of people, including Eva. As they were saying goodbye, Harvath had felt it necessary to warn her. It was important for her to know what was at stake.

Eva, however, was two steps ahead of him. She had already decided she was going to leverage her illness and "play the cancer card."

Her plan was to tell Inessa she didn't know how much time she had left. Because she wasn't going to Russia, it would mean a lot to her to get together for dinner. She wasn't sure she'd still be around if and when Inessa came back. The final step in her plan was to get Inessa slightly tipsy in order to add a little steel to her spine.

By dropping the health bomb on her, it would allow Inessa—in case she'd been invited—to back out of going to Monte Carlo with Tsybulsky. More importantly, if he or any of her security detail thought she was acting strange, she'd be able to legitimately blame it on her concern over Eva's cancer.

It was a win-win, yet it was also something that Harvath never would have asked Eva to do. The fact that she had offered to, unsolicited, only reinforced that bringing her on board had been the right idea.

He could only hope that Inessa would be as tough and as reliable. A key moment was coming and she would need to absolutely knock it out of the park. If she didn't, everything else would be all for naught.

He had dwelled so much on how to make her disappear that it had been practically impossible to think of anything else. In his head, however, he had slowly begun to hear the voice of his mentor, Reed Carlton—the man who had taught him everything he knew about the art of espionage. Had Carlton been standing in front of him right now, he would have been encouraging him to slow down and keep the plan simple.

One of the Old Man's favorite stories had been "The Purloined Letter," by Edgar Allan Poe. Though a mystery about a letter stolen from the French queen's boudoir, in Carlton's mind it embodied the essence of tradecraft. An unscrupulous minister switches a letter with a fake and uses information from the original to blackmail the queen. And no matter how many times the police tear apart the minister's home, they cannot find the letter.

Eventually, it's the prefect of police who figures out that the minister is such an adept student of human psychology that he has hidden the letter in plain sight. Despite the cops searching all the places they would have hidden such a valuable item, it had actually been sitting right out in the open.

The idea of doing something similar with Inessa was tempting. The more he had thought about it, the more it had grown on him. He knew it was incredibly dangerous, which was why he would work to shield her from as much of the fallout as possible. The only thing missing from his operation was a contingency plan.

Harvath knew from bitter experience that all too often Murphy, of the eponymous law, liked to show up and scatter a game's pieces, if not completely flip the board over. There was no guarantee as to whether he'd show up for this operation, but they had to be prepared.

What bothered Harvath the most was that Inessa was being left exposed. He'd gamed out the situation a thousand different ways, but it always ended the same. There was no way to fully protect her. To do that they would need a person on the inside, and that kind of infiltration took weeks, if not months. There was no way they'd be able to accomplish it in a matter of hours. Unless he was struck by a bolt of genius, it would just be part of the operation that they would have to accept.

Which brought him to Grechko. He planned on telling the Russian as little as possible. The man was not entitled to a say in how things were going to go down. He had made his number one priority clear—if Inessa said yes, he wanted to fix it so that neither Tsybulsky nor anyone else ever came looking for her. That was all Harvath owed him, and it was all he was prepared to do for him.

As he watered down what he planned to say to the defector, his phone chimed. It was a text from Eva.

Inessa had agreed to meet.

CHAPTER 27

With the news that Inessa had accepted Eva's invitation, the operation kicked into the next gear.

Before speaking with Grechko, Harvath had wanted to run everything by Sølvi. The Russian was her defector, after all.

But when he tried to grab her, she was already late for her call with Oslo. Nicholas had established an encrypted video link from the makeshift debriefing room in the basement. It had been lined with soundproof blankets. In addition, Nicholas had added a loop of white noise to help mask her audio. Until she was ready to tell her superiors where she was, she didn't want to reveal any information about their location. Once the NIS had uncovered the mole, then they could begin discussing her return to Norway with Grechko.

This left Harvath with only one option. Rounding up Ashby and Palmer, they hopped into the Range Rover and headed in to Saint-Jean-Cap-Ferrat. He needed to get the lay of the land for himself.

Only two and a half kilometers in size, the tiny peninsula looked like a slightly misshapen version of Italy. It was home to sixteen hundred people and some of the most expensive real estate in the world. Winston Churchill, two American presidents, artists like Matisse, Chagall, and Picasso, countless royalty, business tycoons, and a myriad of actors, actresses, and authors had all vacationed there. The coolest visitors in Harvath's opinion, however, were the Rolling Stones.

They arrived in the summer of 1971, looking to escape a ton of personal and financial problems back home, including a relentless press that hounded them day and night. At a sixteen-room mansion named Villa

Nellcote, overlooking the ocean, they installed a mobile recording studio and began laying down songs for their 1972 album, *Exile on Main Street,* which would go on to be considered one of the best albums of all time.

Harvath asked Ashby to pull it up on her phone and play it through the Range Rover's speakers. Just because they were on the job, that didn't mean they couldn't have a little background music.

It started off with one of Harvath's favorites, "Rocks Off," and a few songs later slid into another, "Tumbling Dice." Next to funk music, there was nothing Harvath liked more than classic rock and roll. And the more the artists pushed the limits of their genre, like Parliament-Funkadelic and the Rolling Stones, the more he liked them.

The Stones put Saint-Jean-Cap-Ferrat on the map as a star-studded, celebrity sanctuary. And as more luminaries flocked to this part of the French Riviera, the real estate prices only continued to soar.

Most of the homes were hidden behind stone walls, wrought-iron fences, and massive hedgerows. Harvath had Palmer drive them past Tsybulsky's, which was out at the end of the Pointe du Colombier, along the Chemin de Saint-Hospice.

All you could see of it was the front gate and glimpses of a few rooftops. Had Palmer and Ashby not been out earlier on the Promenade des Fossettes with the drone, all they would have had were a few satellite images of the estate to go on.

Having crossed Tsybulsky's house off his list, Harvath now wanted to go back to the port and check out the restaurant where Eva and Inessa would be getting together.

He asked Palmer to drop him off a couple of blocks away, as it was best they not all be seen together. There was also another reason why Harvath wanted to head to Muse on foot: it would allow him to take a look at Tsybulsky's boat.

The great thing about the small Port of Saint-Jean-Cap-Ferrat was that, unlike many marinas in the United States, none of its docks were off-limits to the public. There were no gates that required an access code. You could walk down any and every pier, admiring the watercraft, and no one could tell you to get lost.

Even better was the fact that Tsybulsky had the hottest vessel in the harbor. As a result, everybody wanted to see it up close. There was a constant stream of pedestrians stopping to take photographs. The boat was a floating piece of art and Harvath was immediately drawn to it.

Dubbed the Tecnomar for Lamborghini 63, it was 63 feet long, could reach 63 knots, there were only 63 of them made, and the number 63 was meant to commemorate the founding of Lamborghini by Ferruccio Lamborghini in 1963.

The word *sleek* didn't begin to do the stunning craft justice. It looked like it had been plucked from a hundred years in the future and dropped into the azure blue waters of Saint-Jean-Cap-Ferrat. With its razor-sharp lines and stealthy, high-tech aesthetic, it was a yacht designed to turn heads and break necks.

Both because of its appearance and its V-12 engines, it reminded Harvath of what a Lamborghini Sián FKP 37 would look like if it were turned into a high-performance, luxury speedboat. As much of a dirtbag as Tsybulsky was, his yacht was first-class.

Harvath hung back and took in the scene from a respectable distance. He didn't need to end up in anyone's social media photos. From where he stood, he could see everything he wanted, including Tsybulsky's crew. Ashby's description of them had been spot-on. Dressed in white polos and blue shorts that appeared two sizes too tight, they all looked like they were on steroids or human growth hormone—popular drugs of choice for ex–Russian Special Forces soldiers now in the private security market. For these guys, and their employers, bigger was always better.

Carrying a to-go cup with a camera hidden inside, Ashby had been able to record her entire visit to the boat. Within minutes of being handed the cup's SD card, Nicholas had identified the crew members and had accessed their military records. As Eva had warned, these were not good men. All were ex-Spetsnaz, and all had been involved in unprovoked violence and unlawful killings from Syria and Ukraine to the Central African Republic.

Having seen enough, Harvath headed back down the dock and continued toward his ultimate destination.

When he arrived at Muse, he approached it from the side, skirting the outdoor terrace, which even at this time of the afternoon was still three-quarters full.

Inside, he found an empty seat at the bar and sat down. The décor throughout was nautical chic—lots of bright white and navy blue, with stainless-steel accents here and there. Even the mahogany bar had been designed to resemble the deck of a classic wooden boat.

Hung upon the walls were enormous black-and-white photographs of Saint-Jean-Cap-Ferrat over the decades, from small fishing boats to gangs of glamorous models on matching Vespas.

A sliding glass wall overlooking the water had been retracted and a light breeze blew through the restaurant.

Harvath ordered a local craft beer. Out of the corner of his eye, he could see Palmer and Ashby at a table, studying menus.

The idea was that they would spend about twenty minutes getting to know the place. Harvath would leave first and then Palmer and Ashby would come pick him up where they had dropped him off.

The barman brought Harvath's beer along with a glass of water and a small dish of marinated olives, before moving on to take care of another customer.

He could see why this was Inessa's favorite spot. The location was perfect and the views really were amazing. If they hadn't been here for such sensitive work, this would have been exactly the kind of place he'd love to bring Sølvi to.

Not counting the glass of wine outside the cottage back in Norway, they hadn't had anything resembling a relaxed, unguarded moment since he'd returned. They needed one. They were long overdue.

She knew that his desire to not let one of his deceased wife's killers go unpunished had nothing to do with his love for her. She also knew that regardless of what Grechko was dangling, he was here to make sure she was successful. He also wanted to keep her safe.

There was no doubt in his mind that she understood all these things, but he also knew better than to take it for granted. They needed a long, uninterrupted discussion and he needed to hear it from her.

He also needed to discuss the $50 million sitting in a Swiss bank account that the CIA had tried to blackmail him with. When it came to the money, there was an ethical line there and it was important that she understand on which side he stood. Perhaps Eva's involvement, if they were able to successfully pull this thing off, might better help Sølvi appreciate his position.

Dinner at a place like this, followed by a walk along the port, would be a nice way to begin a discussion like that. If they were to spend the rest of their lives together, it was a critical conversation to have.

After a few more minutes of studying the restaurant, Harvath polished off his beer and paid his check.

He walked back and checked out the men's room, marking the location of the kitchen and the ladies' room as he passed.

When he was done, he popped upstairs for a quick look at that dining room and then exited the restaurant via a different door than he had entered.

Pretending to be following a map on his phone, he did a loop around the building, taking several subtle photographs, before walking back down to the harbor and to the pickup point where he met Ashby and Palmer.

"All good?" he asked, hopping into the back seat of the Range Rover.

"I'm a little bit worried about line-of-sight issues," Ashby responded. "What if Inessa's security detail sees Grechko get up and follow her?"

"We're going to have him move first. Eva won't tip Inessa off until she gets the text from me," Harvath replied.

"What do we know about Inessa's detail?" Palmer asked as he pointed their vehicle toward Eze.

"According to Eva, she normally travels with a four-man team," said Harvath. "Two guys come inside with her and sit at a nearby table. One remains outside with the car. The fourth is a floater. All ex-Spetsnaz."

"So, the floater could be anywhere."

"We'll need to stay on our toes."

"How many people total are we bringing?" Ashby asked.

"Were you and Palmer able to get a reservation?"

Ashby shook her head. "We asked on the way out, but they're booked solid. We're on the waiting list. They told us to grab a seat on the terrace if we find one, or something in the bar."

"That's going to be my strategy as well," said Harvath. "I'll be with Grechko. You two will be wherever you can find a spot. And I'm going to have Staelin and Haney nearby in the G-Wagon."

"So, we're five, plus Grechko," said Palmer.

Harvath met his gaze in the rearview mirror and nodded. "That's the plan. If everything goes right, we'll be back home, sipping champagne by eleven o'clock."

CHAPTER 28

They returned to the safehouse just as Barton and Preisler were on their way out. The CIA's yacht broker had come through. A boat, fully fueled, was waiting for them in Nice.

Seeing Harvath arrive, Barton paused in the driveway and waited for him to get out of the Range Rover.

Once he did, he walked over to him, held up his phone, and showed Harvath what the broker had been able to secure. "Only you could arrange something like this," he said.

"Like it?" Harvath asked.

"Are you kidding me?" Barton replied. "We'll have no problem keeping up with Tsybulsky."

"Good."

"And, as I've seen the seven-figure price tag, I promise to do my best not to scratch it or run it aground."

Harvath smiled. "Not my problem. The CIA's picking up the tab. Just complete your part of the mission. That's all I care about."

"Roger that," said Barton as he and Preisler threw bags into the trunk of their vehicle and headed out.

Now that he was back at the villa, the first person Harvath wanted to see was Sølvi. He found her sitting on the veranda, cup of coffee in hand, staring out toward the small slice of the Mediterranean that was visible from their location.

"Everything okay?" he asked, stepping out to join her. "How'd your call go with Oslo?"

"Not well," she replied. "But I suppose that was to be expected."

Harvath pulled up a chair and sat down next to her.

"They gave me twenty-four hours to surrender myself," she continued, "along with Grechko."

"And what did you tell them?"

"I told them that until they caught their mole, Grechko and I were safer where we were."

"At which point they assured you that they could keep both of you safe, right?"

Sølvi nodded. "'Just tell us where you are,' they said, 'and we'll come get you. We'll put you anywhere in Norway you want. No one will be able to touch either of you.'"

"Then what happened?"

"Then it got nasty," she replied, exhaling. "If I don't comply, they'll consider it an act of treason, my career will be over, they'll revoke all my military benefits, as well as everything I've accrued at the NIS, et cetera."

"Could be worse," Harvath said, trying to make her smile. "In the U.S. they also would have threatened to take your parking space."

Sølvi chuckled. "It's already gone. They also deactivated my security badge and have flagged my Norwegian passport."

"They're playing hardball."

"Wouldn't you?"

Harvath nodded. "I've been in a similar situation. All I can say is, you just have to do the right thing—even if it's in opposition to what your government is asking you to do. In the end, it'll all work out. Trust me."

"I do," Sølvi said, reaching out and taking his hand. "But I don't want to think about Oslo. Let's talk about something else. How's everything coming together on your end?"

"You want the short version, or the truth?"

Sølvi chuckled again. No matter how rough things were, he could always make her laugh. "Split the difference for me."

"Inessa has agreed to meet Eva for dinner, and we've found the perfect spot. Plenty of ingress and egress points. The conversation is going to have to be quick, but it should be enough time for Grechko to make his case."

"And if she agrees?"

"If she agrees, we make sure no one, including Tsybulsky, ever comes looking for her. That's what Grechko wants, right?"

"Why does that sound like a loaded question?"

Harvath, still holding her hand, leaned back in his chair and stared out toward the ocean. "Just want to make sure we're both on the same page."

Sølvi looked at him. "You're up to something," she said. "I can tell. What is it?"

"How much do you know about Arkady Tsybulsky?"

"Billionaire oligarch. Makes his money from mining. Close friend and confidant of the Russian president."

"Correct," Harvath replied. "In fact, Russia's war effort in Ukraine is heavily dependent upon the raw materials that Tsybulsky supplies. His aluminum, titanium, nickel, and iron ore are critical to Moscow. Without them, you can't build airplanes, helicopters, armored vehicles, missiles, and a whole host of other weapons and weapons systems."

"You're certainly knowledgeable when it comes to Tsybulsky."

"The file Holidae gave me to read before we left was quite detailed. Suffice it to say that Tsybulsky was incredibly rich before Russia invaded Ukraine. Since the invasion, his wealth has exploded. Not only that, but according to the CIA, he was one of the people who had strongly encouraged Peshkov to launch the war."

"The Ukrainians must hate him with a passion," she said.

"You have no idea," Harvath replied.

"What's your plan?"

"I've decided we're not going to make Inessa disappear."

"You're not?" Sølvi replied, drawing her hand back, somewhat surprised.

"No. Instead, we're going to make her problem disappear."

"You're going to kill Tsybulsky?"

Harvath, who had turned to look at her, turned back to look at the ocean. "*I'm* not going to kill him."

Even though his head was turned to the side, she could see that look in his eye again. "Forget splitting the difference. Tell me the truth."

Harvath turned to face her again. "I promise you. I will tell you the full truth, when the time is right."

"What's wrong with right now?"

"I'm doing you a favor."

"By keeping me in the dark? How does that help me?" she asked.

"It'll help you keep your job."

"You mean the job that they've told me is out the window this time tomorrow?"

Harvath smiled at her. "Plausible deniability is invaluable. You've got that right now. Trust me, you don't want to throw it away."

"I think I should be the judge of that. Grechko is my defector."

"Yes, he is. And I want you to be able to focus on him."

"Please tell me you're not trying to patronize me."

"I'm not trying to patronize you," he responded. "I'm trying to protect you. Believe me."

"How can I believe you when you don't trust me?"

"I trust you implicitly. If this all goes according to plan, you can knock me afterward for being overly cautious. But, if anything goes wrong and we can't contain it, you don't want Norway needlessly getting dragged into this. I'll only be gone a few hours. Once I'm back, you can ask me whatever you want." Winking, he added, "Within reason."

Though she didn't want to, Sølvi surrendered. She could have fought a bit harder and maybe have extracted a bit more information from him, but at what cost?

They needed to trust each other—and not just when it was easy. It was when things were difficult that it mattered most.

She took his hand again. "Just promise me one thing."

"What's that?" he asked.

"That you won't make me a widow before we're even married."

Harvath smiled at her as his phone chimed. "You've got nothing to worry about."

Looking down, he saw it was a text from Staelin. He and Haney were about to arrive with the Ukrainian commandos and would meet him at the caretaker's cottage.

He leaned over and gave Sølvi a kiss. "I've got to get going."

"What's up?"

"The package I ordered has arrived."

CHAPTER 29

Stopping to grab Nicholas and the dogs, Harvath drove down to the caretaker's cottage to greet the new arrivals. He had decided to keep them out of sight from Sølvi and from Grechko. There was nothing to be gained from either of them being read in on this part of the operation.

As he and Nicholas entered the cottage, he could see that the dining table was stacked with the commandos' equipment.

"Why don't you just swim into the harbor and stick a mine to the bottom of his boat?" Haney asked, examining the men's gear.

"Because his hull is a composite of fiberglass and carbon fiber," the first commando, whose name was Max—short for Maxsym, replied. "Magnetic mines won't work."

"Why not use suction cups?"

"Too much drag," the second commando, named Petro, answered. "Once the boat gets underway, the attachment to the hull begins to fail. Even before the boat pops out of the hole and gets on plane, the mine will be ripped away."

"Huh," Haney replied, as he went back to looking at their kit.

"Thank you for coming," Harvath said, as he and Nicholas introduced themselves and shook hands with the commandos.

"Thank you for the opportunity," Max responded. "Arkady Tsybulsky has been a priority target for us since the war began."

"With the support we receive from France," Petro added, "I always assumed that taking him out here was a nonstarter."

"It still is," said Harvath.

Both men looked at him, uncertain as to whether they had heard him correctly.

"Everything's going to happen next door, in Monaco," Harvath explained. "And I can't stress this enough—territorial integrity is key to this operation. Monaco has the world's shortest coastline, only 2.38 miles, so our timing has to be perfect. If we pull this off, your country is not only going to get massive international headlines, but every single Russian oligarch, no matter where in the world they are, is going to be terrified to even so much as stick a toe outside their front door. Most important, Ukraine won't risk losing French support for carrying out an unsanctioned operation within their territory. That's why this has to happen in Monaco."

Max and Petro nodded. That was all the clarification they needed.

Staelin, however, had a question. "I've been wondering something," he said. "Why not just wait until Tsybulsky comes back to his boat from the casino and take him out, along with his whole detail? We'd have the element of surprise. We could do it right there at the dock, hose down any blood, and then drive the boat and the bodies out into the Med and sink them."

"We might have the element of surprise," Harvath replied, "but we'd also have an audience. That boat draws too much attention. We're going to have to wait until it leaves the harbor in Monaco."

"And you're convinced there's no way we can smuggle some sort of bomb on board?"

"If we'd had more time, maybe. But we don't. There's going to be ex-Spetsnaz manning that boat from now until it leaves Monaco for the return trip to Saint-Jean-Cap-Ferrat. Any element of surprise we do have would be blown if we got caught trying to plant a bomb."

Staelin was a thinker. That was definitely to his credit. One of his repeated truisms was that the mind was like a parachute: it had to be open to work.

His impulse to continually probe and brainstorm for the best ways to accomplish an assignment made him one of the strongest contributors to the team. Harvath always had time for his ideas.

And he was right: Planting a bomb—had they the time to pull it off—would have been an excellent way to take care of Tsybulsky. They could have even thrown the Ukrainians a bone and given them the credit without having even been on scene. Unfortunately, that wasn't what the universe had handed them. "Easy" didn't appear anywhere on tonight's list of mission options. As team leader, Harvath ultimately had final say in how and what would be done.

To that end, there was one element to the assignment that only he knew about. He had not shared it with Sølvi or anyone else. Even Nicholas wasn't aware of it.

Regardless of what Inessa decided, the CIA had authorized Harvath to assist the Ukrainian commandos in taking out Tsybulsky. Langley wanted the oligarch gone just as much as Kyiv did and this kind of opportunity was too good to pass up. The ultimate call was his, but the Agency had made it crystal clear where they stood on the matter.

There were multiple pieces to synchronize between the Inessa op in Saint-Jean-Cap-Ferrat and Tsybulsky in Monte Carlo—cars, boats, lookouts, et cetera, but so far so good. Things were coming together.

Harvath wanted to give the commandos some time to finish checking their gear and told them he'd be back with the rest of the team in about forty-five minutes for a final mission briefing.

The only person who wouldn't be at the meeting would be Barton. After picking up their boat in Nice, he would be piloting it to a small harbor just north of Eze and waiting there for the commandos. He already knew his instructions.

After making sure the commandos had everything they needed, Harvath, Nicholas, and the dogs returned to the Range Rover for the short drive back to the villa.

"How are you feeling about everything?" Nicholas asked as Harvath started the engine and put the SUV into gear.

"As good as can be expected," he replied.

"Good," the little man said. Then, after a long pause, apropos of nothing, stated, "This is going to be my last assignment."

Harvath looked at him in surprise. "You're quitting?"

Nicholas shook his head. "Not quitting. Just not doing fieldwork anymore. Putting aside my physical condition, and the fact that the dogs are getting older, it's a younger man's game."

"Speak for yourself," Harvath joked.

The little man smiled. "People with PD don't have the longest of life expectancies. I've got Nina and the baby now. I want to make the most of whatever I've got left. FaceTimes from hotel rooms and safehouses halfway around the world aren't real life. They just don't cut it."

Harvath understood where he was coming from. In fact, he had a lot of respect for his friend's decision. "It won't be the same without you."

"Yes, it will. You won't even notice that I'm gone. I'll still be the voice in your ear."

"Do the powers that be know about your decision?"

Nicholas shook his head. "Not yet. I plan on letting them know when we get back. What about you?"

"What about me?"

"Over the summer, when you had burned through all your vacation and sick days so you could stay in Olso with Sølvi, I thought that might be it. But when they threatened to pink-slip you if you didn't come back, you actually started packing your bags. I've got to tell you, I was surprised."

"Why?"

"Beside the fact that you outkicked your coverage in landing a woman like her?"

"Yeah," Harvath replied with a grin, "beside that."

"You've got the two things people would kill for—a mountain of money and excellent health. Yet for some reason, you'd rather keep throwing yourself in front of bullets and oncoming trains than enjoy yourself."

"Maybe that's *how* I enjoy myself."

"If it is," Nicholas replied, "it's because you don't know any better."

Harvath pretended to check his watch. "Is this session only fifty minutes, Doctor, or do I get the whole hour?"

"Don't tell me you didn't enjoy the summer. You and Sølvi even got to have Marco come visit. That must have been terrific."

Having his deceased wife's son—the little boy that he loved like his own—stay with them had been beyond terrific. What's more, Sølvi had been wonderful about it, including having the grandparents along. She was a natural with Marco. There were times when it was just the three of them at the cottage on the fjord that he felt life couldn't serve up anything more perfect.

"It was a good summer," Harvath admitted.

"Bullshit," Nicholas replied, a smile on his face. "It was a great summer. Every time I spoke with you, I could hear it in your voice."

"That's because you always called after five o'clock."

"I always know I'm over the right target with you when the jokes start flying. Your sense of humor is your escape hatch."

"Damn it," said Harvath, as they pulled up to the villa. "We're back already. Well, good talk. Let's not do this again soon."

"Everybody's replaceable, Scot. Keep that in mind. Even you. You don't have to stop what you're doing, but you can change how you do it. They can't force you to be in D.C. If you want to be with Sølvi, go be with Sølvi. You've earned the right to dictate your own terms."

"Thanks, Doc."

Nicholas shook his head as he opened his door. Harvath was never going to change. "Just think about what I said. Okay?"

CHAPTER 30

Maggie Thomas held the White House in high esteem. To her it not only represented the pinnacle of political power but was also a shining symbol of what America stood for.

The character of the person who sat in the Oval Office was exceedingly important. They set the tone for the nation and were a projection to the rest of the world of how the United States saw itself. In her estimation, Paul Porter was an excellent president.

She had come to that decision based on who the man was, not on his party affiliation. Maggie prided herself on her lack of political bias. It was something else she had inherited from her grandmother, and it had served her well in D.C.

The only lens through which she viewed politics was "will the issue in question serve the interests of the American people and make the country better?" That was it. Plain and simple.

Over the course of his presidency, Porter had been faced with difficult foreign policy challenges. Each time, he had stepped up, done the right thing, and told the American people the truth—regardless of the consequences to his career. His courage, humility, and steadfast dedication to integrity were not only refreshing, but they also inspired fierce loyalty in the people who worked for him.

"Nervous?" Conroy asked as they entered the West Wing and headed toward the Cabinet Room.

"No," Maggie replied. "I've briefed the president before."

Steady as a fucking rock, Conroy thought to himself. *Good.* Competence and sobriety were exactly what they needed right now.

"POTUS likes you," the DDO stated. "So, there's nothing to be nervous about."

"Andy, I'm not nervous. And whether he likes me or not is inconsequential. That's not what I'm paid for."

"You're right," Conroy conceded. "I apologize. I guess I may be the one who's a little bit nervous."

In the middle of the hallway, Maggie stopped and looked at him. "You? Why?"

"I hear the president's team is extremely unhappy with the lack of visibility on Belarus. They've sharpened one of the fence posts along the South Lawn and are shopping for the right head to put on it."

"Who told you that?"

"I've got a source inside the administration."

"Of course you do," Maggie replied. "Whoever it is, they're lying to you."

"What are you talking about?"

"If we're correct, the world is a hair's breadth away from Russia detonating a nuclear weapon. As unhappy as some on President Porter's team may be with our penetration of Minsk, he's not going to begin swapping out horses in the middle of the river."

"Why not?"

"Because it's too dangerous. We're one intelligence report away from the DEFCON status being raised. Playing musical chairs at the Agency isn't going to fix things. Not right now. Trust me, Porter's a pragmatist. If we continue to provide him with the best available information, he'll make the right decisions. He's not going to allow himself to be distracted with personnel issues."

"I hope you're right. It would be a shame to let you have all the fun."

"Right," Maggie said dryly, as she started walking again. "Especially when there's more than enough 'fun' to go around."

Upon entering the Cabinet Room, they saw that the members of the National Security Council were already seated at the large mahogany table. As Conroy knew several of them, he walked over to shake hands and say hello.

While Maggie had briefed the president before, it had always been in the Oval Office. This was her first meeting in the Cabinet Room. A bit of a history buff, she had read up on it during the ride over from Langley.

Each of the cabinet member's chairs has a brass plaque on the back of it with the name of their position. The president's, which is dead center on the east side of the table and is two inches taller than the others, has a plaque that reads, THE PRESIDENT.

The table had been a gift in 1970 from President Richard Nixon. All things considered, it seemed an odd item to have retained, but considering what it would have cost to replace, it was probably better for the taxpayers to leave it where it was. It also admittedly intrigued Maggie to wonder if any of the recording devices Nixon used to secretly tape conversations in the Cabinet Room involved this very same table.

Glancing around the room, she could identify dozens of places where current technology could be incorporated to covertly capture both audio and video. There was no doubt that even Nixon would be shocked by how far things had come.

The room was formal, but comfortable. A rich carpet woven with oversize stars and olive leaves covered the floor. On the walls were portraits of past presidents, each painting personally selected by President Porter himself.

A row of windows, with views out onto the Rose Garden, bathed the room in midmorning light and added a touch of momentary tranquility to the space.

Then, without any fanfare, the door to the adjoining Oval Office opened and the president stepped inside, followed by his national security advisor. Everyone in the Cabinet Room rose to attention.

"Good morning," Porter said, bidding the attendees to be seated. "We've got a lot to go over, so let's get started."

They all took their seats and shifted their attention to the national security advisor as Porter handed him the reins.

After a couple of quick housekeeping issues, the NSA transitioned to the reason the meeting had been called. The United States and its allies were growing increasingly concerned, not only about the apparent presence of nuclear weapons in Belarus, but also Russia's intent to use them.

He then invited the Director of National Intelligence to speak.

The DNI ran down the recent intelligence discoveries by the CIA, including Harvath's revelation that at least two oligarchs close to Peshkov—Nekrasov and Tsybulsky, along with their families, had been summoned back to Russia and his Black Sea complex immediately.

Then he let the other shoe drop, updating everyone on that morning's satellite imagery and the findings from the Belarus desk. The impact of the discovery rippled around the table. It was the most disturbing piece of intelligence yet to come to light.

Once the NSC members had enough time to digest the images, the DNI introduced Maggie and asked her to give a quick analysis of the situation. Clearing her throat, Maggie thanked the DNI and launched into her assessment.

"Since its invasion, Russia has used a myriad of nuclear threats, both implicit and explicit, in an effort to influence foreign decision-making and erode Western support for Ukraine. We believe that these threats, along with Russia's possible nuclear force deployment to Belarus, raise the risk of an actual nuclear weapon being used to the highest level in decades.

"As the global community works to minimize these risks, Russia has blocked consensus on the Nuclear Non-Proliferation Treaty, suspended the new Strategic Arms Reduction Treaty, and withdrawn its ratification of the Comprehensive Nuclear-Test-Ban Treaty. We don't see this as mere saber-rattling by Moscow. We believe that President Peshkov and the Kremlin are transmitting a clear signal that they are no longer bound by any rules regarding their nuclear weapons.

"Put aside for a moment what belligerents like North Korea and Iran are taking away from this. Think about what China is learning. Any calculation they're making about an invasion of Taiwan now includes consideration of how long NATO took to respond to Ukraine. Not only was NATO slow out of the blocks, but it was also slow to escalate the types of munitions and equipment being sent, all out of fear that Russia 'might' resort to the use of nuclear weapons.

"We are now in an era where our previous norms have been shattered. Perhaps irreparably so. The one consistent throughline, however is Peshkov. He doesn't hide his intentions. He tells the world what he is going to do, and then he does it, whether that's 'liberating' the Donbas and the Crimean Peninsula, or his full-on invasion of Ukraine. He's actually one of our best sources of intelligence. We should take him at his word. Especially when it comes to his intention to use nuclear weapons. He's not bluffing. He's telling us what's coming next."

Maggie took a moment to let that sink in as she got a read of the room. No one spoke. Every set of eyes was glued to her.

Knowing she was about to shake the building down to its foundation, she chose her next words with the utmost caution. "We believe, with a high degree of confidence, that Russia intends to use a limited nuclear weapon, *imminently*."

CHAPTER 31

Universally, there was shock and horror around the Cabinet Room table. Every participant in the meeting had questions. Everyone, that is, except for President Porter. For the moment, he felt it best to sit back and listen.

The secretary of defense was the first person recognized. "Define imminent," he said.

"It could be a day," Maggie admitted. "It could be a month. We don't know. A lot depends on what happens on the ground."

"Meaning?"

"President Peshkov has multiple scenarios in which he is prepared to use one or more of his nuclear weapons. The phrase Moscow has been voicing most frequently of late is that Russia has the right to utilize these weapons if its *sovereignty* is threatened."

"Sovereignty?" the vice president asked. "Meaning if they fear an invasion?"

Maggie turned to address the VP. "It's a catch-all term. While President Peshkov and the Kremlin have been pushing out domestic propaganda claiming that the West is at war with them and wants to destroy Russia, we also believe that sovereignty extends to all of the Ukrainian territory it currently holds in the east, as well as the Crimean Peninsula. Any move to recapture these areas could constitute, by President Peshkov's definition, a threat to Russian sovereignty."

"Absolute insanity," the attorney general stated. "It's like a kindergartner grabbing another child's toy and saying that because he holds it, it now belongs to him and he doesn't have to give it back."

Maggie didn't disagree.

"I know this question has previously been asked, but it's worth bringing up again. Is Peshkov nuts?"

"It's a fair question," Maggie replied. "And one that we have devoted a lot of resources to answering. Technically speaking, President Peshkov's health status is considered a national security issue and is one of the most closely guarded secrets in Russia. That said, we believe he is suffering from some form of cancer and has been undergoing treatment.

"We all remember that long table he was seen sitting at for meetings during Covid. He'd sit at one end and his guest would sit way down at the other. It was obvious, even to nonmedical professionals, that he was going to extraordinary lengths not to contract the virus. We believe that was because he was immunocompromised due to his cancer treatments and therefore much more susceptible to adverse outcomes from Covid.

"Our analysts also noted that many of his televised appearances looked to have been pretaped, in bulk and—"

"Excuse me," the energy secretary said. "In *bulk*?"

Maggie nodded. "If you know anyone who has been through a rough bout of chemotherapy, you know that some of the treatments can really sideline you. We believe this has been happening to President Peshkov and, to project an air of status quo strength, he recorded multiple interviews and speeches over the past year in advance. There have been small tells we're able to pick up on, but one of the most interesting was when the Russians forgot to have him do a wardrobe change.

"In a recent speech televised on a Monday, Peshkov announced fresh attacks on Ukraine, only to be seen again on TV that Thursday, in the same suit and tie, discussing economic policies for the upcoming year.

"There have been other things our analysts have noticed. His face has appeared swollen of late, possibly due to prescription steroids given to counteract many of the effects of cancer and its treatment. There also appears to be some facial paralysis on the left side.

"Finally, his right arm seems to have developed some sort of a tremor, which he's working very hard to conceal. When he's seen walking, he swings the arm in an almost exaggerated style. It's a marked difference from past video we have of him. When he's seated at a desk, he grips the desk for the entirety of the appearance with his right hand. If he's seated solely in a chair, the chair has arms and he grips the arm the whole time."

The VP looked at her. "All of these symptoms are from his cancer?"

"We're not sure," Maggie replied. "The facial paralysis may be from a stroke and the tremor could be from Parkinson's."

"But is he nuts?" the AG asked, circling back to his question. "Does he have dementia? Is he psychotic? What can you tell us about his current mental state? If we're not dealing with a rational actor, we need to know that."

"Of course," said Maggie. "What I can tell you is what our experts believe. In the diagnosis of psychopathy, President Peshkov overpresents in three categories: aggression, narcissism, and lack of empathy. That doesn't necessarily make him crazy, but it does make him extremely dangerous. Psychopaths are known for being charming, manipulative, and cunning. Three traits that definitely apply to President Peshkov."

"So what are you telling us? He's Ted Bundy, but with nukes?"

A chorus of uncomfortable laughter resonated around the table.

"In that Bundy was a highly intelligent psychopath, I think you can draw a parallel, but I wouldn't get too hung up on trying to draw a comparison. The important thing to remember when considering President Peshkov's mental state is that he is incapable of being negotiated with. To be clear, he'll 'appear' to agree to treaties and the like, he'll even sign them, but they don't mean anything to him. They're a tool to manipulate whoever's on the other side. The only thing he understands, the only thing that he respects, is superior force.

"But, to this assessment, let me add one important cultural clarification. We can't view President Peshkov through a strictly American, or Western, lens. His behavior, while abhorrent to us, is in keeping with Russian norms. Life has always been cheap in Russia. As a nation, its leaders have always been willing to throw as many bodies as necessary at a problem, especially in warfare, until that problem ceases to exist. The only thing that matters to them is a successful outcome. Death and destruction, even of their own people, is secondary. President Peshkov has an even lower threshold when it comes to killing Ukrainians."

"To that end," the secretary of state asked, "what other triggers might cause the Russians to use a tactical nuclear weapon in Ukraine?"

"One of the scenarios we're looking at," Maggie explained, "is massive unrest in Russia. In order to preserve his power, President Peshkov might feel the need to bring the war to a rapid close. He could use nuclear weapons to achieve that."

"But the fallout," the secretary of energy interjected, "would not only endanger Russian troops, the radiation could blow back into Russia itself, not to mention multiple client states."

"For which President Peshkov would blame the United States and NATO. Either he would claim we and our allies were about to launch our own nuclear first strike, or that he learned a massive invasion was pending and he needed to push us back. No matter what his assertion would be, no one in Russia is going to challenge it. His citizens will be told his version of events, it will be repeated ad nauseam by the Russian press, any dissenters will be jailed or assassinated, and that will be that."

The secretary of state asked, "Any other trigger scenarios we should know about?"

"If the battlefield tide turns against Russia badly enough, that's one. If Russia loses many significant ships from its Black Sea Fleet, that's another. And a third, which could contribute to internal unrest, is if Ukraine continues to successfully strike targets inside Russia. Anything that erodes the image of President Peshkov as a strong leader who defends Russia and the Russian people could trigger his use of nuclear weapons."

With that, Maggie rested her case.

A few more questions trickled in and once they had been answered, President Porter adjourned the meeting. As the participants stood to leave, Porter asked Maggie and Conroy to join him in the Oval Office, along with the national security advisor.

"Good job in there," Porter said to Maggie as the door closed behind them and they all sat down on the couches facing each other.

"Thank you, Mr. President," she replied.

"As you said, we're operating with a high degree of confidence that President Peshkov has placed tactical nuclear weapons in Belarus and is prepared to use them, correct?"

"That is correct, sir."

"I want to hear your thoughts on how we change his mind."

"I'm not an economist," Maggie replied, "so I can't comment on any further sanctions that could successfully be brought to bear."

"Nor is that what we're looking for from you," the national security advisor replied. "If Peshkov only responds to power, what power would you threaten him with?"

Maggie took a moment to think before responding, "First, I don't think we should threaten him directly. But we could do so indirectly."

President Porter looked at her. "Go on."

"President Peshkov likes to tell us what he's going to do. I think you should do the same, Mr. President. But do it through surrogates."

"Explain."

"We know the Russians study our media, the same way we study theirs. We should gather up a team of retired, high-ranking generals and arm them all with the same talking points. We should see them on every cable and broadcast news program stating that President Peshkov's threat to use nuclear weapons is absolutely untenable and that the United States will not stand for it.

"Then, when the host asks what the response should be if Russia does use one, each surrogate should say, 'I no longer advise the White House, but if I did, my plan would be to kill every single Russian soldier in Ukraine, including within the illegally annexed territory in the Donbas and the Crimean Peninsula—all via our nonnuclear and far superior military platforms. Simultaneously, we would sink President Peshkov's entire Black Sea Fleet. Right down to the rowboats.' Finally, I would make sure the surrogates made it crystal clear that whatever bases, be they Russian or third party, that were involved in nuclear weapons being used in Ukraine, they will be completely destroyed as well."

President Porter looked at his national security advisor. "Appropriate?"

"More than appropriate," the man replied, before turning back to Maggie. "But what if the Russians don't get the message?"

"I would suggest that as the surrogates are out delivering their remarks, the secretary of state should be in the air, en route to Moscow. I can give you a list of the top five people who have the greatest influence on President Peshkov. Only one of them is in the government. The other four are in private industry. If the SecState can convey to them what the overwhelming response will look like, it may end up landing in President Peshkov's ear. If it does, it might do so in such a way that he pays attention."

"And if he doesn't?"

"If, despite all our efforts, President Peshkov ignores our warnings and detonates a nuclear weapon in Ukraine, we need to unleash a response so severe that not only will Russia never use a nuclear weapon again, but nobody else will either."

CHAPTER 32

When politely asking for the underground parking garage's CCTV footage hadn't worked, Gibert had used an emergency terrorism provision to fast-track a warrant.

While he waited for the magistrate to sign off, he had left two of his most intimidating officers on-site to make sure no "accidents" befell the server in his absence. He also didn't want anyone else touching the doors that led from the Métro tunnel into the electrical/mechanical room, as well as into the garage's stairwell.

Gibert didn't necessarily think any of the employees had anything to do with Jadot's killer getting away, but there was a fierce antipolice sentiment that ran through certain segments of the French population. He wouldn't have put it past any of them to destroy evidence if they knew it could hurt the cops.

Once the warrant came through, the garage dithered until their lawyer arrived. But as soon as he saw the paperwork, he told his client to hand over everything the police had asked for.

Gibert had his cell phone out and was dialing Brunelle before he'd even hit the sidewalk.

They went back and forth over whose office to use, ultimately agreeing that her equipment was better. He joked that if he used lights, sirens, and sidewalks, he could probably be there in two days.

Paris traffic had always been a nightmare but had only grown worse in the last ten years. Being on the Île de la Cité, a stone's throw from Notre Dame Cathedral, la Crim's offices were right in the heart of

Paris. The DGSI, on the other hand, was in the northwest suburb of Levallois-Perret.

It was only about four miles from the center of Paris, but at certain times of day, if you didn't have a helicopter, it might as well have been on another planet.

Gibert had been taught about the area as a little boy. It was popular with impressionist painters, particularly the northern part of Île de la Jatte, an island in the Seine. What had most captivated him, however, was that Levallois-Perret was where Gustave Eiffel had his factory. And from that factory came two of the most iconic landmarks in the world—the Eiffel Tower and the Statue of Liberty.

Parking his vehicle, he passed through a series of security checkpoints, presented his credentials at the main desk, and waited for Brunelle to come downstairs.

The building that housed the DGSI was sleek and modern. The lobby was lined with polished granite and expensive seating areas. All the staff moved with purpose. No one dawdled. There were no T-shirts or shirt sleeves. No neckties had been loosened. No upper shirt collar buttons unbuttoned. Everyone was dressed in perfectly pressed business attire. It looked more like the headquarters of a fancy international investment bank than a domestic security agency. It was also a far cry from the cramped, centuries-old building that housed the Brigade Criminelle.

"Want anything from the café?" Brunelle asked as she signed Gibert in and led him toward the elevators.

"Are you buying?" he asked.

"Seeing as how you made the drive, sure."

They ordered two coffees to go, during which Gibert joked about the DGSI being the only law enforcement department where the employees didn't make their own.

When he added that they probably didn't clean their own guns either, Brunelle responded, "Of course not. That's why we have armorers."

He couldn't tell if she was joking, as he couldn't see her face. She had already picked up her coffee and was headed toward the elevator.

Upstairs, she invited Gibert to leave his bag in her office as they took the portable hard drive with the security camera footage from the garage down to MoMo.

"No coffee for me?" the young man asked as Brunelle arrived at his desk and set the drive down.

She ignored his remark and introduced her guest. "MoMo, Inspector Gibert. La Crim. Vincent, this is Mohammed Motii. He's a digital forensic specialist for our Computer Analysis Response Team."

The two men shook hands. Then, looking at the drive, MoMo asked, "What do you need?"

"Our man with the limp. The one who disappeared down an airshaft shortly after leaving the National Archives. We think someone was waiting for him in a nearby parking garage and helped smuggle him out. The drive has the garage's CCTV footage," she replied, tapping it. "We want to see what it captured."

"That's it?"

"For the moment."

"Plug and play," he stated, attaching a cable to the drive. "This'll be the easiest thing I do all day."

The drive whirred to life and on one of his monitors, MoMo displayed a security grid with the garage's multiple camera feeds.

"Where do you want to start?" he asked.

"Let's start with vehicles exiting the garage shortly after our man disappeared," she replied, giving him a time frame to search.

"Busy morning yesterday," MoMo stated as he scrolled through footage of at least fifteen cars leaving. "Any parameters to help narrow it down?"

Brunelle thought for a moment. "Get rid of any hatchbacks. They would have hidden him in a trunk."

"Okay," he replied. "That takes out two, which means we're left with thirteen vehicles."

Gibert leaned in closer. "Do any of the cameras provide more of a profile view? Having someone in the trunk might cause the car we're looking for to ride lower."

MoMo shook his head. "What you see on the screen is what we've got."

"Maybe we should take a closer look at the comings and goings of the drivers themselves. It'll take a while to match them to their cars, but I don't see that we have much choice."

The young man looked at Brunelle. "Hypothetically, there might be a faster way."

Brunelle nodded. "Do it."

"Do what?" Gibert asked.

"You'll see," she responded.

Within moments, MoMo had used the AI software to match the drivers with their vehicles and to pinpoint when they had parked and walked out of the garage on foot, and when they had come back.

Brunelle then said, "Jadot was murdered Sunday evening. How many of the cars arrived during that day and then left on Monday morning?"

"Four," MoMo responded, isolating the vehicles, along with footage of their drivers walking in and out of the garage.

"What about gait recognition? Do any of the drivers match our suspect—with or without his limp?"

The young man typed in a command for the AI, but then shook his head. "No match."

Gibert smiled when he recognized what software they were using. "None of this will ever be admissible in court."

"It's never going to see a court," she responded. "The minute we step away from this desk, it's all going to be deleted."

"We just don't have the storage capacity to hang on to these training simulations," MoMo said grinning as he tried something else. "If our suspect snuck into the garage via the Métro tunnels, maybe that's how he snuck out in the first place."

"Meaning someone might have driven into the garage with him in the trunk, left the empty car there, and then drove back out with him once the job was finished?"

"Exactly."

Brunelle and Gibert watched as the young man accessed the network of street cameras and zeroed in on the feed showing the faux façade airshaft on the Rue de Chapon. MoMo then pulled up the footage from Sunday and set the AI loose.

The moment he engaged it, the AI got a match. Their suspect could be seen exiting the little blue door. MoMo's hunch had been correct.

Now that they knew how the suspect had traveled to and from the National Archives, they only needed to figure out which vehicle was his.

"This one," said MoMo, enlarging an image of a chalk-colored Peugeot sedan. "And here's the footage of the driver."

"Can you get a better shot of his face?" Gibert asked.

The young man shook his head. "Nope. He paid close attention to where the cameras were and made sure we wouldn't get a good look."

"Just like his partner at the archives," Brunelle stated. "These people knew what they were doing."

"Like I said," Gibert remarked. "Professionals. Can you zoom in on the license plate?"

MoMo did and Gibert texted the number to his office. And though la Crim wasn't using AI, yet, he received an answer back rather quickly.

"The vehicle was stolen sometime early Sunday morning. It was discovered last night in Seine-Saint-Denis. Torched. It took longer than it should have to extinguish the flames. Firefighters believe some kind of special accelerant was used. I wouldn't hold out much hope for recovering any evidence."

"Think there are any witnesses?" Brunelle asked.

"In Seine-Saint-Denis? Who will talk to the police?" Gibert replied, shaking his head. "Less than zero."

MoMo chuckled.

"Why are you laughing?" the cop asked.

"Because you're wrong," the young man answered. "It's not that the people from Seine-Saint-Denis don't want to talk with the police. It's that the police don't know how to talk with the people from Seine-Saint-Denis."

Gibert looked at him. "How would you know?"

"Because I'm from Seine-Saint-Denis. If there are any witnesses there, you need the right person to get them to talk."

"And who would that be?"

Dead serious, MoMo responded, "Me."

CHAPTER 33

G ibert wanted it clear, for the record, that he didn't just think this was a bad idea, he thought it was terrible.

Considering MoMo's family history, he was one of the last people they should be going into Seine-Saint-Denis with.

His father, an immigrant from Morocco, was an ultranationalist who wanted to lock the door behind him, pull up the drawbridge, and cut off any further immigration to France. He supported a host of political candidates who were widely despised across the immigrant-heavy population of Seine-Saint-Denis. When certain politicians wanted to make it look like they had broad support in the Muslim community, they often called on MoMo's father to comment on TV or help fill seats at rallies.

MoMo's uncle, on the other hand, occupied the exact opposite end of the spectrum. He was an extremely religious Salafi-Jihadist who wanted to see much more immigration, particularly from the Islamic nations of North Africa. He was a proponent of sharia law and a known agitator who specialized in riling up Muslim neighborhoods and getting masses of protestors into the streets.

How MoMo had ever passed the background checks and had been hired by the DGSI was beyond Gibert, though the cop suspected the young man's language skills and tech proficiency probably outweighed his family's political volatility.

Nevertheless, no one in Seine-Saint-Denis loved both MoMo's dad *and* his uncle. Residents always hated one of them—usually with a passion. Riding into town with anyone from MoMo's family was like showing up at a natural gas plant with a flamethrower. Not only was someone likely to get burned, but the whole experience was probably going to be explosive. Gibert suggested they might be better off by simply abandoning the idea and taking turns slamming their heads in his car door. He was only half-joking.

A third of the 1.6 million people in Seine–Saint-Denis lived below the poverty level. Islamism, crime, and drugs were rampant throughout. They were at their worst in the dreaded Le Franc–Moisin neighborhood, which is where the burned-out, once-chalk-gray Peugeot had been found. Gibert was going to make an additional joke about not having packed enough hollow points for the trip, but it would have been a lie. His trunk was loaded with additional guns and ammunition.

After a quick stop at the DGSI café for MoMo to grab a chai, they piled into Gibert's vehicle and headed up to Seine–Saint-Denis.

Though Brunelle hadn't said anything, he could sense her trepidation as well. She liked to play the cold, unflappable federal agent, but she wasn't stupid. Far from it. Brunelle had cut her teeth as a street cop. She knew the reaction white faces got in certain Parisian neighborhoods. With the recent death of an immigrant teen at the hands of law enforcement, white faces with badges would likely draw an even more hostile response.

They needed to get in, maintain the lowest possible profile, and get out as soon as possible. In the absence of a couple of riot brigades backing them up, even the mildest of situations could quickly escalate and they could become trapped. Temperatures were running extremely hot.

It was technically a misnomer that Paris had "no-go" zones; neighborhoods that police were locked out of or refused to go into. What there were, however, were areas considered "combustible" and likely to produce civil unrest with little to no provocation. In these neighborhoods, police officers, firefighters, and ambulance crews had been attacked, simply for doing their jobs, and now refused to respond to calls without sufficient backup. Le Franc–Moisin was one such area.

Gibert and his colleagues at la Crim likened it to the old Kurt Russell movie *Escape from New York,* where the entire island of Manhattan has been turned into a maximum-security prison. Getting in wasn't the problem. It was getting out, unscathed, that was the challenge.

Having only shared a bed with Brunelle, not a firing range, he had no idea if she could shoot. And, even if she could, was she any good? Dropping into the hornet's nest with one person who couldn't defend themselves, much less two, was a recipe for disaster. He prayed that the pair could carry their own weight.

As they drove, no one spoke. Not even MoMo. He just sat in back, sliding his straw in and out of the plastic lid covering his chai.

The sound was getting on Gibert's nerves. "Do you mind?" he asked, locking eyes with the young man in his rearview mirror.

MoMo, unaware that he was annoying the inspector, apologized and stopped making the sound. "I do things like that sometimes when I'm tense."

"What's wrong?" Brunelle asked from the front seat. "Why are you tense?"

"Officially, this is my first time in the field."

"Great," Gibert lamented as he changed lanes.

"You're going to be fine."

"We hope," the cop added.

"Ignore him, MoMo," Brunelle advised. "Everyone's a little tense their first time out. But you grew up in Seine-Saint-Denis. You know the people. That gives you an advantage. You've got nothing to worry about."

The young man appreciated her reassurance. He also hoped that she'd be proven correct.

He kept in touch with enough of his childhood friends to know how on edge everything was. People were still angry. In the aftermath of the young teen being shot, there had been violent demonstrations. Shops had been looted. Buildings burned. Despite the passage of a couple of months, tensions remained only a few degrees below the boiling point.

When they arrived, no one needed to see a sign announcing they had crossed into Seine-Saint-Denis. You could sense it. The cars, the people . . . even the graffiti was bleak. Then they drove into Le Franc–Moisin and things really got dark.

It looked like the riots had happened only yesterday. Scorched façades of buildings had yet to be repainted. Broken windows had been left un-repaired. Piles of rubble remained uncleared.

Over it all hung a thick, soot-riddled, grimy pallor. It was as if the neighborhood itself had been consumed by a terrible case of tuberculosis; unable, even momentarily, to prop itself up and drag a damp cloth across its face.

Gibert arrived at the charred remains of the stolen Peugeot and pulled over. There was barely anything left. It looked like it had been hit in a missile strike.

"Now what?" he asked, putting his car in park and turning off the engine.

"Now we find a Khalah," replied MoMo. "One of the neighborhood *aunties.*"

"You mean a local busybody."

"This is why no one wants to talk to you. You have no respect for anyone."

"Look around this place," Gibert responded. "It's a war zone. Hard to have respect for people who don't even respect themselves."

"You're a real asshole," MoMo said as he climbed out of the car. "You know that?"

"Trust me," Brunelle stated as she also stepped out of the car. "He doesn't have a clue."

"For fuck's sake," said the cop. "Can we just focus on what we're sup-posed to be doing here?"

MoMo and Brunelle ignored him as they walked over together to ex-amine the Peugeot.

Having seen more than a few burned-out cars in his day, MoMo wasn't particularly impressed. Instead, he was interested in who was looking at them as they looked at the car. It took him a moment, but then he found a window and a pair of eyes.

"Be right back," he said, before crossing the street and approaching a building on the other side.

Brunelle continued to investigate the Peugeot.

When Gibert joined her, she remarked, "That was one hell of an ac-celerant. Look at how badly everything's melted."

"If the goal was to destroy evidence," he replied, his head on a swivel, taking in their surroundings, "that's the way to do it."

"Let's hope MoMo has some luck," she stated.

Nodding toward a group of young men who had gathered up the block and were checking them out, he added, "And let's hope it's soon."

It only took MoMo about five minutes, and when he came back he had struck gold.

"Come with me," he said.

"Where are we going?" Gibert asked, his eyes still on the group of young men.

"The soccer field around the corner."

"Why?"

"You'll see."

Worried that the kids there might disperse if the trio rolled up in an unmarked police vehicle, MoMo convinced Gibert that they should leave his car behind and walk the short distance. The cop wasn't crazy about the idea, but understanding its merits, agreed to go along with it.

When they arrived at the field, a half-dozen kids were playing soccer. MoMo walked over to where their sweatshirts and jackets were in a pile on the ground and said, "Boom."

"'Boom'?" Gibert repeated. "*Boom* what?"

"What else do you see?" MoMo asked. "Besides the jackets and sweatshirts?"

The cop looked. "A bunch of empty energy-drink cans."

"*Brand-name* energy drinks. Not cheaper knockoffs. And what's going on out on the field?"

"They're kicking a soccer ball around."

"Notice anything about the ball?"

Gibert looked. "No. Should I?"

"It's brand-new."

"These kids have come into a little bit of money," Brunelle responded.

"Precisely," said MoMo. "And they're about to come into a little bit more. Which one of you has some cash on you?"

"I only have credit cards," said Brunelle.

Reluctantly, Gibert reached for his wallet. "How much?"

"Twenty each will probably do it."

"No way," the cop replied. "Here's fifty. They can take it or leave it."

"An asshole *and* cheap," said MoMo as he snatched the fifty-euro note and strode onto the field.

Brunelle stifled a laugh as she and Gibert watched MoMo go chat with the kids.

Soon enough, he pulled out his cell phone and showed them something, presumably CCTV images of the two men they were looking for. One of the kids then took out his own phone and showed something to MoMo.

They chatted for a few more minutes before MoMo handed over the fifty euros and walked back to Brunelle and Gibert.

"The men we're looking for parked a second vehicle here. They paid those kids to keep an eye out and make sure nothing happened to it."

"That was their getaway car," said Gibert. "After they torched the Peugeot."

MoMo nodded.

"Did the kids tell you anything about the men themselves?" Brunelle asked.

"They were in their forties. Spoke terrible French. Heavily accented. One of the kids said the men sounded Russian. And one was walking with a limp."

"Definitely our guys," Gibert replied. "Anything about the other car?"

MoMo smiled and held up his phone. "One of the kids took a picture of it."

CHAPTER 34

Harvath's plan was to have everyone in place before Eva and Inessa arrived at the restaurant. In his experience, people already seated in a venue attracted a lot less attention than people walking in.

Parked at the bar, he sipped a beer and enjoyed a plate of grilled octopus as he quietly monitored all phases of the operation via his phone.

Just north of Eze, in the harbor of Beaulieu-sur-Mer, Barton had picked up Preisler and the Ukrainian commandos, and had sailed up the coast for Monaco.

Back in Saint-Jean-Cap-Ferrat, Palmer and Ashby had hung around the port until they had seen Tsybulsky and his security detail board his yacht and depart.

Once the vessel had cleared the outer wall of the harbor, Ashby texted Harvath and then she and Palmer walked up to Muse, where they had been able to secure an indoor table. Leaning slightly to his left, Harvath could see them from where he was sitting.

Outside, several doors down from the restaurant, Staelin and Haney sat in the G-Wagon, keeping watch over the entrance. On the stool immediately next to Harvath was Grechko.

Despite the space being the perfect temperature, the Russian defector had a film of perspiration across his brow.

"Here," Harvath said as he handed him a cocktail napkin. "Wipe your forehead. You're sweating."

"Thank you," replied Grechko, taking the napkin. "I must look rather foolish to you. A man of my age, giving up everything for a younger woman who might not want anything to do with him."

"I suppose in a perfect world," Harvath stated as he took another sip of his beer, "when two people need to jump, they jump together. But life isn't always perfect, is it? Sometimes one of those people must have enough trust for both of them and jump first."

The Russian liked the sound of that and nodded in approval. "Well said. Thank you."

"You don't need to thank me. I'm just doing my job."

"You're actually showing human compassion," the Russian remarked. "Technically, you could sit there and not say a word to me and it wouldn't violate the spirit of our agreement."

Harvath chuckled. "I think you give me too much credit. Inessa's security team is going to be armed to the teeth. I don't want to be sitting next to the only guy in a climate-controlled bar who's sweating. Feel free to chalk it up to my healthy self-preservation instinct."

"Fair enough." Grechko smiled. "I know you're not very fond of Russians."

"I don't have a problem with Russians, per se. What I have a problem with is the Russian government and the people who work for it."

"As I no longer work for Moscow, where does that leave me?"

"I don't know yet. We'll have to see."

Raising his wineglass, Grechko clinked it against Harvath's beer. "Here's to seeing where things end up. For all of us."

Several moments passed.

"So," the Russian said, looking to make conversation. "You and Sølvi, eh? How'd that happen? Where'd you meet?"

"Listen," Harvath replied. "A couple of moments ago, when I was nice, and I gave you a little encouragement? Don't make me regret that. Okay?"

"Understood," the man responded, taking another sip of his wine. "She's a beautiful woman. Tough too. And smart as hell. I can see why you're attracted to her. It must be hard, though, living in America with her in Norway. I would think that—"

Harvath raised his hand, ever so slightly off the bar—just enough to get Grechko's attention—and said, "I now officially regret being nice to you."

The man smiled. "You both have a similar sense of humor."

"I'm not joking."

"Fine. What about the dwarf? Tell me about him."

"First," Harvath replied, as his eyes scanned the room, "we don't use that word with him. It's considered an insult in English. He prefers to be called a little person."

"But isn't that his code name? His nom de guerre?"

"Close. People referred to him as the 'Troll.' Which, technically speaking, isn't much better."

"I apologize for the inaccuracy," said Grechko. "How do you refer to him?"

"He goes by the name Nicholas."

"Like the saint."

"Exactly."

"Interesting," the man replied. "The wonder worker."

Harvath hadn't heard that description before. *Wonder worker?*

"In the Russian Orthodox Church, Saint Nicholas is a sort of super-saint. He's known as a protector—especially of sailors, children, and the poor. He's also known for his generosity. He's renowned for secretly helping poor families by leaving out bags of gold. This is where the Santa Claus story comes from. Many Russian churches are named for him. He's considered a one-stop shop when the faithful need a saint to pray to. From safe travels to healing the sick, he's the guy."

"Interesting," Harvath stated.

"Why do you think your colleague chose this name?" Grechko asked.

Harvath knew why Nicholas had chosen the name, but he sure as hell wasn't going to tell some supposedly "former" Russian intelligence official. Besides, it wasn't his place to reveal it. That kind of personal information belonged to Nicholas. If he wanted to share it with this guy, that was up to him. And so Harvath simply shrugged in response.

"Perhaps it's because Saint Nicholas was such a strong defender of the faith."

"Sure," Harvath stated, laughing to himself. "Let's go with that. Nicholas, Defender of the Faith."

"Are you a churchgoer, Mr. Harvath? Do you believe in God?"

Sølvi had warned him that Grechko was always "on," a perpetual spymaster, constantly probing for information, looking for ways to stick his boot in the door and leverage himself inside people's minds.

"What I believe," said Harvath, "is that certain men leave the intelligence game, but the intelligence game never really leaves them. Know what I mean?"

"Touché," the Russian replied.

Another long pause ensued before Grechko asked, "You're positive that she'll be here tonight?"

Harvath nodded, taking a bite of his octopus.

"But *how* do you know? Did you talk to her?"

"A little bird told me," he responded.

As soon as he said the words, Muse's front door swung open and a hardened security team ushered in a glamorous, exceptionally attractive Russian woman.

As she passed, Eva Nekrasova pretended not to notice Harvath while also throwing him a discreet wink.

CHAPTER 35

Even in the midst of her cancer battle, Eva still electrified every room she walked into. She was a force of nature.

And while the women of polite South of France society may have frozen her out of their circles because they resented her wealth and beauty, to anyone else, having her around was like basking in the presence of a classic movie star. She was elegance and glamour personified.

Harvath could only imagine the energy she had summoned to be here. On top of that, she looked fantastic. There was no hint that she was undergoing treatment. Every millimeter of her was perfect. Her shitbag husband had zero idea how lucky he was.

"Who the hell is that?" Grechko asked.

"My little bird," said Harvath as he looked at his watch. "It's time for you to hit the men's room. Lock yourself in that stall and don't move until I come get you. Just as we discussed. Understand me?"

The Russian nodded and, after knocking back the rest of the wine in his glass, headed for the restroom.

No sooner had Eva been seated at the best table in the house than the arrival of another statuesque woman, also with her own security detail, sent a hush rippling across the room.

The moment Harvath saw Inessa Surkova, he understood why Grechko had sacrificed everything for her. He also understood why the defector was so concerned that, should she ever disappear, Tsybulsky would go to the ends of the earth to find her and bring her back.

In a word, the woman was stunning. But *stunning* wasn't descriptive enough. While men stole glances of Eva so as not to upset their wives, when Inessa passed through the room, they openly and admiringly stared, unconcerned with the consequences, and were completely unaware that their wives were staring as well.

She had the tightest jawline Harvath had ever seen and cheekbones so high, they rivaled the Andes. A silk dress of emerald green clung to her body and left little to the imagination. Her walk was infused with the kind of confidence only seen on the catwalks of Paris or Milan. How this woman had ended up a courtesan and not a high-fashion model was beyond Harvath.

As she passed, she glanced in his direction and he thanked God that he had already dispatched Grechko to the men's room. Had she seen him sitting there at the bar, before she really knew why Eva had asked her to dinner, there was no telling how she might have reacted. It could have ruined everything.

Harvath watched as Eva stood to greet her. The two women kissed on both cheeks, embraced, and, drawing their chairs closer together, sat down.

A waiter brought over the champagne Eva had ordered. It was a gorgeous bottle of Krug, just like the one Harvath had bought for Sølvi, which was still sitting in her fridge back in Oslo, waiting for them to enjoy.

Expertly removing the cork, the waiter poured a small amount for Eva. She took a small sip and nodded. After filling both of their glasses, the man left the two friends to catch up.

Eva had told Harvath that she wanted to get Inessa loosened up before springing the surprise on her. She believed that having a little alcohol in her system would help keep her calm.

And just in case Inessa got angry and stormed out, Eva wanted to have had a few moments with her to say goodbye.

Harvath deferred to her wishes. Eva not only knew women better than he did, but she also knew Russian women much better.

When their glasses ran dry, Eva didn't wait for the waiter to return. Grabbing the bottle from the bucket, she refilled them and proposed another toast.

As they clinked glasses, Eva placed her left hand on the back of her neck and gave Harvath a signal. *Five minutes.*

Texting the team, Harvath let them know that everything was in motion. He laid a couple of bills on the bar and headed toward the men's room.

The best thing about Muse was that it was a vintage building that had been updated and added on to over the years. In a previous life, back when Saint-Jean-Cap-Ferrat was a fishing village, it had been a cannery.

The frosted windows of the men's and women's bathrooms opened onto a narrow gangway, which led to a service area where fresh fish used to be offloaded from boats in the port and brought in for processing. It wasn't exactly the balcony from *Romeo and Juliet,* but it was better than trying to hide a man and a woman in the same stall at a busy, popular restaurant.

Entering the men's room, Harvath waited for one guy at the urinal and another at the sink to leave, before knocking on the door of Grechko's stall.

When the Russian unlocked it, Harvath stepped inside, and then closed and locked the door behind him.

Hopping up onto the toilet, he carefully swung the window open, and after checking to make sure the coast was clear, pulled himself through and dropped down into the gangway.

There was a pallet nearby and he propped it against the wall to provide Grechko with a makeshift ladder.

Once the Russian was in the gangway, Harvath pulled out his phone and swiped to the camera feature to record a video.

"Short and sweet. Got it?" he asked.

Grechko nodded and Harvath began recording. A few seconds later, it was done. He checked to make sure the audio was intelligible and then, grabbing the pallet, walked down to the window for the ladies' room, where he texted Ashby.

Having seen the dress that Inessa was wearing, he was glad that he had set things up the way he had. There was no way she could have climbed down into the gangway. Leaning the pallet against the wall, he texted the video to Eva.

Once the message had been sent, all he and Grechko could do was to be patient and wait. She was either going to come, or she wasn't.

As far as Harvath was concerned, the only thing better than her showing up and telling Grechko she wanted nothing to do with him would be her choosing not to show up at all. Both of those outcomes would make his night a lot easier. *Easier,* however, didn't appear as if it was going to be in the cards for him.

Moments later, he heard the window of the women's room being opened. Looking up, he saw Ashby poke her head out. When he flashed her the thumbs-up, she returned the gesture and disappeared back inside.

Harvath stood back so Grechko could climb the pallet and be as close to eye to eye as possible with the woman who had now taken Ashby's place in the window.

Before the defector had even started speaking, Harvath knew what Inessa's answer was going to be. He could see it just by looking at her.

After Eva had shown her the video, it must have taken every ounce of self-control she had to calmly get up from the table and walk slowly back to the ladies' room.

Instantly, their hands reached out for each other's. Inessa was overcome with emotion.

"How did you find me?" she asked in Russian, tears welling up in her eyes.

Grechko explained that they didn't have much time and launched into his speech. Harvath, though he spoke a little Russian, could only pick up a few words here and there. The defector was speaking very quickly.

When he came to the end of what he had to say, Inessa Surkova didn't need to ponder her answer. She had rehearsed it in the quiet of her heart a million times. "Etogo ya i zhдaла," she replied, the tears now streaming down her face. *This is what I have been waiting for.* "Ya ne mogu predstavit' svoyu zhizn' bez tebya." *I can't imagine my life without you.*

Inessa had a ton of questions, especially as she was supposed to leave for Russia in the morning. Grechko explained that the details were still being worked out and that Eva would be their go-between.

Harvath looked at his watch and motioned to wrap it up. If Inessa was gone too long, her security team would start getting suspicious.

They kissed and she disappeared back inside the ladies' room. Ashby closed the window and locked it from the inside as Grechko hopped down off the pallet.

The man was overjoyed. "Thank you," he exclaimed, pumping Harvath's hand.

"Don't thank me yet," Harvath replied, trying to temper his expectations. "That was the easy part. From this point forward, things are going to get a lot more dangerous."

CHAPTER 36

Maggie wasn't used to Conroy popping his head into her office. Normally he summoned her to his. But with the situation in Belarus as it was, everyone at the CIA was on edge. Moving around, checking on other departments, conversing with "the troops," were all ways Conroy dealt with the stress.

"May I come in?" he asked.

"Of course," she replied. Putting the cap back on the highlighter she'd been using, she returned it to the mug that held the rest of her pens. It had been a gift, years ago, from her husband. Upon it was printed an inside joke, *If you can't say anything nice, say it in Russian.*

It was just one of the many unique items in her office, which her colleagues had nicknamed "The Overlook" after the hotel in the Jack Nicholson movie *The Shining.*

The sobriquet was not so much in reference to the hotel itself, but rather the hedge maze outside. Though the walls were lined with large, interactive touchscreen display monitors, Maggie was old-school.

She preferred blackboards, whiteboards, and bulletin boards—none of which were subject to crashing.

As such, her office was crammed with them. Some were on easels. Many were on wheeled stands. Others still were propped up on the furniture. When she was in full-blown research-and-analysis mode, like she was now, her workspace could be downright unnavigable.

Clearing a chair for her boss, she invited him to sit, asking, "What's up?"

"After our meeting at the White House, the national security advisor shared your suggestions with the rest of the National Security Council. The secretary of defense wants to take things a step further and President Porter would like to know your thoughts as to how the Russians might react."

"Okay," Maggie replied, leaning back in her chair. "I'm all ears."

"Under its 'nuclear sharing' program, the United States stores a limited number of lower-yield, tactical nuclear weapons in five NATO countries—Belgium, Germany, Italy, the Netherlands, and Turkey. The SecDef thinks we should add another country to that list."

"Which one?"

"Poland."

The consummate poker player, Maggie didn't allow anything about her body language to belie her reaction. What the secretary was suggesting was highly provocative.

"I see where he's going with this," she replied. "Russia placed nukes on Ukraine's doorstep via Belarus, so why don't we place nukes on Belarus's doorstep via Poland."

"Precisely. As these are aircraft-dropped B61 gravity bombs, there's less flight time from Poland to Russian targets, no inflight-refueling requirements, which could make fighters vulnerable to long-range Russian air-defense systems, and it would demonstrate NATO's commitment to its eastern flank."

"My initial thoughts are that it would definitively piss the Russians off. Big-time. We're talking along the lines of how we felt during the Cuban Missile Crisis. The Kremlin would absolutely see it as escalatory. They would be immune to the argument that the move is commensurate with what they've done in Belarus. It would also play right into their propaganda that NATO is at war with Russia and readying to invade. But on top of all that, Poland is just a bad choice."

Conroy looked at her. "What do you mean?"

"For starters, they don't have any place to properly store nuclear weapons. The five other NATO members we work with have WS3 underground storage vaults, which themselves are built within hardened aircraft shelters."

"We can't spend the time and the money building those?"

"Sure," Maggie replied. "Let's say we do and, once they're complete, we shuffle some of our existing arsenal around and place a few tactical nukes in Poland. The minute we do, they'd become targets for preemptive attacks by the Russians, who have Iskander-M ballistic missiles based just north in Kaliningrad. They can hit almost any location in Poland within minutes and with little to no warning."

"Then we up our Patriot missile batteries wherever the nukes get housed," he replied.

Maggie shook her head. "There are only two major Polish air bases that fly F-16s, which are what we'd be looking at for this kind of mission. Both of those bases are also within range of Kaliningrad's S400 antiaircraft missile systems, as well as their radar. Not only would the Russians know the Poles were coming, but they'd start shooting at them.

"By contrast, the base we use in Büchel, Germany, has a longer warning time of attack and NATO planes can take off outside the range of Russian air defenses. I could keep going, but the final hurdle, as I see it, is something called the three no's."

"What's that?"

"In 1997, a document called the 'Founding Act' established relations between NATO and Russia. In it, NATO members asserted that they had no intention, no plan, and no reason to ever deploy nuclear weapons on the territory of new NATO members. The Russians may lie, cheat, and obfuscate when it comes to their side of international agreements, but what does that make us if we do the same? As far as I'm concerned, incorporating Poland into the nuclear-sharing program doesn't make any sense. Especially not in the short term."

"Then what would?"

Maggie thought about the question for a moment before getting up from her desk and walking over to a large board with a map affixed to it that stretched from side to side. Tapping her finger on it, she asked, "What if we went back to a NATO member we've worked with before? Someone with all the infrastructure already in place who knows each and every one of our protocols."

"The Brits."

She nodded. "It made sense, when we were reducing our nuclear footprint almost two decades ago, to remove them from the sharing list. They've got their own nukes and, while they're all submarine-launched, they didn't necessarily need ours. But a lot has changed since then. Adding the air component back in ups their deterrence profile."

"What's more," Conroy added, "it should be relatively drama-free getting them back on the list. They were already previously approved. A unanimous membership vote for Poland might take a little longer, especially with what pro-Russian pricks the Hungarians have been."

"Don't get me started on them," Maggie lamented. "Listen, smarter people than me will make the call on how feasible Poland is. At best, though, it'll be a medium-term solution. Will it anger the Russians? Like I said, it absolutely will, but they're going to raise all the same issues that I did. It might not pass the smell test for them. They may think we're bluffing."

"How do you think they'll react to us putting nukes back in the UK?"

"No matter what we do, the Kremlin isn't going to be happy. If we send nuclear weapons back to RAF Lakenheath, Moscow will publicly accuse us of escalation and fomenting war. It's what they do. But privately, they'll see it as a sound strategic move. We'll be signaling that we're fully prepared to climb the escalation ladder. As they move up a rung, so will we."

"But will it stop them?" Conroy asked.

He waited for her answer, which she was reluctant to give.

"Maggie?"

"You want to know what I really think?"

The man nodded.

"You're not going to like it."

"Out with it."

"Okay," she replied. "But first, please close the door. I don't want this going department-wide."

CHAPTER 37

"Russia isn't going to stop," she stated flatly, as Conroy closed the door to her office and returned to his seat. "They might enter into a ceasefire at some point, but only for the purposes of regrouping and resupplying before launching fresh attacks."

Her voice held a chilling certainty that sent a shiver down his spine. "Is this just . . . intuition?" he asked. "Or something more?"

"It's the truth, Andy. Russia believes it's facing an existential crisis."

"Existential?"

Sitting back down, Maggie pointed toward the map. "Look at it. Russia's a vast expanse of flat plains. A dream target for any invader, a nightmare to defend. They need geographic choke points, physical bottlenecks where they can funnel enemy forces and crush them with concentrated firepower. If you can plug those gaps, you've got a chance at preserving your territory. Russia knows this intimately.

"Every time they've been invaded, the attackers have come through one of nine key gateway territories. This is why their history is so expansionist. They needed a solid, outer perimeter. And after World War Two, they finally had it. The Soviets controlled all nine choke points. But with the USSR's collapse in 1992, they lost all but two. Ever since, they've been fighting to reclaim them."

Conroy absorbed the information, the weight of it settling on him. "So Peshkov's not just playing Cold War nostalgia. This is bigger."

"Much," Maggie stated, her voice grim. "This is about their very survival."

"Who's next on their potential hit list?"

"Estonia, Latvia, Lithuania. It's anyone's guess. They need to plug every single gap. That includes Moldova, Romania, Poland, the Caucasus region, even Central Asia. Without controlling those gateways, Russia will remain vulnerable, and their fear of invasion will never die."

"But why now?" Conroy asked. "Is it Peshkov's health? Is he in some demented race with the Grim Reaper?"

"Sure, some of it is ego," she agreed. "But the primary force driving Peshkov and the Kremlin is demography. In plain English, Russia is dying."

"Because of the numbers of men being fed into the meat grinder in Ukraine?"

Maggie shook her head. "This started well before Ukraine. Back in the 1990s, after the Soviet Union collapsed, the death rate doubled and the birth rate was cut in half. Fast-forward to the war in Ukraine and about a million and a half Russians under age thirty-five have fled the country—most of them young men escaping the draft—two to three times as many as those who agreed to go fight.

"The pool of fighting-age men who are still in Russia is much smaller than what the Soviet Union had at its disposal. So, for the Kremlin, it's now or never. This is the last generation of soldiers that they'll be able to effectively field. If they don't get a hold of those choke points now, it's over. The next time they're invaded, they won't be able to put enough troops on the battlefield to effectively fight.

"On top of this, their economy is crumbling. Their education system collapsed shortly before the USSR did. The last generation with any decent technical training just turned sixty. They're quickly running out of competent people to maintain their railways, their nukes, their airplanes, their military equipment; you name it.

"The worse life gets, the less people want to have babies and the worse the demographic situation becomes. There's no other way to say it, they're in a nosedive and about to reach terminal velocity.

"That's why Peshkov isn't going to stop. He and the Kremlin can read the writing on the wall. It's over for them. If they don't push, and push hard, Russia is finished. Worse still, it will have happened on their watch."

Conroy could feel the knot tightening in his stomach. "Making it all the more likely that they'll employ nuclear weapons to forestall that outcome."

Slowly, Maggie nodded. "That's the lens we need to be looking at all of this through. It's also why we need to be so damn careful. The Russians' backs are against the wall. One wrong move, and they'll take us right down with them."

CHAPTER 38

Harvath left Ashby and Palmer to keep an eye on things in Saint-Jean-Cap-Ferrat. If anything went sideways for Inessa, or Eva for that matter, he wanted people in place who could step in immediately.

Hopping into the G-Wagon, he and Grechko caught a ride back to the safehouse with Haney and Staelin.

Hearing them arrive, Sølvi stepped out of the villa. She was glad to see him back. "How'd it go?"

"Excellent," he replied, giving her a quick kiss and letting his hand linger against her hip. "Phase One complete."

"Congratulations," she said, as much to Harvath as to Grechko, who had climbed out of the Mercedes and was walking by, still smiling.

"Thank you," the Russian responded. "I wonder if we have any champagne in the house. I feel like celebrating."

"No champagne until we all get back," Staelin ordered.

"Yeah, it's bad luck," said Haney. "We wait until the mission's over. Then cigars, champagne, whatever anybody wants."

Looking at his watch, Harvath said to his teammates, "On the road in fifteen, okay?"

"Roger that," the two men replied as they headed inside with Grechko, leaving Harvath and Sølvi alone together outside.

"You must be pleased with how things went," she said.

"I am," Harvath replied. "The moment she saw him, I knew what her answer was going to be."

Sølvi smiled. "True love."

Harvath smiled back. "Now all I have to do is pull off one more magic trick, and then we can catch our breath."

"How can I help?"

He loved her for asking and had no doubt that if there had been something he needed, she would have stepped up and done it without hesitation.

"You," he replied, giving her another kiss, "don't need to do anything. I've got a pack of extremely hungry wolves, all waiting to be set loose. Just focus on Grechko and what you need to get done. We can talk about next steps when I get back."

They shared one more kiss before heading into the villa. Sølvi went down to ready the debriefing room while Harvath walked back to the library to catch up with Nicholas.

"How's everything looking in Monaco?" he asked.

As the dogs stood up to greet him, he spent a couple of moments scratching them behind the ears before coming around the desk to look at the little man's monitors. On them were multiple CCTV feeds.

"Tsybulsky is at his poker table in the Monte Carlo casino," Nicholas answered, "and his boat is being actively gawked at by a small crowd in Port Hercule."

"Where's Preisler?"

"When Barton pulled into port, he helped berth their boat, then grabbed a cab and took up a surveillance position outside the casino. He'll let us know as soon as Tsybulsky leaves."

"Sounds like everything's right on schedule," said Harvath. "Well done."

"Before you go, we really should discuss a plan B."

"Tsybulsky's boat is never going to make it back to Saint-Jean-Cap-Ferrat."

"But what if it does?" Nicholas pushed. "What's the plan? You'll have to take him before he reaches his house. Once he's inside, the degree of difficulty skyrockets again."

Harvath placed his hand on his friend's shoulder. "We discussed this. It needs to happen in Monaco. Doing it in France isn't an option. We're going to make it work. Trust me."

Nicholas didn't agree, but it wasn't his decision to make. Shaking his head, he replied, "You're the team leader."

He knew his friend didn't approve, but he had made up his mind. Changing the subject, he asked, "Can you show me where Barton and the commandos will be waiting?"

The little man pulled up a map of the Port Hercule harbor and highlighted where the boat was moored. He then indicated where Haney and Staelin would be dropping him before proceeding to their rendezvous point with Preisler, near the casino.

After going through everything else on his list, Harvath had Nicholas walk through it with him one more time. He wanted to make sure that they hadn't overlooked anything.

When he was confident that they had it all covered, he said, "It looks like we're good to go."

Nicholas nodded. "If there's anything else you need, I'll be right in your ear."

It brought Harvath back to their earlier discussion when they were returning from the caretaker's cottage. There was definitely something else he was going to need, but not just yet. That particular item could wait.

Saying goodbye to his friend, he retreated to his room to grab a couple of items before walking back outside to where Haney and Staelin were already waiting for him.

Staelin unzipped the oblong backpack they had prepared for him and Haney walked him through all of its contents. In addition to the wet suit and snorkeling gear that had been purchased in nearby Beaulieu-sur-Mer, there were gloves, a robust multi-tool, a diver's headlamp with multicolored lenses, a fistful of plastic zip ties, and, most important of all, a handful of the HEL-STAR marker lights the team used on their helmets to recognize each other in the dark.

Completely waterproof, the lights had built in tie-down points and could be run for hours in infrared mode. They were exactly what he needed and would be absolutely critical.

Placing the rest of his gear into the pack, he zipped it up, and nodded at his teammates.

This was it. It was now time to head up the coast for Phase Two.

CHAPTER 39

Monaco

They dropped Harvath along the appropriately named Quai des Etats-Unis and let him walk the rest of the way.

Slinging his pack, he skirted the edge of the glittering, horseshoe-shaped harbor and took in the evening air, which had grown considerably cooler.

He saw everything from small sailboats, no bigger than twenty-five feet long, to massive megayachts, which were over three hundred feet.

It was good to see that in the billionaire's playground of Monaco, Port Hercule still had room for the little guy.

The boat the CIA had helped arrange was right where Nicholas had said it would be. Painted graphite black, the thirty-eight-foot BRABUS Shadow 900 looked like a long, sharp knife bobbing gently on the surface of the water.

Its twin Mercury Marine V-8 four-stroke engines were capable of speeds over 60 knots. Its supercar-style helm included a sophisticated touchscreen information display, which provided the boat's main navigation, G-shock monitoring, engine management, multiple driving-assist features, and, similar to inflight systems, supported passenger screens with current speed, air temperature, and water depth.

From the hand-stitched leather seating to its blacked-out chrome, the craft was both sleek and luxurious. It was immediately obvious to Harvath why this was the same company famous for taking already high-end Mercedes-Benz vehicles to the next level.

Hopping on board, he shook hands with Barton and the two Ukrainian commandos, Max and Petro, before getting a quick update.

To help them track and target Tsybulsky's vessel, Harvath had volunteered to slip into the water and attach the HEL-STAR marker lights with zip ties. Barton, however, was worried about the distance Harvath would have to swim.

"I'm not saying you can't do it," he stated. "I'm just asking why you would want to. Even with a wet suit."

Part of his development as a team leader had been learning when to listen and when to speak. He had a lot of experience, but it didn't mean he had cornered the market on good ideas. That had already been proven in the short amount of time they'd been in France.

"What are you thinking?" he asked.

Opening his tablet, Barton pulled up satellite imagery of the harbor and walked Harvath through his idea. "If you can make it to this point, we can trail a rope as we head out of the port. You grab on to it and we'll tow you until we get just beyond the last pier. Then we'll bring you aboard and nobody will be any the wiser."

Barton was using his head. There were more than a few cameras around Port Hercule. Like Ring doorbell cams, they had become ubiquitous on even the smallest of vessels. If Harvath got into or out of the water anyplace other than their boat, there was a good chance it was going to be captured on video.

Even though he could keep his mask on, he knew that it was best to avoid being recorded whenever possible. If that meant swimming farther than he preferred or treading in cold water waiting to be picked up, that would always be the best way to go. Now all he had to decide was which option he wanted to take.

Examining the image and calculating the distances and time in the water, Harvath weighed his options. Then his phone, along with Barton's, chimed. Someone had added a message to the team's encrypted group text. It was from Preisler. Tsybulsky had cashed in his chips early and was on the move.

Harvath and Barton both looked at each other and said the same word in unison: "Fuck."

They then looked back down at the tablet. Harvath used his fingers to move the imagery around until he found what he was looking for.

Zooming in, he said, "Right here. The gas dock. I'll dump off the port side."

"What am I supposed to tell them?" Barton asked. "We stopped there on the way in and already fueled up."

"You'll come up with something," he replied, opening his backpack and pulling out everything he needed. "Let's get moving."

Within minutes, Barton was ready to go. As Harvath got into his wet suit and prepped the rest of his gear, Barton activated the running lights, fired up the engines, and, after making sure all systems were functioning, had the commandos cast off the lines.

Moving toward the gas dock, he radioed Nicholas a SITREP to bring him up to speed on what they were doing. Phase Two had officially begun.

The gas dock was not its own stand-alone structure. It was at the end of a long pier and resembled the crosspiece on the letter *T*.

Barton slowed as he neared and placed his engines in neutral. Glancing toward the stern, he caught a glimpse of Harvath as he slipped over the side and entered the water without making a sound.

CHAPTER 40

With each stroke, Harvath was reminded of the pain he felt throughout his body. *This is what you get,* he thought to himself. This is what happens when you're the first to volunteer for everything.

He didn't need to be doing this part of the operation. Technically, he could have "volunteered" Barton, or any of the other guys, for it. But that wasn't who he was. And maybe that was his problem.

It was one thing to not ask the members of your team to do anything you yourself wouldn't do. That was called leadership. It was something else entirely to never ask them to do the hard things because you were too busy doing them yourself.

Not allowing people to undertake difficult tasks was not only selfish, but also robbed them of the opportunity to better themselves. Trusting people to perform to the best of their ability, and then letting them do so, was likewise part of leadership. As he swam, he wondered if that was a lesson he should more tightly embrace. It certainly couldn't hurt to explore.

Pushing the pain and ruminations from his mind, he focused on his objective and, kicking his flippers even harder, picked up the pace.

The harbor stretched for over forty acres and had enough berths for seven hundred vessels. Had Barton not gotten him as close as he had to Tsybulsky's boat, he would have been swimming for a good ten or fifteen minutes longer.

Moving silently past the hulls of the enormous yachts was like threading his way through a pod of giant steel beasts, sleeping in the cold, dark water. As they groaned against their moorings, he could feel the vibrations ripple across his body. There was an otherworldliness, an eeriness to it all.

The quiet, black stillness of the harbor, however, soon receded as he closed in on Tsybulsky's vessel.

Gathered along the pier, groups of people gawked and took pictures, making enough noise to echo off the neighboring boats. They added a layer of audible camouflage to Harvath's approach. They also helped keep the crew distracted—something absolutely critical to his mission as the LED hull lights had been activated and were illuminating the water around the yacht's stern. The stern area was where he needed to zip-tie the HEL-STARs.

The Tecnomar for Lamborghini 63 was designed with an open tail and a series of steps that ended right above the water level. The final step was its widest and functioned as the swim platform. Beneath it, at both the port and starboard edges, was another design element—a trio of narrow carbon-fiber tubes. Painted red, white, and green to honor the car manufacturer's Italian heritage, they resembled pool railings. They were the only attachment points he could access from the water.

Knowing Tsybulsky could be back at any moment, he worked fast. After three deep breaths to saturate his lungs with oxygen, he took a final breath and soundlessly slipped beneath the surface.

The LED hull lights pushed illumination from the stern outward, so he ducked under the middle of the boat and swam aft. The lights were so bright, he didn't even need his headlamp.

While being careful not to be illuminated or to cast a shadow, he pulled one marker light at a time from the mesh bag at his waist and zip-tied them in place to the outermost tube on the port side. After activating them in IR mode, he swam back to where he had started, quietly broke the surface, and filled his lungs once more with air.

Once he was ready, he slipped back underwater and repeated the process, this time on the starboard side.

Satisfied with the job that he had done and confident that the HEL-STARs were securely in place, he swam away from Tsybulsky's boat and out toward the middle of the harbor, where Barton would be picking him up.

Using his pain as motivation, he leaned into it and propelled himself with as much speed as his legs and his flippers would muster.

Several minutes later, when he arrived at the rendezvous point, he activated his own HEL-STAR and waited for the team to detect his IR beam through their night vision. It didn't take long. Soon enough, he could hear the rumble of the big V-8s as the BRABUS Shadow approached.

As they slowly moved past, one of the commandos tossed him a line. Harvath grabbed hold and pulled himself up close against the hull as Barton piloted the craft toward the mouth of the harbor.

Even though his muscles were tired and he was dipping into his reserves to maintain his grip, it felt good to no longer have to be kicking. All he had to do was hang on a little longer.

The moment they cleared the final dock, Barton put the BRABUS in neutral and they pulled Harvath aboard. As he pulled off his mask and fins, one of the Ukrainians tossed him a towel. He was halfway out of his wet suit when Barton put the boat back in gear and headed for the open ocean. They needed to be in place and all set up before Tsybulsky passed.

Because of the contours of the coast, the most direct route back to Saint-Jean-Cap-Ferrat was a straight line that resembled traveling from two o'clock to seven o'clock across a watch face.

Charting this course, Tsybulsky would exit the harbor, point his yacht southwest, and move parallel to Monaco's shoreline before being taken out into deeper water as he crossed the Golfe de Saint-Hospice. It was Harvath's job to make sure he didn't get that far.

Out of the wet suit and back in dry clothes, he joined Barton at the helm where he focused on the touchscreens—particularly the digital navigation features. He wanted a precise picture of the boat's exact location at all times.

Activating the BRABUS's electronic chart plotter, he pulled up the port at Saint-Jean-Cap-Ferrat and activated it as their destination. Tsybulsky's captain had likely done the same and it would allow them to better anticipate his movements.

Harvath watched as Max and Petro assembled their equipment. He recognized the Accuracy International AX50 ELR from having seen it at the caretaker's cottage. It was a .50 BMG (Browning Machine Gun), extremely long-range antimatériel rifle. Weighing in at almost twenty-eight pounds, the weapon boasted impressively low recoil and incredible accuracy. It was capable of taking out targets at an effective range of 2,500 meters, or more than twenty-seven football fields away.

The fact that it fired the high-explosive incendiary/armor-piercing projectile known as the Raufoss Mk 211 only further endeared the weapon to his heart. The round was manufactured by a Finnish-Norwegian company called Nammo, and the word *raufoss* was Norwegian for "red waterfall." A pretty good omen in his book.

Topping it all off, the rifle had been outfitted with an AWC Thor Turbodyne titanium suppressor, a Schmidt & Bender scope, and a HISS-XLR ThermoSight. The entire package probably cost more than most people's cars.

As the commandos continued to ready their gear, Harvath scrolled through the digital navigation system.

Pointing to a spot up ahead, he drew Barton's attention to the map and said, "X marks the spot. This is where we're going to do it."

CHAPTER 41

Lined with plush cushions, the bow of the BRABUS was designed as a luxurious, oversized sun pad. It was a far cry from the cold, unforgiving landscapes Max and Petro usually found themselves in—more like the Ritz than a sniper's perch. Despite the incongruity, they hauled their equipment forward and began setting up their new "office."

After Max's rifle, the only thing nearly as expensive on board were two pairs of thermal binoculars from Newcon Optik. They were like pieces of alien technology. The devices could see through smoke, fog, and countless forms of camouflage. They also had built-in laser range-finders that could measure distance, azimuth, and inclination for far-off targets—all necessary features for Petro, who was the team's spotter and would be helping Max zero in on Tsybulsky.

For Harvath, however, there was one additional feature that was critical to the mission's success. Everything seen by the binoculars could be recorded and then exported to a peripheral device, such as an iPhone, and subsequently uploaded anywhere—including to social media.

Standing at the darkened stern of the BRABUS, he peered through his binoculars. Scanning the yachts leaving Port Hercule, he searched for the telltale pulses of infrared light from the HEL-STARs he had attached to Tsybulsky's vessel.

There was an intermittent breeze, and Harvath could feel the boat begin to roll beneath his feet. A light swell had formed. Max and Petro already had a highly complex and difficult ask. Any change in the environment, no matter how small, was only going to make their job harder.

The team was wearing noise-reduction headsets with boom microphones connected to their individual radios. When Harvath identified Tsybulsky's Lamborghini 63, *Hermes,* exiting the harbor, he gave the team the heads-up.

While examining the yacht earlier in the day, he hadn't noticed a FLIR camera that would allow its crew night-vision capability. That didn't mean that there wasn't one, perhaps cleverly incorporated somewhere into the vessel's design. There was also the possibility that they had a handheld unit of some sort like what Harvath was using. But even if they did, there was no reason to have it out unless there was an emergency. Just to be safe, Max and Petro had covered themselves with a Predator brand, spectralflage ghillie blanket, which helped reduce both their IR and thermal signatures.

Harvath's hope had been to point the BRABUS perpendicular to the shore, and to engage the *Hermes* as she passed in front of their bow. Not only would it give Max a good, clean profile shot with the .50-cal, but if he missed, the coastline in this area was nothing but concrete seawall and rocky cliff face. There was no worry that any errant rounds would strike and kill innocent bystanders.

All of that was for naught, however, when he saw what Tsybulsky's boat did next, forcing him to recalibrate.

Instead of a nice, leisurely cruise back to Saint-Jean-Cap-Ferrat, someone had decided to drop the hammer.

There was a roar as the throttles were pushed forward and the enormous V-12 engines leapt to life, like a pair of lions being released from a cage.

"We're going to have to chase him," Harvath stated over the radio.

"Roger that," Barton replied. "Everybody hang on."

That Tsybulsky might come out of Port Hercule and decide to put the pedal to the metal had been on Harvath's list of possibilities. The *Hermes* was a Lamborghini, after all. You didn't spend millions of dollars on a yacht like that if you didn't enjoy speed.

Harvath had no idea why the Russian hadn't stayed longer at the casino, and he didn't care. All he knew was that they needed to keep the man in their sights. *Literally.* Leaving the BRABUS's running lights extinguished, Barton gave chase.

Lying on a floating platform, correcting for wind, while trying to time the up and down of swells, all in order to shoot at a boat as it passed by, was already a monumental undertaking.

Now, however, Max and Petro were going to have to pull it off while speeding after said boat. What's more, their shots would no longer be focused on the side of the yacht, but rather its tail.

Harvath had been concerned that it could come down to this, which was another reason why he had attached the infrared marker lights. Not only would they help positively identify Tsybulsky's boat, but they could also help dictate the area within which Max would have to deliver his rounds. Petro knew how far above the waterline to instruct Max to be aiming to effectively hit their target. The HEL-STARs allowed him to establish dead center.

The pain-in-the-ass factor in all of this, though, was how fast they were moving. To be fair, once the BRABUS had popped out of the "hole" and was up on plane, the craft was a lot more stable. But it was far from perfect. Speed could be a real hindrance to accuracy.

The other issue, which the commandos couldn't be bothered with, was that they were now running parallel to the coastline. If one of their shots went wide, someone on the water ahead of Tsybulsky could be killed.

Harvath tried not to think about it. Right now, he had one eye glued to the navigation screen and their GPS location. The biggest problem with the *Hermes* going like a bat out of hell was that they were very quickly going to leave the territorial waters of Monaco and be back in France. The commandos needed to start slinging lead.

"Light 'em up," Harvath ordered over the team's headsets. "Send it!"

Seconds later, the first round from the antimatériel rifle screamed out of the suppressed barrel and rocketed toward the stern of the *Hermes*.

It was perfectly placed and tore right through the rear sun pad area, which covered the engine compartment.

Petro radioed that they had scored a direct hit and then began helping Max set up his next shot.

Once again the heavy rifle fired, and once again they scored another direct hit. Peering into his thermal binoculars, Petro walked Max through his next shot, which, thanks to a sudden rise in the bow, went straight through the Lamborghini's cockpit and shattered its windshield.

Harvath watched through his binoculars as pandemonium erupted on board the *Hermes*. Smoke was pouring out of her manifolds and her engine compartment. More importantly, she was slowing down.

Aware that they were under attack from the rear, several of Tsybulsky's men appeared at the yacht's stern, armed with automatic weapons, and began firing.

"Get us as close to them as you can," Harvath told Barton, concerned that they were quickly running out of territorial runway.

Hailing Max, who had fired his two last shots and was now inserting a fresh magazine, he told the sniper to keep putting rounds on the *Hermes*. He didn't need to tell Petro that it was now his time to shine.

No longer concerned about remaining hidden, the commando cast off the camouflage blanket and moved quickly back to the cockpit area of the BRABUS.

Flipping open the lid of a rectangular storm case, he punched several buttons, activating the device inside, and then flashed Harvath the thumbs-up.

Looking through his binos again, Harvath could see not only that the red waterfall rounds had disabled the Lamborghini's V-12 engines, but also that the engine compartment was actively on fire. Crew members sprayed fire extinguishers into the space, trying to put out the flames.

Worried that Tsybulsky's people might have already radioed for help and, seeing that they were almost at the maritime border with France, Harvath slapped the helm's console and commanded Barton to go faster.

The former SEAL gave Max a warning up front and then sliced out of the yacht's wake, pushing the throttles as far forward as they would go.

As the BRABUS's deep V-hull cut through the waves, Harvath counted down the remaining distance on the GPS, finally ordering Barton to come to a stop.

"This is it. We launch here," he stated. "Petro. You're up!"

As the commando used a set of nylon straps to lift the device out of its case and lower it into the water, his colleague had readjusted himself at the bow and was firing anew at the *Hermes*. Little did Tsybulsky or his men know that something much worse than high-explosive incendiary/ armor-piercing rounds was headed their way.

The unmanned surface vehicle, or USV for short, that Max and Petro had brought with them was something new. It was similar to the jet-ski-based, waterborne drones that had proven so effective against the warships in Russia's Black Sea fleet, but smaller. Called a *Vodyanyk* and based on a reworked sea scooter known as SEABOB, it packed a considerable payload and was quite fast.

Not fast enough, however, to catch a vessel that was underway at speed. Ukraine's USVs were meant to target ships that were either docked or moving quite slowly. That was why Tsybulsky's boat needed to be stopped before they could send the USV after it.

"Twenty seconds to contact," Petro announced, using a ruggedized tablet to remotely pilot the *Vodyanyk*. "Fifteen . . ."

Harvath watched through his binoculars, digitally recording everything.

As Petro announced, "Impact in five, four, three . . ." all eyes were on the *Hermes*. When the explosive-laden USV rammed into it, the detonation was instantaneous.

As a roiling fireball climbed into the night sky, the shock wave from the enormous blast sent a wall of water all the way out to the BRABUS, soaking everyone on board.

Minutes later, putting their boat in gear, Harvath and the team piloted through the flaming wreckage of the *Hermes,* making sure everyone was dead.

There were no survivors. Everything had happened in Monaco's territorial waters. Nothing had crossed the line into France. The operation had been a success.

CHAPTER 42

"You're a bad Muslim," the young man stated. He was seated behind a laptop covered with stickers acquired at French hacking conferences. "We never see you at mosque anymore."

"You know I changed mosques," MoMo replied.

"Yes. Allegedly, you go to the same one as my cousin. I asked him, but he says he hasn't seen you in months."

"I've been busy."

"Too busy for Allah?"

MoMo held up his hand. He wasn't interested in rhetorical questions. "Amir, please. I didn't come here for a lecture."

"Correct. You came for my help. And that's what I'm giving you. I don't want you to lose your way."

"I'm not going to lose my way."

"Says the brother who no longer goes to mosque."

In the interest of getting what he wanted, MoMo relented. "If I promise to go to mosque this week, will you shut up and help me?"

"How many *times* this week?" the other man asked.

MoMo was losing his patience. "You know what? Forget it. Instead, I'm going to go back to my office and tell the DGSI that I saw someone moving a bunch of bomb-making equipment in here."

"Into my *mother's* home? How dare you."

"Give it a rest, Amir. You and I both know your mom moved back to Morocco three years ago. Which means you're not only squatting in this rent-controlled apartment, but I bet if I looked into it, your mom is still collecting social assistance funds. Funds meant for *residents* of France. So let me ask you, does she have direct deposit, or do you cash her checks and send the money directly back to Rabat?"

The young man shook his head. "As I said, you're a bad Muslim."

"With apologies to you and Allah, peace be upon him, I'm also a French citizen. And as such, I have a duty to uphold the oath I swore when I joined the DGSI. You took a similar oath, remember?"

Amir did remember. He had been a highly skilled cyber specialist for the Agence nationale de la sécurité des systèmes d'information, or ANSSI for short, where he worked in the national cyber incident-response center. But despite his pious pose, Amir loved money, which was why he had allowed himself to be wooed out of government service by a French company at the forefront of artificial intelligence.

MoMo didn't begrudge him the move. For a handful of kids in their old neighborhood, computers were their way out. While other children were practicing their soccer skills, dreaming of becoming professional athletes, MoMo and Amir were learning how to program and code.

As his frustration with cracking Brunelle's flash drive had continued to build, he had thought of Amir—especially in light of the successes they'd had in using the AI software to track the initial movements of Jadot's killer. He'd also gotten a taste of being in the field and he liked it.

If he were being honest, the fact that he still hadn't been able to track down the Russians' getaway vehicle, the one they'd fled Seine-Saint-Denis in after torching their stolen Peugeot, was also weighing on his mind. He wanted to prove he had good investigative instincts and that he should be entrusted with more fieldwork.

All of that was what had brought him to the little apartment in Paris's posh 7th arrondissement. How Amir's mother had finagled her way into it was beyond him. A stone's throw from Napoleon's tomb and the Rodin museum, the unit couldn't have been situated in a more perfect location.

"Your uncle wouldn't agree with how you're comporting yourself," Amir stated, attempting a stab at his conscience.

"And my father wouldn't agree with you and your mother ripping off the French taxpayer," MoMo replied, parrying the blow. "So let's just leave our families out of this and focus on the reason I'm here."

With an almost imperceptible tilt of his head, Amir conceded the point. He knew what he and his mother were up to. It wasn't just wrong, it was illegal. Flagging him as a potential terrorist was probably the least of the things MoMo could do to make his life a living hell. He decided that discretion was the better part of valor, especially when it came to someone he had grown up with in the old neighborhood.

"Fair enough," said Amir. "Did you bring the device with you?"

Pulling it out of his pocket, MoMo handed it over.

The other man looked at it in disbelief. "Somebody stored national security information on a flash drive disguised as a key fob? You've got to be kidding me."

"Pretty clever if you ask me," MoMo replied. "Probably the last place anyone searching for national security information would ever look."

Amir plugged it into his laptop's USB adapter and logged into his work account. "Let's see what we've got."

"You can use your Sirocco program to break it, right?"

"As long as we do it before Sirocco becomes fully sentient and destroys all of humanity," Amir joked, playing upon the public fear of his company's new large-language-model chatbot.

Capable of self-improvement, Sirocco was revolutionary in the AI field. It possessed the ability to evolve on its own, independent of humans. Getting "smarter" solely by being asked questions was no longer its modus operandi. Sirocco now actively sought out information, broadening its intelligence.

Where it was really making strides was in math—one of the biggest weaknesses in AI models. And one of the ultimate puzzles to be solved with math was encryption. It was rumored that Amir's company had cracked the global gold standard: AES-192 encryption.

It was a feat that even the biggest supercomputers could never achieve. Now, with a laptop and access to the right software, it might be banged out in a matter of moments.

"You're lucky," Amir stated. "Whoever encrypted this key fob was good, really good, but he wasn't perfect."

"Meaning?"

"He didn't anticipate me, and Sirocco, cracking his flash drive."

Turning his laptop around, he showed MoMo what he had done. "We're in."

CHAPTER 43

"Jesus, MoMo," Brunelle exclaimed as she looked at her screen. "What the hell did you unlock?"

"Pretty messed-up, right?"

Normally, she wouldn't have allowed anyone from work to come to her apartment, but MoMo had insisted. *Emphatically.* And now she understood why. He had done so with very good reason.

"Has anyone else seen these?" she asked.

"Only my friend Amir. But he's okay. He used to be with ANSSI."

Brunelle immediately reached for her phone. "Auberge 71322," she said when her call was answered. "I need a button and fade from the following location."

Looking at MoMo, she stated, "Give me the name, address, and a physical description of your friend."

Unnerved, but understanding the urgency, MoMo complied.

"Do you know if he's armed?"

MoMo shook his head. "I don't know."

"Full tactical team," Brunelle said into her phone. "They have priority. Make sure we get his laptop and any digital storage devices. I don't care how messy it gets. If anyone steps in your way, flatten them."

MoMo was aghast. Brunelle didn't care. "He accessed his company cloud?" she asked. "While in control of the flash drive?"

"Yes," the young man admitted, "but I didn't think this was going to—"

Brunelle cut him off as she continued to relay information over the phone. "We're also going to need to do a full lockdown on the subject's place of business. Shut off the power and kill their generators. I want all internet access disabled. This is going to be a political firestorm, so call in every single one of our lawyers. I'll be in the command center as soon as I can get there."

"Don't do this," MoMo implored. "I grew up with Amir. He's a good person."

"He could be a *great* person for all I care. Right now, none of that matters. All I'm concerned with is containing what may have leapt out of the Pandora's box you just opened."

"Wasn't opening it my job?"

"For fuck's sake, MoMo," Brunelle replied. "Your job was to *unlock* it. Not to read through all of it. You know that. Opening it was *my* job."

He was ashamed. "You're right," he admitted. "I'd hit a wall on the flash drive and thought that this might help move us forward."

"It's a huge breakthrough," she said, softening her tone. "But in the future, things need to be contained within DGSI. When sensitive material escapes into the wild, recovery efforts can get quite feral."

"Will Amir be okay?" he asked. "He was only doing me a favor. He didn't intend to do anything wrong."

Brunelle was about to respond when she heard the sharp *chirp chirp* of a police Klaxon downstairs announcing that her ride had arrived.

"Your friend's going to be fine," she ended up saying. Gathering what she needed, she herded MoMo toward the door.

"What about me?" he asked as she kept pushing him toward the stairwell.

"Keep your mouth shut. Don't touch your phone until I call you. And if you reach out to your friend Amir and tell him we're coming," Brunelle warned, "I'll kill you myself."

CHAPTER 44

S omeone could have dropped an atom bomb on the driveway behind him and Harvath would have kept on walking into the villa, and heading straight for the bar. Right now all he cared about was Sølvi and a glass of bourbon. Everyone else, especially his blackmailers at the CIA, could go fuck themselves.

As he passed the library, Nicholas looked up from his desk, but even the dogs seemed to know better than to engage. Something about Harvath had changed. He had brought a piece of the operation back with him. A bad piece.

Hitting the bar, Harvath grabbed the first bottle he saw, snatched up a glass, and headed out to the terrace.

Not long after, Sølvi came up from the basement debriefing room and, realizing that he was home, followed him outside.

As she passed the library, Nicholas caught her attention and tried to wave her off. "He needs space," the little man said.

Sølvi smiled, ignored his advice, and kept walking. Stepping out onto the terrace, she found Harvath on one of the chaise lounges and sat down next to him.

The greatest thing about their relationship was that most of the time they didn't need words. With a look, they could tell what the other was thinking. That said, this wasn't one of those times. The moment required a modicum of communication.

"Should I be concerned that you went right for the bourbon instead of the champagne?" she asked.

Head back, eyes closed, he took a sip of his drink and replied, "I think I'm out."

"Of what?"

"Everything."

Interesting, she thought.

Nudging him for his glass, she took a long, slow sip and allowed her fingers to linger over his as she handed it back.

"What about the name Grechko has for you? The last person supposedly responsible for your wife's murder?"

Taking another sip of his drink, he replied, "Maybe I'll give it to Johnson. It was his idea, after all, to go after Tsybulsky. And he was right. It was a good idea. Not to mention that Johnson's like the Terminator. We may make fun of how much stuff he breaks in the process, but he never stops until his target has been flatlined."

Sølvi didn't doubt it. Johnson was intense. He was the axe murderer of the group. No matter how many times you thought he was down, he always got back up. To this day, she still couldn't believe that he was married to a lovely woman who worked in a children's bookstore.

The idea that she was putting books in innocent little hands while he was out putting bullets in bad guys' heads was a circle that took a little work to square. Nevertheless, they were very happy together.

Which brought Sølvi back to Harvath. Outsourcing a job like this, regardless of how competent Johnson was, didn't sound like him. He had sworn to make every person pay for his wife's murder. Now, with one name left, he was going to walk away? No, that definitely didn't sound like him.

"You're not really going to give this to Johnson," she said.

"Of course not," Harvath responded. "I'll crawl into the darkest cave in the coldest, most remote corner of Siberia if I have to. Believe me, I am going to find this guy and I am going to take him apart. I'd just like a couple of days off before I do. Even my eyelids feel like sandpaper."

Stress, anger, exhaustion . . . it was all there. And rightfully so. He'd been through a lot.

There was also his sense of humor, which she was grateful to see. It was an important part of how he healed and processed things.

"You mentioned Tsybulsky," she said, changing the subject. "Ready to fill me in?"

Opening his eyes, Harvath picked up his phone and checked his flight-tracker app. The private jet that was returning the commandos to England was only minutes away from leaving French airspace. "Just about," he replied, standing up. "Where's Grechko? You're both going to want to see this."

"We're taking a break from his debrief," she answered. "I think he's in the kitchen getting something to eat."

"Perfect. Let's get Nicholas and that bottle of champagne. We're about to have reason to celebrate."

CHAPTER 45

As Harvath opened a bottle of Ruinart Blanc de Blancs and filled four glasses, Nicholas had his laptop on the counter and kept refreshing a Telegram account called Stratkom ZSU. It was a Ukrainian military channel, approved by the army high command, that was known for breaking news about successful military operations, especially when they could include spectacular video. And in this particular instance, they really did have some spectacular video.

The understanding with the Ukrainians was that they wouldn't publish the Tsybulsky story until the jet with their commandos had successfully left France. Once it had, the post went live.

Grechko was floored. He'd had no idea what Harvath and his team were planning. Right up until this moment he had believed that they were going to fake Inessa's disappearance and help smuggle her back to Norway.

"My God," he stated. "Tsybulsky's dead?"

Harvath raised his glass and clinked it against the defector's. "Problem solved. Congratulations."

Sølvi nodded approvingly at Harvath. "Well done," she stated, clinking glasses with him.

"Don't look at me," he replied, smiling. "From what I'm hearing, it was the Ukrainians."

"Carried out just off the coast of Monaco. Very clever," said Grechko. "The principality provides little to no support to Ukraine and is quite limited in conducting any sort of investigation. You averted an international incident and gave the Ukrainians a very high-profile win."

"I have no idea what you're talking about," Harvath responded, taking another sip of his champagne. "But I will say this—I hope the Norwegians are paying you a lot of money. From the little bit I saw, Inessa has excellent, and expensive, taste."

The Russian grinned from ear to ear. "It doesn't matter. Now that Tsybulsky's dead, she's rich."

"She's in his will?"

"No. In order to avoid sanctions, he put all of his foreign holdings in Inessa's name."

Now all of the shell companies out of Cyprus that Holidae Hayes had found made sense. "Please tell her I'm sorry about the boat," said Harvath.

Grechko laughed. "I'm sure it's insured."

"So the estate on Saint-Jean-Cap-Ferrat is hers too?" Sølvi asked.

"Plus the chalet in Switzerland, and the flat in London, and a penthouse in New York City. She's going to need a team of accountants to sort it all out, but she'll have no problem affording them. Her life has just taken a dramatic turn."

"To the perfect crime," said Nicholas, raising his glass. "Za zda-ró-vye."

"Za zda-ró-vye," they all replied.

When Nicholas excused himself to go walk the dogs, Harvath topped off their glasses and suggested that Grechko join him and Sølvi on the terrace. He wanted to get this next piece of business finished.

They took seats around a glass table and, without wasting time on small talk, Harvath got right to the point.

"I believe you have a name and a location for me," he said.

Grechko took a long, slow sip of his champagne. "I assume you're familiar with a unit of Russian military intelligence referred to only by a number. 29155?"

Harvath nodded. "I am."

"Their missions include assassinations, sabotage, and other covert activities—like interfering in elections and fomenting riots—aimed at destabilizing foreign countries, particularly those in Europe. They were responsible for the poisoning and attempted murder of Sergei Skripal and his daughter, Yulia, in the UK. Skripal was a former GRU officer who had become a double agent for MI6."

"They used a nerve agent," said Harvath. "Novichok."

"Correct. They used that same nerve agent on Alexei Navalny. They've also used a radioactive material called polonium-210. This is in addition to all the other tools of the dark arts—guns, knives, garrote wires, rooftops, and open windows. They can be highly sophisticated and also downright brutish. They can also be sloppy. And that's where the name I have for you comes in."

"I'm listening."

"Perhaps it was a product of being based in Europe and being so far away from Moscow, but the unit got careless. Several members were caught on CCTV footage. Several more didn't change cell phones often enough, which allowed their movements to be tracked. Missions had to be scrapped. Assignments were abandoned. The powers that be back at the GRU were not only angry, but also embarrassed, which only made them more angry. They decided to send in a man named Colonel Ivan Kapralov.

"Kapralov had served with Spetsnaz GRU in both the Second Chechen War and the Russo-Ukraine War. In both actions, he tortured, maimed, and killed a lot of people. Men, women, children, the elderly—you name it. For his service, he was awarded Hero of the Russian Federation.

"He was loathed within the GRU. His fellow intelligence officers wanted him out of the building and as far away from them as possible. As he had earned 'preferred status' from the Kremlin, he was put in charge of unit 29155, and sent off to Europe. When it came time to prepare the operation to snatch you from the United States and bring you back to Russia, Colonel Kapralov was put in charge of selecting the team and drawing up the mission plan. He authored the rules of engagement, which called for any witnesses to be killed."

"Including my wife," responded Harvath, his jaw tight.

Grechko nodded.

"Where do I find him?"

"They're based near Paris. Six of them in a safehouse. The location changes every couple of months."

"Do you have an address?"

The Russian shook his head. "No," he replied. "But I have the next-best thing."

CHAPTER 46

A s her workday had begun so early, Maggie had no problem leaving the office a little before five o'clock.

Per Holidae Hayes, Scot Harvath's operation had been a success. Arkady Tsybulsky was dead.

There would be tons of Russian media reports to sift through and analyze—the most important of which would be clipped and waiting for her in the morning. Her overnight team was more than capable of handling the surge without her. If anything rose to the level of needing her personal attention, they knew where to find her.

Driving home, she parked the old Volvo in the garage, changed clothes, and hopped on her bicycle. She needed to pick up a few things for dinner and a brisk bike ride was the perfect way to clear out some of the cobwebs.

In order to avoid rush-hour traffic, she stuck to the side streets. It added a little time to her journey, but not much. She was happy for the additional physical activity.

As she pedaled, she allowed her mind to wander. There were so many things that she and Paul had been forced to put on hold or cancel since the Belarus situation had popped up—a literary festival on Nantucket, the opening of a favorite chef's new restaurant in Nashville, use of a friend's cottage in upstate New York . . .

None of them were devastating losses and they both understood the demands of her job. In times of crisis, she needed to be not just available, but also physically present. She was the leader of Russia House. That, as Paul liked to joke, was why she got paid the "big" bucks.

In all fairness, the bucks weren't that big, which was what made Paul's joke all the more amusing. Quite frankly, if not for her grandmother's disciplined investing and subsequent largesse, Maggie and Paul would never have been able to afford the kind of lifestyle they enjoyed. Their house and the large parcel it sat on were easily worth several million dollars.

That wasn't to say that having to cancel plans didn't come with a sting. It did. And even though he would never admit it, Maggie was certain that the sting was felt even more acutely by Paul. Travel was in his blood. He absolutely loved it. The bigger the trips, the better.

But the little trips had their place as well. They were escapes. Worlds away from their lives as civil servants, the sojourns functioned as release valves, allowing them to blow off steam and just be themselves. That was particularly important for Paul, who worked "in" a department rather than over one, like Maggie.

She knew that being so incredibly bright made it difficult for him to take orders from people who were less intelligent. Not that Paul ever complained. He didn't. Not once. He was an absolute stoic. But when she listened to stories about his day, she could read between the lines. It was as if she could *almost* hear him say it.

If she had to put a word on it, the trips were a reward. They were a reminder that they didn't live to work. They worked to live. And considering how many people she knew in D.C. who came home and did a swan dive right into their liquor cabinet, there were much less healthy ways than travel to deal with a job that you might not be in love with.

So, if at the moment they couldn't travel, she was determined to double down on the other things they loved and still could engage in. Chief among them was food. More to the point, it was cooking—either together, or for each other.

Paul had cooked her a fabulous breakfast this morning, only to have it be interrupted by Maggie's office. She was determined to make it up to him. To that end, she planned to make one of Paul's favorite dishes: Paella de Marisco.

The key to the perfect paella was the quality of the ingredients, especially the rice and saffron. There was a specialty butcher in McLean who not only could source excellent rabbit for when Maggie made the less well-known Paella Valencia, but also offered an outstanding selection of fresh seafood.

Knowing that she would need to keep the chicken, mussels, clams, shrimp, and any fish she purchased cold for the ride home, she had attached extra-large panniers to her bike, so that one of them could be filled with ice.

For dessert, Paul loved her crème brûlée. But instead of doing it in the traditional manner, this time she wanted to do it with a twist. Maybe cardamom and coconut or rosewater and pistachio. She'd have to see what ingredients the nearby grocery store had.

Then there was the wine. Maybe a rosé from Castilla La Mancha or a Cava from Catalonia. It would depend on what the wine store had in stock. She hoped they had something good. Paul would be happy with either of those. A nice Godello or a Verdejo would also be a terrific pick.

She was so busy contemplating her options, she failed to notice a silver minivan lurch out of its driveway, until it was too late.

Breaking hard, Maggie attempted to swerve, but slammed into the right rear quarter panel.

The impact echoed down the street as she tumbled to the pavement unconscious.

CHAPTER 47

Brunelle arrived just as the tactical team was getting ready to make entry. A plainclothes agent had quietly awakened the building's concierge and gotten the key for Amir's apartment. There would be no need for battering rams or blowing doors off hinges—although the team was prepared for such eventualities if they became necessary.

Falling in at the rear of the stack, Brunelle followed the team up the stairs. They paused just outside Amir's door.

Because this was a dynamic entry, speed, surprise, and domination were the goals.

When the team leader gave the signal, the breacher slipped the key into the lock and twisted it slowly to the left. When the lock released, he pushed the door open and stood aside, at which point the team flooded into the apartment.

They found Amir in the second of the two bedrooms, sitting in his underwear and a T-shirt at his computer. The tactical team yelled at him to get down on the floor.

Once they had him secured with flex cuffs, they slapped a piece of duct tape over his mouth, yanked a hood down over his head, and began bagging up all of his computer equipment.

Brunelle helped with the search of the apartment, making certain that the officers had also retrieved Amir's phone. From start to finish, the entire operation had taken less than six minutes.

As they prepared to leave the apartment, a call came over the radio from the plainclothes agent outside. Gibert had arrived. Brunelle told the agent that she'd be right down.

After issuing a handful of instructions to the team, she exited the building and found Gibert standing near his car.

"Plainclothes lookout," he said, nodding toward the agent. "Another in an unmarked tactical van double-parked down the street. Obviously, you're here for a party. The only question—is it about to start, or is it already over?"

"A little bit of both," Brunelle admitted as she looked at her watch. "Listen, I need a favor and I don't have a lot of time."

Gibert laughed. "Of course you do. Why else would you call me up in the middle of the night and tell me you needed to see me right away. What's the favor?"

Wanting to get out of earshot of the plainclothes agent, she asked, "Can we walk?"

The cop agreed. As they walked, he pulled a pack of cigarettes out and offered her one. She accepted. He lit hers and then his own.

Brunelle took a deep drag.

Satisfied that the plainclothes agent was far enough away, she exhaled and said, "I know why Jadot was murdered."

Gibert was stunned. "Why?"

"Powell was right."

"The CIA station chief?"

Brunelle nodded. "Remember when he said that Jadot was worried the Russians might have burrowed deep into the French government? He was spot-on. It's bad."

"How bad?"

"The Russians have spies inside the ministries of Interior, Armed Forces, Justice, Foreign Affairs, and Finance. Jadot uncovered evidence that even the DGSI and the DGSE have been compromised."

"My God," the cop exclaimed. "That is bad. *Very* bad."

"It gets worse. Jadot also implicated one of the president's closest advisors, the minister of foreign affairs. It's a shitstorm and there's not going to be an umbrella big enough to protect any of these people. Jadot found all the receipts—bank statements, money transfers, all of it."

"And this was what he was bringing to Powell? This is why he had asked for the breakfast? The one he never showed up for?"

Once again, Brunelle nodded. "Somehow, someone figured out that he was onto it and had him killed."

"With an ice axe," said Gibert. "Just like Trotsky."

"Sends a message, doesn't it? *When you cross Russia, you do so at your peril.*"

"A hell of a message," the cop agreed. Taking his cigarette out of his mouth, he picked a piece of tobacco off his tongue. "Where'd all this information come from?"

Brunelle held up the key-fob flash drive she had taken from Jadot's apartment. "From this."

"What's that?"

Taking it apart she showed him. "I removed it from Jadot's key ring."

"After lecturing *me* on professionalism? After I told *you* not to touch anything at the crime scene? Jesus, you really are a piece of work. When were you going to tell me?"

"As soon as I knew whether it had any value, which is why you're standing here right now."

"And what exactly is going on here?" he asked.

"When I figured out that the fob was a flash drive, I set MoMo loose on cracking it. When he couldn't crack it, he overstepped and, without permission, brought it to someone who could. That someone is about to be escorted out of the building with a bag over his head."

"You're taking him into custody?"

"These are exigent circumstances," she replied. "He needs to be kept someplace quiet. Someplace safe. At least until we can figure all of this out."

"Even for you, Karine, this is really pushing the outer edge."

"I'm just trying to do my job. But I can't do this part alone. Will you help me?"

The cop feigned ignorance. "Help you with what?"

"You're going to make me say it?"

"No," said Gibert, fishing for his phone, "I'm going to record you saying it. Just to cover my ass. I'm not losing my career over this."

"Can we please take two seconds and not make this about you?"

"About *me*? You're the one who's asking for a piece of crime scene evidence to be logged as if it never went astray."

"Not just logged," she replied, acutely aware that she was pushing her luck. "I'm also going to need it backdated and cataloged as having been signed out to me for analysis."

"Is that all?" Gibert dryly asked.

"Vincent, if Jadot is correct, this isn't just a colossal breach of national security, it's one of the biggest scandals in French history. If we can't use what's on that drive, then the Russians will have won."

The cop remained quiet and took another pull on his cigarette.

After several moments of uncomfortable silence, she gave in. "Okay," she said, "you're right. I shouldn't have removed the drive from the crime scene. I'm sorry. Happy?"

"No," he replied. "I'm not happy about any of this. But I am going to help you. There's just one small thing I want in return."

Brunelle didn't like the sound of that. She had little choice in the matter, however. Without Gibert's cooperation, she was dead in the water.

"Fine," she replied, as the DGSI's unmarked van rolled up and double-parked in front of the building. They were about to bring out Amir. She needed to get going. "What do you want in return?"

"It doesn't matter now," the cop replied. "When all of this is over, I'll tell you what it is. Until then, I expect you to honor your word. You keep me in the loop. Understand? The moment you track down the Russians' getaway car, or you learn anything else about Jadot's killer, I want to know about it. Are we clear?"

"Crystal," Brunelle replied.

With that behind her, she turned and moved quickly back to the tactical team. What lay ahead at the DGSI command center would be some of the most difficult and important work she had ever done. The implications of taking down so many members of the French government were practically unfathomable.

On top of that, they still needed to locate the getaway car and apprehend Jadot's killer.

As the team loaded Amir into the van, Brunelle climbed in behind him, praying that nothing came along to screw any of it up.

CHAPTER 48

The fastest high-speed train from Nice to Paris made the journey in about five and a half hours. A private jet could do it in forty-four minutes. Harvath had chosen the jet.

After some additional back-and-forth with Grechko, he had gotten Holidae Hayes on a secure call and gave her the rundown of everything he wanted. This wasn't going to be a CIA op. It wasn't, technically, even going to be a Carlton Group operation. This was a personal undertaking, but he couldn't do it without the quiet help of both organizations.

Once Hayes had confirmed his list of requests, he disconnected the call, dragged himself up to his room, and fell into bed with Sølvi.

The next morning, after checking his emails, he came downstairs to find Nicholas and Preisler cooking breakfast. Someone must have made a run to the village because there were all sorts of fresh baked goods. With a notebook tucked under his arm and a pencil behind his ear, Harvath said good morning to everyone, grabbed a cup of coffee, and stepped out onto the terrace.

Haney and Staelin, their own coffee cups in hand, were sitting at the glass table and he joined them.

"You should have stuck around last night," said Staelin. "Once we got back, we opened several more bottles of champagne."

"I appreciate you guys driving the Ukrainians back to the airport," he replied. "Sorry I didn't stay up to celebrate."

"You missed out," Haney added. "Did you know there's a tabac down in the village that sells Cubans? Johnson bought two boxes."

"You deserve it. The op was very well done." Then, changing the subject, he asked, "What's the latest from Ashby and Palmer? How are things down in Saint-Jean-Cap-Ferrat?"

"They sat on Tsybulsky's estate until just before dawn. After the news broke about the boat being blown up, security was increased on the house, a couple more guys were added at the gate, but that was it."

"And this morning?"

"Gage and Morrison went down to relieve them. Doesn't look like anything has changed. According to Nicholas, the private jet back to Russia hasn't been canceled."

That didn't surprise Harvath. Tsybulsky's security guys were likely in serious disarray. With their client missing and presumed dead, next steps would be difficult to manage. Unless they had reliable law enforcement sources within Monaco, which they probably didn't, the only information flowing their direction was what they could pull from the internet. Hopefully, Inessa had done as Grechko had instructed and had dug in her heels and was refusing to even consider leaving France under the circumstances.

Pulling out his phone, Harvath sent Eva a text, asking her to update him with any information regarding Inessa. Then he turned his attention back to his teammates.

"As long as Inessa plays her cards right, she'll be fine."

Staelin took a sip of his coffee and asked, "What about Sølvi? Any clue when she and Grechko are going to be able to go back to Norway?"

Harvath shook his head. "NIS gave her an ultimatum. They want her back ASAP. She's not ready to do that, though. Not until they've nailed the mole inside her organization. For now, she's going to remain off the radar."

"That seems like a smart move," stated Haney. "Does that mean we're staying? Because I can think of worse places to have to be a babysitter."

"It's up to you," Harvath replied, flipping open his notebook and taking the pencil from behind his ear. "I've got one more job. The CIA's station chief up in Paris is offering me some of his guys, but I don't want his guys. I want *my* guys."

"What's the job?" asked Staelin.

"One of the Russians responsible for Lara's death managed to get away and—"

"I'm in," the man said, not even waiting for Harvath to finish his sentence.

"Me too," said Haney.

This was one of the biggest reasons why Harvath did what he did. The loyalty of his teammates meant the world to him. All they needed to know was that he was going after one of his wife's killers. That was it. They didn't need to know where, or how many of the enemy would be there when they arrived. Harvath was going and so would they.

Stepping out of the villa carrying plates of food, Preisler and Johnson walked over to the table and set them down.

"What are we talking about?" asked Preisler.

"Harvath's got a lead on an additional person involved in Lara's murder," said Haney.

Johnson looked at him. "When do we leave?"

"I'm with Johnson," Preisler stated. "I'll meet you all in the driveway. I just need to grab my gear."

"Thank you," Harvath said as a sea of painful, bittersweet, and vengeful emotions churned inside him. "For the record, that was the right answer."

His teammates smiled. A couple laughed. They knew him well. Without a sense of humor, they'd all be lost.

As they ate their breakfast, Harvath jotted down a few notes. Taking these four with him to Paris, he'd be leaving five more behind to help guard the villa—Gage, Barton, Morrison, Ashby, and Palmer. Nicholas and the dogs would also stay behind, as would Sølvi and Grechko.

He didn't like cutting the team in half. If anything happened to any one of them, he wouldn't forgive himself. And if anything happened to Sølvi, he knew that would be a pain he'd be unable to bear.

But while all that was true, he also knew that he couldn't allow anyone involved in Lara's murder to go unpunished. His joke about sending Johnson had been just that—a joke. There was only one person who
could, and rightfully should, settle this score.

After finishing breakfast, he gathered his things together and went to
say goodbye to Sølvi.

Grateful for all that had been done, Grechko had agreed to start their
debrief early, which was why she had been out of bed before Harvath. He
was loath to interrupt, but she had left him a note asking him to come
find her before he left.

He knocked on the debriefing room door and waited in the basement
hallway for her to step out.

"Hey," she said, closing the door behind her and wrapping her arms
around him. "You were out cold when I woke up. How did you sleep?"

"I slept well, but not nearly long enough," he replied, giving her a kiss.

"Getting ready to leave?"

"The guys are packing up now. We're going to take two of the cars.
Barton and Gage are driving and will bring them back."

"Who's going up to Paris with you?" she asked.

Harvath rattled off the names.

Sølvi smiled. "You're taking the A-team with you."

"All ten of us are the A-team and I'm leaving you with five. You're in
good hands. Don't worry."

"Listen, I've been thinking about something."

There was something about her tone that suggested maybe he didn't
want to hear this. "Do we need to talk about it now, or can it wait?"

"I want to cancel the wedding."

"What?"

"After this is all over, I want as little drama as possible. Let's just elope.
Bali. Barbados. Buenos Aires. I don't care. You pick the spot. How does
that sound?"

To be honest, it sounded fantastic, but it wasn't a decision he wanted
to make under duress. "I am one hundred percent open to the idea," he
replied. "Let's talk about it when I get back."

"You promise?"

"That I'm coming back," he teased, "or that we'll talk about it?"

"Both."

He gave her another kiss. "I promise."

They stood in the hallway for a few more moments, holding each other. Finally, they broke off their hug.

"Do what you need to do," she said. "I'll be waiting for you."

Giving her one last kiss, Harvath went back upstairs, picked up his bag, and rallied his teammates.

He wanted this operation done with as soon as possible. It was a chapter from his life that needed to be welded shut. Once it was, he would be able to move on.

As much as he wasn't looking forward to it, however, there was one consolation: he intended to fully vent his rage. He wasn't going to stop until he had purged every last ounce of anger from his body. Consider it highly kinetic therapy.

Harvath was going to make this as painful for the Russians as possible.

CHAPTER 49

It was late morning when they landed at the Paris Le Bourget Airport. A storm had just moved through and the wet tarmac looked like it had been slicked down for a movie scene.

They taxied for a few minutes before pulling into a large, private hangar. Waiting for them, alongside a convoy of three vehicles, was Ray Powell, the local CIA station chief.

"Welcome to Paris," the man said, extending his hand as Harvath descended the jet's airstairs.

He was a bit tweedy for Harvath's taste, but knowing that it took all kinds to keep the Agency running, he reserved judgment and shook the man's hand.

He briefly introduced the other team members and then oversaw the offloading of their gear.

Once everything had been loaded into the vehicles, Powell suggested Harvath ride with him, so he could be briefed on the rest of the intelligence he had requested.

As the station chief piloted the black Citroen C5 out of the airport and headed for the Périphérique road, he removed a folder and handed it to Harvath. "Here's everything else we were able to pull together for you."

Opening it, Harvath saw a picture of his target right up top. Colonel Vladimir Elovik was Russia's military attaché to France. He operated out of the Russian Embassy in Paris's westernmost arrondissement, the 16th, and lived just across the Seine in a suburb called Suresnes.

"Elovik travels with two FSB bodyguards. Per your question, he doesn't receive any protection beyond that, nor does he receive a police escort."

"Good," Harvath replied.

"We've got you set up at an Agency safehouse in Nanterre. It should have everything you need. If it doesn't, you'll have to improvise."

"Roger that."

"And a word to the wise," said Powell. "My guys refer to that area as Transylvania. When night falls, you don't want to be caught out wandering the streets if you know what I mean."

Harvath nodded and continued to peruse the folder.

"The upside though," the station chief continued, "is that the people in that neighborhood don't care for the police. They mind their own business. As long as you and your team keep a low profile, nobody's going to bother you."

"Just the way we like it."

"I've also included some satellite imagery. You'll see I highlighted possible routes as well as suggested areas to engage the target."

Harvath flipped to the main image and studied it. "Lot of places somebody could get lost in here."

"Better to have them and not need them, right?"

"Exactly," he responded. The tweedy chief was growing on him. "What about these three bridges you've marked?"

"Elovik's most direct path home from the embassy is via the one in the middle. But we don't know how competent his security detail is. Maybe they run surveillance detection routes and change things up every night, or maybe they don't. You're going to have to adapt on the fly."

"Understood. What about the DGSI? I know the French rotate surveillance on Russian diplomats. Will there be a team on him tonight?"

"You guys are going to have to figure that out for yourselves," said Powell. "This isn't supposed to have any American fingerprints on it. For the sake of operational security, I haven't pinged anyone—not even my most trusted DGSI contacts."

Harvath appreciated his attention to detail. Powell was both smart and thorough.

"What about the special items I asked for?"

"Very difficult to come by, especially on short notice, but we got them. It's all waiting at the safehouse."

If Powell had, in fact, rounded up everything on his list, Harvath was going to recommend the man for a promotion. Though he didn't know how much better one could do than Paris station chief. It had to be one of the best assignments Langley had going.

At Porte Dauphine, they got off the Périphérique and drove down the broad, apartment-block-lined Boulevard Lannes and past the Russian Embassy.

In a city of such striking architectural beauty, the Russian Embassy was positively ugly. It was even worse than the FBI's headquarters in Washington.

Built in the brutalist style, the embassy was a three-story concrete monstrosity that took up an entire city block. Not only was it ringed with an iron fence, but the French police had erected barricades so that pedestrians, and more than likely protestors, couldn't access the sidewalk. There was plenty of security, including cameras and uniformed law enforcement officers.

The narrow streets on each side had been closed to through traffic and were posted with manned checkpoints.

Drawing Harvath's attention to the first checkpoint, Powell explained, "The embassy has an underground parking structure. Vehicles exit from the rear of the building and come out here."

"There isn't a road in back?" Harvath asked.

"There is, but it's been closed off as well. The city even went so far as to build concrete embankments back there. Essentially, three out of the four streets surrounding the embassy are off-limits to anyone but embassy personnel. To get in or out, you have to go through a police checkpoint."

"I don't see any parking along here. How are we going to have eyes on in order to know if they turn left or right?"

Powell smiled and pointed out the Piscine Henry de Montherlant across the street. "Public pool. We've got a hidden camera up on the roof. It allows us to monitor who comes and goes. You'll be parked about a block over. As soon as Elovik's car leaves, I'll let you know if he's headed north or south."

"What about CCTV cameras in the park? Are we going to have to be concerned about those?"

Powell shook his head. "The Bois de Boulogne is over two thousand acres. That's two and a half times the size of Central Park. They would need an army to watch that many cameras."

"So their answer is no cameras at all?"

"In the city proper, where they're worried about terrorism, they've grudgingly given way to more and more cameras. But out in the woods, on the edge of the city? It's highly unlikely that it would be a terrorist target, so they figure why bother?"

Harvath couldn't argue with that logic. Until AI had completely taken over and was watching everything, all the time, human-monitored cameras only made sense in areas where they were actually needed.

He supposed he should be grateful. Even New York City had invested in cameras for Central Park. Granted, they were placed strategically at entrances around the perimeter, but they were still there, always recording. And the software system the NYPD and the Department of Homeland Security used to tap into and analyze feeds from across the city was downright scary. It was like something out of a sci-fi movie. He didn't know how younger spies were going to be able to ply their trade in a few years.

The good thing about his Bois de Boulogne plan, however, was that even if he and his team were spotted, it wouldn't matter. They were going to be perfectly disguised.

Powell entered the park and, one by one, showed Harvath the three different bridges and the routes the military attaché and his bodyguards might take. Then they crossed the river and drove past Elovik's house in Suresnes. From there it was less than five klicks to the CIA safehouse in Nanterre.

When they arrived, Harvath was impressed. It was an old, out-of-business auto shop and looked like an absolute shithole.

The front of the property had a high, graffiti-covered wall, topped with barbed wire. Removing a remote from under his armrest, the station chief retracted the metal security gate, revealing a small outer parking area and a squat commercial building with three service bays.

"What do you think?" he asked, as the other two vehicles followed them in.

"I think you knocked it out of the park," Harvath replied.

"Good. There are a couple additional features that I'll show you once we get inside."

Climbing out of Powell's Citroen, Harvath took in the sight lines. They were in some sort of warehouse district and none of the structures were high enough to let anyone observe what they were up to. Once the front gate had closed, they were all but invisible to the outside world.

As the team got out and started unloading their gear, Harvath followed the station chief into the shop. It wasn't exactly the Ritz, but it didn't need to be.

Despite being old and run-down, it was at least clean. There was a closet-sized bathroom with a toilet and sink, a break room with a couch, table, small fridge, microwave, and coffeemaker, and a parts area that had been converted into sleeping quarters with several cheap bunk beds.

The pièce de résistance was down a narrow flight of stairs, beneath the shop. There the Agency had set up a makeshift interrogation chamber.

High-intensity construction lights, portable DJ speakers, a stainless-steel surgical table, ten-gallon water jugs, pulley systems mounted to the ceiling—they hadn't missed a thing. Right down to the lone metal chair in the center of the space—it was all there.

Opening a hard-sided Storm case, Powell revealed two video cameras, digital audio recorders, and several tripods to mount everything on.

"The entire structure is outfitted with high-speed, encrypted Wi-Fi," he said, handing Harvath a small piece of paper with the log-in and password.

"How many cameras are there?" Harvath asked. "Besides the three I saw outside."

The station chief led him to a small office off the interrogation chamber. Inside was a desk with a wide flat-screen monitor. Moving the mouse to wake it up, Powell tapped several keys saying, "Same password as the Wi-Fi, but in reverse." The screen then lit up with the feeds from all of the cameras.

"Nothing down here?" Harvath asked.

The CIA man shook his head. "None. You can turn any of the cameras on and off from this workstation."

"Backed up to the cloud?"

Powell nodded. "But we'll scrub everything when you guys are done."

Sure you will, Harvath thought to himself. They had already blackmailed him once. He didn't intend to give them another opportunity. "What about the vehicles?"

"Right this way," the station chief said, taking him back upstairs and into the service area.

Sitting there were two unmarked Renaults—a windowless panel van and a sedan. They were both painted in the deep navy blue popular with French law enforcement and security services.

"Go ahead," Powell encouraged him. "Take a closer look."

Since the van was closest, Harvath checked it out first. Sliding its side door open, he looked inside.

Everything was set up just the way he had requested. Moving around to the driver's side, he opened the door and tested the blue strobe lights mounted behind the grille, as well as a quick squawk from the Klaxon. Inside the enclosed space, it was ear-piercing.

Leaving the van, he walked over and checked out the sedan. "No strobes?" he asked, not seeing a switch.

"Gumball," Powell responded, referring to a single, spinning light that could be manually attached to the roof via its magnetic base. "The cops use them all the time in Paris. Very authentic. There's one on the trunk."

Harvath gave the sedan's Klaxon a quick blast, making sure that it was operational. It was. In fact, it sounded even louder than the one on the van.

"What about the raid vests?"

"Also in the trunk," said the station chief.

Walking to the rear of the car, Harvath popped the lid and looked inside. Next to the box containing the blue gumball were five tactical vests, all emblazoned with emblems from the Research and Intervention Brigade, or BRI for short.

The BRI was a highly specialized police tactical unit responsible for hostage rescue, as well as taking down France's most violent criminals.

Except for their SWAT teams, it was a plainclothes unit, which spent most of its time hiding out among the public.

When it was time to spring into action, they donned balaclavas, the black tactical vests, and special police armbands, which Powell had also been able to secure. They carried their pistols in military-style thigh holsters worn right over their jeans.

Whether on TV, in movies, or the news, there wasn't a single French citizen who couldn't recognize the BRI. Everyone knew that they meant business and not to get in their way. Even beat cops kept their distance, unless directly instructed to engage.

The station chief had delivered all the items on Harvath's wish list, right down to clean license plates.

"Anything else we can do for you?" the station chief asked.

"I think we're good," said Harvath, offering his hand. "Thank you."

Powell shook his hand and after handing over a couple of gate remotes said, "You know how to reach me if you need me. Here's hoping you don't. Good luck."

After the CIA man had left and the gate had closed, Harvath shut down all the cameras and set to work finding any others that Powell might have "forgotten" to mention. He also had his team scour the vehicles for hidden surveillance equipment, including tracking devices.

As they worked, he made contact with Nicholas and provided him remote access to the safehouse workstation, which could be used as a springboard into the CIA's cloud. He wasn't leaving any box unchecked when it came to covering his tracks.

Stepping back into the service area, he saw Mike Haney doing an inventory of everything in the van.

"All good?" Harvath asked.

Haney flashed him the thumbs-up.

Harvath checked in with the rest of the guys, making sure they all had what they needed. This was going to be an extremely dangerous, two-part assignment. And once it began, the clock would start racing against them.

CHAPTER 50

Out of all the cracks in her plan, Brunelle had been most worried about MoMo. As it turned out, she didn't need to be.

He wasn't happy, of course, about Amir being taken into custody, but he understood why it was necessary, as well as what his role had been in it.

Gibert had lived up to his end of the bargain, sneaking the flash drive into the evidence log. Once his text had arrived, confirming that it had been done, she had finally been able to breathe.

The DGSI command center had been a hive of activity overnight. A small cadre of trusted agents had been handpicked by Director General de Vasselot to work the assignment. As they did, they were gripped with a universal terror—in addition to the names already on Jadot's list, how many other government operatives had the Russians co-opted? Had Jadot uncovered them all? Or were there more? And if there were more, how many of them were from right inside DGSI?

Those operatives identified by Jadot had been placed under immediate surveillance. The director general didn't want to move on anyone, not yet. She wanted to have a solid plan in place first. Brunelle agreed with her. If they weren't exceedingly careful, they could blow the entire thing. The moment that happened, they would lose any opportunity to fully grasp the scope of how badly the French government had been penetrated, as well as to bring every bad actor to justice. It was a highly sensitive situation that required patience and cunning.

Brunelle was also still bound and determined to nail Jadot's killer. Unfortunately, the fates were not cooperating. The getaway car had all but vanished into thin air. The farther one moved from the heart of Paris, the fewer traffic cams there were. MoMo suggested that the Russians might have even pulled off somewhere and switched license plates, making their search all but impossible. Even the AI software had come up empty.

Nonetheless, she refused to throw in the towel. The reason they had yet to generate any new leads was simply that they were not looking in the right places. There was always evidence. You just needed to adjust your eyesight in order to see it. She wasn't going to stop until she uncovered something.

At the same time, de Vasselot expected her attention to be fully focused on Jadot's list. Brunelle had uncovered it, after all. How they handled this bombshell was going to impact both the DGSI and Brunelle's long-term career. This was a quintessential make-or-break moment if ever there was one.

Though she could strategize with the best of them, determining how to move against so many well-connected people, all at once, with no one knowing it was coming, was proving almost impossible to wrap her brain around. Whom could they trust to make the arrests? Would they apply for warrants, or use provisions in the terrorism code? There was even a law going back to the 1940s, created in the aftermath of the Nazi-collaborating Vichy government, that DGSI's lead attorney thought could be dusted off and put into play.

At every turn, the director general made space for her to weigh in. Brunelle could see what was happening and she was grateful for it. A brilliant, successful woman who had risen to head one of the most powerful law enforcement agencies in France, de Vasselot was allowing another up-and-coming woman the opportunity to take her shot and make her mark. It was beyond generous.

Brunelle, however, was not going to win any politically correct plaudits with her ideas. She wanted to kick in the door of every single traitor, drag them out of their beds, and livestream their interrogations. Part of her even wanted to let citizens choose from a menu of punishments and vote via text message. She wasn't a total anarchist, but when it came to dealing with people who were willing to sell out their country to an enemy like Russia, she was definitely open to exploring a wide range of remedies, including the unorthodox.

Her punitive desire to inflict maximum pain and consequences aside, if she could help plot the DGSI's next steps, it would cement her as a superstar. The trajectory of her career would be all but guaranteed.

Think, she told herself. *How do you gather up that many people all at once? How do you outsmart so many intelligent and talented people?* There had to be a way.

Suddenly, it hit her. You don't outsmart them. You allow them to outsmart *themselves.* You hand out ropes spun from golden thread and watch as they turn into nooses.

Pulling de Vasselot aside, she said, "I think I may have an answer for you. But first I need to ask—does the president trust you? I mean *really* trust you."

CHAPTER 51

Andrew Conroy had sat by a few hospital beds in his day, but this was the first time he'd done so while warming up an "I told you so."

Paul had reached out to him last night and had filled him in on Maggie's accident. She was being taken in for surgery and wouldn't be available to see visitors until the morning.

Conroy had arrived bright and early, giving Paul a chance to go down to the cafeteria for coffee and something to eat.

When Maggie opened her eyes and she saw her boss sitting there, she ordered, "Don't say it. Not a word."

He ignored her issuance. "A handlebar hernia," he remarked. "Never heard of that one before. It's got to be an Agency first."

"Don't rub it in."

"What have I been telling you about that bicycle?"

"You never liked it."

"Correction," said the DDO. "I hated it. And this is why. I always knew something like this was going to happen."

Maggie winced as she struggled to get comfortable in the bed.

"Here," Conroy said, handing her the remote.

After adjusting everything, Maggie relaxed. "Thank you."

"You're welcome. So, I thought we'd discuss your medical leave."

She looked at him. "I haven't requested any yet."

"Well, don't bother. I've already denied it. Preemptively. That place ceases to function without you. We can't afford your absence right now."

Maggie smiled. "It's nice to be needed. That said, those handlebars made some pretty aggressive contact with my abdomen. The surgeon said I'm going to need at least two weeks of bed rest. I don't know how I'm going to get into the office."

"If you're willing, the president has offered you full use of his suite at Walter Reed Medical Center. We'll assign an around-the-clock security detail. You can have any materials you want from the office and any staff as well. There's a secure conference room with encrypted communications where your people can work. There are also the executive living spaces, which will be made available to Paul. As soon as the doctors say you're ready to be moved, we'll transfer you via Marine Corps helicopter. All you have to do is agree."

"You make it rather hard to say no."

"Listen, Maggie. I'm sure you'd rather be recuperating at home. In any other situation, I'd prefer that for you too. Unfortunately, this isn't any other situation. You've got President Porter's ear and you also have the respect of his national security advisor. We need all hands on deck to thread this needle with Russia and Belarus. Nobody has the experience and insights that you do. Without you in the picture, I worry that some of the louder, less-informed voices will start taking up all the air in the room."

"Like I said," Maggie repeated. "It's nice to be needed."

"So, that's a yes?"

"Of course I'll want to speak with Paul first, but yes. Please tell the president that I appreciate his generosity."

"Terrific," Conroy said. "I'll get everything in motion. As soon as you know what people and materials you want, we can get those balls rolling too. In the meantime, I need to ask you about a particular Russian diplomat."

"Which one?"

"Russia's military attaché to France."

Maggie inhaled a sharp breath. "Colonel Vladimir Elovik. He's a very nasty piece of work. Why are you interested in him?"

"Scot Harvath is about to make contact. And it isn't going to be a polite social call."

"Well, Elovik's file speaks for itself. Like I said, he's a nasty piece of work. His colleagues call him the 'Porcupine' because he surrounds himself with pricks. Seems to have an affinity for bad actors and people of low character. Feels right at home around them. Whatever business Harvath has with Elovik, tell him to be very, very careful."

CHAPTER 52

Something was eating at Harvath, but he couldn't put his finger on it. Something just felt off.

Perhaps it was having to rush another job. He knew all too well that just because the Tsybulsky op had been successful, it didn't mean that this next one would.

Hits that were daisy-chained, where the intel gleaned from one operation led immediately to the next, required a tremendous amount of luck. There was a lot of room for error. No matter how much care you took, Murphy seemed to be waiting around not just one corner, but *all* of them.

Harvath was reminded of a friend who, years ago, had been killed right at the finish line. It was July Fourth weekend and they had been chasing a team of terrorists through New York City. At the very end, right when they had cornered the key figure they were after, Harvath's buddy, Bob Horrigan, had been shot.

They had been running and gunning for hours. From one battle to the next, they kept pushing through their mental and physical exhaustion. Then, right when they could see light at the end of the tunnel, Bob had been hit by a figurative train.

It didn't matter that Horrigan had been an elite Delta Force operator and that he had been on countless high-risk missions throughout his storied career. In the end, the world's best training and hard-won experience hadn't been enough to save him.

Harvath had always wondered if it was bad luck or simply the law of diminishing returns. Had Bob's number just come up or had they pushed too hard for too long?

By the same token, night after night during the wars in Afghanistan and Iraq, teams had daisy-chained from dusk to dawn. It wasn't the preferred method of doing business, but it produced results, which was why it was done. Sometimes, people got hurt. But when the clock was ticking, often there was no other choice. Which was where Harvath was now.

He tried to let the feeling roll off him. If there was nothing he could do about it, it was pointless to dwell on it. He needed to focus forward.

The Russians being the Russians, they observed a strict 5 p.m. end to their workday, meaning that many of them began leaving the embassy at 4:30. Harvath and his team would have to be in place well before that.

Having checked and rechecked their weapons, radios, and equipment, Harvath called for a brief break. It was important that everyone get a little pre-mission relaxation. A chance to breathe and decompress before going hot could reap substantial benefits if things got bad. If there was one truism in their business, it was that a rested operator was a resourceful operator.

While Powell had stocked the fridge in the break room with bottled water, there wasn't much else. In one of the cabinets, there were bags of salty snacks—pretzels, chips, and peanuts—but that was it.

Johnson offered to run out for food, but couldn't find any takers. No one was really hungry. Not now.

As Preisler put on coffee, Harvath kicked off his boots and closed his eyes for a few minutes. Being able to quiet his mind and block out his thoughts before an assignment had always been one of his greatest skills. Even if only for a few minutes, he always came away feeling refreshed and much sharper.

He sat in that meditative state for a good fifteen minutes before the smell of the coffee became too tempting to ignore any longer. Getting up, he grabbed a mug and then sat down next to Staelin, who was studying the satellite imagery at the table.

"See anything interesting?" he asked.

Staelin, who would be driving one of the vehicles, shook his head.

"Just running the routes. Do we have any clue how busy the Bois de Boulogne is going to be?"

Harvath shrugged. "It'll be rush hour, so expect it to be busier. Other than that, I don't have any additional intel."

"At least we're not trying to grab the guy in the center of downtown Paris. That'd be a nightmare."

Harvath agreed. He had done a handful of operations like that. They were incredibly complicated and took a long time to orchestrate. Crowds and chaos could work to your advantage, but only if you retained control over all the other elements in the operation. If not, you very quickly became a rat being chased through an increasingly dangerous maze. He had no desire to get anywhere near that sort of scenario.

When the time neared, he gave his teammates a fifteen-minute warning. It had been agreed that all weapons and police gear would be kept out of sight until Elovik had been spotted and they were ready to begin their pursuit. There was absolutely no reason to risk drawing any attention before that.

He sent Nicholas a text, letting him know that they were ready to roll. The little man, who had hacked himself deep into the CIA's security system, confirmed receipt and began streaming bogus feeds from the safehouse cameras to the Agency's cloud. No one in the Paris station or back at Langley would have any record of what Harvath and his team were about to do.

Opening the garage bay doors, they backed the two navy blue Renaults into the small parking lot area and paused as they awaited Nicholas's next move.

Each of the vehicles was outfitted with a tracking device so that Nicholas could not only monitor their progress, but also cover their movements. The less evidence available to anyone—be it the CIA, the Russians, or the French—the better.

While the little man couldn't wipe every single, individually operated camera the team passed, he could interrupt the feeds from those controlled by the French authorities, particularly their traffic cameras. It would be next to impossible to fully grasp what had happened, if they couldn't pick up any trace of the vehicles.

As soon as word came back that Nicholas was ready, Harvath gave the order for the team to roll.

They crossed the Seine via the Pont de Puteaux, cut through the Bois de Boulogne, and popped out a few blocks from the Russian Embassy near the Porte de la Muette.

Passing the Embassy of Bangladesh, they hung a left on Boulevard Flandrin and found places to park right before Rue Dufrenoy. Now it was simply a waiting game. The moment Powell saw Elovik's car, he would let them know.

At 4:55, they received word. The Russian military attaché was on the move. His car had turned right onto Boulevard Lannes and was headed south.

Elovik, however, wasn't alone. An additional embassy security vehicle—carrying two men—was trailing right behind him.

As Harvath had feared, Murphy had now arrived on scene.

CHAPTER 53

"Nothing has changed," Harvath radioed his teammates as they began their pursuit and donned their raid vests and police armbands. "We stick with the plan. Keep following and wait for my command."

After the team in the van confirmed Harvath's order, Staelin, who was driving the sedan, looked at him. "Why the extra security all of a sudden?"

"Our operation in Monaco may have had a bigger impact than we anticipated."

"And now we've got double the Russian vehicles and double the Russian personnel to contend with," Staelin said. "The plan is going to have to change. Preisler and Johnson can't cover down on four guys across two cars."

"They won't have to," Harvath replied. "You and I will be responsible for the embassy security vehicle. Like I said, nothing has changed."

Technically, that was a change—a big one. Harvath and Staelin were supposed to remain with the sedan, prepared to handle any additional problems or threats that might roll up during the takedown of Elovik. But that was no longer an option.

As a former Delta Force operator, Staelin both appreciated the situation and the role that improvisation would need to play in its successful outcome. Nodding his head, he responded, "Roger that."

Up ahead, the two embassy cars turned right again and headed toward the Bois de Boulogne. Harvath and his team kept them in sight as they stayed a safe distance behind.

At the last red light before the park, Harvath instructed the team to ready their weapons and balaclavas.

When the light turned green, Elovik's vehicle and its security escort entered the Bois de Boulogne.

It was a good thing that Harvath and his team had given the Russians plenty of space. They were actually being professional and had run multiple surveillance detection routes—going all the way north to skirt the park's large lake and then doubling back at the Pavillon Royal. Despite their precautions, they appeared to have no clue that they were being followed.

With the element of surprise on his side, Harvath could pick any spot and any moment he wanted to spring his trap.

As the Russians crossed the Allée de Longchamp and headed into a densely wooded section of the park, they were sixty seconds away from one of the best ambush spots. Harvath alerted the team. That's where they would take Elovik.

Rolling his balaclava down over his face, he pushed the button to extend the retractable brace of his Flux Raider X PDW and made sure a round was chambered.

Looking at Staelin, he said, "There's a cutout in the shoulder up ahead."

"I remember it from the satellite imagery," the man replied.

Harvath nodded. "Let's get close, but not too close to the second car's rear bumper. We'll get out at the same time. I'm going to do a passenger-side approach. You'll be taking the driver."

"Good copy," Staelin replied as he rolled down his own balaclava.

Reaching into the bag at his feet, Harvath removed Staelin's MP5 SD, verified that it was charged and ready to fire, and then balanced it on his lap.

Studying the maps feature on his phone, he counted down over the radio, "One hundred and fifty meters . . . One hundred meters . . . Fifty meters . . . Now!"

Smoke from burning rubber filled the air as Haney slammed the van into the opposite lane, lights strobing and Klaxons blaring. As soon as he passed the Russians, he crossed back into their lane to box them in.

Staelin accelerated and Harvath watched the speedometer needle climb, willing the Renault to close the distance. Attaching the gumball to the roof, Harvath lit it up and activated the sedan's Klaxons. He could practically hear the Russians cursing in their cramped embassy vehicles as Haney and Staelin bullied them off the road, and forced them into the cutout.

Before the van had even come to a full stop, Preisler and Johnson had leapt out. They were both armed with suppressed Heckler & Koch UMPs.

Quickly they surrounded Elovik's vehicle, pointing their weapons at the security agents in the front seat.

As Staelin brought the Renault sedan to a stop and jammed it into park, Harvath handed him his weapon, opened his door, and rushed the security vehicle.

Speed, surprise, and overwhelming force of action was the intent. No matter what happened, they didn't want to give the Russians a single moment to think, much less react.

Closing in on the passenger in the front seat, Harvath trained his Trijicon red-dot sight on the back of the man's head.

"Hands!" he yelled in French, as Preisler and Johnson did the same at the vehicle in front. "Raise your hands!"

Suddenly, the world exploded. A spray of bullets erupted from the tree line, ripping through the air all around him.

"Contact right!" Harvath yelled, returning fire and diving behind the embassy security vehicle.

A sickening thud came from up front. Preisler's voice crackled over the radio, laced with panic. "Man down. Johnson's hit."

Harvath whipped around, his heart hammering his ribs. He struggled to see Johnson and gauge the severity of his injury.

As he did, figures poured out of the embassy vehicles, their Kalashnikov PPK-20 submachine guns spitting fire.

He and his team weren't ambushing the Russians. The Russians were ambushing *them*. They had walked right into a trap.

CHAPTER 54

Heavy rounds chewed through the thin metal skin of the van as Haney lunged for his suppressed HK417. Ignoring the danger, he aimed through the passenger-side window and unleashed his own withering barrage of gunfire into the tree line.

In the cutout behind him, Harvath and Staelin were a blur of controlled chaos. Retreating behind their bullet-riddled Renault, they returned fire with deadly precision, allowing Preisler the ability to drag Johnson to safety as, one by one, they picked off their attackers.

A young Russian, barely in his mid-twenties, was the first to fall. Taking a bullet to his throat, he crumpled to the ground, his Kalashnikov clattering uselessly beside him.

Next was a grizzled man in his forties, his skin like cracked leather. Receiving two shots to the chest, he collapsed like a cheap lawn chair behind the embassy security vehicle.

Having neutralized the closest threats, they immediately engaged the Russians in the lead car. An enormous man with a shaved head and a thick black beard leaned out of the passenger seat and fired his weapon on full auto, tearing up the hood of their Renault and splintering its windshield.

Harvath waited for the onslaught to pause and then, risking a peek around the side of the sedan, caught the man as he was reloading his weapon. He double-tapped him through the bridge of his nose and his left eye, killing him instantly, and painting the inside of his vehicle with bits of brain and bloody bone.

Moving to take out the driver, Staelin rolled away from the Renault just as a volley of bullets tore up the position he'd been occupying a millisecond earlier.

The driver—a thin man with a tight crew cut—quickly took cover behind his engine block and changed magazines. It wasn't, however, enough to protect him.

Lying in the dirt, Staelin fired at the man's boots, ripping apart both of his feet. The driver dropped to the ground, screaming, and made himself an even bigger target.

From the Russian's abdomen to his lower jaw, the ex–Delta Force operative opened up on him and painted a lethal racing stripe right along the driver's upper body.

The round that went through the driver's jaw—shattering his face—kept going through the roof of his mouth and into his brain, killing him and bringing his screaming to an end.

That left only one more possible combatant—the Russian military attaché.

"Where's Elovik?" Harvath demanded.

No one knew. He hadn't been seen since the shooting started.

"Probably hugging the floorboards in the back seat of that lead vehicle," said Staelin, rejoining him behind the Renault.

"No way," Harvath replied. "He's a decorated combat vet. We need to get up to that car and figure out what's going on. Ready?"

The man nodded.

Harvath began counting backward from three, but before he could get to one, another fusillade exploded from the trees.

Aborting their launch, they tightened up behind the Renault and waited for Haney to return fire. But the shots never came.

Instead, Haney put out a distress call over the radio. "I'm hit," he stated. "Fuck."

"How bad?" Harvath asked.

"Bad."

Damn it, Harvath thought to himself. *First Johnson and now Haney.*

"Can you still fight?"

"Negative," Haney replied. "Trying to get my tourniquet out. There's a lot of blood."

There was only one thing Harvath could do. Collapsing the stock and holstering his PDW, he laid out a plan to Staelin. "I want you to give me your MP5. All the extra mags too. When I give the command, you're going to clear the Russian security vehicle and then move on to Elovik's. I'll lay down cover fire for you."

"And if Elovik's in there?"

"If he's armed, shoot him. If not, pull him out of that car by his throat and wait for me. Understood?"

Once again, Staelin nodded. After handing his MP5 and spare magazines over to Harvath, he drew his pistol and made ready to move.

Inserting a fresh magazine into the submachine gun, Harvath confirmed a round was chambered, then flicked the firing selector to three-round bursts. Getting himself into place, he looked at Staelin and ordered, "Now!"

The moment he gave the go command, Harvath popped up from behind the Renault and began strafing the tree line.

He tore through it like the world's deadliest weed whacker. Pieces of bark, branches, limbs, and leaves went in all directions. Wherever the enemy shooter was hiding, he wanted to be certain the sniper couldn't pick his head up.

"Car one clear!" Staelin announced over the radio. "Standing by."

"Reloading!" Harvath declared as he ducked back behind the Renault and inserted a fresh magazine into the MP5.

When he was all set, he repeated the go command, "Now!" And as Staelin took off running, he popped back up and began spraying the woods all over again.

"Car two clear!" Staelin reported. "Elovik KIA. Standing by."

Harvath dropped back behind the Renault once more and asked, "Was he armed?"

"Affirmative."

Harvath had no idea who had killed the Russian. Preisler and Johnson had both gotten off a couple of shots as they had been backing away. Alternatively, it could have been fratricide—the Russians were notoriously undisciplined in high-stress situations. Or Elovik could have simply popped his head up at the wrong second and been caught in the crossfire. None of it changed the fact that he was dead.

It also didn't change the fact that until they eliminated that sniper in the woods, Harvath and his team would remain pinned down, unable to escape.

If the police hadn't been alerted to the gunfight yet, any moment someone was going to pass by, see bodies and battle-scarred vehicles, and call it in. Observing the BRI conducting an arrest was one thing. A blood-bath like this was something entirely different.

Harvath was now faced with a very dangerous task.

Radioing Staelin and Preisler what he wanted done, he swapped in a fresh magazine and took several deep breaths.

He was about to head into the woods to take out the sniper.

CHAPTER 55

Right now, Harvath was wishing he had the rest of the team with him. At the very least, having Ashby or Palmer, especially if one of them had brought the drone, would have been a game changer. As it stood, he didn't even have so much as a smoke grenade to help mask his movements.

What he did have, however, was the extremely thick tree cover. The same tree cover that the sniper was using so effectively to his advantage. All Harvath had to do was find the sniper before the sniper found him.

On his command, Preisler, who had both his and Johnson's UMPs, and Staelin, who had picked up Haney's 417, would begin shooting to help cover his mad dash into the woods. Once past the tree line, he would be on his own.

Keying his radio, he made sure everybody was ready. When both men confirmed they were in position, he counted down from three, and the moment Staelin started firing, Harvath took off running.

It was everything Sølvi wouldn't have wanted him doing—sprinting across an open piece of ground, into an unknown environment, which was under the control of an opponent he could neither identify nor pinpoint. Other than that, she would have assured him, it sounded like a terrific plan.

For the brief moment that he had weighed his options, he had consoled himself with the fact that there really was no other choice. Somebody had to do it and, Harvath being Harvath, the thought of asking anyone else to step up hadn't even occurred to him. You had to send the best man for the job, and in his mind, that was *always* him—regardless of how beaten his body, exhausted his mind, or difficult the assignment.

With Haney having directed Staelin and Preisler on where to focus their fire, Harvath managed to make it into the trees without being shot.

His lungs burned and he took the briefest of seconds to catch his breath and steady his heart rate. Everything from this moment forward would depend on him being absolutely silent and completely in control. The first task on his list was to gain the upper hand over the sniper. Removing the satellite imagery, he identified his position and then his first waypoint. He felt fairly confident that the shooter had probably made one very serious mistake. If he was right, the balance of power was about to shift substantially.

Pushing into the now-silent woods, he carefully chose his steps, making sure not to put weight on anything that would snap, crack, or otherwise give him away. It was bad enough that he didn't know where the sniper was. Drawing audible attention to himself could only make the situation worse and possibly even get him killed.

With his weapon up and ready to engage, he swept back and forth as he moved, as well as up and down. There was no telling where the sniper might have established his hide site.

Harvath made it all the way to the next break in the trees without making any contact. But the moment he stared out into the clearing, he saw exactly what he had hoped to see.

Judging by the imagery, there was supposed to be a trailhead with a small parking area, which was exactly what he found. And in that parking area was a lone SUV, which he was willing to bet belonged to the sniper.

From here the sniper could have easily unloaded his gear, disappeared into the trees, and hiked the likely short distance to his hide. All Harvath had to do now was pick up his trail.

Based on where Haney believed the shots had been coming from, Harvath began his search. Luckily, it was in the opposite direction of the established trails, which were so well traveled that it would have been all but impossible to pick up the sniper's figurative scent.

It took Harvath a few moments, but soon enough he saw it. There was a mound covered in tall grasses, a narrow band of which had been bent and recently broken. It was all that he needed to see.

Figuring that he had the element of surprise on his side and would be long gone before anyone investigated, the sniper hadn't tried very hard to cover his tracks. His path, while not exactly a piece of cake, had been easy enough for Harvath to follow.

Closer and closer he crept until finally, he didn't dare move another muscle. At this point, he could begin to make out the ambush site through the trees. The outlines of the shot-up vehicles were definitely visible. It was time to force the sniper to reveal himself.

To do that, someone other than Harvath was going to have to take a pretty big risk. As Staelin had already stabilized Haney and was closest to the dead Russians, he had offered to do it.

With Preisler laying down a volley of cover fire, which was aimed well into the tree canopy so as not to accidentally hit Harvath, Staelin ran back to Elovik's vehicle.

Using it for cover, he peeled off his balaclava and put it over the head of the dead driver. Then came the hard part.

Planting his feet, he grabbed hold of the body from behind and keyed his radio to let Harvath know he was in position. A bona fide CrossFit fanatic, Staelin credited the program with helping him to maintain his edge. But even in spite of all the dead lifts he'd done in the gym, he never thought he would actually do one in the field, much less that his life and the life of his teammates would depend on it.

Out in the trees, Harvath crouched down, his senses on fire, ready to take out the sniper. He then keyed his radio two times in quick succession, transmitting the signal for Staelin to act.

Upon hearing the clicks over his earpiece, Staelin tightened his core, pushed hard with his legs, and drove the corpse upward so that its masked head peeked above the hood of the vehicle, offering the sniper an irresistible target.

No one moved. No one spoke. No one dared even breathe. The entire team remained quiet. Seconds passed. The sniper refused to take the bait.

How the hell could that be? Perhaps he had already fled and was no longer in the trees. Maybe the vehicle Harvath had seen in the parking area wasn't actually his.

A dozen possible scenarios were racing through Harvath's mind when, suddenly, he heard the *pop* of a twig snapping directly behind him.

Faking to his left, he applied pressure to his trigger and began firing as he lunged right and spun 180 degrees.

The sniper's bullet missed his head by a millimeter, but Harvath's rounds found their target, slicing through the man's groin and lower abdomen.

Before the sniper could bring his weapon back to bear, Harvath fired again and again—driving three rounds center-mass through his heart, and two more, just for good measure, directly into his forehead.

The man fell to the ground, his rifle discharging one final time as he landed. Thankfully, Harvath wasn't in the path of the bullet.

"Target neutralized," he said over the radio. Patting down the sniper, he found the man's car fob, cell phone, and a Russian diplomatic passport. "Be prepared to roll," he added. "I'm heading your way. Black Dacia Duster. Don't let Johnson shoot me."

"Fuck you," Johnson replied through gritted teeth, the pain evident in his voice.

Having dropped the Russian corpse and gone back to tend his wounded comrades, Staelin radioed, "We're going to need additional medical. What's the plan?"

"I'm working on it," said Harvath, who could already hear the wail of Klaxons off in the distance.

As he rushed back to the sniper's vehicle, he pulled out his phone and sent Nicholas a text: Haney & Johnson shot. Need medical. Also need new safehouse. DO NOT contact COS Powell. DO NOT contact CIA. REPEAT do not contact Powell/CIA.

With that, he hopped into the SUV, started the engine, and sped out of the trailhead parking lot.

Moments later, he came flying into the cutout and skidded to a halt next to the van. "Did you guys check the bodies?" he asked as he helped Staelin load an extremely pale Haney, tourniquet around his right arm, into the back seat of the Duster.

"Negative."

Once Haney was safely in the SUV and Staelin had gone to help with

Johnson, Harvath hurried over to search the dead Russians, starting with the pair from the embassy security vehicle.

Just like the sniper, they were also carrying diplomatic passports. After matching the photos to their faces, he put the passports in his pocket and ignored their phones. The devices would only serve as homing beacons for a subsequent Russian reprisal.

Moving quickly to the lead vehicle, he checked the photos against the two dead security agents, peeling the balaclava off the corpse Staelin had propped up, and then pocketed their passports as well.

But when he went to roll the deceased military attaché over, he got a huge surprise. It wasn't Elovik at all.

Taking out his phone, he pulled up the photo he'd been given, just to confirm that he wasn't mistaken. He wasn't. It definitely wasn't the attaché.

Grabbing the man's passport, Harvath gathered up the team's gear from the two Renaults and hustled back to the Duster. Johnson had just been placed inside and the cops were almost on the scene.

As he tossed the gear in back, climbed into the SUV, and put the vehicle in drive, he had two priorities. The first was to get his injured teammates medical attention ASAP. The second was to settle the score with the person who had set them up.

The fact that Elovik hadn't been part of that embassy convoy was the final piece of the puzzle. He knew exactly who he needed to go after and was already formulating a plan for how he was going to make Ray Powell pay.

CHAPTER 56

B reaking the news that the government had been infiltrated by Russian spies had not been easy. As director general of the DGSI, de Vasselot had requested an emergency meeting with President Mercier at the Élysée Palace and had insisted, for national security reasons, that no one else be in the room.

It was a highly unusual request, but Mercier had agreed, with one caveat. His chief of staff would be present. Seeing as how de Vasselot was bringing a second, she could hardly disagree.

Once the terms were set, she assigned Brunelle the job of drilling down on the chief of staff. They had to be absolutely certain he hadn't been compromised by the Russians as well. Karine was working on getting confirmation right up until the moment they walked into the president's office.

Sixty seconds before they were waved in, she finally received a text from MoMo reading: He's clean. She and de Vasselot both breathed a sigh of relief. With that concern out of the way, they could focus on Mercier.

To his credit, the French president's reaction had not been to protect himself and his political career. Instead, it had been to protect the country and the French people. That didn't mean, however, that things had gone smoothly.

While Mercier had come out of the gate strong and was proving himself to be the right man at the right moment for France, his chief of staff was growing increasingly uncomfortable with unilateral action.

He understood that the breadth of the Russian spy ring was yet to be fully determined. The fact that one of the president's own cabinet ministers—the minister of foreign affairs, one of Mercier's closest friends and advisors—might be compromised spoke to the danger of the situation. Basically no one could be trusted. But if no one could be trusted, how could the government even operate? Did the presence of a cancer, even an aggressive and metastasized cancer, mean the body needed to shut down and stop functioning?

Of course, neither de Vasselot nor Brunelle thought the cancer analogy was an apt description for what they were up against. They weren't asking for the government to be shut down. They were asking the president to keep the loop closed until they could get a fuller picture of what they were dealing with. Or, to put it in a way the chief of staff could better relate to, this wasn't cancer—it was something highly pathogenic like tuberculosis or Ebola. It had spread rapidly and, for all they knew, it was still spreading. There was no way to tell who had it and who didn't. So, for the time being, it was better to assume that everyone was infected, at least until they could begin ruling people out.

The chief of staff was not only concerned with making sure they adhered to French law, but also how all of this would impact Mercier's political future. The president would either emerge the hero or the villain of this crisis. It was the chief of staff's job to make sure Mercier was protected. Part of that was achieved by spreading the risk around, by soliciting multiple opinions and having lots of stakeholders with ample skin in the game. That was democracy. That was how things were done in France.

"Five names," said Brunelle.

"Excuse me?" the chief of staff replied.

"Give us a list of five names. Five people, the minister of foreign affairs notwithstanding, whom you and the president believe you can trust and who will provide you the best possible counsel. We'll clear them first. How does that sound?"

"They'll each want their chief of staff cleared as well."

Brunelle looked at her boss and, once she nodded, replied, "Done."

"What then was the other item you wanted to discuss?" President Mercier asked. "You said something about needing a favor. From me?"

The director general nodded again and looked at Brunelle, allowing her to take point.

"Mr. President," Brunelle began. "Are you familiar with something called the prisoner's dilemma?"

"Where two prisoners are held separate from each other and offered a lighter sentence if they inform on their compatriot?"

"That's the one. Yes. We'd like to conduct a version of it with the officials suspected of spying for the Russians."

"And?" Mercier replied.

"We can't just go round everyone up. It would be all over the news and the Kremlin would know we're on to them. We're going to have to be a little more creative."

"Okay. So, what exactly would you need from me?"

Taking a deep breath, Brunelle cleared her throat and replied, "Mr. President, we'd like to use you as bait."

CHAPTER 57

"No way," Maggie exclaimed as one of her Russia House analysts handed her a sealed manila envelope that she had couriered herself from CIA headquarters in Langley.

Unwilling to wait for the doctors to make their rounds at the hospital in McLean, Conroy had begun greasing wheels and rattling cages right away in order to get Maggie approved for release. The moment everything had been signed off on, he'd had a helicopter airborne from Andrews.

All in all, it had taken less than an hour from his first phone call until Maggie had arrived at the secure presidential medical unit at Walter Reed. From that point forward, it was a matter of staffing and getting the conference room up and running.

Sitting in her hospital bed at the front of the room, she opened the envelope with more than a little zeal. It wasn't exactly child-on-Christmas-morning energy, but it was close. When a hunch in the intelligence game paid off, it was something worth being excited about.

Pulling out the large, glossy photos, she splayed them in front of herself. "I'll be damned," she said, looking at each one. "Hello, Balthazar, you beautiful, flaxen-haired bastard."

"Pleased?" the analyst asked.

"Beyond pleased. Where were these taken and how did you get them?"

"We've been watching Peshkov's mistress, Valentina Usova—monitoring her phone and email traffic. Turns out she's been communicating with a woman fifteen kilometers up the coast from Pushkin's palace, in a town called Dzhankhot. And what would you guess this woman does for a living?"

"Something with horses," said Maggie.

The analyst smiled. "Yep. Boards them. Trains them. Teaches people to ride them. Soup to nuts, she's the go-to person in the area for all things horsey."

"How'd you get the photos?"

We have an asset in St. Petersburg with a cousin farther up the Black Sea coast in Gelendzhik. Our guy made a call to his cousin, we Cash App'd some Bitcoin their way, and voila—several hours later, we've got calendar-quality portraits of Valentina's pride and joy, as well as his very expensive trailer, which the cousin found parked behind the barn."

"Well done," Maggie stated. "*Very* well done. Has Conroy seen these?"

"Not yet," the analyst replied.

"Well, you're going to brief him when he gets here and he'll make the call on whether or not these go to the DNI and on to the president. In the meantime, I want you to write up a full report. Do you have a laptop with you?"

The analyst patted her bag and nodded.

"We're using the first lady's suite for our overflow offices. Head over there and tell them I sent you. And once again, you did a great job."

Smiling, the analyst exited the conference room.

As soon as the young woman had left, Maggie began tapping the nearest photo with her index finger. "What's your game, Peshkov?" she asked aloud. "Are you really going to start World War Three, or do you have something else up your sleeve?"

Opening up her encrypted email system, she banged out a quick message for Holidae Hayes at the Oslo station. There was a question she needed answered.

Something had been bothering her and the more she thought about it, the more nervous she became.

CHAPTER 58

G etting behind the wheel of the SUV, Harvath selected the fastest route out of the Bois de Boulogne and stepped on the gas.

From the back seat, Staelin relayed updates on both Haney, who had taken a round straight through his right arm, and Johnson, who had taken a bullet in the back, somewhere above his left hip, and which had not exited.

Staelin was alarmed not only by Haney's blood loss, but by Johnson's possible internal bleeding and organ damage. They didn't want some guy with a staple gun and Crazy Glue, they needed an actual surgeon with proper tools and medicines. And they needed that person to work with them off the books. Showing up at a regular hospital with gunshot wounds was out of the question. It was the fastest way, short of dialing 1-1-2, the European version of 9-1-1, to summon the police.

Crossing the Seine via the Pont de Suresnes, Harvath wove through traffic, merged onto the Quai Léon Blum, and, flipping a mental coin, elected to head south. He had no idea yet where they were going. All he knew was that they needed to put as much distance between themselves and the shoot-out as possible. Soon enough the French cops would be erecting barricades and casting a dragnet over the city.

Being outside the city limits proper would be a good initial means to avoid police, but it wouldn't make any difference if he couldn't get Haney and Johnson the medical attention they needed.

As he swung around a slow-moving car in front of him, Harvath's phone vibrated with a call. Pulling it out, he answered it and put it on speaker.

"What have you got?"

"La Clinique Saint-Raphael," Nicholas replied. "It's a six-bed, short-stay surgical center. Facelifts, tummy tucks, and rhinoplasty are their bread and butter. The surgeon who runs the place, a guy named René Jourdain, used to do covert, off-the-books medicine for the CIA until he got PNG'd for selling prescription meds to embassy employees. He's a bit of a wild card, but he's the best I can do on short notice."

That was all Harvath needed to hear. "Text me the address and make sure he has Haney's and Johnson's blood types ready to go. We'll be there as soon as we can."

Harvath's mental coin flip and decision to go south had paid off. Jourdain's clinic was located at the southern edge of Paris, in the 13th arrondissement. He wasn't crazy about having to cross back into the city, but he had no choice. All he cared about at this moment was getting there in time.

He drove as fast and as aggressively as he dared. It was an extremely difficult needle to thread. The last thing they needed was to get pulled over.

When they arrived at the small clinic, Jourdain and his two most-trusted nurses were waiting for them. The facility was currently empty with no new patients expected for the next two days. Haney and Johnson were taken directly to separate surgical suites. There was no exchange of names, no paperwork.

Staelin scrubbed in, ready to assist with either patient, or both if need be. Preisler left to dispose of the SUV, as well as the BRI raid vests. Harvath familiarized himself with the building, including possible evacuation routes in case the team had to leave in a hurry. If it came to that, which he prayed it wouldn't, they were going to be well and totally screwed. Neither Haney nor Johnson could be safely moved at this point.

It had been hours since Harvath had had any pain meds and, finding a water cooler, he poured himself a cup and swallowed the last two from his pocket. He made a note to get a few more from Jourdain before they left. With the little bit Nicholas had revealed, he had a feeling the doctor would let him have anything he wanted.

After taking his meds, he checked back in on his injured teammates. Johnson's situation had been deemed the most urgent, so Jourdain had taken him right into surgery. Haney was stabilized, given three units of blood, and now was being prepped as the next up.

When Harvath stuck his head into his room, Haney reminded him, "This is the second time you've gotten me shot."

The first time was in North Africa. It was hard to believe that it had only been a couple of years ago. So much had happened since then.

"Well," Harvath replied. "Third time's always the charm."

Haney gave him the finger and turned his attention back to the nurse who was helping to get him ready.

With Johnson in surgery and Haney soon to follow, there wasn't much Harvath could do. Walking down the hall to Jourdain's office, he made himself comfortable.

In a small cabinet, he found that the doctor had a well-curated liquor collection. He must have known someone in the business because he not only had a bottle of Blanton's, but also a bottle of Colonel Taylor. They were both excellent bourbons. Harvath poured himself two fingers of the Colonel Taylor and sat down on Jourdain's couch.

Pulling out the Russian diplomatic passports, he photographed each one and sent them to Nicholas. He didn't know if they would be helpful or not. That wasn't his department. Shortly after sending them, his phone rang.

"How are the guys doing?" Nicholas asked.

"Johnson's in surgery. Haney's up next, but they think they can do him under local anesthetic."

"You know this is the second time you've gotten him shot."

"It's like a frickin' conspiracy with you guys," said Harvath. "For the record, Mike got shot by *terrorists* in North Africa and *Russians* in France. Neither was my fault. He's a bullet magnet."

"Speaking of fault," the little man replied, changing the subject. "Are you sure you want to go after Powell?"

"He set us up. He got two of my guys shot. I'm more than sure."

"Okay. I'm going to text you the address of his apartment. Anything that happens after that is up to you."

"Understood," said Harvath.

"You're still going after Elovik, though, right?"

"Absolutely. But first Powell. We can't trust anything he's told us thus far. I want to apply some pressure and make sure we're getting the truth."

"How much pressure?" asked Nicholas.

"That'll be up to Powell. If he cooperates, it'll go quickly."

"And if he doesn't?"

"If he doesn't . . ." Harvath said, pausing. "It's going to be very long, very painful, and he'll spend every second wishing it was over."

CHAPTER 59

The evening light slanted through the apartment windows and splayed across the floor, pushing back against the deepening shadows. It was perfect. *Absolutely* perfect. Like something out of a Michel Setboun photograph.

Ray Powell hated the idea of losing the apartment. But unless Harvath was found, and found soon, he would have no other choice. He would have to go on the run.

That was the only reason he had returned to his residence on the Rue des Écoles. His cash, his fake passports, his Beretta pistol . . . all of it was kept in a safe under a false floor in his bedroom closet.

He had learned early on in his career that you never cached anything personal at the office—at least not anything you weren't prepared to walk away from. Tides could turn quite quickly, especially in the intelligence game. When they did, it paid to be prepared.

There were a half-dozen places he could flee to, none of which the CIA would ever suspect him of having contacts in—Argentina, Namibia, Angola, Oman, Vietnam, or Kyrgyzstan. Of course, the Russians would also take him, but it would come at a cost. He'd have to sing for his supper every day for the rest of his life.

After milking him dry of everything he knew, they would put him on a propaganda tour, weaponizing him back against the United States. All the while, he'd be living in state-run housing on an inconsistent, quasi-survivable stipend. *No thanks.*

Besides, he wasn't in this for the politics. He was in it for the money.

He was at the pinnacle of his career. As station chief, he was the law in these parts. While he reported to CIA headquarters back in Langley, there was no one physically overseeing him. Simply put, things weren't going to get any better than they were right here, right now. *This* was the time to feather his nest.

That's why he had said yes to the Russians. He understood them. He understood not only what they wanted from him, but also what they needed. The Chinese, on the other hand, were too dull, the North Koreans too obnoxious, and the Iranians too fanatical. The Russians you could deal with —bang out all the details, get rip-roaring drunk together, and then be back to business again the next morning. They were nuts, but there tended to be a method to their madness.

Madness. It was a good word for what he was experiencing right now. He hadn't signed up to be operationally involved with the Russians. His job was to be on the lookout for intelligence that the Kremlin might find valuable and to pass said intelligence to them via his handler. That was it. End of story.

Now he had not only sent a covert American tactical team into an enemy ambush but was also about to help mount a secret enemy manhunt for the survivors.

It was insane, Wild West stuff—except that in this scenario, he was the rogue Indian helping the U.S. Cavalry hunt down members of his own tribe.

But true to his nature, Powell had made sure that he was being paid. *Handsomely.*

As soon as he learned American operatives were coming for Elovik, he had sold that information to the Russians at triple his usual rate.

Luring Harvath and his teammates into the ambush had brought another payday. But the Russians had drawn the line at forking over any further cash until the manhunt was successful.

They weren't stupid. The Kremlin and the Russian president himself had been after Harvath for years. Every time they thought they had him, he had slipped their grasp. Until his head was delivered to Moscow in a cooler, the Russians wouldn't part with another ruble.

What's more, Elovik and his superiors figured Powell had an even greater incentive than money to find Harvath—the preservation of his own skin.

Since the Russians had a healthy, professional respect for Harvath, the moment they heard their operatives had been slain in the failed Bois de Boulogne ambush, they knew that it was only a matter of time before Harvath realized who had betrayed him. It was in Powell's best interest to get to Harvath before Harvath could get to him. But time was running out.

Pulling his weekender bag from under his bed, he unzipped it and began packing enough to get him through the next several days—shirts, trousers . . . the works.

In the bathroom, he hurriedly stuffed his razor, toothbrush, and other assorted items into his dopp kit and then tossed it into his weekender.

After adding a heavy sweater, a sport coat, and an extra pair of shoes, he was ready to go. Zipping up the bag, he set it in the hall near the front door and returned to his closet.

Kneeling, he hooked his index fingers behind the false floor panel and popped it out, revealing a small, biometric safe underneath.

He placed his thumb over the sensor, the light went from red to green, and there was a click as the lock released and the lid opened.

There would be no time to sort through the contents. He would be taking all of it, right down to the gold coins and preloaded debit cards.

As he lifted the lid and reached for his pistol, his heart seized in his chest. The safe was empty.

But then he heard the hammer of his Beretta being cocked and things went from bad to much, much worse.

"Don't move," a voice said from behind. "Don't even fucking twitch."

Scot Harvath had gotten to him first.

CHAPTER 60

"I want you to know that it wasn't personal," said Powell, still on his knees and not moving a muscle.

"Of course not," Harvath responded, masking the rage he was feeling. "It was just business."

"Exactly."

"Out of curiosity, what did the Russians pay you? What was my life and the lives of my teammates worth to them?"

"I'll split it with you," Powell offered, attempting to bargain his way out. "Better yet, you can keep it. All of it. One hundred and fifty thousand dollars."

"From one hundred million to one hundred and fifty thousand. I'm beginning to think the Russians are losing interest."

"They're not. Believe me. It was fifty thousand for the information. One hundred thousand more to lure you to the Bois de Boulogne. All of which, like I said, is yours."

Harvath now realized what had so bothered him on first meeting Powell. It wasn't that the chief of station was too tweedy, it was that he was too smarmy. Just beneath the surface, there was a casual unprofessionalism about him that Harvath had allowed himself to ignore as the CIA man lulled him into a false sense of security with his well-thought-out planning, a halfway-decent safehouse, and his ability to source police-like vehicles and accoutrements. It was a mistake Harvath wouldn't make again. Ever.

"Forget the money," said Powell, still negotiating. "Or don't. What I mean is, I know what you really want."

"What's that?"

"Elovik. Unit 29155. He's the key; the only way you can get to them."

Skeptical, Harvath replied, "And you're going to help me get to Elovik."

"I think, all things considered, that would only be fair."

"Why do I need you? You've already told me where he lives. Suresnes."

Powell, his back still to Harvath, shook his head. "That's an FSB safehouse. It was also a trap. If you showed up there, it was going to be another ambush."

"So where is he?"

"I can show you."

Harvath laughed. "Nice try, asshole. Not interested."

"I'm serious."

"So am I. You're going to have to do better."

"May I turn around?" Powell asked.

"Slowly," Harvath replied. "Hands behind your head."

The station chief obeyed his orders. Keeping his hands behind his head, he turned very slowly around.

"If you were going to shoot me, you would have done it already. So, why don't you tell me exactly what you want, and we can figure out some sort of arrangement."

"A, I still may shoot you," said Harvath. "And B, you know what I want. Where do I find Elovik?"

Powell was still in a mood to negotiate. "What assurances do I get that if I tell you, you'll let me live?"

"Nothing in life is guaranteed, Ray. The only way you can help yourself is by helping me. This is the last time I'm going to ask. Where's Elovik?"

The station chief needed to buy himself some more time. He knew the only way to do that was to cooperate. And cooperation meant telling the truth.

"There's a small command center at the Russian Embassy. He's there. Monitoring the situation and dealing with the fallout from Moscow."

"I'm not interested in storming a hardened diplomatic facility guarded by local law enforcement. Where does he live?"

"In the Eighteenth. Near Montmartre," said Powell, shaking his head. "But he won't be there. Until he knows you've been neutralized, he's going to remain at the embassy. It's SOP for them."

A plan started to form in Harvath's mind. "And once he believes I've been neutralized?"

"Then things will be safe enough for him to come out. Why? What are you thinking?"

"I assume you gave Elovik the location of our safehouse?"

Powell dropped his gaze and nodded.

"So, there's been surveillance on it, likely still is, and the Russians will be aware that none of us have returned."

"I would assume so," the CIA man responded. "But I still don't under—"

Harvath cut him off. "Where's your car?"

"It's parked outside."

"Let's go," said Harvath, waving the pistol and motioning for the station chief to get up.

"Where are we going?"

"That's none of your concern. I'll explain when we get there."

CHAPTER 61

There were countless, incredibly dangerous unknowns that Harvath needed to solve for. How many men would the Russians send? Four seemed to make the most sense. But what if they sent six? Or twelve?

What kind of pre-attack surveillance would they conduct? Would they attempt to send someone in to get the lay of the land and carry out a head count? Or would they launch into battle the minute they received the information?

Most important of all, could they even be relied upon to take the bait? Would Powell be able to sell it in such a way that the information wasn't just probable, but irresistible?

The only way to secure the outcome he wanted on that last question was for Harvath to be absolutely clear to Powell what would happen to him if he failed.

Elovik was protecting one of the men responsible for his wife's murder and Powell had been protecting Elovik. As far as Harvath was concerned, that put them all in the same category. He would gladly mete out the same punishment to the station chief that he planned on delivering to the Russians.

Though he was still wrestling with the idea of letting Powell walk away at the end of this with his life, it was the only way to get the man to turn in his best performance. And they were going to need it.

In essence, what Harvath was planning was one very intense piece of stagecraft, for which he was dreadfully understaffed.

He had achieved much more with much less at times in the past, but this was different. He had two of his guys lying in hospital beds and he was going to put them right in the path of an oncoming truck.

As Haney had only been under local anesthesia for his surgery, he was fully with it and was able to consent to the plan. Johnson, on the other hand, wasn't one hundred percent there. He'd been slow to wake up. He was also on a bunch of pain medication.

Harvath didn't like leaving those two to fend for themselves, but he didn't have anyone who could sit in their rooms and pull guard duty. For his plan to work, he was going to need both Staelin and Preisler. He was also going to need an incredible amount of luck.

Despite Elovik's background, the fact that he hadn't accompanied his shooters to the ambush in the Bois de Boulogne told Harvath the guy was not very hands-on. He was more management than labor.

In one respect, that was a good thing. He wouldn't be bunched up with his men if and when any bullets started flying. On the other hand, someone would have to keep eyes on him at all times. He was the reason all this was happening. If he tried to bolt the moment something happened, everything would be for naught. The team had come too far and had suffered too much to have that be the outcome.

Once Harvath had mapped out what he wanted to do, he and his teammates then had to allocate their remaining equipment.

They had burned through a lot of ammo at the ambush. Rolling into a renewed gunfight with such low stocks was asking for trouble. But, as Harvath had made clear, their only alternative was to abandon the mission. No one wanted to do that. And they knew that had Johnson been fully awake, he wouldn't want it either. The team would have to conserve what ammo it had and make the best of their less-than-optimal situation.

What they did have going for them was the element of surprise. But, of course, that was exactly what they had thought going into their encounter with the Russians in the Bois de Boulogne, only to have the tables dramatically turned.

While they were always ready for anything, that was a twist they had not seen coming. If the team was honest, there had been a bit of operational arrogance at play; a belief that they had the upper hand and because of that, maybe they hadn't had their eyes open wide enough. Though he doubted that being sold out by the CIA station chief was on anyone's bingo card.

Nevertheless, they had to be prepared for everything to go sideways. The Russians were brutes, pretty low-level strategic thinkers, but they weren't total morons. As soon as Powell contacted him, Elovik was going to be wondering if it was a trap. Was the CIA man being honest with him, or was someone, most likely Harvath, standing behind him with a gun to his head, telling him what to say? It was guaranteed that if the Russians took the bait, *they* were going to come in with their eyes wide open.

Harvath, however, would be ready for them—no matter what. He still had a few tricks up his sleeve, and he was prepared to use all of them. He wanted this to be over tonight. All of it.

It was a lofty order, but if the team did everything right, there was a chance—albeit slight—that they could pull it off.

They weren't Harvath's preferred odds, but he reveled in jobs no one else could do. Success, as he always said, was the only option. He owed it to himself, his team, and especially to Lara to see this through and make the Russians pay.

But in order to do that, he was going to have to do something he didn't want to—relinquish control. He would have to trust his team with some of the hardest and most dangerous parts of this assignment. Everything came down to managing Powell and Elovik. If that part of the plan fell through, it all would fall through.

He was thinking again about "The Purloined Letter" and hiding in plain sight. He was also thinking about how the best lies were those that contained the most truth.

To trap Elovik, they were going to need to tell him a story that was all but impossible to refute; something that made so much sense, he'd be a fool to doubt it.

As he had stood in Powell's apartment, holding the station chief at gunpoint, the lie had begun to form in Harvath's mind. It was simple, which was another hallmark of a good lie. It also offered the most likely explanation of events, which Elovik would immediately recognize as being the most probable course that Harvath had taken. Once the pieces had been put in place, all that was necessary was for Powell to make contact with his paymaster.

They communicated, in English, through an encrypted messaging app that allowed Harvath to see both sides of the communication and script the station chief's responses.

Posing as Powell, Harvath relayed the following: Of the five-man American tactical team, three had been killed in the ambush. Harvath and another surviving team member were seriously injured. They were receiving medical attention in Paris, from an off-the-books provider previously employed by the CIA. For five hundred thousand dollars, Powell would reveal their location.

After hitting send, Harvath sat back and waited for the military attaché's response. It didn't take long for the Russian to come back with a counteroffer.

The Kremlin, he claimed, was only interested in Harvath. He offered seventy-five thousand dollars, but Powell would have to snatch Harvath himself. Elovik wasn't interested in launching another operation and potentially losing more men. He was already up to his eyeballs trying to figure out how the Russian ambassador was going to explain away a bunch of dead embassy employees in the Bois de Boulogne.

No deal, Harvath texted back. He's wounded. This is your best chance to get him. Tell Moscow I get the full $500,000 or I walk.

It was a game of financial chicken. The Russians would expect Powell to play hardball. They also knew that Powell needed Harvath to be eliminated. If Harvath survived, Powell would never be safe.

Stand by, Elovik replied.

After what felt like an hour but in reality was twenty minutes, Powell's phone vibrated with another text.

The embassy only has three hundred thousand dollars cash on hand, the military attaché texted. Moscow says take it or leave it.

Harvath sat back and let Elovik twist in the wind, wondering what Powell's reply would be. Finally, he texted back, Deal.

The Russian's response was immediate. Send me Harvath's location, details on the doctor, etc. We'll arrange your payment once we confirm his whereabouts and condition.

Harvath chuckled. They were either testing him or they really didn't give Powell much credit. Only a fool would hand over prime intel hoping to get paid after the fact. Spies referred to it as the "prostitute principle." In which the perceived value of services rapidly diminishes after said services have been rendered.

Negative, Harvath texted back. We do it in person. Café Apate. 13th arrondissement. One hour. Once the intel is confirmed, you hand over the money.

It was a ballsy move, but it backstopped the lie. It made Powell look nervous, perhaps even desperate. He had a good hand, and he was playing it for all it was worth. That was something the Russians would recognize and appreciate. Had the situation been reversed, Elovik and every one of his superiors would have done the same thing. When life gave you an opportunity, you took it.

Once the military attaché had confirmed the meeting, Harvath left Staelin in charge of Powell, exited the Clinique Saint-Raphael, and walked to Café Apate on the corner.

He took a seat at an outdoor table and ordered an espresso. When the waiter returned inside, he pulled out his own phone and texted Preisler, who had opened one of the clinic's windows and was sitting behind Haney's HK417 rifle.

Ready? Harvath's text read.

Ready, Preisler replied.

Ok, then. Take your first shot. Light me up.

CHAPTER 62

Brunelle had ignored the first call from Gibert, as well as the second, letting them both go to voicemail. She was too busy and couldn't be distracted right now. Whatever he was calling about could wait.

Then a text had come in telling her that it was urgent and that she needed to stop sending him to voicemail and to take his call.

Stepping out of the conference room she was in, she phoned him back. "What is it, Vincent?"

"I've got six dead Russians in the Bois de Boulogne. All embassy employees."

"Jesus," she replied, lowering her voice. "What happened?"

"A huge gunfight. Multiple calibers. Based on the corpses and the vehicles, our people are guessing hundreds of rounds were fired."

"Who were the other shooters?"

"We don't know yet. But get this, one of the Russians was found with a long gun, a couple of hundred yards away in the woods. We think he was a sniper of some sort."

"What the hell is going on?"

"Could be any number of things," Gibert responded. "All the Russian diplomatic outposts are crime hubs. This might have been a drug deal gone bad."

"Are you guys in la Crim seeing a lot of drug deals involving snipers?"

"Plenty of gangs and cartels have been recruiting vets. They pay a lot for their expertise. Small unit tactics and all that."

"Okay," Brunelle conceded, "but you're not calling me because you think this is some drug deal gone bad. What is it about your crime scene that made you dial my number?"

"The cars," Gibert stated. "There are four in total. All shot to shit. Two trace back to the embassy. The other two are a bit more interesting."

"Interesting how?"

"Both were stolen. A blue Renault sedan and a blue Renault panel van. Guess where they were stolen from?"

"I have no idea," said Brunelle.

"The same neighborhood as our burned-out Peugeot from Jadot's murder."

"That's one hell of a coincidence."

"Yeah, I thought so too. But it gets even more interesting. Each of the Renaults was outfitted with lights and sirens. The van had strobes mounted behind the grille and, in the sedan, we found a gumball."

"They were made to look like police vehicles?" she asked.

"Correct. They were found on the side of the road in a cutout, not far from the Allée de Longchamp."

"How are they parked?"

"In a straight line," Gibert stated. "Fake police van, embassy car, embassy car, fake police sedan."

"Were the Russians trying to make it look like they had a police escort?"

"I don't think so."

"Why not?" Brunelle asked.

"Because the Renaults had bigger bullet holes than the embassy vehicles. We think those shots came from the sniper."

"So, based on that, we can assume the fake police vehicles belonged to the opposing party."

"Right now, I'd say that's safe to assume," the cop stated. "Which leaves us with two possible options. One, posing as police vehicles, the Renaults pulled the Russians over."

"To what end?"

"To rip them off. They posed as cops to get the upper hand, shot all six of them, and then took the money or the drugs—depending on who was on what side of the deal."

"Which doesn't track," said Brunelle, "because to have a sniper positioned in the woods, the Russians would have had to have known ahead of time where they were getting pulled over."

"Agreed. And that brings me to option two. This was a prearranged meeting. The Russians, however, had decided to double-cross their fake police friends and staged an ambush, but got outgunned."

"That's much more believable, but why was the other party posing as cops and what does this have to do with the Russians who stole the burned-out Peugeot?"

"Now you know the real reason why I called you. I need your help."

She was shocked, but surprisingly pleased, to hear him admit it. "I appreciate you calling me. Listen, I'm going to tell you right now that the Russians will want to control this internally. You're likely to receive little to no cooperation from the embassy."

"No kidding. None of the victims were carrying identification. Cell phones, yes, but ID no. As we don't have all the scary Big Brother tools that you do, we could only use facial recognition from airport entries to identify them."

"Send me whatever you have and I'll get MoMo on it."

"Speaking of which," said Gibert. "Still nothing on the getaway car?"

"No," Brunelle replied. "But something tells me that we have just gotten one step closer."

CHAPTER 63

“A what?” Maggie asked, as her boss dropped a stack of folders on the conference room table and made himself comfortable.

“A loyalty test,” Conroy repeated. “Can we get some coffee in here?”

After a staffer disappeared to fetch a carafe, Maggie said, “Expound on that.”

“It’s pretty simple. Regardless of the propaganda Peshkov and the Kremlin put out, Russia is getting its ass kicked in Ukraine. Nobody knows that better than the people closest to the top—Peshkov’s inner circle. That’s also where the biggest challenges to his power are likely to come from.”

“So, he brings everyone down to Cape Idokopas for what?”

“The world’s biggest fireworks show!” replied Conroy. “His own version of the Trinity test.”

“A light dinner, a little dancing, and then he just airdrops a tactical nuke over the Black Sea?”

“Exactly.”

“Did POTUS give you this idea?”

Conroy shook his head. “It came up in discussion with the national security advisor.”

“I think he’s been watching too many Godfather movies.”

“If you’ll pardon my French, it *is* the ultimate dick-measuring contest.”

“I don’t disagree,” Maggie replied.

"Peshkov will call it a 'test' but in actuality he's throwing the West a don't-fuck-with-me-in-Ukraine brushback pitch."

"And conceivably, by doing it over the Black Sea, outside Turkish maritime claims, he wouldn't be triggering a wider war with NATO."

The more they discussed it, the more convinced Conroy was becoming. "Can you imagine an event like that?" he asked. "It would serve the same effect as a detonation in Ukraine, but Peshkov would reap the added benefit of forcing any of his would-be usurpers to watch. 'Look at the power I have,' he'd be telling them. 'Challenge me and it'll be the last thing you ever do.' He could then put on a screening of *Oppenheimer* afterward and let everyone keep their goggles. The guy would be untouchable."

Handing out atomic goggles as some sort of sick party favor was definitely in keeping with Peshkov's profile. That said, Maggie wasn't crazy about her boss falling in love with this theory. It was always dangerous to get too attached to any one idea and she decided she needed to throw a little cold water on it.

"Based upon the size of the device he chooses, the fallout could be limited to about a kilometer in all directions. The Turks, however, will go apeshit. They'll never let another Russian vessel transit the Turkish Straits again. This would be across the board, including commercial ships, on top of the already current prohibitions in place against the Russian Navy. Peshkov would be a fool to do it. It would be absolutely devastating for Russia and would destroy all the work Moscow has done in building bridges with Ankara."

"All right then," said Conroy as the staffer came back in with the coffee. "I'll make sure to let the national security advisor know that you're a strong no on the possibility of a nuclear demonstration over the Black Sea."

"Anything's possible," said Maggie. "I just think that on the list of probabilities, this one's highly unlikely."

The DDO poured himself a cup of coffee and offered one to Maggie, who declined.

"So, we're still looking at a tactical nuclear weapon being detonated somewhere inside Ukraine. Is that the position we're operating from?"

"At the moment, yes," Maggie responded. "That's where the evidence is pointing."

"In that case, you'll be glad to know that President Porter is taking your advice. He has lined up former high-ranking military figures for all the Sunday shows. He is also dispatching the secretary of state to Moscow to deliver an in-person warning. If you can give me the list of Peshkov influencers you think he should be meeting with, I'll make sure it gets passed along."

"Absolutely. In the meantime, I've got a follow-up report for you," said Maggie, handing him a folder.

"What's this?"

"We've found Balthazar. Valentina Usova's horse."

Conroy took the folder and opened it. "Where?" he asked as he flipped through the photos.

"A town called Dzhankhot. It's about fifteen kilometers up the coast from Pushkin's palace."

"You were right."

"We got lucky," Maggie replied.

"What do they always say? Better to be lucky than good?"

She nodded. "In that case, let's hope we're about to get lucky again."

"What's up?" Conroy asked as he set the folder down.

"We're starting to pull on a new thread. Something in the debriefing of Leonid Grechko. It may be nothing."

"Okay. But if it's *something,* what kind of something is it?"

Maggie took a deep breath. "We're looking at the possibility that Russia might be looking at striking outside Ukraine. Somewhere in Europe."

CHAPTER 64

From the beginning, Powell had been the Achilles' heel in Harvath's plan. No matter how many ways he came at the problem, he couldn't find a better way to solve it. The station chief was necessary to flush Elovik out into the open, but he absolutely couldn't be trusted.

One wrong word, one wrong facial expression, and the CIA man could torpedo the entire operation. If tipped off that something was wrong, Elovik would rabbit. He wouldn't just walk, he'd run away—and it would be a very long time before they could get him to show his face outside the embassy again. That meant the meeting in the café was critical. But how could they guarantee that Powell would live up to his end of the bargain?

In a perfect world, Harvath would be sitting right next to him, sticking a gun in his ribs. This, however, wasn't that world. Elovik was expecting Powell to be alone.

The next-best scenario was to have someone at a nearby table, also with a gun, who could see and hear everything that was going on. But, as he was a known commodity to the Russians, Harvath automatically ruled himself out. Even if he could have come up with some sort of passable disguise, there simply wasn't enough time. That left either Staelin or Preisler.

Either man could have handled the job, but Preisler, who was of Danish descent and had spent loads of time visiting family in Europe whiling away hours in local cafés, was his first choice. And though Staelin, who came from solid Teutonic stock and would have easily blended in, was no stranger to European culture, his expertise would be make-or-break at the clinic.

Once all the roles were established, the ground rules were then explained to Powell. When everything was over, Harvath was going to let him walk. The contents of his safe, minus the Beretta, would be returned to him and he could keep any and all bank accounts he had established. It was agreed that in exchange for his life, he would drop off the grid and never be heard from again.

If he didn't comply with the terms of the agreement, Harvath would hunt him down and there wouldn't be any negotiating the next time. He would kill the station chief on the spot.

Harvath also made it clear that if the CIA man did anything to spook or warn Elovik, that if for any reason the Russian military attaché abandoned their meeting, it would be grounds for his immediate termination. To emphasize the point, Harvath told Powell to look down at his chest.

The station chief was sitting outside Café Apate, at the same table Harvath had been. Preisler, who was sitting nearby, had handed Powell his phone so that Harvath could provide the CIA man with a final recitation of the ground rules.

Upon being instructed to look at his chest, Powell glanced down and saw a tiny red dot hovering over his heart.

"Just know," said Harvath, who was now perched behind Haney's rifle in the fifth-floor window across the street, "that I'll be watching you too. Don't do anything stupid."

With that, Harvath turned off the laser and disconnected the call.

Taped next to the window was the range card Preisler had drawn up. In addition to the distance to the café table, it listed several others Harvath had thought might be useful once he was situated in the team's makeshift overwatch position. Having a general knowledge of how far away a target was made for better accuracy. Shooting in a civilian area was incredibly dangerous. If he had to take a shot, he wanted to make sure that as much guesswork as possible had been removed. The only blood he wanted to see spilled was Russian blood. And of course, Powell's, if the station chief stepped out of line.

With twenty minutes left until Elovik was expected to arrive, Harvath did a final walk-through with Staelin.

Between the two of them, and their knowledge of chemistry, they had been able to scrounge multiple ingredients inside the clinic and hastily prepare several improvised devices.

Considering what the Russians were likely to throw at them, anything that might slow down their assault and help even the odds was more than welcome. In this situation, neither the Marquess of Queensberry nor the Geneva Convention applied.

After conducting a check of their weapons, comms, and other essential equipment, there was nothing else to do except wait. The Russians were going to have to come to them.

Five minutes later, Harvath received a text from Preisler. A vehicle resembling the Russian embassy cars they'd encountered in the Bois de Boulogne had just made its second pass of the café. Inside were four men in suits.

Back behind Haney's rifle, Harvath had seen it too, though he hadn't been able to distinguish anything about its occupants.

Looks like our guys, Preisler texted. Possibly an advance team.

Roger that, Harvath replied. Stay frosty.

A couple of minutes later, one hour on the dot since Harvath had communicated with him, a different car came to a stop in front of the café and out of it climbed Elovik.

Activating his radio, Harvath announced to the rest of the team, "Game on."

CHAPTER 65

A s Elovik exited his vehicle, his eyes took in everything, especially the multiple customers sitting outside the café. Among them, three men and two women looked like they might be pros, but he couldn't be sure. In scenarios like this, he was always hypervigilant. As a result, his overactive mind could perceive threats that weren't necessarily there. It was a weakness, to be sure, but it had also helped keep him alive for a very long time.

Joining his counterpart at the small, marble-topped table, he stated, "I don't like this, Ray. Our current circumstances are quite undesirable. This was not how I wanted things to unfold."

"I didn't either," Powell admitted, scanning the pavement. "Believe me."

There had been two other men in Elovik's vehicle, neither of whom had gotten out. Instead the car had rolled forward and pulled into a nearby loading zone, where it was currently idling. The other vehicle, the one that had twice circled the café, was nowhere to be seen.

"All the way over here," Elovik continued, "I was tempted to pull the plug and tell my men to turn around."

"Yet you didn't."

"My government would have been most displeased with me if I had. Particularly, my president. The opportunity to capture his son's killer has quite an allure. Not the least of which is the opportunity to be recognized as a Hero of the Russian Federation."

Even before being ensnared by Harvath and pressed into service, this kind of banter had never appealed to Powell. There was no reason to act like he enjoyed it now. "Where's the money?"

"Right to the point," Elovik replied. "How American of you."

"I'm sorry. Did you expect drinks first?"

"A drink wouldn't hurt. It would give us something to do while my men confirm the authenticity of your information."

"Fine," Powell relented. "Anything but vodka."

Snapping his fingers, Elovik got the waiter's attention and waved him over. "As a rule, I don't like to celebrate before a job is done. But for some reason, I feel extra confident tonight. Let's have champagne."

"Order whatever you like. You're buying."

After a little back-and-forth with the waiter about the wine list, the Russian settled on a vintage and the waiter headed inside to retrieve two glasses.

While they waited, Elovik probed what had happened in the Bois de Boulogne. "Six dead Russians and only three dead Americans. Seems somewhat disproportionate, doesn't it?"

"I warned you," Powell replied. "The Americans were all ex–Special Forces. A couple of them were even Tier One operators."

"Which was why I sent some of my best."

"Well, apparently your best weren't good enough."

"Good enough to take out three of yours," Elovik responded with a smile.

"If, at any point, you want to say 'thank you,' feel free to just spit it out. If it wasn't for me, you never would have seen Harvath coming."

"My dear Ray. We did thank you. One hundred and fifty thousand times. And you're about to get three hundred thousand more. Perhaps it is you who owe us some thanks."

Powell shook his head. "This is the problem with Russian economics. To you guys, hundreds of thousands of dollars are like winning the world's biggest lottery. You think you can retire and maybe, in Russia, four hundred and fifty sets you up for the rest of your life. But in American economics, four fifty is nothing but a really good year."

Elovik smiled. "Who said anything about retiring? We expect you to have a long, deeply involved career at the CIA. In fact, we're going to help get you to deputy director. That's when you'll really begin making money."

The station chief, not a fan of being bullied, was choking back the urge to tell his handler to fuck right off when the waiter appeared with two glasses of champagne and set them on the table.

"Santé," the Russian said in French, picking his up and clinking it against Powell's. *To health.*

The station chief didn't respond in kind. Instead he raised his glass in the attaché's direction and took a long, smooth sip.

It was a decent champagne, made even more delicious to Powell by the fact that his handler actually thought he had something worth celebrating.

"Well," Elovik stated, setting his glass down. "Now that we have our drinks, I think it's time that you give me what I came for."

Removing a cocktail napkin from his pocket, the station chief placed it on the table and slid it across to him.

"You've got to be kidding me," the Russian replied, picking his head up and looking across the street at the building that housed the Clinique Saint-Raphael. "I thought you chose this neighborhood because it was off the beaten U.S. Embassy path, or you had a safehouse around here or something. That's where Harvath is? Right now?"

"My hand to God," Powell replied, not raising his hand.

"Who else is in there?"

"Patient-wise? Only Harvath and one of his teammates. I don't know how many staff. Probably pretty sparse. One nurse. Maybe two? It's the overnight shift."

"How did Harvath find this place? He didn't get it from you, did he?"

The station chief shook his head. "I haven't heard from him since I dropped him off at the safehouse. From what I understand, his own organization kept working with the surgeon who runs the place after we fired him. Sometimes the intelligence world is small."

"Quite," Elovik agreed. "Do you know anything about the building? Service elevators? Stairwells? Airshafts?"

"Not part of my purview. Our security guys handle that stuff. I just made sure the bills were paid."

"Understandable," the Russian replied as he pulled out his phone and took a picture of the cocktail napkin with the address written upon it. Typing out a quick text message, he attached the photo and hit send.

"Now what?" Powell asked.

Sitting back in his chair and raising his glass, Elovik said, "Now we enjoy our champagne."

CHAPTER 66

I f Harvath had been truly honest with himself, he had only partially relinquished control. Stepping into the sniper role and occupying an overwatch position allowed him to be two places at once.

He could be in the window, with a view across the street, enabling him to protect and assist Preisler, and he could also be available to back up Staelin, should anything go down. In essence, he had figured out how to have his cake and eat it too.

Harvath had only one rule of engagement. If the Russians went on the offensive, then any Russians in or around the operation could be considered rightful combatants and therefore fair game.

As his phone vibrated, he looked down at a text from Preisler. Elovik just transmitted your location. Look sharp.

Harvath texted back a thumbs-up and then radioed the rest of the team. If an attack was coming, it was coming soon.

As Harvath manned Haney's suppressed 417, Staelin was monitoring a bank of CCTV cameras at the front desk.

Four minutes after Preisler's last text, he texted again. Three vehicles just pulled up. South side of your building.

Acknowledging receipt, Harvath then hailed Staelin. "We've got company. South side. Three vehicles."

"Good copy," Staelin replied. "I see them. They're debussing now. Looks like twelve men in total."

"Twelve?" Harvath replied. "Who's back watching their embassy?"

"They're going to be down to cooks and computer specialists soon. Here we go. They're approaching the lobby door."

"Which I made sure was fully locked. If they breach that barrier, it's on. We go hot."

"Jesus," said Staelin, leaning in closer to watch his monitor. "One of these guys just pulled a sledgehammer out from under his jacket."

There was a pause as Staelin continued to watch the events on the ground level unfold. Then his voice crackled back across the radio, "Breach. Breach. Breach. They just made entry."

"Roger that. We're live."

"Confirmed," Staelin replied. "They're breaking into four-man teams. One is headed for the north stairwell. Another is crossing the lobby toward the south stairwell. And, if you can believe it, it looks like these idiots are going to send the last team up the elevator."

"It's the Russians," said Harvath. "I can believe anything. Just make sure there's something there to greet them."

"Roger that," the ex–Delta Force operative stated, getting up from the front desk. "I'm going to position one."

"Good copy," said Harvath as he texted Preisler. Contact. You're cleared hot. 10 seconds out.

When Preisler sent him the thumbs-up, Harvath began counting down from ten. Flipping the fire selector on the 417 from safe to single shot, he snugged the butt of the weapon up against his shoulder and consulted the range card taped next to the window.

As soon as he saw Preisler stand up and approach the table where Powell and Elovik were seated, he sighted in his target and took a deep breath.

Exhaling, he pressed the rifle's trigger. *Good hit,* he murmured to himself as it shattered the windshield of Elovik's vehicle, idling in the no-parking zone. He followed it up with five more, moving back and forth between the driver and passenger.

He then watched as Preisler, who already had the Russian military attaché on his feet with a pistol jammed tightly into his side, steered him out of the café and down the block.

True to their arrangement, Powell—who had laid money on the table to pay their tab—was walking right alongside. When they reached the embassy vehicle, the station chief popped the trunk and removed the briefcase with his payment; then the trio disappeared around the corner to where Harvath had parked the CIA man's Citroen.

As soon as they were no longer visible, Harvath closed the window, transitioned from Haney's 417 to Johnson's H&K UMP submachine gun, and let Staelin know he was coming.

With only one, half-loaded backup mag, he was going to have to be judicious with how much lead he slung.

That said, if the handful of improvised devices they had created ended up working, they might be able to tilt the field to their advantage, regardless of how outmanned they now found themselves.

Racing down the hallway, Harvath tagged up with Staelin not far from the elevator and the front desk area. The Russians coming up the elevator were going to be first on the floor. It was critical that they not gain any ground.

"We good?" Harvath asked as he drew even with him.

"If we're not," Staelin replied, "we're about to find out."

Ahead of them, the elevator indicator chimed, and each floor indicator lit up as the carriage approached.

Finally it arrived at the fifth floor, and when it did, Harvath announced, "Showtime."

When the doors started to open, he and Staelin pulled the tabs on their homemade diversionary devices and slid them across the floor toward the elevator.

As the four gun-wielding Russians inside were revealed, the fuel-air explosive devices detonated. There was a bright flash, followed by a muted *boom*.

Though not the overwhelming flashbang effect Harvath had been hoping for, it was enough to temporarily blind, if not stun, their attackers.

Not wanting to waste a single moment of their advantage, he and Staelin sprang from their hiding places and, guns blazing, fired rounds of two shots in rapid succession known as controlled pairs. None of the Russians made it out of the elevator.

As the four men lay dead or dying, Harvath helped himself to one of their Kedr machine pistols and, adjusting the fire selector, delivered four quick head shots just to make sure. With that, it was time for Harvath and Staelin to split up.

It had been decided that Harvath would take the north stairwell and Staelin the south. Pulling the stop button so the elevator couldn't return to the lobby, the two men hustled in their separate directions.

In the middle of Harvath's hallway, next to a purposefully overturned supply cart, lay a metal box about the size of a loaf of bread. Two long, un-insulated wires, which were hopefully difficult to see, connected it to a jerry-rigged detonator.

Taking up his position in an exam room, Harvath used a small mirror, placed across the hall, to watch the stairwell.

It was hard to hear anyone approaching over the continuous ringing of the elevator alarm. The attackers could be right behind the north door, having a full-blown conversation, and he wouldn't have known. His only confirmation of their arrival was going to be visual. And so he watched, and waited.

Finally, he saw the stairwell door crack open and figured one of two things was going to happen next. Either these guys were going to toss out a flashbang or an actual grenade first, or they were going to push right out of the stairwell, ready to get their gunfight on.

As he hadn't noticed any of the men in the elevator carrying grenades, he assumed it would be the latter and gripped the detonator a little bit tighter. Then he heard Staelin through his earpiece.

"Someone just tossed a smoke grenade into my hallway," he radioed.

Harvath was about to reply when the north stairwell door was opened a bit farther and he got treated to a smoke grenade as well.

The device was pitched in a long arc, clattered to the ground, and rolled as it began spitting out thick white smoke only a couple of yards from Harvath's position.

He gave them three seconds to exit the stairwell and all be in the hall together before depressing the switch on his homemade detonator.

Nothing happened.

Checking the wires, he tried again. *Nothing.* Pulling the wires out and reattaching them, he tried one more time. *Still nothing.*

From the south hall, Harvath heard Staelin's device detonate. He could imagine the tsunami of shrapnel—nails, screws, scalpel blades, and hypodermic needles—that were slashing through the smoke and ripping into the flesh of the attackers who had exited the south stairwell. Within seconds of the device going off, gunfire began.

Harvath had a decision to make: lean out the door and start firing blindly, or wait for the Russians to come to him. As it turned out, the decision made itself.

The room he was hiding in was beginning to fill with smoke. He had a couple of seconds left, at best, before he wasn't going to be able see anything. That was when a gun barrel appeared at the door frame.

Letting the UMP fall in its sling, Harvath used both of his hands to wrench the man's weapon down and away. Simultaneously, he delivered a blistering headbutt, which caused the man's vision to dim.

Rocking unsteadily on his feet, the Russian looked like he was ready to fall over. Harvath helped push him in that direction by slamming the man's weapon into the base of his skull and knocking him unconscious.

Patting him down, he found that the man was carrying an unusual Russian Brutalica knife in his waistband. It was jet black, resembled a straight razor on steroids, and now belonged to Harvath.

With three more Russians in proximity, a head shot would have only brought them running and was therefore out of the question. Instead Harvath put the knife to work. *One down.*

Slipping out of the exam room, Harvath crept to the office across the hall, ready to take down his next Russian. The space, however, was empty.

He was about to twist to his left to step back into the hall when he heard the metallic click of a weapon's hammer fall. Harvath had had no idea that the guy had been right there. It was the second time in a matter of hours that had happened to him. He pivoted hard to get off the Russian's line of attack.

Whether the *click* had been the result of a misfire or the man not having seated a round wasn't Harvath's problem. Not getting shot was.

As the man slapped the bottom of his mag to make sure it was fully inserted and went to recharge his weapon, Harvath shot him twice with his UMP—once in the chest and once in the head. The attacker fell to the hallway floor, dead. *Two down.*

The smoke had largely dissipated by this point and when the remaining two Russians swept back into the hall to see what had happened, they easily identified Harvath as a target and began firing. The gunfight was on.

Diving back into the room he'd just been in, the Russians' bullets tore up the walls and floor, missing him by mere millimeters.

He scrambled to take cover behind a heavy wooden desk as dust, splinters, and shredded papers filled the air.

Round after round ripped through the walls and the doorway as the Russians focused their fire on him and kept getting closer. Raising his UMP, he tried to anticipate where they were, and fired back.

For a moment, he forced the Russians back and their guns fell silent. Then another smoke grenade was loosed, and it landed only a few feet away from him. His attackers were about to make a final, deadly assault on his position.

Having mapped the entire building, he knew going out the fifth-floor office window was a nonstarter. There wasn't enough of a ledge to provide a foothold and there were zero handholds. Unless he could get out the doorway before they pushed in, he was going to be worse than trapped; he was going to be dead. He had only seconds to figure out what to do. Suddenly, he thought of the Brutalica.

Pulling out the knife again, he picked a lower section of wall behind the desk and cut into it. Once it had been properly scored, he kicked through the drywall, yanked the insulation, and repeated the process on the other side. He then slipped through the narrow opening into the empty office next door. The tables had been officially turned.

Gun up, ready to engage the enemy, he moved to the door. From the south stairwell, he could hear the sounds of Staelin's ongoing, intense firefight. He needed to get down there to back him up, but first things first.

The smoke had poured into this office, but less so, and it was already starting to vanish. Any moment the Russians were going to make their move. So was Harvath.

Risking a look into the hall, in between the weakening curtains of smoke, he could see two figures massed near the other door. The attackers were getting ready to make entry. As they did, Harvath began applying pressure to his trigger.

The moment they charged into the office, Harvath sprung into the hall and went straight after them.

CHAPTER 67

The Russians sprayed the room with bullets. Had Harvath been anywhere inside that space, even if he had remained behind the wooden desk, his life would have been over.

Using the doorway to conceal as much of himself as possible, he opened up on the Russians and let his own bullets fly. Each one found their target. He shot the men multiple times, cutting them down where they stood, and finished the job with a head shot apiece, just to make sure. *Three and four down.*

Removing his almost spent magazine, he inserted his lone backup, which was half-empty and headed quickly to assist Staelin.

"Moving to you," he radioed.

"Hurry up," Staelin replied.

Making sure to rapidly clear each doorway he passed, he got down toward the south stairwell area as fast as he could.

As soon as he neared, he could see what the problem was. Staelin was pinned down behind a large column. Two Russians were firing on him. A third was on the ground, covered in blood. There was no sign of the fourth.

Taking cover, he radioed for Staelin to get ready. Then, with the first Russian in his sights, he gave the order to move and began firing.

Neither of the Russians was aware that Harvath was there. He caught the first Russian with two rounds to the upper chest and one to the base of the throat.

As the man dropped to the ground and Staelin scrambled out from behind the column, Harvath adjusted his aim. He was about to engage the second Russian, who had just spun in his direction and was preparing to fire.

Before he could, Staelin executed an incredibly difficult shot. At great risk to himself, he had moved toward the threat, not away from it, and leaning hard to his right, had double-tapped the man in the head. It was one of the most audacious maneuvers Harvath had ever seen.

He thought about administering a head shot of his own to the Russian who had been lying in the pool of blood, but it wasn't necessary. Staelin's homemade claymore mine had torn the guy to shreds.

Looking around, Harvath asked, "Where's the fourth guy?"

Staelin looked but didn't see him either.

Harvath gave the signal to fall in behind him. They were going to have to clear every single room until they found him.

As they moved down the hall, Harvath noticed a trail of blood splatter. Their fourth Russian was not only injured, but was also leading them right to him.

Ejecting his magazine, Harvath did a quick check to see how many rounds he had left. Eight was better than zero, but not by much. At least they only had one more attacker to neutralize.

Harvath's optimism, however, began to crater the moment he saw a shift in direction of the blood droplets. The Russian hadn't been looking for a room to hide out in; he had headed back to the south stairwell. Harvath immediately picked up his pace and Staelin followed.

Carefully, they pushed the door open and, guns raised, stepped into the stairwell. The fifth floor was the top floor of the building. The blood didn't go toward the roof access, it went down the stairs toward the next level. With Staelin covering their six o'clock, Harvath followed.

When he saw the blood pooled outside the door for the fourth level, his own blood went cold.

The fifth floor had been a decoy—a clinic belonging to a different physician entirely, whose offices had been closed while the staff was on a medical education retreat. The fourth floor was where Jourdain's clinic was located and where Haney and Johnson were recuperating.

As he grasped the blood-soaked door handle, Harvath heard a gunshot ring out from the other side.

Throwing the door open, he and Staelin heard two more shots as they charged into the clinic, its reception area empty, and rushed to the aid of their comrades.

There was blood all over the floor and, as they got closer to the source, Harvath's heart rate began to elevate.

Somehow the Russian had been drawn right to Johnson—the most grievously injured and the most defenseless person on their team.

Applying pressure once more to his trigger, Harvath raced for Johnson's room, his heart pounding in his chest.

Swinging into the doorway, he expected to see the worst—Johnson dead and a badly injured Russian, whom Harvath would instantly kill, very much alive.

Instead, he saw the opposite—Johnson was very much alive, the Russian was very much dead, and standing in the corner, protecting his teammate, was Haney. He was bracing the Flux PDW that Harvath had given him against his good shoulder.

"Shot him two times," he said, referencing the Russian. "But he wouldn't go down. The third time, however—"

"Was the charm," Harvath replied, finishing his sentence for him.

Drawing the Russians into the building had been the only way to flush Elovik into the open and separate him from as many of his security forces as possible. It had been done at a considerable risk, but it had paid off.

The next step in Harvath's plan came with its own potential downfalls—not the least of which being their inability to, once again, escape before law enforcement arrived.

He had also worried that Jourdain and his two nurses wouldn't go for it, but offering to significantly increase the amount of money they were being paid had eliminated all resistance.

While Jourdain and the nurses took Johnson and Haney to the underground parking facility, Harvath and Staelin dumped the dead Russian back in the stairwell, rolling his body down a level, and then returned to the fifth floor to retrieve Haney's 417, and so that Harvath could plant something on one of the bodies.

After sanitizing Jourdain's clinic, bagging up the medical waste from Johnson's and Haney's procedures, which would be thrown in the back of one of the nurse's cars, they went down to the garage, where Harvath hopped in the passenger seat of the lead vehicle, Staelin did the same in the third vehicle, and they all departed the underground parking facility together.

As they drove, Nicholas kept track of their progress remotely, scrubbing footage from each of the traffic cameras they passed.

From Jourdain's clinic, it was a half-hour drive to the village of Les Molières and the team's new safehouse.

The director of Bastide Lumière, a luxury assisted living community in the countryside southeast of Paris, was a long-standing business partner of Jourdain's. Whenever his clinic was full, or he had patients who required extended stays, Bastide Lumière, or in English the luminous country house, was where he placed them.

The property was over two hundred bucolic acres with an eighteenth-century chateau as its main facility. Scattered throughout the woods were smaller houses for residents who were capable of independent living. There was a full modern medical clinic, a spa, two golf courses, tennis courts, a restaurant, a movie theater, and all the other amenities one would expect from a high-end development of its kind.

Harvath and his team had been booked into a cluster of cottages as far away from the rest of the structures as possible. And while Haney had said no to a hospital bed, one was definitely waiting for Johnson when they got there.

One of the nurses would stay in the room next to his to keep an eye on him, while Haney would receive the same care from the other nurse. Jourdain, as requested, would remain on property to oversee everything.

With Haney and Johnson settled in, Harvath left Staelin behind to protect them, borrowed Jourdain's car, and drove to an even more remote part of the property to meet up with Preisler.

When he got there, he stepped out of the vehicle and took a deep breath. The evening air was cool and smelled of pine. It was quiet. Peaceful.

For a moment, Harvath was almost able to forget that he was in the middle of an operation.

Almost.

CHAPTER 68

Knocking on the side of the maintenance shed, Harvath waited for Preisler to roll the sliding door back. When he did, the first thing he noticed was Powell's Citroen sitting off to the side of the large space.

"Do you want to bring your vehicle in?" Preisler asked.

Harvath shook his head. "It'll be okay outside."

Standing aside, Preisler let Harvath enter and then slid the door closed behind him.

"Any problem getting here?" Harvath asked.

"Negative," Preisler replied. "Neither of those assholes wanted to ride in the trunk, but other than that, everything went fine."

Harvath had figured as much. He and Preisler had predetermined a secluded spot for Preisler to pull over. Upon which, Powell was enlisted to help secure Elovik and place him in the trunk. After that, it was Powell's turn. The less each of them was aware of, the better.

Powell already knew Harvath's reputation and what he was capable of. Inviting, or even forcing him to watch the interrogation, was pointless. By and large the station chief had served his purpose. When Harvath was ready to put him out with the trash, he would do so. Right now, he had some very personal business to attend to.

Unlike the woodsy scent outside, the maintenance shed smelled like diesel fuel and old motor oil. The concrete floor was cracked and covered with decades of stains. Iron trusses ran overhead, and snatches of moonlight spilled through the dirty glass skylights. Parked at the far side, a yellow snowplow looked old enough to have served as a troop transport in World War II.

The place had character. It had served a purpose in life. And though it was a little aged and a bit worn down, it was still doing its job. Harvath respected that.

He also respected the touch of modern that had recently been added, and which Preisler now drew his attention to. Mounted to one of the trusses was a two-ton electric chain hoist. Its remote hung from a thick, black cord. Underneath, a table with two chairs had been set up.

"Hands over his head or keep them behind his back?" Preisler asked, a wry smile on his face.

Harvath smiled back. Even the most inexperienced police officers didn't pull up on cuffs to get a suspect to his feet when his hands were behind his back.

What's more, with equipment like this it wouldn't take much to tear the arms out of someone's sockets. Between the screaming and the passing out from the pain, the interrogation they were planning could go well into overtime. Nobody, especially Harvath, wanted to be here a minute longer than they needed.

Nodding at the Citroen, he said to Preisler, "Time's a-wasting. Let's get Vlad out."

Opening a trunk with one prisoner inside, much less two, was a lot like opening a soda you'd left in the presence of a vindictive sibling. You never knew how explosive the result was going to be.

As seniority had its privileges, Harvath motioned for Preisler to hand him his Taser and then stood back as the junior operative popped the lid.

Thankfully, especially for Preisler, whose job it had been to properly secure the two men, nothing happened. Powell and Elovik were right where he had left them—hands and feet secured, hoods over their heads, and pieces of duct tape across their mouths underneath. Harvath had been quite clear that he didn't want these two comparing notes and making plans for some great escape. They were no longer masters of their own destinies. Harvath, and only Harvath, would decide what happened to them.

Grabbing Elovik, who had been placed in the trunk first and was therefore farther back, Preisler dragged him across Powell and pulled him out.

Preisler then removed his knife and cut away the plastic restraints from Elovik's ankles so that he could walk.

Guiding him to the table, he sat him down in such a way that his hands, which had been bound behind his back with flex-cuffs, were slipped over the rear of the chair.

As Preisler went to stand next to the Citroen, Harvath removed Elovik's hood and peeled the piece of duct tape from his mouth.

The Russian didn't speak. He just blinked as he tried to adjust his eyes to the light.

On the table was a tall plastic bottle of water and a stack of cups. "Thirsty?" Harvath asked.

Elovik nodded.

Harvath poured a cup and then held it to the Russian's lips so he could drink. The man nodded again when he'd had enough and Harvath set the cup back on the table.

"Thank you," the military attaché replied.

"You're welcome," said Harvath, keeping his demeanor relaxed.

Having control over an interrogation required, first and foremost, control over oneself. Psychologically, it was important that the Russian understand that Harvath held his fate in his hands. The outcome, good or bad, would depend on how Elovik comported himself.

"It appears Mr. Powell was happy to play us both," the Russian offered. Looking up at the heavy steel hook hanging from the hoist, he added, "Is that meant for me?"

Harvath smiled. "That's up to you. But to be honest, I hope it won't be necessary. If that's where we arrive, then this conversation has really gone off the rails."

"Agreed," the Russian replied, stealing one more glance at the winch. "Where would you like to start?"

"Normally, we'd be talking about your background and things like that."

"Building rapport."

"Exactly," said Harvath. "Except that I'm not that interested in your background."

"From what Powell told me, I understand you are interested in Colonel Ivan Kapralov, the commander of unit 29155."

"That's correct. What can you tell me?"

"Quite a bit, I would imagine. More to the point, however, I can tell you where to find him."

"Then we're off to a good start," Harvath replied. "Where is he?"

This time it was Elovik's turn to smile. "Perhaps we can first discuss what a successful outcome of this conversation looks like. Beyond us not having to employ anything suspended from the ceiling."

"Such as?"

"Such as, what does my life look like after we're done chatting? Do we shake hands and I return to my embassy?"

"That depends," said Harvath. "Is that how you want this to end?"

"Maybe. What did you promise Powell?"

"I promised that he gets to keep breathing."

The Russian smiled again. "At a minimum, I would expect the same."

"If you prove helpful to me, I might be able to arrange that."

"What if I could prove helpful not just to you, but also to your government?"

"Are you looking for some sort of an overall deal with the United States?"

The military attaché nodded.

The man definitely had Harvath's attention. But Harvath had his own agenda. "To work out a deal, we'd need a station chief. And all things considered, I don't think Powell is in a position to help anyone. Why don't we start with why I'm here. We'll call it a mutual gesture of good faith. You tell me where Kapralov is, and I'll agree to let you keep breathing. Fair enough?"

"Do I have a choice?"

Harvath couldn't have been more serious as he looked at the man and replied, "No."

"Colonel Kapralov and his men are in Norway."

"Where in Norway?" Harvath asked, working to conceal his surprise.

He had entertained the possibility that the assassination unit might be on an assignment and that he'd either have to wait for their return, or chase after them. What he hadn't foreseen was that they would be in Norway.

"Near Oslo," Elovik answered.

"Why? What are they doing there?"

"Several days ago, a high-level Russian intelligence official, named Grechko, defected. A team was sent to kill him. They failed. Kapralov and his men were dispatched to finish the job."

"And you know precisely where I can find them?" Harvath asked.

"Of course. I helped set up their safehouse."

"That's helpful," said Harvath, who, knowing what he had in the palm of his hand, began pressing for more information. "I've got to imagine, though, that the Norwegians have this guy Grechko locked down tight. They're not going to leave a high-value defector sitting on a park bench somewhere. How is Kapralov supposed to find him?"

"We have someone inside Norwegian Intelligence. An asset I developed myself," the Russian responded proudly, before shifting gears and adding, "But something's wrong. The Norwegians have misplaced him."

"Misplaced?"

"After the first team tried to kill him and were all wiped out, Grechko and the agent debriefing him disappeared. They're assumed to still be in Norway. No one, however, knows where. Kapralov and his team are on hold until the location is uncovered."

"Interesting," Harvath replied, feigning indifference. Switching gears, he posed a new question, a plan forming in his mind. "Why don't you run me through what intel you have that you think my country might be interested in."

"I assume since Powell is no longer viable, that you have another station chief in mind we could speak with?"

Harvath nodded, itching to get outside and place the call. "I think I have someone who will be very interested."

CHAPTER 69

Brunelle had gone to see the Bois de Boulogne crime scene for herself and had been standing next to Gibert when word came in of another gunfight. This time in the 13th arrondissement.

According to the dispatch officer, there were two dead Russian Embassy employees in a car near the Café Apate and a dozen more inside a medical building across the street.

Having seen enough in the Bois de Boulogne, she hopped in Gibert's car and they rolled, lights and sirens, to the 13th.

The two Russians shot to death in the front seat of their embassy car were shocking to behold. The brazenness of it reminded her of mafia killings in Italy. Barriers, to shield the scene from view, were only just being erected when they arrived.

Inside the building was even worse. *Much* worse. It looked like a war zone—especially the victims of what appeared to be some sort of homemade, shrapnel-laden bomb. Brunelle couldn't even begin to imagine how painful it would have been to die that way. One of the men had not only absorbed a ton of shrapnel, but also appeared to have been shot multiple times before retreating down the stairs and succumbing to his wounds.

Another man had received neither shrapnel nor bullets but had had his throat cut from ear to ear and had bled out on the floor. The scene was one of pure, unadulterated carnage.

What wasn't obvious, however, was who had done the killing. Similar to the site of the first gun battle, where only the fake police vehicles had been left behind, there was basically no additional evidence that might help identify the other shooters.

None of it made any sense. And it was about to get even weirder.

As the first detective on the scene, Gibert had authority to examine the bodies. He and Brunelle were bent over their third corpse when the cop pulled a stack of passports from the man's pocket. Opening each of them, he showed them to Brunelle.

"My God," she said. "Those are from the dead Russians in the Bois de Boulogne. Why does this guy have them?"

"I have no idea. The deeper this goes, the more bizarre it gets."

"What is going on at that embassy? Some kind of internecine warfare?"

Gibert shook his head. "I don't think I've ever seen anything like it. Two different groups of Russians, both slaughtered, and no sign of who did it."

"What's your gut telling you?" she asked, genuinely meaning it this time, rather than tossing it off as a flippant barb as she had two mornings ago in Jadot's kitchen.

"It looks like these guys have evolved. They sent a lot more personnel this time."

"Doesn't appear to have made any difference."

"No, it doesn't," the cop replied. "Whoever they're up against are good. *Very* good."

"I agree," said Brunelle. "But *who* are they? Other Russians? French? Why the gangland-style combat? What the hell are they fighting over? And what does any of this have to do with Jadot's murder?"

Gibert shrugged. They were all good questions. He just didn't have any good answers. He didn't even have any bad answers.

"And why the medical clinic?" she asked, throwing more questions on the pile. "What's the connection with the Bois de Boulogne?"

"That one," the cop replied, "I think I can answer. Or at least I can make a relatively well-informed guess. The Russians came here in search of one, or more, of their enemies who was injured at the last gunfight. They bulked up the size of their force and came in hard, smashing through the lobby door and charging up the elevator and both stairwells."

"But their opponents were waiting for them," Brunelle continued.

"They set up IEDs and, along with their guns, were able to take down twelve men and disappear."

Gibert nodded. "We'll want to send a bulletin to every hospital in the city. We'll also want to start pulling CCTV footage. Nobody simply *disappears*."

"I'll get MoMo going on the footage right away," she said as her phone started to ring. Pulling it from her pocket, she looked at the caller ID. "Speak of the devil.

"Agent Brunelle," she stated, activating the call and raising the phone to her ear.

She listened for several moments as MoMo filled her in on the startling information he had just learned.

"Are you *sure*?" she stressed. "I'm talking, absolute, one hundred percent, watertight certainty. Because if you're wrong, we're worse than fucked. President Mercier is going to bring back the guillotine."

After a few more words back and forth, Brunelle said to MoMo, "Send it to me. I want to see it for myself."

With that, she ended the call.

"What was that all about?" Gibert asked.

"I'll tell you in the car."

"Where are we going?"

Taking out her pistol and making sure a round was chambered, she replied, "To conduct the biggest bust of our careers."

CHAPTER 70

I t was a briefing President Porter would have preferred to have had in person, but given Maggie's condition, he agreed to do it via encrypted video link.

There had been some discussion as to whether the National Security Council should be summoned for the meeting, but in the end it was decided to limit it to the president, his chief of staff, the national security advisor, the Director of National Intelligence, and Maggie.

Her boss, Andy Conroy, had pushed her latest findings right to the top. As soon as the CIA Director read them, he pushed them further up the ladder. It was clear to everyone that POTUS was not going to want to wait to read them in tomorrow morning's PDB. He would want to be informed immediately.

Once all of the participants were on the call, President Porter said, "Maggie, it's all yours. You have the floor. Take it away."

"Thank you, Mr. President," she replied. "In your digital briefing books, you can see the photos and read the update on Balthazar, the horse belonging to President Peshkov's mistress, which was found just up the coast from Peshkov's Black Sea complex.

"More importantly, I have included secure links to portions of Norway's debriefing of ex–Russian intelligence official Leonid Grechko. Per our arrangement with the Norwegian agent conducting the debriefing, we're allowed to monitor the proceedings and to ask questions via our station chief in Oslo, Holidae Hayes.

"In Grechko's most recent session, we asked that he be pushed on the

Russian nuclear weapons that had been placed in Belarus, as well as Moscow's intentions. You can listen to Grechko's responses yourself, but the gist of it is that his office was charged with developing intricate false-flag operations, as well as highly sophisticated propaganda in the run-up to a tactical nuclear weapon being detonated."

"So, they're definitely going to do it," the chief of staff stated.

"It's an option," Maggie clarified, "but it's continually looking like one they plan to exercise."

"What are the false flags and propaganda about?" the national security advisor asked.

"Moscow," Maggie replied, "wanted Grechko to have plans ready to paint NATO and its Western allies as increasingly more aggressive and belligerent actors set on destabilizing Belarus and collapsing their government."

"To what end?" the advisor asked.

"According to Grechko, the idea was to feed the narrative that the West planned to invade Belarus and force it into NATO."

"That's absurd."

Maggie nodded. "Agreed," she said. "But it gets worse. As the false-flag operations and fire hose of propaganda were rolled out, the Belarusians would understandably be nervous and on edge. It's against this backdrop that a missile launched into NATO territory could ultimately be characterized as 'accidental.'"

"What?" the chief of staff replied. "As in 'Whoops, we didn't mean to press that big red button'?"

"Essentially, that's the concept," said Maggie. "However, there are several steps that would have to happen before that. Belarus would need to raise its posture, the warheads would have to be unstored from their depots and loaded onto missiles, those missiles would have to be loaded onto launchers, et cetera."

"But all of that could happen in a matter of hours," the Director of National Intelligence observed.

"That is correct."

"Those are Russian missiles, they'd be tipped with Russian nuclear warheads, and there'd conceivably be Russians somewhere in the launch chain," said the chief of staff. "How does President Peshkov think he'd escape accountability?"

"He doesn't," Maggie responded. "At least not fully. But there's a big gray area that he believes he can manipulate. Instead of taking all the heat, he'll blame-shift to Belarus, which'll be seen as having actually launched the missile. In essence, it would allow Russia to dodge a significant amount of the international condemnation while, Peshkov believes, scaring Western populations into pressuring their governments into dropping their support of Ukraine."

"Unbelievable," the chief of staff angrily stated. "The guy's going to use a cutout to do his nuclear dirty work."

"Not if I have anything to say about it," President Porter replied. "Did Grechko mention any possible targets?"

"Only one," said Maggie. "J-Town."

As she had in her meeting with the full National Security Council, Maggie once again stunned her listeners into silence.

J-Town was shorthand for NATO's key logistical hub near Jasionka Airport, outside Rzeszów, Poland, just sixty miles from the Ukrainian border.

Billions of dollars in Western military equipment and ammunition passed through J-Town on its way to Ukrainian forces. The site was critical to the war effort. If this indispensable gateway was struck, it would dramatically turn the tide in Russia's favor.

President Porter was first to break the silence. "That leaves us with just one question," he said. "How do we guarantee this attack does *not* happen?"

Looking into the camera on her monitor, Maggie responded, "Having listened to all of Grechko's interview, I have a couple new ideas. But they're potentially very dangerous and come with a lot of risk."

CHAPTER 71

Holidae Hayes landed at Paris Le Bourget Airport in a slate-gray Bombardier Global 8000 business jet. In her hand was an American passport filled with stamps, under the assumed name Elovik had requested.

With everything to his satisfaction, the Russian had thanked her with a smile and boarded the plane. Harvath walked up the steps right behind him, barely acknowledging the Oslo station chief.

Langley wanted her to begin debriefing Elovik right away, but first she wanted to have a few words with Harvath. Directing the Russian military attaché to an enclosed, private area at the rear of the aircraft, she told him she'd be with him in a minute.

Despite the late hour, she looked all business. Her red hair was pulled back tight. She wore a dark pantsuit. To top it all off, she sported a pair of expensive heels.

"This is for you," she said, handing Harvath an envelope.

He had been pocketing the pain-relief packets in the forward galley. "What's this?"

"An official letter from the Treasury Department. They've released all holds on your Swiss account and have waived any taxes, penalties, or fees."

Folding the envelope in half, he slid it in the back pocket of his jeans.

"You're not going to read it?" she asked.

"Do I need to?"

"No, but I figured you'd want to make sure."

"I'm good," he said, excusing himself so he could slide past her and grab a bottle of water.

"Are we really going to end things this way?"

"What way?" he asked, fishing a bottle from the fridge.

"You're choosing to shoot the messenger."

"I don't know what you're talking about."

"For fuck's sake, Harvath," she replied. "I had a job to do. I took no pleasure in it. I told you, I wanted to go with the carrot, not the stick."

Setting the water on the counter, he looked at her. "I get it. I just thought we were better friends than that."

"We *are* friends."

"I don't shiv my friends."

"Nobody shivved you. In fact, I made Langley scale way back. They wanted twenty-four-hour surveillance on you. Plus, a full listening and video package installed at Sølvi's apartment. Not only did I tell them to forget it, but I also told them that if they tried to force my hand, I'd resign."

When Harvath didn't respond, she continued. "I made it clear that they needed to trust you, like I do. In fact, I figured that if you're half the man I believe you are, the first thing you would have done was to fill Sølvi in."

Harvath tried to suppress a grin, but Hayes, who was a master at reading people, caught it. "You motherfucker," she said with a smile. "I knew it."

"At some point," Harvath replied, "and it doesn't have to be right now, I want to know whose idea it was to blackmail me."

Running her index finger down his water bottle in a move that was quasi-erotic and considerably off-putting, she replied, "Obviously, as a professional intelligence officer, that's not something I could ever do. Not even for a really good friend."

Harvath was about to respond until he watched her use the condensation from the bottle to write three letters on one of the shiny maple cabinets—*DDO.*

"So?" she asked. "Are we good?"

"Gooder than good," Harvath joked, pulling her in and giving her a hug.

"It's an hour and forty-five to Oslo," she said as they separated and began walking back to start Elovik's debrief. "Get some rest. You've still got a long night ahead of you."

Despite how angry he'd been, Harvath knew that focusing on Hayes was, as she had put it, shooting the messenger. Would he have handled things differently? Of course, but they were two different people with two different ways of doing what they thought was necessary. To tell the truth, she was one of the best, most solid people he had ever dealt with in the CIA. If the rumors were true, and the president was reelected, she'd probably make a fantastic ambassador. Part of him, however, hoped that she would stay exactly where she was.

Popping two packets of pain meds, he carried his bottle of water to the first chair he saw and, exhausted, dropped into it.

As the forward door closed, he could hear the engines spinning up. Pulling out his phone he texted Staelin for a SITREP.

It had been decided that Haney and Johnson should remain behind to convalesce. Once they were both ready to travel, a plane would be sent to bring them back to the United States. Until that time, Staelin and Preisler were in charge of their protection.

When Harvath's phone chimed with a response that everything was good, he gave permission to release Powell, tilted back his seat, and closed his eyes.

Hayes hadn't been kidding. He had an incredibly long night still in front of him. As he fell into what would be a very short sleep, the last thing his mind pinged off before going silent was that if his story was ever written, how might he be remembered?

CHAPTER 72

*S*cot Harvath was an asshole. That was the first thought that had gone through Ray Powell's mind when he was released from the trunk of his Citroen.

He had been left by the side of the road, two klicks away from the nearest suburban train station, with only his house keys and a ten-euro note in his pocket.

Technically, Harvath had kept his word, but only just barely. Powell, for whatever reason, had expected more.

At the very least, he had expected Harvath, upon his release, to give him back his false passports. And maybe, if Harvath was a halfway-decent human being, to also hand over the rest of the contents of the safe from his bedroom closet. Minus the gun, of course.

To his credit, Harvath, in his own sadistic way, had done just that, but not without making Powell jump through a few more flaming hoops.

Instead of allowing the CIA man to begin his life on the run by heading for the closest airport or seaport, Harvath had made it so that the station chief needed to return to his apartment in the center of Paris.

There, Harvath had informed him, wrapped in a garbage bag and tucked in his freezer, was everything Harvath had pulled from his safe. Minus the gun, of course.

Without his phone, there was no one Powell could call for help. The emergency numbers that field operatives were required to memorize were useless. There was no way he could phone the embassy or Langley for assistance. He was completely and totally on his own.

Taking the first available RER train, he had then transferred to the Métro, changing lines twice before resurfacing two blocks from his apartment.

He was burning extremely valuable time. If Harvath or, God forbid, the Russians were looking to screw him, resurfacing in Paris was the absolute last thing he wanted to do. In fact, part of him wondered if the journey was even worth it.

That was his self-preservation instinct talking. When his professional instincts kicked in, he knew the contents of that bag in his freezer were indispensable. Passports, cash, gold coins, and debit cards were crucial to his ability to disappear. Only once he was safely ensconced in another country could he partially let down his guard, breathe a little easier, and begin accessing the money he had hidden away in his multiple international bank accounts.

Walking up to his building, he maintained his vigilance, covertly keeping his eyes peeled for any signs of surveillance. Per his training, he had conducted multiple surveillance detection routes since boarding the RER. He had scanned every face on the Métro, had changed carriages multiple times, and had gone so far as to take the long way home once exiting the subway system. To his relief, he hadn't seen anything.

Entering his building, Powell couldn't be bothered to wait for the elevator. Instead he bounded up the stairs, taking them two and even three at a time.

When he arrived at his floor, he moved down the hall comforted by the fact that he didn't need to waste time packing. Prior to Harvath's arrival, his weekender bag had been fully prepped.

At his front door, he pulled out his keys, opened it wide, and hurried inside. His bag was right there where he'd left it. All he needed was the garbage bag fucking Harvath had shoved in his freezer.

Charging into the kitchen, he threw open the freezer, fully expecting to see it, but it wasn't there.

He was about to curse Harvath out when a woman's voice from the living room said, "Looking for this?"

Powell spun to see both Brunelle and Gibert sitting there, a garbage bag between them on the coffee table.

"God damn it," the station chief swore, pissed beyond measure that his apartment had been breached twice in one night.

"Raymond Alan Powell," Brunelle continued, reading the arrest warrant that had been signed off on by her boss, Director General Audrey de Vasselot, "By the power vested in me by the Republic of France, I hereby place you under arrest in connection with the killing of Jean-Jacques Jadot."

Pausing briefly, Brunelle then added, "We also want to discuss your possible involvement in the death of France's ambassador to Beirut."

The station chief looked at the bag on the table, looked at Brunelle, and then looked at Gibert.

For a fraction of a second, Powell weighed his options. But no sooner had he started thumbing his mental scale than he knew what he had to do.

Dropping his shoulders in resignation, he slowly moved out of the kitchen and stopped at the threshold of the living room. He was surrendering.

Brunelle and Gibert were finally able to let their guard down too. It had taken a tremendous amount of work to get to this point, and it was all but over. They could finally breathe a collective sigh of relief.

That was when Powell ran.

"Son of a bitch!" Gibert exclaimed as he scrambled for his radio.

Leaping off the couch, ignoring her colleague's shouts to wait, Brunelle pulled her pistol and gave chase.

For someone fifteen years–plus her senior, he was fast as hell. She yelled repeatedly for him to stop, but Powell ignored her.

As she ran, she was driven by the anger she had felt over the evidence MoMo had sent her. Using the AI software, he had been able to ascertain that Powell had been involved in both the theft of the Peugeot used in Jadot's killing, as well as the Renaults in the Bois de Boulogne shoot-out. The fact that he was attempting to flee only confirmed his guilt in her mind.

When he neared the stairs at the end of the hall, she realized she wasn't going to catch him. So, raising her weapon, she attempted to control her breathing, took careful aim, and fired.

The shot was dead-on, shattering a large, ornamental cap atop a newel post just in front of him, showering the CIA man with splintered pieces of wood.

He might have been able to outrun her, but outrunning her well-placed bullets was not going to happen. Coming to a full stop, he held his hands out at his sides where she could see them.

"I want them in the air," she demanded. "Over your head. Way up!"

The station chief complied.

Moving forward, she holstered her weapon, took out her handcuffs, and reached for Powell's right hand. But just as she did, he swung his left elbow behind him and hit her in the face so hard, she felt sure he had knocked a couple of her teeth out.

The pain radiated across her skull and for a second she thought she was going to black out. Refusing to lose consciousness, she shook it off and fought back.

She grappled with the station chief, trying to maneuver him into a joint lock or some other pain compliance technique, to subdue him and bring him under control.

Attempting an aikido wrist reversal, she lost her grip as Powell wrenched his arm free and violently pivoted to get away from her. But as he did, he lost his balance.

Brunelle lunged to catch him, but only caught the hem of his shirt, which tore from her grasp as he went over the railing and plunged six stories to the lobby below.

He landed with a sickening thud. Brunelle, too stunned to speak, peered over the railing at Powell, his arms and legs akimbo, as a crimson pool of blood began to spread out like a halo around his cracked head.

Looking from the corpse to the upper floor from which he had fallen were several of Gibert's officers who had been waiting outside but had rushed in when he had hailed them over the radio.

Her face ashen, she continued to stare down at the body. As she did, Gibert, who had just arrived at the railing, placed his hand on top of hers.

"I saw everything," he said. "It wasn't your fault."

She appreciated his words, but for several moments couldn't speak. When she finally recaptured her ability, she said, "He was a huge break in our case. Now he's dead."

"You got the list. That's the most important thing."

"I know, but I also want answers."

"Unfortunately, that's not always the way this business goes," he responded. "Sometimes you get nothing and your case doesn't even get solved. But you got something. Be grateful for it."

She knew he was right and was about to say as much when her phone vibrated. It was a text from Director General de Vasselot. With President Mercier's cooperation, everyone they had identified on Jadot's list as being on Russia's payroll had been assembled at the Élysée Palace. They had each been told that an international incident was brewing and that their specific expertise was required. As they arrived, they were all kept separate from each other.

De Vasselot was ready to spring the trap. She wanted Brunelle there when it happened.

CHAPTER 73

The safehouse being used by Colonel Ivan Kapralov and his unit 29155 members was a secluded cabin, deep in the woods, forty-five minutes north of Oslo.

Upon landing, Harvath, Elovik, and Hayes had walked into the private aviation terminal where Chief Inspector Borger was waiting for them. Holidae handed over their passports and the man drove off to get them processed.

A staff member had taken Hayes and Elovik to one of the private suites, where personnel from the CIA's Oslo station had already assembled. Hayes thanked Harvath, wished him good luck, and told him to reach out if he needed anything. She then disappeared inside with her newly minted Russian defector.

Harvath was then shown to the same room he'd been given two days ago when he had arrived from Poland. Inside was the rest of his team from the South of France.

Along with Sølvi and Grechko, they had closed up shop in Eze and had all flown up together.

Despite being a little outside the twenty-four-hour window that she'd been given by the Norwegian Intelligence Service, Sølvi's employers had been more than happy to extend her deadline a few hours—especially if it meant identifying the traitor in their midst.

After some serious horse trading with Holidae Hayes, Elovik had been willing to give up the name of his mole inside the NIS.

The Russian military attaché was an intelligence gold mine and he had struck a very lucrative deal with the CIA. For giving up everything he knew, he would receive not only a new identity and a generous annual stipend, but also a condo on the beach in Miami with deeded parking and a convertible Mustang. As long as he continued to cooperate, he'd be set for the rest of his life.

Once the Bombardier was catered, prepped, and refueled, he'd be on his way to a safehouse and a thorough debriefing back in the United States. It was Holidae's job to make sure he and the operatives traveling with him got off the ground without a hitch.

Because the mole at NIS had been unmasked, Harvath had agreed with Sølvi that it was likely safe for her to return with Grechko. Just to make sure, he had suggested several extra security precautions, which her employers had also agreed to.

He knew that she and Grechko would have been met on the tarmac with a serious security force, who would have whisked them to a highly secure and undisclosed location—this time a military base, which had been one of Harvath's multiple suggestions. The bottle of Krug sitting in Sølvi's fridge would not be opened tonight. That was fine by Harvath. He had one last, extremely important job to do.

According to Elovik, Ivan Kapralov had been injured in a fall after murdering a French DGSE intelligence officer named Jadot. Powell had tipped the Russians that Jadot had uncovered their spy network deep inside the French government. As silencing Jadot was considered a mission of paramount importance, Kapralov had been given the job himself. An arrogant man and a bit of a showboat, he had killed Jadot with an ice axe. He knew that the similarities with the 1940 assassination of Leon Trotsky would be admired inside the Kremlin.

He sounded like a straight-up psychopath to Harvath and the sooner they put this rabid dog down, the better.

The minute Borger handed Harvath his passport back, the team finished loading the two SUVs Hayes had arranged for them and got on the road. Barton, Morrison, and Gage were in the lead vehicle. Harvath, Nicholas, and the dogs rode in the second car with Ashby driving and Palmer riding shotgun.

As they drove, Harvath had an eerie, unshakable sense of déjà vu. A couple of years back, he'd been on a mission farther north in Norway. The target was a Russian terrorist cell, which had also holed up in a remote cabin. They had booby-trapped the perimeter with antipersonnel mines. It had turned into a total bloodbath. Harvath made a mental note not to repeat those mistakes. He would take things extra slow and pay close attention to every single detail.

The thick tree cover meant their drone was going to be useless. They would have to figure things out on the fly.

Nicholas would hang back with the dogs and function as their mobile command center. Harvath and his five teammates would approach the cabin together and make the final call as to how to take it down once they got there.

Thankfully, the team had brought plenty of ammo. They also had night-vision goggles and the two sets of night-vision binoculars they had used in Monaco. Short of a rocket launcher to blow up the cabin, there was really nothing else he could ask for.

And so, putting his head back, he closed his eyes and tried to relax his mind for the rest of the drive. That bloody image of his prior Norwegian operation, however, kept replaying in his head.

CHAPTER 74

They parked the SUVs as far away as possible. It would mean a good two-mile walk to the target, but they wouldn't have to worry about headlights or the sound of engines giving them away.

Harvath took point and led the team through the darkness. Every quarter mile, he would stop and transition to the extremely powerful night-vision binoculars to get the long-track view. Once he was satisfied that they weren't walking into a trap, he would transition back to his goggles and wave his teammates forward.

It made for a slow and laborious trek, but he didn't care. He didn't want anyone else getting injured. This wasn't an officially sanctioned operation. Yes, the powers that be back in Langley and Washington would be thrilled to deal the Russians and unit 29155 a deadly blow, but at its core, that wasn't what this was about. This was personal. This was about revenge. This was about Harvath.

Granted, his teammates had known and loved Lara. What they were doing for him, he would have gladly done for any one of them. Yet the sense of déjà vu wouldn't let him go. With each step, as they crept closer to the cabin, his sense of foreboding, his sense of danger increased. His intuition was trying to tell him something. He just didn't know what.

Half a mile from the target, he decided to scrap the mission.

"Are you joking?" Ashby asked, as quietly as she could.

Harvath shook his head. "Something's off. I'm calling it. End of mission."

"So, we're just going to turn around and walk back to the cars?" Palmer asked.

"*You're* going to turn around and walk back," Harvath clarified. "I'm going the rest of the way by myself."

"The hell you are," Gage objected. "Per our intel, there's six battle-tested Russians in there. What's the number one rule of a gunfight?"

"Bring all your guns," Harvath admitted.

"And number two?"

"Bring all of your friends with guns."

"Precisely," said Barton. "So stop screwing around and let's Charlie Mike."

Charlie Mike was militaryspeak for *Continue Mission.*

Harvath knew that Barton wasn't pushing back because he was angry. He was pushing back because he was determined. He wanted the Russians to suffer for what had happened to Lara. The alarm bells in Harvath's mind, however, were only getting louder.

"If you're going, we're going with you," Morrison asserted. "End of discussion."

Harvath shook his head. "I'm in charge of this team and if I say I'm going in alone, that's how it's going to be."

"Then I quit."

"Me too," Ashby replied.

"Me three," Palmer chimed in.

Gage flipped Harvath the middle finger as his official resignation and Barton joined him by making an even more obscene hand gesture.

"Maybe you're the one who should go back to the car," Morrison stated. "It looks like you've got a lot of pink slips to process."

Harvath loved these guys, but this was too much. Healthy loyalty was necessary for a unit to successfully function. Blind loyalty could get people killed.

Taking up the point position, Barton stated, "I guess we'll see you up there," as he signaled the team to move out and began walking toward the cabin.

"Fuck," Harvath mumbled under his breath. This was a hell of a bad time to have a sudden outbreak of democracy. There was no telling what he was marching all of them into.

But here they were, unwilling to abandon the mission. Unwilling to abandon *him*. They were going to Charlie Mike whether he liked it or not.

Harvath had been a leader long enough to know that loyalty was a two-way street. If they weren't going to let him go in alone, he wasn't going to let them go in alone either.

Taking back point, he led his team forward.

But with each step, the alarm bells continued to grow louder. He was actively ignoring his instincts, and knew that things would not end well.

Two yards later, something caught his eye. Halting their forward motion, he stared at a tree in the near distance, trying to make out what he was seeing, but it wasn't clear.

Flipping his goggles up, he transitioned back to his night-vision binoculars and suddenly knew exactly what he was looking at—the glow from an infrared trail camera. And where there was one, there were definitely more.

Calling up Gage, who was carrying the other pair of night-vision binoculars, he showed him what he had seen.

"Do you think the Russians put that there?" the man asked.

"Could be the Russians. Could be the people who own the cabin. Could be some nature club," Harvath replied. "Regardless, we don't want anyone to know we're coming."

Raising Nicholas over the radio, he described what they had found. Because the trailcam had an antenna, that likely meant it was designed to broadcast over a cellular network. With a log-in and password, you could access it the same way you would a remote CCTV camera. You could also set it up to push alerts to you, with either stills or video, when it detected movement.

The only thing Nicholas needed to know was how Harvath wanted it handled. Even though trailcams were far less sophisticated technology than CCTV networks, their simplicity made them a bigger pain in the ass to loop video and spoof.

The easiest and most believable solution was to jam cell signals in the area. Not only would the trailcams not work, but neither would the Russians' cell phones. It was a win-win. Harvath instructed Nicholas to get on it.

Seven minutes later, the little man confirmed that the network was down, and the team could advance.

Harvath gave the signal once more to move out and the team continued its cautious journey forward. There were only the sounds of the darkened forest to accompany them.

In any other context, these sounds might have been soothing, but tonight, as they pushed deeper into the unknown, they remained ominous.

A quarter mile out from the cabin, he stopped the team, transitioned to the binoculars, and conducted a final assessment.

He could make out the cabin and three cars parked in front. The chimney appeared warm, but not hot. The Russians had built a fire earlier, but it had been allowed to die down. Maybe they had gone to bed. Maybe they'd run out of wood. At this moment, there was no way of knowing.

As they closed the remaining distance, they stepped off the dirt road and melted into the trees.

He didn't need to advise them on what to do or what to be on the lookout for. They were some of the best operatives he'd ever worked with. They were in their element now. Silently materializing, achieving their objective, and disappearing again was what they did best. Harvath was honored to be among them.

Fifteen yards into the trees, they encountered their first tripwire. Raising his right arm, Harvath held his clenched fist just above shoulder level. It was the command to halt. He then pointed out what he had discovered. Carefully, they all stepped over it. Ten yards later, they found another one. Someone was going to very extensive lengths not to be taken by surprise.

In almost any other scenario, extensive surveillance and thorough planning would have ruled the day. But as the last twenty-four hours had demonstrated, time was not always a commodity in abundant supply. If a window opens and you can hit the target, you *hit* the target. Especially when you don't know when you'll get that chance again.

In a raid where a subject needed to be captured, speed, surprise, and overwhelming violence of action were the keys. In an operation where none of the subjects were leaving alive, Harvath liked to slow things down. In his book, slow was smooth and smooth was fast. When you took your time, your precision spiked. And though he fully intended to maintain the element of surprise, while applying overwhelming violence of action, what mattered most to him right now was precision. Precision would get this job done effectively and allow the entire team to walk out of the cabin alive and unharmed.

After establishing the parameters of the takedown, the most important decision was where your entry point would be and how you intended to conduct the breach. In this case, there was no decision to be made. The safehouse, and Elovik, had done that for them.

Airbnb was the best thing to ever happen to intelligence agency budgets. In an era when more and more money was being diverted away from human operations and plowed into technology, the days of endless, Agency-owned and operated safehouses around the world were over. Short-term home rentals were where it was at. The fact that it could be done over the internet, with little to no notice, and zero in-person contact, was the icing on the covert cake.

With the information Elovik had provided, Nicholas had easily tracked down the listing. It provided not only photos of the home and the property, but also a floor plan, which greatly assisted in their planning. The most useful piece of intel, however, was which door they should use to make their entry.

Coming in through the main door was out of the question. It was big, heavy, and had both a ton of iron fixtures and was additionally secured from the inside with a wooden beam. Without an explosives kit, they weren't getting in that way. The good news was that they didn't need to.

Not wanting to mar the traditional appearance of their cabin, the owners had placed an electronic keypad for guests at the rear of the structure on the kitchen door. Nicholas had made short work of tracking down the home's most recent email, which included the security code. Blowing the door off its hinges wouldn't be necessary. All they had to do was punch in the string of numbers.

They took several moments to surveil the back of the cabin before stepping out of the trees and approaching the kitchen door. They wanted to make sure there was no one keeping watch. As best they could tell, no one was.

With the guns of Barton and Morrison trained on the windows, Gage watching their six o'clock, and Ashby and Palmer covering their flanks, Harvath tapped the code into the keypad, the light switched from red to green, and the lock released.

Verifying that everyone was prepped for entry, he gave a silent countdown with his fingers, twisted the knob, and pushed the door open.

There was a slight, barely audible creak from the hinges. Nothing else. Crossing the threshold, Harvath stepped inside and led his team into the cabin.

It smelled like cigarette smoke and burnt garlic. He had no idea what the Russians had been up to, but he was fairly confident that they weren't going to be getting their security deposit back.

Keeping their eyes and ears peeled, the team was the embodiment of stealth as they flowed soundlessly through the dining room. Crushed beer cans and empty liquor bottles were visible upon the table.

Sitting around a safehouse, waiting to be activated, was one of the most boring parts of the job. Getting hammered to help pass the time, however, was not just unprofessional, it was dangerous. It was also par for the course when it came to the Russians. They were a different breed.

Passing into the living room, they swept their suppressed weapons left to right and right to left, searching for targets. So far, everything was quiet, and they moved on to the sleeping area.

Based on what they knew about the cabin's layout, there were three bedrooms with probably two men in each. Harvath's plan was to split his team into three pairs, position them at the doorways, and launch their attack all at the same time.

He made it to the midpoint in the hallway when a board groaned beneath his foot. The entire team heard it, and everyone froze in place.

They stood there for what felt like a lifetime, listening for any indication that they'd been given away, before Harvath began moving again.

Two steps later, he hit another bad board—this one even louder. And just like before, he froze. With his grip tight on his weapon, he waited.

The shot came through the wall right behind him, missing his head by a fraction of an inch. The crack from the round was deafening. He didn't need to see the hole in the wall to know it was probably from a .45.

Immediately after the first shot had been fired, a barrage of follow-up shots exploded around them.

Knowing how deadly hallways were, the team rapidly retreated to the living room, where they expertly took cover and, upon Harvath's command, returned fire.

The team pumped round after deadly round through the walls and into the bedrooms.

When he signaled for them to cease firing, the team members took turns covering each other while they inserted fresh magazines into their weapons.

Grabbing Ashby and Palmer, Harvath headed back into the hall, in which hung a haze of sawdust and gunsmoke.

He covered Palmer as he swept into the first room, firing two controlled pairs at the already injured and bloodied occupants. Without wasting a single moment, they moved to the second bedroom—the room from which the first shot had erupted.

It was Ashby's turn and, gun up and at the ready, she swung into the room as Palmer covered her and Harvath, despite having Morrison, Gage, and Barton securing any necessary retreat from the living room, kept an eye on their six o'clock.

A half-dressed man with a large handgun lay dead on the floor. His colleague lay dead in his bed. Ashby placed a shot in each of their heads, just to make sure.

Backing out of the room, Ashby joined her teammates and the trio proceeded to the end of the hall. Based on the floor plan, this was where the master bedroom was located and where they expected Kapralov to be. It was now Harvath's turn at bat.

With Ashby covering him, he swung into the room and drilled a bleary-eyed Russian fumbling with a Saiga automatic shotgun.

He traced the room with the front sight of his weapon, but there was no sign of Kapralov. Stepping fully inside, he checked the closet, under the bed, and then the bathroom, where the window was wide-open.

"Kapralov's on the run," he said, climbing out the window. "I'm going after him."

"Right behind you," Ashby announced, following him.

They spread out, each searching in a different direction.

Unable to pick up anything through his goggles, Harvath was about to flip them up and pull out the binoculars when Ashby radioed, "I've got him."

"Where?"

"Twenty-five meters east of the cabin. He may have a limp, but he's moving at a good clip. I'll stay on him until you can catch up."

It was the moment of truth. Harvath was finally going to scratch the last name off his list. His revenge would be complete, and he could allow Lara to rest in peace. But something inside him had shifted.

A leader who didn't believe his team was every bit as good as he was wasn't really a leader at all. Harvath's team wasn't just exceptional, they were even better than he was.

"Do you have the shot?" he asked.

"Affirmative."

"Take it."

"Are you sure?" Ashby replied.

Harvath had never been more certain about anything in his life. "Take the shot," he stated. "That's an order."

CHAPTER 75

K arine Brunelle looked up as she heard a hiss, and the door of the sensitive compartmented information facility opened.

Poking her head out, Director General de Vasselot said, "You can come in now."

Brunelle stood, adjusted the pleats in her skirt, and entered. She had never been to the American Embassy before, much less the highly secretive CIA offices within, and had changed her outfit four times that morning.

It was stupid, and she knew it. All that mattered was that she appear professional. Afterward, however, she had another meeting, and it was important to set the correct tone for that one as well.

The SCIF was similar to the ones at the DGSI. The only difference was that this one seemed to be a little more modern and up-to-date.

Once the door had closed, de Vasselot made the introductions. "Karine, I would like you to meet James Jansen. Jim is now acting station chief until the CIA decides who should succeed Ray Powell."

Brunelle shook hands with Jansen, accepted a seat, and declined coffee.

"Congratulations on your promotion," he said, sitting down at the conference table across from her. "Fastest assistant deputy director in DGSI history."

"Thank you."

"And she reports directly to me," de Vasselot added, "so you'll be see-ing a lot of her."

"I look forward to it."

Brunelle smiled politely, her hands folded in front of her. She hadn't been told what the meeting was about but had figured it was probably going to center on Powell's death. She hadn't been looking forward to it and had barely slept at all last night.

"As we conveyed to Director General de Vasselot," Jansen contin-ued, "we want to apologize for the actions of Raymond Powell. Neither the CIA nor the United States holds you, in any way, responsible for his death. In addition, we want to commend you for your work. You did an amazing job."

This was not what Brunelle had been expecting. "Thank you," she managed to say.

"With that, I wanted to make myself available to answer your questions."

"What questions?"

"Any questions you may have. If they're in my power to answer, I will."

She looked at him. "*Any* questions?"

"Yes," Jansen replied. "*Any* questions."

An hour after saying hello to James Jansen, Karine Brunelle said goodbye and agreed to meet with Director General de Vasselot back at DGSI head-quarters later that afternoon.

Leaving the embassy, she skirted the Place de la Concorde with its Luxor Obelisk and headed in the direction of the Palais Garnier to a small bistro called Les Bacchantes. It took its name from the Greek tragedy by Euripides. Gibert had selected it as a good spot for an early lunch, but she couldn't help but wonder if it was also supposed to be somehow symbolic of their romantic relationship.

She found him at a quiet table in back. As she approached, he stood and pulled out her chair. The moment she was seated, the waiter arrived with a bottle of champagne—and it wasn't an inexpensive one either.

"What's this?" she asked.

"We're celebrating," Gibert replied.

"Celebrating what?"

"Your success. All of it."

"I had a little help," she admitted.

"Then we're toasting *our* success and I'm doubly glad I selected such a good vintage."

After Gibert had tasted the champagne and the waiter had filled their glasses and left the table, he proposed a toast, "To success."

Raising her glass, Brunelle clinked it against his. "To success," she repeated.

"So," the cop asked, after savoring a nice long sip, "how'd your appointment go?"

"Remember when Powell died, and I worried we were never going to get any answers?"

Gibert nodded and took another sip from his glass.

"Well, I've got answers now," she continued. "Lots of them."

"Good thing I picked such a nice, quiet spot. Tell me all of it."

Brunelle took another sip herself and then launched into everything she had learned. Twenty minutes later, the waiter refilled their glasses and took their lunch orders.

When he had left the table again, Gibert said, "But who killed all the Russians in the Bois de Boulogne and at that medical clinic?"

"That was one question I was not given an answer to. Powell's replacement, this man Jansen, hinted that the Kremlin has some sort of a beef with another foreign intelligence service."

"And the passports in that one dead guy's pocket?"

Brunelle smiled. "Meant to throw us off the track and keep us guessing."

"What about how Jadot's killer had a key that allowed him to disappear behind a faux façade for a Métro airshaft?"

"Allegedly, he was an incredibly resourceful assassin."

"*Was?*"

She nodded. "I'm told he's dead too. Along with his getaway driver."

"So, somebody got to them before us."

"Correct."

"But why is France ground zero for all of this?" Gibert asked. "Why can't these people handle business in their own respective countries?"

"Apparently, it had something to do with Elovik, the military attaché."

"Who was the mastermind behind the entire spy ring," said the cop, shaking his head. "Was there anything that guy *wasn't* into?"

"According to our sources, he's now vanished, so we may never know."

"What was his raison d'être? Why set up that spy ring? Did it have a military purpose of some sort?"

Brunelle nodded. "By recruiting spies in our government, Moscow bragged that they could get their hands on any classified NATO intelligence it wanted, particularly as it applied to Ukraine. And, post-Brexit, with Britain out of the EU, the Russians are very nervous about the leadership role they see France growing into. The Kremlin about lost its mind when President Mercier suggested French troops could soon be sent to Ukraine."

"So Jadot was poised to expose everything, but made the mistake of turning to Powell, who was on Russia's payroll and sold him out."

"Correct," she replied. "But as you wisely said, the best thing about this was that we got the list. Without it, we never would have known who the traitors were."

"And without you," the cop said, "the government might never have come up with such a clever plan to bring them all in at once, get as many as possible to confess, and control the fallout."

"I don't know how much fallout we contained. It's still a massive scandal."

"Don't undersell what you did. It could have been much worse. Playing to their egos and gathering them up in one fell swoop was a stroke of genius."

"We got lucky," Brunelle admitted.

Raising his glass, Gibert proposed another toast. "To luck."

Clinking her glass against his again, she took another sip.

"How's MoMo?" he asked after swallowing his champagne.

"He's good."

"What about his buddy, Amir?"

"Still pissed-off, but he'll get over it," said Brunelle. "Which brings us to why we're here. Outside of Amir's apartment, when you agreed to log the flash drive into evidence for me, you said you wanted a favor in return. Your text said that meeting you for lunch today would be that favor. What does that mean?"

"It means that I want to apologize. *Properly* apologize. I am sorry for lying to you. I should have told you the truth about my wife. I didn't. That was wrong. I still think you're a little bit crazy, Karine, but you are the most intriguing woman I have ever known. I wish our circumstances had been different. Someday, I hope you can forgive me."

"Thank you," said Brunelle. "I was very hurt. Still am to a degree. But as long as we're apologizing, I'm sorry if I caused you any unnecessary pain."

Raising their glasses, they clinked. There was no toast. There didn't need to be. It was an act of détente; of something very painful, for both of them, finally being laid to rest.

CHAPTER 76

O f all her grandmother's extraordinary accomplishments, that remarkable woman had never welcomed a United States President into her home. Maggie knew that if she could see her now, she would be incredibly proud of all that her granddaughter had achieved.

Maggie also knew that she had only reached these heights by standing on the shoulders of all the women who had come before her. It may have been a shopworn expression, but there really was no better way to phrase it.

"How's your recovery coming?" President Porter asked as he joined Maggie in her den.

"It only hurts when I laugh," she replied. "And lately, there hasn't been much to laugh about."

"That's why I came. I wanted to give you the latest Russia update myself."

"I'm impressed, Mr. President. Normally I get the information before you do."

Porter grinned. "That's true. After all, it is your job. But seeing as how you're convalescing, I think I can give you a pass. Just this once."

Maggie smiled back and gestured to the President to help himself to some of the appetizers Paul had prepared. She had no idea how he had done it on such short notice. One minute the White House was calling on the phone, the next minute President Porter was standing at their door. Maggie had barely had time to make herself presentable.

"Thank you," he replied, helping himself to a few buckwheat blinis with smoked trout, crème fraiche, and red grapes. "And thank you for all of your help throughout this situation."

"Of course, Mr. President. As you said, that is my job and I take it very seriously."

"I know you do, and the country owes you a sincere debt of gratitude."

Maggie was deeply honored. "Thank you, sir."

Porter paused to take a bite of the smoked trout and when he closed his eyes in enjoyment, Maggie knew Paul had scored a direct hit. The president was an avid fly fisherman and had probably eaten more trout, more ways, than any other politician in D.C.

"This is amazing. Maine smoked trout?" he asked.

The man's palate was impeccable. "Indeed. Very good, Mr. President," she responded.

"Tell Paul that if he can come up with any more recipes like this, I'll fast-track him for a Medal of Freedom."

Maggie chuckled. "He's going to be insufferable, but I'll let him know how much you enjoyed it."

"My love of your husband's cooking notwithstanding, let me get to the reason why I came. Putting the generals on all the Sunday shows a few days ago played *very* well. Not just here in the U.S., but around the world. It was an absolute home run."

"Thank you, Mr. President."

"But where you really shined," Porter continued, "where you went supernova, was in the recommendations you followed up with. And yes, they ticked a lot of people off. That's how I knew you were on the money. If you're taking flak, it's probably because you're over the right target.

"When the secretary of state arrived in Moscow in the wake of the Sunday shows, the Kremlin was already agitated—as you had said they would be. But when he informed them of the new Patriot missile systems being deployed to the Baltic states, the temperature in the room really started to rise.

"Next came the 'courtesy' announcement that all restrictions against Ukraine using Western weapons systems to strike inside Russia were being lifted. In fact, the SecState asked me to give you a special thumbs-up for suggesting that we inform the Russians that the Ukrainians were going to be encouraged to target Russia's own equivalents of J-Town: Belgorod and Rostov-on-Don."

"They didn't like that, did they?" Maggie asked with a smile.

Porter smiled back. "Not at all. But what finally tipped them over was the assurance that if Moscow detonated a nuclear device in Ukraine, Ukraine would automatically be admitted to NATO and NATO would be at war with Russia.

"Additionally, the SecState informed Moscow that any nuclear device that landed in NATO territory would be treated as if it came from Russia. It didn't matter if it was launched from Belarus or was ridden in on a moped from Chechnya. Russia would face the West's full wrath and bear the brunt of the consequences."

"And?" Maggie asked hopefully.

"And, we just learned that Russia is going to announce their withdrawal of tactical nuclear weapons from Belarus. Naturally, they're spinning it as a show of good faith and an effort to reduce tensions in the region, but here at home, we know it's because Maggie Thomas scares the hell out of them."

"Thank you, Mr. President."

Porter looked at her. "No, Maggie," he said. "The thanks go to you. You've been right every step of the way. This was exactly how we should play it. I'd throw you the world's biggest parade, but I think it's better to celebrate this a little closer to home."

Standing up, the president walked to the doors of Maggie's study and opened them wide. Standing on the other side was the entire National Security Council, Maggie's closest colleagues from Russia House, and Paul, holding up her favorite bottle of champagne.

CHAPTER 77

Since all of the people Sølvi would have invited to the wedding were already on this side of the Atlantic and almost everyone Harvath would have invited were also here, they had decided to go through with it and get married in Oslo.

Even Haney with his bad wing, which he kept blaming Harvath for, and Johnson, who had just been cleared for travel, had been willing to fly up from France. Preisler and Staelin had come too.

For everyone on the other side of the Atlantic, the Carlton Group had generously offered up its private jet.

Having the wedding in Oslo had made everyone happy, especially the men in Sølvi's family, who Harvath was convinced would have strapped him to a sinking Viking longboat had he attempted to go through with an elopement.

Nicholas and Nina were thrilled to be able to show off their new baby. Gary Lawlor, interim director of the Carlton Group, had shown up with a bottle of Pappy Van Winkle that was so expensive it had to be kept under armed guard. Even Holidae Hayes was in attendance.

Shortly before the big day, she had reached out to Sølvi with an early wedding gift. The CIA didn't have a spy inside the Norwegian Intelligence Service. They had learned about Grechko's defection through a series of intercepted Russian communications, all of which she turned over, in full. It was a first step in mending fences—both professional and personal.

Sølvi had gotten to know and love Lara's beautiful little boy Marco, as well as Harvath's wonderful former in-laws, but a snap wedding wasn't in the cards for them. They had just been to Oslo for a fabulous visit several months ago. Pulling Marco out of school in Boston and coming back so soon was too overwhelming. Harvath had figured as much. Nevertheless, he had extended the invitation, but with a nice get-out-of-jail-free card, which they had politely availed themselves of. As far as everyone was concerned, they were there in spirit.

The ceremony had been officiated at the palace by the king of Norway, who had recently recognized Harvath for bravery.

The reception took place atop the Thief hotel, where Harvath had originally proposed to Sølvi. Twice, the exceptional staff had to put the call out for more champagne and more oysters.

When it was time for the newlyweds to depart, they said goodbye to their beloved guests and headed down to the water, where Harvath's same boat was waiting at the swim platform to take them to the cottage out on the fjord.

Tired of doing anything that smacked of responsibility, Harvath had arranged for a captain to transport them.

As he and Sølvi relaxed in the open air of the stern, a wool blanket keeping them warm, he pulled out the bottle of Krug that had been sitting in her refrigerator.

"Right here?" he asked, echoing his lurid invitation of several nights ago, "or up in the cabin under the bow?"

Sølvi smiled. "Per Viking law, I'm not yours until we've fully crossed one body of water together."

"Good thing I'm patient," said Harvath, as he peeled away the foil, loosened the cage, and removed the cork.

He handed Sølvi a pair of glasses, poured the champagne, and then offered up a toast. "I love you. Thank you for not subjecting me to any of those weird Norwegian traditions like cheese, wooden shoes, or ribbons."

Feigning offense, Sølvi slapped his chest and said, "What kind of oddballs do you think we are? The Dutch are the ones with the wooden shoes."

"Okay," Harvath said with a smile. "Then thank you for not making me do anything weird with ribbons or cheese."

"You're welcome, but we're going to revisit all of this at midsummer."

He loved pulling her chain and loved even more that she pulled his right back. They really were a wonderful pair. First they kissed and then they clinked glasses.

"So," she said, loud enough that Harvath could hear over the engines but quiet enough that the captain couldn't, "what's next? Any loose ends?"

His mind had already been spinning back in Eze about how he and Nicholas could hide his money once he had gotten it away from the U.S. Treasury. Now that it was safe, he had space to breathe, relax.

"Part of me," he replied, "wants to go after the guy at the CIA who blackmailed me."

"And the other part?" Sølvi asked, leaning in closer.

"Now that I have it all back? I guess the other part of me wants to take the money and run."

Leaning the rest of the way in, she kissed him; long, hard, and deep. When she finally pulled her lips away, she asked, "Do you trust me?"

Harvath didn't even need to think about his answer. "Without a doubt."

"Then let's run," she said, kissing him again. "Let's run as fast and as far and for as long as we can."

ACKNOWLEDGMENTS

The idea for *Shadow of Doubt* came from a fascinating article I had read about a French spy scandal in the 1960s known as the "Sapphire Affair." Much like Jean-Jacques Jadot discovers, many of the corridors of power in Paris at that time were alleged to have been penetrated by the Russians. Thriller author Leon Uris based his 1967 novel *Topaz* on a fictionalized version of these events, which Alfred Hitchcock turned into a terrific film.

As I do with every novel, I want to begin these acknowledgments by thanking you, my magnificent **readers**. Each year, it is an honor and a delight to take you on a new adventure with Scot Harvath. I hope this has been one of your favorite books yet!

To all the superb **booksellers**—thank you. I simply couldn't do what I do without you. The joy of reading that you help instill in people every day makes our world a better place.

One of my oldest and dearest friends, **Sean Fontaine**, was once again a fabulous resource. He has not only a wonderfully dark sense of humor, but also a depth of knowledge developed over an impressive career in some of the most dangerous corners of the globe. Thank you, Sean. I hope to see you for some brown water soon.

I also need to thank another very good friend, **Knut Grini** of the Norwegian Police Service. I was supposed to spend part of the writing of this novel as his guest, in a particularly special location. I blew it. I will not make that mistake again and hope that I can get a rain check this summer. Takk for hjelpen, min venn!

Ex-CIA analyst and thriller author **David McCloskey** is not only a terrific writer (*Damascus Station, Moscow X, The Seventh Floor*), he's also an all-around great guy and helped me with some CIA-related material. If you haven't read his books yet, do yourself a favor and start. Thanks, David.

Of all the research I did for this novel, discovering geopolitical strategist **Peter Zeihan** was my favorite part. His assessments of world events, particularly as they pertain to Russia, are absolutely fascinating. I cannot recommend his excellent, easy-to-digest YouTube videos, or his bestselling books, including *The Accidental Superpower* and *The End of the World Is Just the Beginning*, highly enough. When you hear Maggie Thomas discussing Russia, that is me attempting to channel some of Mr. Zeihan's positions. The concept of Russia trying to solve its geographic problems with military solutions was something I had not previously considered and found both intriguing and highly compelling. Go check him out. You will be much more knowledgeable as a result. Thank you, Mr. Zeihan.

It is impossible to list all of the excellent research materials I uncovered, but I do want to call out the following, which were invaluable for helping me understand key elements of the conflict and the role played by nuclear brinksmanship: "Russian Nuclear Calibration in the War in Ukraine" by Heather Williams, Kelsey Hartigan, Lachlan MacKenzie, and Reja Younis as published by the Center for Strategic & International Studies; "The U.S. Should Store Nuclear Weapons in Poland" by John Vandiver as published in *Stars & Stripes*; "U.S. Nukes in Poland Are Truly a Bad Idea" by Steven Pifer as published by the Brookings Institution; "By Sending Nuclear Weapons to the United Kingdom, Could the United States Be Fueling Nuclear Proliferation" by Janani Mohan as published by the *Bulletin of the Atomic Scientists*; and "Petraeus: U.S. Would Destroy Russia's Troops If Putin Uses Nuclear Weapons in Ukraine" as published in *The Guardian*.

Jon Karp, President and CEO of Simon & Schuster, is the spectacular captain of our ship. I was honored when he asked me to speak at the S&S hundredth-anniversary celebration this year. What an incredible run our publishing house has had. Thank you, Jon, for all that you do for each and every one of us. Here's to a hundred more years of success!

My extraordinary editor, publisher, and friend, **Emily Bestler**, has been such a critical force in all my books. She has been with me since Day One and her sage counsel is felt in every line and on every page I have ever written.

Thank you, Emily—especially for your patience. Where would I be without you?

All of the incredible people at **Emily Bestler Books**, especially **Lara Jones** and **Hydia Scott-Riley**, are invaluable when it comes to getting my books published from start to finish. There are so many elements that need to be anticipated, attended to, and accomplished. This team nails all of them, every single time. Thank you!

The dynamic duo formed by my Atria publisher, **Libby McGuire**, and my associate publisher, **Dana Trocker**, is unbeatable! These two terrific pros work around the clock to help me bring my books to more and more readers every year. I am always so grateful to be working with you both. Many, many thanks.

A new year, a new book, and another 365 days with the best damn publicist in the business, **David Brown**. As an author, you can write the best book in the world, but without an incredible publicist like David, no one is going to hear about it. Thank you, DB, for everything you do for me!

One of the greatest things about being an author at Simon & Schuster is all of the remarkable people I have been blessed to become friends with. Chief among them, I am very thankful for the marvelous **Gary Urda**, senior VP of sales for Simon & Schuster. He and his superb **team** are the engine that keeps everything humming. Thank you, Gary!

If you have read me in paperback or have seen me on a store shelf in paperback, that's thanks to the phenomenal **Jen Long** and her astounding **team** at **Pocket Books**, who are always hard at work. I cannot fully express how much I appreciate all of you. Thank you.

I dedicated this book to **Al Madocs** who, along with **Christine Masters**, **Jason Chappell**, and the rest of the **Atria/Emily Bestler Books production departments**, are absolutely brilliant. Any mistakes in my books are mine, but there are a lot fewer of them because of the dedication and professionalism of these amazing people. Thank you all.

The fantastic **Atria/Emily Bestler Books and Pocket Books sales teams** continue to crush it day in and day out. They never take no for an answer and never rest on their laurels. Without an all-star sales team, nothing else matters. My thanks go out to each and every one of you.

The fabulous **Jimmy Iacobelli** and all the team members at the awe-inspiring **Atria/Emily Bestler Books and Pocket Books art departments** have done it again! Every single year, they blow me away with new covers. They are absolute pros and I am so grateful. Thank you.

The stellar team at the **Simon & Schuster audio division**, including **Chris Lynch, Tom Spain, Sarah Lieberman, Desiree Vecchio**, and my longtime friend and narrator, **Armand Schultz**, have once again delivered an award-winning audio edition. It is a joy to watch (and of course listen) to them work. Thank you for yet another masterpiece.

My glorious agent and dear friend, **Heide Lange** of **Sanford J. Greenburger Associates**, was there for me, yet again, at every turn with this book. She made sure I was stocked up on great chocolate, great coffee, and lots and lots of terrific advice. Thank you, Heide, for everything. You mean the world to me.

I also want to thank the rest of the exceptional **SJGA team**, including **Iwalani Kim, Madeline Wallace**, and **Charles Loffredo**. A million thank-yous would still never be enough! You are the glue that holds everything together. Thank you all for your poise and your professionalism.

The remarkable **Yvonne Ralsky** delivered another stellar year! The number of things Yvonne does for me so that I can focus on writing are immeasurable. I am grateful for everything, but particularly for her deep and abiding friendship, as well as for all the laughs!

We had a big Hollywood announcement this year and for that, as well as so many other things, I want to say an equally big thank you to my dear friend and the megalodon of entertainment attorneys, the wonderful **Scott Schwimer**. Here's to finally getting Harvath to the screen. Thank you, Scottie!

And last, but absolutely not least, I want to thank my incredibly splendid family. Even though we now form a household of adults, all with busy lives, they never missed an opportunity to love, support, and encourage me throughout the writing of this book. I owe a special debt of gratitude to my wife, **Trish**, who is my very first reader and an unparalleled editor. I love you all!